MW01688102

Clockwork Universe: Steampunk vs. Aliens

Other Anthologies Edited by
Patricia Bray & Joshua Palmatier

After Hours: Tales from the Ur-Bar

The Modern Fae's Guide to Surviving Humanity

Clockwork Universe: Steampunk vs. Aliens

Edited by

Patricia Bray
&
Joshua Palmatier

Zombies Need Brains LLC
www.zombiesneedbrains.com

Copyright © 2014 Patricia Bray, Joshua Palmatier, and
Zombies Need Brains LLC. All Rights Reserved.

Interior Design (ebook): April Steenburgh
Interior Design (print): C. Lennox
Cover Design by C. Lennox

Cover Art "Steampunk Octopus" by Alex Broeckel

ZNB Book Collectors #1

All characters and events in this book are fictitious.

All resemblance to persons living or dead is coincidental.

The scanning, uploading, and distribution of this book via the Internet or any other means without the permission of the publisher is illegal and punishable by law. Please purchase only authorized electronic editions of this book, and do not participate or encourage electronic piracy of copyrighted material.

Kickstarter Edition Printing, May 2014
First Printing, June 2014

ISBN-10: 1940709008
ISBN-13: 978-1940709000

Printed in the U.S.A.

Copyrights

Introduction copyright © 2014 by Patricia Bray

"The Cavorite Job" copyright © 2014 by Ian Tregillis

"Gracie's Fire" copyright © 2014 by Leah Cutter

"Quinta Essentia" copyright © 2014 by Bradley P. Beaulieu

"When Comrade Ekaterina Died for the Motherland"
copyright © 2014 by J.R. Hargenrader

"A Clockwork Alien" copyright © 2014by Jeanne Cook

"Heart of the Empire" copyright © 2014 by Jason Palmatier

"The Red Queen and the White" copyright © 2014 by C.B. Pratt

"The Wizard of Woodrow Park"
copyright © 2014 by Jean Marie Ward

"Of War and Wings" copyright © 2014 by Tansy Rayner Roberts

"Airship Down: A Sound and Fury Adventure"
copyright © 2014 by Gail Z. Martin & Larry N. Martin

"Steamsuit" copyright © 2014 by David J. Fortier

"Fingers of Steam, Veins of Gold"
copyright © 2014 by Brad Hafford

"Heart of Clockwork" copyright © 2014 by S.C. Butler

"Lady Antheia's Guide to Horticultural Warfare"
copyright © 2014 by Seanan McGuire

Table of Contents

Introduction by Patricia Bray	1
"The Cavorite Job" by Ian Tregillis	2
"Gracie's Fire" by Leah Cutter	27
"Quinta Essentia" by Bradley P. Beaulieu	39
"When Comrade Ekaterina Died for the Motherland" by J.R. Hargenrader	65
"A Clockwork Alien" by Gini Koch	75
"Heart of the Empire" by Jason Palmatier	96
"The Red Queen and the White" by C.B. Pratt	119
"The Wizard of Woodrow Park" by Jean Marie Ward	132
"Of War and Wings" by Tansy Rayner Roberts	152
"Airship Down: A Sound and Fury Adventure" by Gail Z. Martin & Larry N. Martin	164
"Steamsuit" by David J. Fortier	191
"Fingers of Steam, Veins of Gold" by Brad Hafford	209
"Heart of Clockwork" by S.C. Butler	227
"Lady Antheia's Guide to Horticultural Warfare" by Seanan McGuire	246
About the Authors	266
About the Editors	270

Signature Page

Patricia Bray, editor:

____

Joshua Palmatier, editor:

____

Ian Tregillis:

____

Leah Cutter:

____

Bradley P. Beaulieu:

____

J.R. Hargenrader:

____

Gini Koch:

____

Jason Palmatier:

____

C.B. Pratt:

____

Jean Marie Ward:

____

Tansy Rayner Roberts:

____

Gail Z. Martin & Larry N. Martin:

____

David J. Fortier:

____

Brad Hafford:

____

S.C. Butler:

____

Seanan McGuire:

____

Alex Broeckel, artist:

____

Introduction

When I first discovered science fiction, I was drawn to it by a sense of wonder. And of course there was the appeal of all the cool toys—ray guns and spaceships, robots and time machines, all the things my teenage life was sadly lacking. Steampunk has that same feeling of endless possibilities. What if things had turned out just a bit differently, or Jules Verne had been writing science fact instead of science fiction?

When it came time to propose the first anthology project for Zombies Need Brains press, Joshua Palmatier and I were immediately drawn to the idea of a steampunk project. Taking our inspiration from classic nineteenth century science fiction adventures stories, we asked authors to imagine what would happen when aliens discovered a Steampunk Earth. Would the first encounters be peaceful or violent? Would humanity emerge triumphant or be defeated? Would Earth even recognize the threat before it was too late?

We found a half-dozen authors who agreed to anchor the project, and inspirational cover art by Alex Broeckel. Then we solicited submissions to fill out the anthology. Choosing the final story list was incredibly difficult, we had far more good stories than we could use. In the end we narrowed it down to fourteen stories which best fit the original concept, while representing a range of settings and themes. You'll find stories from bestselling authors to those making their professional debut. From steampunk cities to remote wildernesses, with stories ranging from light-hearted humor to horror, there's something for everyone.

Enjoy!

Patricia Bray

The Cavorite Job

Ian Tregillis

It wasn't until the alien tripod burst forth from the mountainside forest, lambent energy beams sizzling through the monsoon-soaked air like billion-candela spotlights celebrating a West End premiere, and rather inconveniently piercing the *Black Shiva*'s envelope of hydrogen lifting gas—the very same airship from which, it was important to note, she currently dangled by swollen fingertips from a rain-slick rope ladder—that Captain Sujata Malhotra finally accepted what others on the crew had sensed from the beginning: they never, ever should have taken this job.

"Wellington!" she bellowed into the teeth of the storm. "You thrice-damned scalawag! I'll cut your—"

But she had scant opportunity to express her displeasure, for the very next moment the remnants of a tropical cyclone in the Bay of Bengal slammed into the *Shiva*. The ship, already spiraling earthward like a wounded pigeon, now jinked to port hard enough to snap the ladder like a whip. And, not inconsequentially, tearing said ladder from her grip.

It was later remarked, by those in a unique position to witness these events, that Captain Sujata fell less like a wounded pigeon and more like an anchor weight filled with piss and rage.

* * *

The setting sun had turned a dusky red to port, like the meat of a blood orange suspended abeam of the *Shiva*, as they crossed the last few miles of ocean between Ceylon and the mainland. It was the final leg of a long loop around the Indian Ocean to meander through the Malay Archipelago. The Malay route was a favorite, combining as it did two of Sujata's favorite things: a plethora of ships fat with trade, and a dearth of octos. For now, at least, the aliens and their chromium-plated tripods seemed to avoid the deep ocean around the Spice Islands.

As usual, they had crossed paths with several airships of foreign registry; these they relieved of troublesome ballast. It was a purely humanitarian gesture, of course, aiding ships in danger of sinking to the bottom of the sky. The *Shiva* had a moral obligation to help given its active role in the sinkings, and the fact that naval vessels had become a rare sight ever since the octo invasion had sent so many loyal tars to the darkness above and below. As a result of its humanitarian largesse, the *Shiva* lumbered to port with holds near to bursting.

Sujata watched from the bridge, feeling the *thrum-thrum-thrum* of the engines through the soles of her boots.

Turcotte, her helmsman and navigator, eased the *Shiva* toward port with one hand on the wheel and the other holding a shaving mirror. He'd spent half the voyage admiring the tattoo he'd acquired in Sumatra to commemorate winning a no-rules Kuntao cage tournament held behind a particularly colorful house of ill-repute outside Bandar Lampung. It was, she had to admit, a noteworthy accomplishment given that Turcotte had entered the competition armed only with a vague knowledge of the Malaysian martial art that barely extended beyond its pronunciation. On the other hand, they were entering some of the most crowded airspace she'd seen since before the first tripods had landed in London. Seemed like half the empire had fled to India to prop up the Raj.

"Mr. Turcotte! If I see that looking glass in your hand one more time before we dock, I swear upon all that is good and holy that I will personally insert it so far up your nethers that you will shit marbles from now until Boxing Day."

The mirror disappeared into a pocket of Turcotte's cargo trousers. He turned a dial on the helm and muttered into a speaking tube; moments later the engine rhythm slowed to a lethargic *whoom-whoom-whoom*. The lowering sun sent the *Shiva*'s shadow lancing across the ocean. And it evoked little flashes of light from the darkening continent. Like the glint of sunlight on cavalry sabers. Or alien tripods.

The captain sighed. Everybody knew it was only a matter of time before the octos turned their tentacles to the more far-flung corners of the Empire.

Damn you, Jack Scaly.

Turcotte saw it, too. “Bloody octos,” he muttered.

Sujata yanked the speaking tube from its clamp above the helm. “Vi! Ready the guns.”

The deck lurched four times in rapid succession. A quartet of armaments each the size of an elephant’s thigh slid out of recessed compartments around the airship. Turcotte adjusted the trim. If the weaponeer lost the reins, the kick from those buggers could overpower the engines and push a ship like the *Shiva* halfway to the stars. If loaded with white phosphorus rounds and a bit of luck, they could pierce an octo tripod and set it ablaze. Merely loaded with regular munitions, as they were at the moment, they could shoot clean through the House of Lords. Or so it was said; fortune hadn’t favored them with an opportunity to try it.

The chain guns were, technically, illegal for any ship not on the naval register. But navy scrap could be had for a song these days. At least, those bits that hadn’t burned up in the atmosphere or been melted by Jack Scaly’s energy beams. (*Damn you twice, Jack Scaly.*) Besides, the *Shiva*’s letter of marque afforded them a certain amount of latitude.

The speaking tube turned the weaponeer’s voice into a raspy whisper. It said, “Guns away, captain. Trouble?”

“None whatsoever. But load whatever’s left of the phosphorus belts before going to regular shot.”

Meanwhile, Turcotte used another to speak to the engine room. “Spin ‘em up, de Vries. Full power on standby.”

The engineer’s response came out of the tube clearly enough for Sujata to hear: “Really glad there’s no trouble whatsoever up there.” The deck rattled in time to the turbines’ acceleration.

By now the sun had melted halfway into the horizon. The ruby-red sky cast a softer illumination across the source of the metallic flashes. An array of cannon and the gleaming spires of a new Tesla palisade ringed the Madras aerodrome. No tripods, no octos. Just new preparations for their arrival. Turcotte exhaled.

Sujata issued the order to stand down. “Mr. Turcotte, find us a berth so we can get down there and get rich off our hard-earned and entirely legal cargo.”

The whine of turbines shook the deck as one by one the guns flopped back into their niches, unused and unneeded. But Sujata’s gaze didn’t waver from the perimeter defenses as the gloaming draped them in shadow. The Madras ‘drome hadn’t been armed to the teeth when they departed two months earlier. But now it was, meaning the octos had landed on the subcontinent. It was only a matter of time before the tripods thrashed their way across the Raj, tearing bloody great furrows in civilization as they had in Europe.

Damn you thrice, Jack Scaly.

* * *

A sweaty man in a tweed suit, grossly overdressed for the subtropical heat, met them at their birth. Wellington was their contact with HM’s government, or what was left of it, back in London.

First the ‘drome gets new anti-octo defenses. Then Wellington drops in unannounced, thought Sujata. *All the shit is rolling downhill, isn’t it?*

Body language reflected a similar wariness among her lieutenants as they gathered around Wellington. It ranged from scowls and glowering (Turcotte, though to be fair the tattoos did much of the heavy lifting for his face) to a carefully affected loucheness (Violet, her weaponeer, who at the moment smelled of black powder and sulphur), to icy civility (de Vries, her engineer, and one of the best things she’d ever stolen from Malaysia).

Sujata said, “Mr. Wellington. It’s not that I don’t enjoy surprises—I don’t—but surely you haven’t come all the way from London just to see us? Flattered as we would be to think otherwise.”

“Aha,” said the bureaucrat. It was his nervous tick, something he did when lying, or stalling for time, or both. “A pleasure as always, captain.”

He's been relocated, she realized. *The situation in Europe hasn't improved.*

"What's this about? We have cargo to unload and mind-altering liquids to drink." This met with grumbling approval from the crew.

"Well. I wonder if you'd be interested in a commission? Nothing dangerous, I assure you. A bit of a change of pace for you, perhaps, something inland rather than over the open sea."

"What's so interesting inland?"

"A warehouse."

"Uh-huh. And would this warehouse also be of interest to Jack Scaly?"

"Oh, goodness, no. Aha. I rather doubt the octos would find it the least bit interesting, if they even knew of this place. Which I'm rather sure they don't. Aha."

That made two *aha*s in the same utterance and three in the half minute since he greeted them. Only a fool would take him at his word.

"Well, Mr. Wellington, I've truly enjoyed our chat, aha, as I always do, aha. But I'm afraid I'll have to decline your very kind offer to spice up our working routine with variety and a complete lack of adventure or danger."

"Ah," said Wellington. He plucked the pince-nez from his face. Then he produced a cotton handkerchief and set about wiping the sweat from the spectacles. The hypnotic pattern on the cotton indicated it had been woven on one of Mr. Babbage's modern successors to the Jacquard loom, according to a mathematical pattern discovered by the Countess Lovelace. It was said the duo turned a pretty penny licensing spinoffs from their mathematical endeavors applying computational engines to orbital calculations for the Royal Navy. They probably had little else to occupy them in the wake of the octo invasion and the rout in orbit.

The government man ran the cloth over the lenses in slow spirals, saying, "Well. I would be a liar if I said I was surprised. An eminently reasonable decision on your part, captain. And, may I just take this opportunity to say that were I in your rather colorful shoes I would doubtless make the same choice."

A look of confusion, tinged with greater or lesser amounts of skepticism, ricocheted from one lieutenant to the next. Sujata intercepted it. "So we're not to be punished for turning down your offer?"

Wellington looked as though she'd just accused him of killing a man for his brolly. "Dear heavens! I should hope not. We in Whitehall are not savages, in spite of what you may have heard. If we were to compromise our principles at the first sign of duress, why, we'd be little better than animals. We were the queen's subjects prior to the octo invasion, we're her subjects now, and we'll still be her subjects when we've driven Jack Scaly back to the inky void between the stars."

Turcotte clapped. "Hear hear!"

"Yes, yes. No doubt," Sujata said. "Well, I wish you luck in that endeavor, Mr. Wellington. Meanwhile we'll be doing what we do best. Good day to you."

She'd turned and gone three strides when Wellington made a single embarrassed cough into his handkerchief. He sounded, for all the world, like a man struggling to put the very best light on the fact his dog had just diddled in the queen's handbag. The crew heard it. Shoulders slumped.

"On a completely unrelated note," he said, "there is, I'm sorry to say, the issue of your letter of marque."

Sujata remembered that she carried a pistol and a saber. But she ran her hands down her braids, counted to ten, and turned to face the government man again. "I'm sure I don't understand. The terms of our agreement are, I'm quite certain, in perfect order."

"Indeed. Indeed," he said. "There can be little question the *Black Shiva* has adhered to the terms of the original letter quite admirably, performing along the way great service to the queen."

"Original letter?" Her hand fell to the pistol at her waist.

"Yes. This is a somewhat, aha, delicate issue. Not something we're proud to admit. But the fact is that the resources required to fight the octos have put quite a strain on the national coffers. The Foreign Office has seen fit to reach out to our continental cousins to strike an alliance that we might together marshal our forces and bring an end to this tiresome invasion rather sooner than later." Wellington brought the handkerchief to his mouth and again emitted that delicate cough. "However, and this is a bit embarrassing, as I'm sure you can imagine, the fact that HM government has sanctioned patriotic privateers such as yourselves to scavenge what you can from the holds of ships flying under foreign colors—the very same colors we now court for this alliance—is, well, awkward. So it has been decided that any active letters of marque shall be rescinded."

A letter of marque was the distinction between a privateer and a pirate; the difference between official sanction and the gallows. The careers were the same, only their ends differed. Privateers could retire; retirement for a pirate meant a long drop and a short rope.

Violet looked ready to choke the man. A vein throbbed in Turcotte's forehead. He'd gone the color of a boiled beetroot. "You unbelievable arsehole."

"My hands are tied, I'm afraid. Although I have heard that certain letters may be reconsidered in situations where mitigating circumstances might apply."

"Mitigating circumstances." Beads clicked when Sujata shook her head. "Such as accepting this warehouse job."

"Oh, captain. It would be untoward for me to speculate."

"Of course."

She sighed. "Very well. Tell us about this warehouse."

"You've changed your mind then? Capital!"

"Yes, I'm all aflutter at the opportunity. So tell us about the gods-damned warehouse."

"Aha," said Wellington. He made to cough again, thought better of it, and folded the silk into his pocket. "Tell me, captain. What do you know of cavorite?"

* * *

After the bureaucrat departed, Sujata studied her lieutenants. Now their expressions ranged from gobsmacked (Vi), to angry (Turcotte), to the narrowed eyes of profound wariness (de Vries).

"Well?"

Turcotte, never one to mince words, said, "I think we tell

him to go bugger himself with a steam-powered badger."

Vi wrinkled her nose. "This doesn't smell right."

"If it's so easy," said de Vries, "why haven't they done this themselves?"

"It does beg the question." Sujata chewed her lip, thinking.

"It's dangerous as hell," said Turcotte.

"Unquestionably."

The engineer said, with the tone of voice like somebody testing the ice on a frozen lake, "One might suppose the warehouse wasn't fully assayed, or that some fraction of its contents was lost in the confusion following the octo landings…" He left it at that. A simple observation, nothing more. Certainly nothing to suggest he was thinking about his share of any potential profits. And that such profits might be astronomical.

"Can't spend money when you're croaked," said Turcotte. The more Sujata chewed her lips, the unhappier he looked. "I reckon you know that, captain, mum."

"Rest assured I do," she said. Long exhalations all around as the officers relaxed. She waited a moment before adding, nonchalantly, "Vi, just out of curiosity, how long would it take to crack open the phosphorus rounds?"

Turcotte sighed. "Hell's bloody bells. She's already making a plan."

Vi ran her hands through her hair; they left sooty highlights in their wake. "We're going to die," she said.

"Well. At least we'll die rich," said de Vries.

"No," said Turcotte. "We'll die with our innards wrapped around our throats, wishing we'd had the chance to be rich."

* * *

Sujata knew what every legitimate independent entrepreneur who occasionally profited from the hardships of others knew about cavorite: that the mere thought of carrying it was a shortcut to a slow and bloody execution.

The mineral, named for its discoverer, some Royal Society egghead, was to the earth's gravitational radiations as a lead plate was to Mr. Röntgen's X-rays. As such, it was central to the Royal

Navy's operations at altitudes beyond those attainable by even the most advanced hydrogen airships. The aetherships designed by Isambard Kingdom Brunel all relied upon a powerful stock of cavorite plating to shield them from the earth's gravity, thereby making them nigh weightless and thus enabling their extra-atmospheric maneuverings.

Which is why hanging was too good for a pirate caught pinching the Queen's cavorite. They'd wreck you good and proper if they found so much as a single anti-dram in the hold. But that hadn't been a worry for months, much less a temptation, as Dr. Cavor's famous discovery was now nothing but a footnote in the history of natural philosophy. All the Queen's cavorite had been lost when Jack Scaly routed the Royal Navy in orbit. By now, half of it was scattered across the celestial spheres; the other half had given rise to some spectacular displays of falling stars over the British Empire, the Czar's Russia, and points beyond. As had the more mundane wreckage of the Royal Navy.

Stealing cavorite was a shortcut to an abrupt end to one's career. It was also, in theory, a shortcut to unimaginable profit: foreign powers would empty their national coffers just for a peek at the material.

So if the *Black Shiva* took this job, and if the warehouse was just as Wellington described, and if the warehouse records weren't entirely accurate (or easily forged), and if it just so happened that some of the cavorite from the warehouse accidentally slipped into hidden compartments in the *Shiva*'s hold through an entirely innocent mistake, and if the crew later found it and accidentally sold it to the highest bidder …

Well, that would be enough money for a smart captain to retire and move somewhere very far away where she didn't have to worry about a brace of alien tripods mucking up her morning tea.

* * *

Wellington gave them a map. The warehouse of T. David England and Sons, Victuallers to the Crown by Royal Charter since the Year of Our Lord 1822, lay hundreds of leagues away in the mountainous forests of the Uttarakhand province. (*An improbably patriotic name*, thought Sujata. She wondered what other names Mr. England had answered to before turning his back on the life of a confidence trickster to enjoy respectable employ as a war profiteer.) Fortunately for the Empire, the richest cavorite mine in the world lay inside its borders; the warehouse was actually a compound comprising a refinery for the raw mineral, a weighing station for the refined cavorite, and a storage facility.

Wellington's map conveniently omitted any indication that the nearest tripod landings had been less than twenty leagues from the warehouse. Strange that Jack Scaly had chosen to land in the hinterlands of the subcontinent; in Europe, the slimy devil had gone straight for the capital cities. When Sujata confronted him about the omission, he pulled out his handkerchief.

"Aha," he said. "An oversight, I'm quite certain. But you needn't worry about the octos, for HM navy will be your beard, yes! Aha. Once we sight the *Shiva* north of the upper Ganges, we'll send a sortie of frigates and corvettes straight into the heart of their nefarious nest. Jack Scaly will have his tentacles full dealing with the righteous fury of loyal tars armed with phosphorus, blades, and a taste for vengeance. That devil will never notice you."

"Oh. Well, that's very reassuring. Aha."

Turcotte used the map to chart a course into the rolling hills of the north. Reports from inland were spotty; Jack Scaly had played merry hob with the telegraph lines. But rumors and grumblings among the denizens of Madras's watering holes put at least four octo nests between the *Shiva*'s berth and the warehouse. Running that gauntlet required creative navigation. So Sujata was content to let Turcotte take the time he needed to do the job right. Besides. It took several days for the crew to offload their cargo and turn it into cash. The cash turned into a spool of steel cable, welding gear, fuel, additional miscellany of varied and sturdy purpose, plus a truly astonishing amount of ammunition, including phosphorus rounds. In spite of the extra weight they took on—in the words of de Vries, the spool alone was "heavier than a pregnant elephant dipped in lead"—they procured only a single bladder's worth of spare hydrogen. They wouldn't need it, if Wellington's figures were correct.

They couldn't be. His figures were absurd.

But Sujata did the math, and Turcotte checked her figures and found them sound. And then they re-did their sums assuming Wellington was a particularly well-dressed opium addict. After that, they revised their calculations downward yet again, on the logical assumption that a cavorite refinery would be paid on a sliding scale pinned to the purity of its product. And the merchant hadn't been born who wouldn't occasionally let his thumb fall upon the scale when there were government guineas to be had. Or, in this case, under the scale.

* * *

On the docks, she had asked Wellington, "How much?"

"Approximately seven hundred thousand anti-stones, with a purity between ninety-five and ninety-seven percent."

Vi said, "That sounds like … a lot."

Sujata did the math in her head; Turcotte, despite having taken no few blows to the head during his tournament, got there a second later. That's why she paid him. His fists weren't without their uses—occasionally his elbows, knees, feet, fingernails, and teeth, too—but she kept him around for his brain. A navigator had to know numbers; Turcotte knew them as though he'd gone on week-long benders through the sleaziest parts of Shanghai with each and every digit and returned with tattoos to prove it.

"That's a displacement of over forty-five hundred tons! Bugger me sideways and call me missus."

"Anti-tons," Wellington said. "Technically."

De Vries cleared his throat. "Captain, this is absurd. That's many times the *Shiva*'s displacement. It's not possible."

Wellington came as close to displaying an emotion as Sujata had ever witnessed. Perhaps he had gas. "We have an entire navy to stock, Mr. de Vries."

Under his breath, Turcotte said to Vi, "Not any more, the way I hear it."

Sujata turned on him. "Stow it," she said. Then to the

government man, she added, "A cynical person—not me, mind you, but a cynical person—might wonder why, if you have all this cavorite sitting around doing nobody any good while Jack Scaly makes a hash of things on earth and in heaven, you haven't scooped it up."

Vi giggled. "And up. And up. And …"

"Aha. Well. As you can imagine, the octos have taken quite an interest in the navy since our engagement above the atmosphere. If we started outfitting a new fleet in the hinterlands of the Raj, Jack Scaly would notice. And set upon us immediately before we had a sporting chance."

"Bloody octos," said Turcotte. "No honor!"

"Yeah. They lack the benefit of an honorable profession like ours," said Sujata. "But if *we* were to offload the warehouse …"

Wellington nodded. "Jack Scaly wouldn't blink twice. Assuming he has eyes to blink, the devil."

* * *

Sujata's stroke of genius—she felt comfortable calling it that, even if the crew hadn't yet come around—was to realize that it would be easier and faster to steal the entire warehouse rather than just its contents. The key was to utilize the cavorite's gravitational shielding properties to hasten its theft. Evenly distributed through the warehouse, it would reduce the weight of the metal dome to the merest fraction of its unshielded value. Meaning that once the foundation piles were severed—courtesy of demolition fuses built from the phosphorus Vi had extracted from the armaments—the *Black Shiva* could lift the entire building, cavorite and all, and feel nothing but the weight of the floor under the cavorite. Unloading the entire warehouse would take a day or more, but the building could be cut free in half the time: a worthy consideration with Jack Scaly prowling the jungles. Further, the anti-gravitational properties of the mineral would lessen the weight not only of the warehouse dome but of everything above it—including the *Shiva* itself, thereby boosting its lifting power.

* * *

The *Shiva* set sail two days later, turning inland just as a particularly unwelcome line of squalls crested the horizon behind them. A tropical depression in the Bay of Bengal set the mercury falling like a perforated frigate. Sujata watched the oncoming storm through her spyglass. Without benefit of the glass, and the *Shiva*'s altitude, the squalls would have been still hidden across the ocean. The storm couldn't surprise them now, but it could still make them unhappy. What a shame that even the strongest wind couldn't blow the octos back to the stars. More stubborn than a sack full of barnacles was old Jack Scaly.

Turcotte stood at the wheel, keeping one eye on the cross winds, another on the engine readouts, and some unseen mystical third eye on the navigation chart he'd marked for the voyage. He somehow also noticed his captain's preoccupation with the receding horizon.

"Trouble, captain?"

Sujata knocked the spyglass against her hip. It telescoped, *clink-clink-clink*ing like fine china to become a tube small enough to fit in her coat pocket. She dropped it there, saying, "I was just thinking, Mr. Turcotte, that this might go down as one of my very best plans. The capstone of our careers."

"Really? Because I was thinking it would probably be the one where we all end up dead."

"Everybody dies, Mr. Turcotte. Even people as pretty as you and me. Well, pretty as me and as … elaborately decorated as yourself."

The deck shivered as a cross-gust shook the airship's lifting body. Turcotte paused to adjust their bearing. This time he did consult the chart, just long enough to convince himself the *Shiva* still lay dead-center in the first of several emerald-green lines zigzagging across Wellington's map. Each segment bisected a blood red line connecting the rumored locations of octo nests.

He said, "This is a terrible idea, captain. We all feel it. Let's say to hell with the octos and science and set course for a place where neither can follow."

"That's the problem, Mr. Turcotte. If you can find me a place where Jack Scaly won't soon follow, we'll set course for it today. But I think you'll find it exists nowhere on the Lord's earth, and certainly not in the heavens above."

"So we're doing this out of patriotic duty?"

"We're doing this because I want to one day retire and spend my afternoons sipping tea in a rose garden without worrying about some accursed octo tripod wobbling over the hills to trample the bushes and incinerate everything else."

"Oh." Turcotte chewed on a fingernail. He worried it for half a minute, then spat the husk through a porthole. "I thought we were doing this to get rich."

"That, too, Mr. Turcotte."

"I suppose that when it comes to finding one's fate, there are worse pursuits."

But Sujata had produced her spyglass again—*snick, click*—and returned her attention to the storm. She pulled the speaking tube from its clamp and said, "Mr. de Vries. Spin up the engines. Give them the reins a bit, let them gallop. Wellington hired us for speed. Let's show him we can deliver."

The tube funneled his response, and a whiff of petrol, to her. "Aye, captain."

Turcotte turned a suspicious eye in her direction as she quit the bridge. "You're sure there's nothing worrying you, captain?"

"Fetch me if you glimpse any tripods," she said. "Otherwise, I'll relieve you in six."

* * *

They sailed for a night and a day. Sometimes their course let the *Shiva* ride the rising wind, earning them precious hours, and other times it put the ship bucking and thrashing straight into its teeth like a suicidal skipjack dead-set on hurling itself down a shark's gullet. The whine of overworked engines became the atonal music by which the plan began to unravel. In other words, it was business as usual aboard the *Shiva*.

The wind put them hours behind schedule. A bit past one in the morning, Sujata and Turcotte stood on the bridge in darkness broken only by the sepulchral glow from the phosphorescent paint on the instrumentation. A hundred yards underfoot the Ganges River gurgled through the lush valleys of Uttarakhand. But nobody could see them. The moonless night that enabled them to glide unnoticed past the octos also rendered them invisible to the sharpest eyes in the Royal Navy. Assuming Wellington's talk about providing a beard hadn't been a skein of lies.

Turcotte asked, "What's the word, captain?"

They had three options. They could descend, drop anchor, and try to hold position until dawn, when navy eyes could spy the *Shiva* and initiate the promised diversion. But that would mean putting themselves at the mercy of the cyclone as the fringes they'd skirted all day and night passed over them. Or they could fire up the arclights and turn the ship into the brightest thing for leagues around. But that would draw attention from humans and octos alike, likely defeating the purpose of the diversion. Or they could stay the course and hope like hell there were enough bright sparks among Wellington's people that the navy would do the sums and catch up soon after sunrise.

Sujata weighed her choices. When the future contained nothing but bad, worse, and worst, it was the captain's job to choose between them.

"We plunge ahead, Mr. Turcotte. No lights."

And so they did. Which is how, two hours later, they soared through the middle of an octo nest.

Sujata, who had given up on sleep until the conclusion of their venture, stood at the wheel. Turcotte, whom she had relieved but never felt entirely comfortable away from the wheel when things were tense, dozed in a chair that hung in a corner of the bridge. The green corpse light of the instrumentation glistened from the drool at the corner of his mouth. He snored loudly enough that she didn't immediately notice how the timbre of the engine noise had changed.

But something pricked her ears. She flung an orange at Turcotte—"Stow it!"—then called down to the engine room. "Trouble down there? No? Idle 'em for a tick."

De Vries's engineers disengaged the rotors. The *chuff-chuff-chuff* of the props faded away, as did the hum of machinery. Deck vibrations faded as the *Shiva* stopped fighting the wind. The world fell silent but for the creak of rigging, the susurration of wind, and the gurgle of a mountainside river.

Yet still a faint grinding persisted; it sounded like a drunken nob trying to disentangle a pile of forks.

Turcotte heard it, too. They looked at each other. The whites of his widened eyes glistened at the same moment the realization struck her. The mechanical noise wasn't coming from the *Shiva*. It came from below. It was the sound of Jack Scaly's tripods massaging each other, as they were oddly wont to do.

"Well," said Turcotte, "we're buggered."

Thoughts racing, Sujata spoke into the tube again. "Deploy the guns! Phosphorus rounds only! Engineering, keep the boilers hot but do *not* engage the rotors!"

A few seconds later the familiar but dreaded quadruple thump of unfolding gun emplacements rattled the deck. Sujata gritted her teeth, hoping the noise wouldn't draw attention from the inhuman invaders massed somewhere in the darkness below. Hoping they wouldn't need the guns at all. Hoping to all seven hells they could drift unnoticed past Jack Scaly and his incomprehensible diversions. Hoping the nest was small, and that none of the monsters looked up.

The seconds scuttled past, single file, ushered by the jackrabbit thumping of her heart.

The world contracted to a disjointed series of sensory impressions. The creak of the *Shiva*'s rigging and metallic grinding of the octos. The jitter of the wheel under her hands as the deployed guns changed the ship's trim and snagged the wind. The sweet smell of a ruptured orange, the peppery scent of the unlit cheroot tucked behind her ear, the sour odor of the sweat trickling from her armpits. Turcotte eased to his feet as though the octos might hear the creaking of his chair. He exhaled, long and slow.

They drifted with the wind, a silent shadow in a moonless sky. Part of her wondered how long they'd have to wait until they reengaged the engines, and whether the cyclone they'd fled would overcome them.

No death beams lanced up from the jungle to cleave them in

two. No tentacles enfolded the airship in a crushing embrace.

After a handful of minutes that felt like decades, Turcotte whispered, “Whew. Thank God for small—”

A thunderous *crack* interrupted him as an octo heat ray sliced through the jungle, and the air, and his relief. The overwhelming scent of ozone wafted through the cabin portholes. Moments later it mingled with smoke and the smell of a forest fire. Flames leapt from a hundred-meter swath of blazing bombax trees like candles on a giant birthday cake. Ruddy firelight illuminated a pair of alien tripods parked in a clearing. Most of their tentacles were knotted together in a writhing mass of limbs, like an orgy of chromium-plated asps. Sujata glimpsed their frantic struggle to break free of each other. The aliens tossed each other back and forth in the effort to unlimber themselves. No wonder Jack Scaly’s beam had swerved wide of its target: they’d been caught with their knickers down.

But once they pulled apart they’d have the *Shiva* dead to rights, skewered between triangulated heat rays.

“Weapons!” Sujata yelled. “Target the octos and fire! Set those bastards aflame before they pull apart!”

The deck juddered underfoot and the ship slewed to starboard when Vi’s crew let loose. Phosphorus rounds etched incandescent streaks in the darkness. A rain of silvery-red meteors traced a line of perforations across the clearing and the thrashing octos. One beast took a rapid sequence of hits across the central pod; the phosphorus burned sun-bright, melting through the unearthly metal. Bluish sparks fountained from the ruptured tripod, a sign that the terrestrial oxygen/nitrogen atmosphere wreaked havoc upon mysterious alien chemistries. The air smelled like a thousand snuffed candles. The punctured tripod flailed twice, serpentine limbs spasming.

Another volley tried to slew across the writhing mass to visit the same justice upon the other octo. But the hail of gunfire sheared through the tangled mass of limbs. The surviving tripod lurched free of its dying partner.

Sujata bellowed, “Engines NOW!”

The octo spun like a dervish to stalk the *Shiva.* A clank shook the airship, and then the deck lurched as the props reengaged. The air sizzled. Sujata slammed the attitude controls to rotate the gimbaled propellers and spun the wheel hard to starboard. Jack Scaly's heat ray flashed so close to the bridge that she could have sworn she saw the heat ripple of scorched air flashing just beyond the portholes. The ray parried the gunners' next volley, vaporizing the projectiles before they could find their target. Sujata jinked the controls again, trying to outmaneuver the alien's invisible beam weapon. But even the fleetest airship was a ponderous thing compared to a tripod. The odor of scorched metal washed through the portholes as the heat beam again sizzled through the night. The airship flung itself upward. Sujata twisted the levers but the portside attitude controls wouldn't budge. A tremendous crash echoed from the forest below at the same moment de Vries cried, "We've lost props one and three!"

"All weapons fire on that bastard before it cuts us in half! All weapons FIRE!"

An incandescent rain of falling stars converged upon the second tripod. The monster thrashed. It ignited another swath of jungle as it struggled to bring its beam to bear on the ship again. Then the phosphorus burned through its skin and the demon went up like a Roman candle.

Damn you, Jack Scaly.

* * *

It was the closest shave in a career characterized by narrow strokes of luck. Less than a yard inward and the heat ray would have sliced through the *Shiva*'s canopy from stem to stern. Unlike a Navy ship, their hydrogen envelope lacked the benefit of mirrored armor. Jack Scaly's beam would have filleted them like a trout.

At sunrise, Sujata donned a harness and went out to inspect the damage with de Vries. She saw instantly there was no point in dropping anchor to recover the fallen rotor pods. The heat ray that sheared two props from the Shiva had melted straight through the fittings and vaporized inches of the best Yorkshire steel. Even if they did recover the lost props, and somehow found them miraculously undamaged by their fall, they had no hope of reattaching them to the ship without several weeks in dry dock. Their choices were to turn around and limp back through the gauntlet of octo nests, or limp the last few leagues toward their destination.

They couldn't afford the repairs, much less new engine pods, without a big payday. And with half their propulsion and maneuverability lost they'd be at the mercy of the weather, as the return course would put them straight at the remnants of the cyclone they'd fled for the past two days. They needed money and they needed to lighten their burden. They needed cavorite.

So they pressed forward.

Turcotte watched the burning jungle recede in the distance. He pointed to the plume of black smoke billowing into the morning sky. "I reckon Wellington's chums know we've been here. As will every octo on the subcontinent."

He had a point. Sujata stationed crewmen from de Vries's and Vi's teams as extra eyes on the final leg of their journey to the warehouse. Vi herself stumbled onto the bridge a few hours later, looking as though she hadn't slept since before the first octo landings in London, and smelling like she'd last bathed a year before that. Sujata took her aside while the lookouts murmured to each other and Turcotte, who had become a font of profanity as he wrestled with the half-crippled airship.

"We spent a lot of phosphorus on Jack Scaly last night," said the weaponeer.

Sujata nodded. "We won't have to do any more fighting. Wellington's people are taking care of that. So open everything we have left." She'd never seen Violet so exhausted; the captain wondered, briefly, whether it was a good idea to have her working with volatile phosphorus in this state. But they'd arrive in a few hours, winds permitting, and what choice did she have?

Vi nodded. "It's done, captain. Just wanted to warn you that we might not have enough left for what you intend."

"One problem at a time, Vi. Now get some sleep."

The weaponeer nearly bumped into de Vries, who entered the bridge just as she departed.

"Let me guess," said Sujata. "Having recalculated the tolerances for our remaining engines, you're worried we lack the lift and maneuverability to carry out my frankly ingenious plan."

The engineer sighed. "Yes. It was quite clever, captain. But we overlooked something. We were counting on the cavorite to augment our buoyancy. But in fact—" Here he rattled a sheaf of papers covered in his precise draftsman's hand. There were equations, diagrams, arrows, and a rather detailed sketch of Turcotte crapping in Wellington's hat. "—It will actually reduce the *Shiva*'s buoyancy."

"What the blue blazes are you prattling on about?" She studied his eyes, wondering if he was drunk.

"The cavorite will reduce the weight of the air around us, along with the weight of our ship. By reducing that differential it reduces the buoyancy."

"You didn't mention this before."

"Where the cavorite helps is with the thrust-to-weight ratio." He rattled the papers again. "And until last night we had a comfortable margin of excess thrust."

"You mean back when we had four engines."

"Yes."

"And now?"

"Now we don't."

* * *

Unmarked octo nests aside, Wellington's map proved accurate. The *Black Shiva* drifted over the secret compound of T. David England & Sons around midafternoon. They found no sign of human activity in the camp, and no sign of tripods lurking in the surrounding forest. Perhaps Wellington had been true to his word and the Royal Navy had drawn their bug-eyed attention. Sujata gave the order to drop anchors and lower belaying lines. Soon the ship hovered over the steel hemisphere of the storehouse while the crew descended to swarm through the camp, only to find it abandoned.

Vi led a team into the warehouse—they didn't waste time being discreet about the break-in—while Sujata and de Vries supervised the men and women who welded a series of iron hooks to the roof of the warehouse. The captain kept one eye on the work and the other on the inky clouds massing in the southeastern sky. They'd limped away from their tussle with Jack Scaly, and now the cyclone was catching up.

Vi emerged from the warehouse. Sujata, standing atop the shallow dome, cupped a hand around her mouth and called down, "Tell me you have good news."

"It's full, captain. If the markings on the crates can be trusted, they support that weasely toff's claims."

Sujata slapped her engineer on the back. "What'd I tell you? This is going to work."

But Vi lingered on the loamy soil below, shuffling her feet and looking uncomfortable. "Uh. There's more." At the captain's exasperated nod, she continued: "They anticipated us. The foundation isn't wood, it's reinforced concrete. The piles are a foot thick and go down at least a yard. We don't have the phosphorus to burn through them. The metal shell is sunk straight into the concrete, so we can't pluck that free, either, without several days' work with sledges and picks."

Sujata pushed her hat far back on her head. Beads clicked together when she ran a hand through her hair. "If we ever meet in the afterlife, Mr. T. David England," she muttered, "you'll know me because I'll be the one stomping on your bollix with most singular dedication."

De Vries shrugged. "It was a good idea, captain."

Perhaps England and Sons had foreseen their strategy. Or perhaps they were more pragmatic, and had realized that storing vast amounts of cavorite in their warehouse would render the dome nearly weightless, thereby making it susceptible to storms and monsoon winds. Hence the reinforcements. This was probably the most solidly constructed building in all of the Raj. Trust a weasel who named himself "England" for business dealings with the Crown to be possessed of a particularly paranoid and devious mind. So they couldn't cut the warehouse loose of its foundation. And even if they could, the concrete slab between the cavorite and the earth (where it wouldn't benefit from the gravitational shielding) grossly outweighed the simple wooden floor they'd planned around. The *Shiva* would struggle to lift the damn thing even if they weren't down two rotors.

De Vries cleared his throat, as though hoping to nudge the captain from an angry reverie. "We have to change tack," he said.

"But stealing an entire warehouse, walls and all, it would have been … I mean, it would have looked …" The captain sighed. "They'd be telling the story in every pub and chophouse from Sumatra to São Paulo. We could have dined out on this one for the rest of our natural lives."

"Sometimes clever is the enemy of practical."

A gust of wind tugged at Sujata's hat. She grabbed it before it went tumbling away. "If we use the cargo nets, we can sling them under the Shiva to compensate for the lost rotors. How quickly can you sketch out the rigging?"

De Vries produced a length of paper from a trouser pocket. "Already done."

"I am pained by your utter lack of faith in my vision," she said. "It borders on insubordination."

"I think of it as anticipating the ship's needs."

Sujata called down to Vi, who still waited below. It took extra effort to make herself heard over the wind rustling through the surrounding forest. "Scratch it. We'll use the cargo nets. Get those crates outside and empty them. We're taking the cavorite, nothing else." To the crewmen welding hooks atop the dome, she said, "Belay that welding. Get topside and lower the cargo nets. And dump the steel cable. All of it. Double time." Then she turned back to de Vries. "Get your rigging in place."

The engineer craned his neck, taking in first the airship bobbing a dozen fathoms overhead, and then the wildly swaying trees in the surrounding forest. She imagined Turcotte on the bridge right now, cursing a blue streak while he fought the rising wind with a crippled airship. De Vries' frown reflected her own misgivings. But they were here now and standing on a fortune.

"We've come this far," she said, as the first swollen raindrops pinged against the warehouse dome. "And we don't have to worry about Jack Scaly, thanks to Wellington's tars. Just wind and rain, and we're no strangers to either."

The reassurances sounded slightly hollow to her own ears. But there was *so much money* in the warehouse.

* * *

So it wasn't until a few hours later, when the octo tripod emerged from the mountainside forest just as the crew struggled to sling the last of the sodden cargo nets under the *Shiva*, that Captain Sujata finally accepted that she never, ever should have agreed to this job. Jack Scaly wielded its heat ray like a carving knife and set upon the *Shiva* without any hint of Royal Navy encumbrance. The first beam pierced the *Shiva*'s lifting body to vent the central hydrogen bladder; the second severed the cargo nets and sent their hard-earned prize crashing into the clearing below.

"Wellington!" she yelled, though the percussive tattoo of the guns drowned out her scream. "You thrice-damned scalawag! I'll cut your—"

But then she plummeted through the wind and rain like an anchor weight filled with piss and rage. Tumbling toward a rapidly approaching earth strobed by lightning and incandescent streaks from phosphorus rounds, she had just a few seconds to question her choices in life.

The cargo nets hit the ground first. They burst open, spreading chunks of high-purity cavorite across the clearing. Including directly beneath Sujata. And the captain, now weighing a hundredth of what she did just seconds earlier, tumbled less like an anchor weight, less even than a wounded pigeon, and more like a feather caught in a gale.

She had plenty of time during her long, slow, and thoroughly dizzying fall to watch Vi's guns pierce the alien tripod and set its innards ablaze. The weaponeer had kept phosphorus rounds in reserve; Sujata wondered if she'd even bothered to open any of them. She also had an unobstructed view of how the two surviving rotors swiveled back and forth to keep the *Shiva* centered over the clearing, taking advantage of the cavorite to render the severely damaged ship airborne. Turcotte fought like hell to compensate for the lost buoyancy, the swirling gale, and the kick from Vi's guns. It gave the captain another idea.

Sujata had descended to within a few fathoms of the ground when the winds pushed her beyond the reach of the scattered cavorite. She tucked and rolled as her full weight reasserted itself, thereby softening her landing in the rain-sodden earth just enough to prevent broken bones.

The crew lowered anchor lines. She didn't dare climb back up until the weather subsided; she'd had enough of rain-slick rope. So she took shelter in the warehouse to wait out the wind and rain, wondering how much of the shattered cavorite she could stick in her pockets, wondering if octos would send another tripod in their direction, and wondering how they would make the rendezvous with Wellington's people. The storm gave her hours alone with her thoughts. Near sundown she decided that, on balance, she hated Jack Scaly even more than Wellington. If it had to come to a choice between a magnificent payday and seeing the octo menace removed from earth once and for all, she'd opt for the latter. Best of all, she knew how to get the cavorite to Wellington's people.

Watching the gunners tear loose on Jack Scaly, and seeing how the *Shiva* bucked and kicked when they did, had given her the solution to their thrust problem.

While the crew patched the hole Jack Scaly had burned through their lifting envelope, Captain Sujata explained her new plan to her lieutenants. She hardly needed to remind them that the trade winds blew generally from the northeast at these latitudes. So if they could but attain sufficient altitude to catch the fastest winds, they could drift back across the subcontinent toward the heart of the Raj. And unless Wellington's people were asleep at the switch (admittedly there was some debate about this), they'd have an eye out for the *Shiva*.

They'd lost half their engines and a considerable amount of hydrogen. But they had gravitational shielding and four very large guns. And so the delivery that would mark a change in humanity's fortunes came heralded by intermittent bursts of gunfire, riding incandescent streamers that cleaved the sky.

They ran out of fuel, and ammunition, several hundred leagues from Bombay. By the time they paid for new engines along with several weeks in a shipyard, and rearmed the ship, and refueled it, the cost of their misadventure grossly outweighed any meager profits. They returned to port poorer than when they'd left.

Yet somehow the *Black Shiva* always held on to its letter of marque even in spite of the alliances that would, eventually, end the war.

Captain Sujata Malhotra and her crew dined out on that particular tale for the rest of their long and storied careers.

Gracie's Fire

Leah Cutter

Mother-of-a-whore my boots hurt. They pinched my toes, chafed my ankles, and the damn heels made my back and calves ache. The best part of every night was finally getting home to the garret above the feed shop and taking 'em off. Even if they was a present from my long-lost husband, god bless his soul, made outta solid black leather with brass hooks and laces, they felt like they was taking orders from the devil himself.

I still wore 'em with a smile. I even practiced walking as gracefully as I could, from one end of The Gold Mine Saloon to the other, across the sawdust and straw-strewn floor, balancing my tray with one hand, like they did at the Barstow Hotel, in the fancy part of town. They did make my hips sway, which garnered attention and more tips. Tips that I saved, tips that were gonna get me out of that garret and maybe buy me my own piece of land someday.

Not that I was likely to get any tips tonight. The saloon was deader than a priest's cell on a Saturday night. The seven-twenty train from Sacramento wasn't coming in: bridge had flooded out (again). As we was directly across the muddy street from the train station, it brought us most of our trade.

As for folks from here in Stockton, well, Lucky Lucy's had just opened down the street—and they had dancing girls.

Mister Thomas didn't much approve of them. He didn't make us strip down to nothing either. I couldn't have worn my dress to church, but it only bared my shoulders, ankles, and arms. I kinda liked the color too, a rich gold across my chest that didn't show the dirt too much, over a black short-sleeved blouse and a hitched up skirt. It showed off that pale Irish skin of mine, and Mister Thomas said the gold matched my green eyes. Nothing worked with my hair of course—I wore it shamefully short, and it was too thick and black to be much use.

The only "special" that The Gold Mine Saloon had to offer was that hulking steam-powered contraption that took up half the bar, another one of Mister Thomas' inventions. Me and the girls done made him get rid of most of thems: the weird, flickering, automatic lights (we all preferred gaslight); the odd moving belt for taking the dishes back to the kitchen (it was nice of him to try and save us some steps, but the pile ups and broken glassware made all our lives hell); and the clockwork automaton that used to run the drink machine (Mister Thomas said it wasn't alive, and its eyes was just glass, but it'd still watch all the girls walk around the saloon, giving us chills).

We had traditional kegs of beer, bottles of cheap whisky, and cheap moonshine—cloudy liquid in big bottles that'd eat anything, even brass, if we tried cleaning with it. I coulda made better, but Mister Tomas didn't want to get into the distilling business, not like that.

However, the machine, well, it could make pretty much any drink. Large glass jars of colored liquid—pink, brown, green, blue, and yellow—stuck out of one end of the sleek brass, like a peacock's tail. At least a dozen knobs, wheels, and gears regulated the flow and temperature of the liquid as it churned through the machine. The twisting spigot on the other end looked like glass, but it was hard as diamond.

That contraption could make damn near anything. Fizzy, sparkling lemonade that tasted like the perfect summer day. Dark, rich wine that reminded you of Mama's stews in deep winter. That odd, blue drink that left smoke on your tongue and tears in your eyes.

A lot of the locals didn't care much for the machine, never buying drinks from it. But sometimes a riverboat hand or a farmer'd get drunk, tell me to make 'em whatever I felt like.

I always got a good tip from that.

Sometimes stupid cowpokes would come in, drunk already, then dare each other to come up with wilder concoctions, and force 'em down.

Then I'd have to shove 'em out the door before they started

puking.

Tonight, though, no one was ordering nothing. Mister Thomas was at his regular weekly poker game—the one I'd rescued him from at least twice over the years—and had left me in charge for the night, as usual. Old Dusky sat at the bar, nursing his customary one whisky. He were a regular, but rarely talked. Just sat, had his one drink, drawing patterns on the bar with his finger. Two businessmen sat in one corner, talking about some land deal they was putting together.

And that was it.

I'd already sent all the other girls home, so it was just me behind the long bar. Me in those damn boots that I daydreamed about burning in the grate at the far end of the saloon. I'd set my mind to close the bar early—kick Dusky out and start moving the businessmen along—when the doors swung open and in came this group of four men.

Well, at first I thought they was men. They was in these big black cloaks with the hoods up, shapeless and hiding their faces. But they were regular height, and didn't look too wide, either.

"Gentlemen," I called out. "We're clos—"

That's when I realized something was wrong.

They turned to stare at me, all of 'em together, like they was one person, really. Peeking out from underneath those black hoods was some of the orangest skin I'd ever seen, like they was pumpkins or something. They had weird black eyes and no real noses. Their lips were thin and chins were long and pointed, with warts, like what a witch would wear.

Course I didn't scream or nothing. Didn't know what they were, had never seen nothing like them before, but they was obviously from out of town.

Wouldn't know real prices for anything, and it weren't like we had anything written down, even if they could read.

And maybe they'd be good tippers, besides.

* * *

I got 'em settled at a table in the center of the saloon. I cut Dusky off, sent him along his way. The businessmen didn't look too happy about the outsiders there, so it weren't too long before they was gone too.

Which left just me and the four newcomers.

"So what'll it be, boys?" I asked, coming out from behind the bar, letting my hips sway just a bit.

None of them paid any attention. They all looked me directly in the face.

That'd never happened before.

"Whissskey," said the first guy. He was a little taller than the others.

I couldn't really read his expression, but he seemed proud of himself.

"Whisky all around?" I asked. They didn't nod, but they didn't disagree either. "I'll bring a bottle. That'll be a quarter eagle." I wasn't about to bring nobody no booze without payment first. At their blank looks, I added "Two-fifty."

It was only two bits more than the regular price. I was just including my tip in the cost.

They had some kind of hissing language they used with each other. Sounded like drunk Mexican to me. The tall one brought out a gold piece from his sleeve and slid it across the table.

I didn't try to count how many fingers he had—as long as he kept them to himself, we was gonna be just fine.

He'd passed me a full eagle—ten whole dollars. "I'll keep this as your tab," I told him, picking up the coin and weighing it. Didn't bother tasting it until after I'd turned away, but it was pure gold as far as I could tell.

I wouldn't have kept the whole thing, if they hadn't spent it all by the end of the evening. I would have given them change. Or at least some of it. My mama may not have been kind, but she did raise me to be fair. Mostly.

I brought 'em back a bottle of the cheapest stuff we had, along with four clean glasses. Then I went back behind the bar, cleaned up Dusky's glass, the businessmen's, and watched my new guests.

They didn't seem quite sure what to do at first. Eventually, they figured it out, pouring the booze into the glasses, then the glasses down their throats.

Maybe they weren't complete strangers, because they swallowed down stuff that would strip the finish off the bar and didn't cough or sputter once.

After they'd finished off a third of the bottle, they seemed to loosen up, as all men do. They leaned back in their chairs, and the tall one even flipped his hood back.

Damn, he was ugly. Bald as a baby's butt, with a dark web of lines growing like tree roots out of the back of his neck and up into his skull. His black eyes shone wet and long, kind of like a horse's. He hissed at the others, getting them to flip their hoods back too.

The others were just as ugly, though I'd been right—Big Baldy was the tallest of the group, and had the strongest features. The others were smaller, not like kids, but not fully grown, either.

I couldn't make heads or tails outta their hissing talk. They did seem worried about something. I sure hoped it wasn't the money, that they weren't thinking about robbing the place. I couldn't get the day's take out of the bar and to the bank until morning.

While they was pouring another round for themselves, I got the revolver Mister Thomas had given me, that I'd taught all the other girls to use. It weren't one of his inventions, no, it was a real Smith and Wesson, a six-shooter, that I made damn sure was kept cleaner than brand new sheets from the Sears and Roebuck Catalog.

I also started up the coals under the big kettle, so I'd have plenty of steam later if I needed it. Mister Thomas didn't approve of us wasting his special coal and heating up the water before a client asked for a drink from the machine, but I had a feeling about these four.

Once Big Baldy and the others had finished their whisky, I came out from behind the bar again. "Want another?" I asked. They was all leaning way back in their chairs now, loose in the way a cowpoke gets after a hard night's whoring.

"Thisss machine," Big Baldy said, waving his hand toward the beast on the bar. "How much for it?"

"Y'all got enough on your tab for more drinks," I told him. "Anything special you want? Or should I just make you something?"

"Make usssss, yessss, make usss ssssomething." Big Baldy pressed his thin lips together, tightly, pushing them outward.

Hell, was that a smile? Or was he making a kissy face at me?

I sure didn't stick around to find out. I went back behind the bar, tightened the ends of the hoses connected to the kettle, then opened up the valves so the steam would rise, powering the machine.

It came to life slowly, despite the head of steam I'd already built up. The bottles gurgled—the blue one especially—as seals formed, making sure nothing leaked. Then the dials started lighting up, one after another, showing temperature, pressure, moisture, and a bunch of things Mister Thomas had told me that I didn't remember and couldn't read, having never learned my letters.

So what would it be for Big Baldy? I paused in my considering, looking over the machine at him. He still leaned back, like a lazy cat, playing with the glass in front of him.

What would make him relax more? I remembered thinking about whoring. Maybe that was what this crew needed. Something that would both relax 'em, and raise 'em up.

I started with the yellow—liquid gold, as Mister Thomas likened it. Then some brown: Those boys needed some earthiness. A touch of blue for whimsy. Then topped it off with the pink, for the frills of the dancing girls up the street.

It didn't take the machine long to process, huffing and puffing as it blended the liquids in its sleek innards, finally distilling the prettiest orange drink at the other end.

I was congratulating myself as I took the first glass over. It looked a perfect match. I was sure to get a big tip from this.

But Big Baldy looked askance at it. "What isss thisss?"

"You asked me to make you something," I shot back.

Mister Thomas would be so mad at me if I wasted a drink from the machine. He sometimes got angry enough to take it out of my wages. I always made it back, though, fixing something that broke either at the bar or in town.

"Ssssomething humanssss, yessss," Big Baldy replied.

Human? Well, hell. These boys really weren't from around

these parts.

Not like I was gonna stop making 'em drinks, though. We even served Indians here at the Gold Mine Saloon.

"Tis human," I told him. "I made it from the machine built by Mister Thomas. You should try it," I coaxed. "Just a sip. I'm sure it's good for what ails you."

Big Baldy glared at me, glared at the glass I offered him, but he finally reached out with those too-many fingers and took the drink.

He brought it to his nose—no idea if he could smell anything through those tiny slits. I was afraid he was gonna unfurl a tongue or something to taste it first, but he brought it to his mouth, taking a small sip.

After Big Baldy smacked his lips together like an old timer who'd lost all his teeth, he finally looked back up at me. "Issss good!"

"One for each?" I asked, nodding at the other gents.

"Yessss! One for everyone here! You too!" Big Baldy said expansively. "Tell usssss your name?"

"Gracie," I told him. It wouldn't harm none, and might keep 'em friendlier, later.

'Cause I could see that keeping 'em friendly now weren't gonna be a problem—that drink had turned Big Baldy into one jovial pumpkin.

* * *

"Now boys, I'm sorry to tell you, but it's closing time," I eventually told Big Baldy and his friends, Frick, Frack, and Nod. I had no idea what any of their names were, but I was plum tired, through and through.

And my feet were *still* killing me.

They'd tossed me an extra eagle, for my troubles. But it weren't enough to keep me going, not when dawn was creeping up outa the east.

"Graccccie," Big Baldy sang out. "Jusssst one more. Pleasssse?"

I'd already planned on that. "Last call," I said. "Last one.

Then, vamoose."

Big Baldy actually giggled at that, like a weird pumpkin child. "Vamooooshhhh!" he said, his hand flying through the air, toward Frick, Frack, and Nod.

They chittered at that, like not quite full-grown giggles.

I knew what I should make them to get them moving along—a drink of home.

It was a gamble. It might make 'em morose. I'd done that once already, mixing 'em a drink with too much of the yellow and not enough brown.

But they still needed to be moseying along.

So I gave them great brown muddy skies, with dots of yellow stars, blue hard rocks and soft pink nests.

Then I mixed up something for me. Started with a solid moonshine base, then mixed in a dash of all the colored liquids.

Mister Thomas had told me once never to add everything in. It would muddy the drink. Too much of everything and not enough of a single taste, a single feeling.

But I wasn't so tired that I couldn't coax that machine to sit up and sing for its supper if I set my mind to it.

The drinks for Big Baldy were all a muddy brown, while mine was the color of fire, red and furious.

I'd actually made this drink one time before, named it after myself: Gracie's Fire.

I merely sipped my cordial, planning to finish it later, while the boys slammed theirs back, as I thought they might. "So it's a good evening to ya," I said as I came back out from behind the bar, tray in hand. I collected their glasses and the empty bottle, then turned back toward the bar.

Big Baldy and the others hissed at each other. I had no idea what language it was, but they sounded more intent now, not so relaxed.

I got myself back behind the bar again, brought the revolver up beside me, and waited.

"Gracccccie," Big Baldy said, standing, swaying.

I took a sip of my own drink, "It's been fun, gentlemen, but I gotta close up, and you have to go."

"Not without you, Graccccie," Big Baldy said.

He made that kissy face again. Shit, he was ugly.

"And your marvelousssss masssshine."

Damn it. I knew they was gonna be trouble sooner or later.

I picked up the revolver and cocked it. "Can't have it. Need y'all to just move along, now."

"Gracccccie, you wouldn't sssshoot usssss," Big Baldy said confidently.

I put a bullet into the floor, directly in front of his feet.

Mama may not have been the best, but she made sure I was well-versed in the essentials: Shooting and moonshine.

Mister Thomas would just have to understand about the hole in the floor.

Big Baldy started, then stood up straight. The others chittered at him. He raised one of his odd, too-many-fingered hands and silenced them.

"I got five bullets still warm and waiting," I told him. "Now, you've been good customers, so let's just leave it at that."

Big Baldy shook his head. "I'm sssssssorry, Gracccccie." He held up some kind of weapon of his own. It looked like a short rifle, but the end was blown out, like a trumpeter's horn.

Now, I'd seen duels out on the street. No one was ever a winner. And while I was fast, I couldn't take down four of them, not before I got myself shot.

I was just gonna have to sweet talk my way out of this. Unfortunately, being sweet wasn't something Mama had ever bothered to teach me.

I kept the gun pointed directly at Big Baldy's chest, while with my other hand I took a sip of my drink. Casual like. Not because I needed the extra courage. Or to prove to myself that I could do this without my hand shaking.

It warmed me from tip to toes, like the sun was already coming up and heating me up on the inside. "Now, gentlemen," I said. "Let's be reasonable about this. I'm sure we can work something out."

Before I could say another word, Big Baldy shook his head. "No," he said.

Then he shot me.

* * *

You know those old houses, out on the prairie, that get abandoned after the fever runs through, or maybe the Indians come in and kill everyone? The way the walls all crumble in, bricks and boards collapsing to dust?

That was how my bones felt. Big Baldy's gun shot out a huge black net that wrapped around my chest, pinning my arms to my sides and making my bones feel like they was all crumbly, nothing solid left inside.

Luckily, I was able to stay upright. Damn boots hurt too much for me to lose feeling with my feet: They was strapped in too tight to turn to dust like the rest of my bones.

Frick, Frack, and Nod all swarmed up over the bar. They made hissing noises at the machine, stroking it and chittering.

Big Baldy looked all too pleased with himself.

But they hadn't pinned my arms all the way, just across my shoulders and my chest. I still had my hands free.

They wasn't paying me no mind.

I didn't have my gun anymore. I'd dropped that when I'd been hit.

But I could still reach my drink.

It was mostly colored moonshine, something these idiots had no idea about.

Mister Thomas could always replace the bar. But he couldn't replace the machine. He'd told me that himself.

With careful, slow movements, I reached for my glass. My hands were shakier than the legs on a newborn calf. I had to watch my fingers to make sure they closed, then tightened, around the drink.

Just as slowly, I brought my hand up and my mouth down, getting a good mouthful of the liquid.

Gracie's Fire.

I didn't swallow it down, though it burned. I took small breaths, afraid the fumes would knock me out.

I took one stumbling step, then another, before I finally reached the lamp on the edge of the bar.

"Gracccccie, where are you going?" Big Baldy asked. He

sounded like he was laughing.

That just made me push my poor, abused feet forward one more step. Then another.

I stumbled around the end of the bar until the lamp stood between me and Big Baldy, then clumsily knocked the lamp off, exposing the flame.

"I won't hurtsssss you," Big Baldy assured me.

With my mouth full, I couldn't tell him, *Too bad. Cause I'm about to hurt you.*

Then I blew that pure moonshine straight onto the flame.

An arc of fire jumped from the light and hit Baldy straight in the chest.

Big Baldy fell back on his ass, screaming, his cloak flaming up nicely. He beat at the flames with both hands, not paying me any mind.

Frick, Frack, and Nod took one look at him, and skedaddled.

Seemed they didn't feel like being toasted.

As best I could, I stripped off that damn net. It was sticky and clung to my fingers like spiderwebs. But I peeled it off and dove for my gun, finally holding it with still weak hands, pointing it right at Big Baldy's chest as he rose up from the ground.

The gun he'd used on me was out of his reach, still on the bar. I picked it up too, pointing it straight at his head. "Keeping this as collateral," I told him. "Now git." I started walking toward him.

Big Baldy's cloak was in tatters. Seemed he was just as orange all over, with weird black lines pulsing over his skin, like a map of a river delta.

"We needsssss the masssshine," Big Baldy complained as he started backing toward the door.

"Then come during business hours and make a deal with Mister Thomas," I told him.

When Baldy stopped moving, I put another bullet in the floor. "Git."

"We will return," he warned, but he left.

I locked the doors behind him and leaned back, taking a deep breath.

I had no doubt they'd come back. But I also had faith in Mister Thomas. Once he'd taken apart that gun they'd left behind, he'd know exactly what kind of drink I should serve 'em next time.

I took another sip of Gracie's Fire, thanking Mama for having raised me right, with a steady hand and a solid appreciation of moonshine.

After I made sure that Frick, Frack, and Nod hadn't broken that damn contraption, I could finally close up the saloon for the night, head back up to my garret.

And take my damn boots off.

Quinta Essentia

Bradley P. Beaulieu

On the day they finally came, Sean Brannon tossed and turned in his bed, his ligature exoskeleton whirring while assisting his movements. The sound of the ligature was nearly, though not quite, masking the childlike whine that escaped him with each turn of his broken body. He rolled and lay in a fetal position, and found Therese an arm's length away—a measure of space that in their early days had always seemed so tenderly close but now felt unbridgeable. He knew she felt his movements, heard every minute manifestation of his pain, no matter how hard he tried to mask it, but she tried to remain asleep while he in turn tried to remain as quiet as he could manage.

Dawn was still a distant dream, but Sean knew he would never get back to sleep now, so he threw off his thin blanket and pivoted himself up, joints howling from the attention the levering of a ninety-pound frame to a semi-upright position required. Placing hands on knees and gritting his teeth, he pushed himself up to a trembling stand. It was worse than normal today. The humidity—he could feel it in the air already—and something else, something more arcane than precipitation.

He was sweating by the time he managed to coax his body into a fully upright position.

"Come back to bed," Therese said, reaching over the ruffled bedcovers with an arm that was well shaped. A *woman* that was well shaped. A woman that had helped him every day since this endless nightmare had begun.

"Go back to sleep," Sean said.

She woke more fully then, raised herself up, arms and shoulders angling unnaturally as she propped herself on one elbow. By the light of gas lamps filtering in through the nearby window, she watched him with pity-filled eyes. This was the worst time of day for both of them. It reminded them how frail he was, and he suspected it reminded Therese how frail *she* was—how frail they all were in light of the ways the world had changed—and Therese was a woman who had never liked being reminded of her own mortality. She seemed ready to argue with him, to coax him back to bed, but then she relented and lay back, turning over with the leaden movements of the deeply fatigued, and fell back to sleep.

As she lay there, snoring softly, Sean forced the suit to work his body. As much as he'd learned to ignore pain, he couldn't stand so much of it at once. He started in increments: toes, then feet, then calves and thighs. Sweat gathered on his brow as he continued with his back and stomach and chest. Then neck and jaw and mouth. His arms and hands were the least painful, but he was careful to move them properly—flexing, then releasing, flexing and releasing—lest he strain a something before he'd warmed up.

Every gradient in movement pained him, as if his muscles were being ripped apart. Even his bones felt like millstones, grinding themselves into dust. But he worked through it all. He couldn't give in to the pain, not even a little. Do that, and he *would* return to bed. He would lie there, crying as the pain consumed him, and Therese would be forced to take him to the University hospital and *they'd* work his muscles for him until he'd gotten past it. If that happened, it would be infinitely worse than what he was feeling now.

By the time he pulled his clothes on—clothes made overly large to fit his ligature—the sun was burning blue along the eastern horizon, across the River Wear. In the distance, the towering haulms the Jovians had seeded twelve years before waved gently in the wind. Jovians, they'd been called, even though no one truly believed the haulms had come from Jupiter.

Like candles on a grand cake, the tips of the haulms were lit brilliant orange by the sun. The rest of their length was dark, like mottled ochre earth. Bits of flake fell away from each, twinkling in the light as they were blown by the wind. The skin of the haulms had been doing this ever since they'd emerged from the earth. The flake was like the bark of the eucalyptus, shedding as it grew, but the haulms were so large now that if the wind came from the north, the streets of Durham would be covered with layer upon layer of it—thin, chalky flakes building until the plows came to clear the streets or the rain dissolved it into a thick yellow slurry that eventually washed away.

A hundred men, hands clasped, would be needed to circle the base of one the haulms. Their roots dug deep, some said as deep below the earth as they towered above. Sean doubted this, though. Some few scientists from the British Society of Engineers had commissioned a dig to determine for certain, but gave up after excavating five hundred feet down. They'd run calculations based on how quickly the roots had narrowed, and determined they could go no further than half a mile down.

No one knew why the Jovians had sent the stalks. No person or government had been contacted in any way. The haulms had simply started to grow—all over the Earth—at an unimaginable rate, reaching up and up until they towered over every territory in the world where vegetation grew.

Sean reached the rail yard just as the sun's first rays were gleaming against the horizon in the east. He headed to a red train that in an hour would carry dozens of workers from Durham up to the fluorite mines, one of the city's major exports, especially since the discovery of quinta essentia some thirty years ago. Standing next to it on a second set of rails was a new train, or more accurately a train with a new power plant, fueled by an ingenious mix of quinta incendia, terra, and unda. It was shiny and bright and green with red trim, a recent prototype granted to the mining company from Morgan College—the University's newest college dedicated to the study of elemental science. The gift made sense. The college, after all, benefited greatly from the fluorite mines. It was the primary doping agent in the lenses they made, the ones that focused the five elements into viable and useful applications.

Sean went to the first of the coal cars sitting next to the steam train and, after rolling back the tarpaulin covering the coal, gritted his teeth and began shoveling the coal into the tender. Pain ran through his arms and legs and back, but the truth of it was it felt good, no matter how much pain there was, for it was loosening his muscles even further, the first of many steps in a long and careful process of physical exertion that would, if he was careful, carry him through the entire day. Even his ligature—the exoskeleton drilled into every major bone used in typical human locomotion—whirred more enthusiastically, providing more than half the effort needed.

"Ah, now," came a voice from behind Sean, "please, Mister Kelly, won't you let me help?"

Sean turned and found Thomison, the old rail yard foreman, standing some paces away wearing his engineer's cap and blue denim overalls.

"Good morning, Thomison."

"I'd say the same to you," Thomison said, wiping his hands on a greasy rag, "but I can see it's going poorly enough already."

"I told you, the activity does me good."

"As you say, but you also said it would make you healthier. Just looking at you, begging your pardon, sir, but it's been seven weeks and you're looking worse'n ever."

"Why, thank you, Thomison. You're looking well yourself."

Thomison bowed his head apologetically. "My father told me never to mince words, not when it might do someone some good. I can't have the men late for work. I'll be speaking to Master Hunt later today. I think it might be best if you went to see the doctor, spent a bit of time at home."

"Thomison, I've seen the doctor. I can assure you, there's no need for it."

Thomison looked as though he was going to argue with Sean, but just then his eyes went wide, his mouth fell open, and he pulled his cap off and clutched it to his chest.

Sean turned, stared up at the thin layer of clouds high above. They were parting, folding backward as something with a dark, mottled surface drove through from above. It was huge. Massive. Larger than a bloody castle and shaped like an island ripped up from the sea. Its smooth top warred with a ragged underside and the strange tendrils hanging down from below. It floated down, down, down toward Durham, and behind it came more. One, then two, then three, then a dozen.

They lowered themselves, each heading slowly but inexorably toward one of the haulms.

Around him, the city was coming alive, more and more coming out from their homes or stepping away from the day's early work and staring up at the wonder of it all. Screams came. Children wailed for their mothers. A gun rang out, and then another, rifles and pistols firing up ineffectually at this new menace. But the Jovians cared for them not at all. To them, the humans running about the ground below were little more than a host of teeming insects, a minor annoyance at best.

The first of the lowering shapes was nearing its chosen haulm. Thin tendrils reached up from the massive stalk. More reached down from the underside of the pod. And they intertwined, multiplying, strengthening, drawing one another closer until it had secured itself in place.

"What's it mean, Mister Kelly?" Thomison asked breathlessly.

"I've no idea," Sean replied, "but I can't imagine it bodes well, can you?"

"No, sir, I cannot."

* * *

Several months after the Jovians arrived, the steady rain of flakes dwindled and then stopped altogether, but something new soon took its place: a fecund smell wholly alien to the forests and bogs and marshes Sean had ever been to—a byproduct, the botanists said, of the pods' tendrils attaching to the tops of the haulms. Sean thought it a poor sign. It meant that the haulms had stopped growing, that the pods were nearing maturity, and that the next steps in whatever plans the Jovians had for Earth were nearing.

Or so it seemed to him.

Winter passed and spring arrived. The pods had been catalogued all over Earth, wherever the haulms grew. In point of fact, as far as anyone knew, not a single haulm had been left untethered, suggesting an intelligence that couldn't be explained away as simple extraterrestrial plant life. Fear of the pods and the hatred they'd initially generated were starting to soften. The pods simply were—a new feature of the landscape all over the world—and people were starting to say it was a *good* thing. What they saw floating above over their cities and countrysides was likely the worst of it, they said. The Jovians had come from wherever they'd come, they'd planted their seeds, and they'd grown. Simple as that. Like petunias. And one day, if the science community was right, they'd find something useful from these pods, something revolutionary. They'd come from another world, after all. Who since the days of Ptolemy hadn't dreamed of this very thing?

Twelve months after the arrival of the pods, there was a breakthrough announcement from the team of botanists who'd convened in Durham. They had been taking weekly samples of the pods using the university's science platforms—the undersides of which had been infused with quinta aeris—and now claimed the husks were slowly hardening, perhaps in preparation for some transformational event. A regrowth, a seeding. No one knew for certain, but it seemed to make sense. It was a natural organism, and so of course would have some way of reproducing itself.

Sean was pounding out a bar of iron, red and fresh from the forge, a new job after Thomison, the rail yard foreman, had seen to it that Sean had been shown the street. The forge suited him just fine. It let him work his body all he wanted—a thing it needed even more in the colder months—and the owner was rarely around to hear Sean's groans, which, even Sean had to admit, were difficult to deal with.

Sean was just finishing the forming of the bar he was working on when he heard footsteps, saw the silhouette of a man in a brown suit standing in the entrance to the forge. He blinked against the lowering sun, trying to see who it was.

And then, like a dark dream suddenly returning in the light of day, he recognized him.

"What the bloody hell are you doing here, David?"

David Lock, a scientist Sean had worked with years ago, stepped into the forge. "I've come because we need to talk, Sean."

"Bollocks, we need to talk …" Despite himself, his atrophied muscles began to shake. The ligature was as silent a piece of machinery as there was, but still it betrayed him, its sensors picking up his movements and whirring in response. "I want you to turn around, right now, and leave."

Instead, David took a step forward. "I didn't make this journey lightly, Sean. I've come bearing news. Critical news. And you're one of the few people in the world who would have any hope of understanding it."

"What, some mad new scheme to restore your chair at the University?"

"Nothing of the sort." David doffed his bowler and gripped its rim tightly. "It's the Jovians, Sean. I think I know why they've come."

* * *

David led Sean to an abandoned shoe factory that had shut its doors a decade ago, but when David pulled the heavy door aside, rollers squealing in protest, he found a science lab within it—a proper, well equipped, elemental science lab. It smelled of leather, as if nothing save burning the warehouse to the ground would ever rid the place of it, but warring with this, and the other echoes of its sweatshop past, were four precise rows of workbenches with dozens of individual stations, glass beakers and blue flames and fluorite lenses all about, nearly an exact replica of the lab Sean had helped David run over a dozen years ago.

Sean found he could go no further than a few steps inside the doorway, which made David stop and stare.

"Are you all right?" he asked.

Memories of their shared past were flooding over him. "It's like nothing's changed …"

David looked chagrined at that. "I work no differently than I did years ago. It makes no sense to alter the configuration." He motioned to the nearest bench. "Please, it's right here."

Still staring in wonder, Sean followed, the sound of his footsteps lost in the vast darkness of the factory's hollow interior. David motioned to a set of three microscopes, indicating that Sean should look into the first. Sean reluctantly leaned down to the leftmost, putting one eye to the black eyepiece. The view showed a tight pattern of tubular green cells backlit by a disk of quinta incendia. "These look like pollen tubes."

"They are," David said. "Can you guess what species they came from?"

Sean stood, his ligature whirring loudly in the relative silence of the place. "I'm not your student anymore. Keep your questions to yourself and tell me why you've brought me here."

David winced, but recovered quickly. "Do you know where I've been for the past thirty-eight months, Sean?"

"I've no earthly idea."

"I've been in the Amazon, studying the plant life there. Did you know there's a higher concentration of haulms in the Amazon basin?"

"I'd heard something about it, yes." In fact, Sean had been reading many of the journals coming out of the university. The pain he experienced day in and day out—not to mention the efforts he went through to keep it in check—prevented him from pursuing the field of botany as he once had, but his love for it was as strong as ever, so he read when he could, keeping up on the field as much as his quiet times allowed him.

"What you're seeing are the pollen tubes of Victoria amazonica, the water lily. They're normal, healthy, rapid-growth cells, yes? Now take a look at the second scope."

"David ..."

"Please, Sean. Just take a look."

The urge in Sean to deny David anything he was looking for was strong, but there was also a fire within him, a strong curiosity for knowledge, especially where it related to the Jovians. He stepped up to the second microscope and bent down, the muscles along his shoulders and spine and hips aching dully from the attention. Within he saw a similar slide of cells. They were shaped the same, but their color was wrong. They were damaged and crumbling, though from what, Sean had no idea.

"What are these?" Sean said as he studied them carefully.

"Those are the same cells exposed to the influence of the haulms' roots."

Sean stood. "Their *roots*?"

David nodded. "At the center of the Amazon basin, we noticed that many of the plants near the haulms looked weakened where they hadn't been only a month or two before. We took careful samples of dozens of different varieties, studying their growth—or in this case, their *decay.* In the middle of the rain forest, one of the most fertile places in the world, Sean, we found that these plants were dying."

"There might be any number of reasons for that."

"Indeed there might be, but we'd been studying that area for nearly two years already. We know its ecosystem intimately, and there was no reason for them to decay in the manner we saw. Rain was plentiful, as always. The nutrient levels in the soil were all within acceptable ranges. We found no traces of toxins." David stepped up to the third microscope. "But what we *did* note was that the phenomenon started a mere few weeks after the arrival of the pods, the rough timeframe we estimate it took the pods to completely fuse with the haulms."

"You're suggesting the pods themselves had something to do with this."

"I am."

Sean pictured the haulms spread high above the basin, the ponderous pods lowering and attaching. Just how conscious were these inscrutable beings? To date they'd exhibited no form of communication—either with one another or with humanity—that earthly science might detect. "Perhaps it's a leaching of the soil near the haulms."

David nodded like a professor to his prized student. "In the early weeks of our detecting the phenomenon, the withering was stronger near the base of the haulms, but since then, the rate of decay in the more remote areas has been strengthening, and now, since that equalization has occurred, the rate of decay has been steadily increasing."

Sean's mind was racing. "The roots… . They're forming a colony."

David's head jerked back. "Very good… . It took us a long while to confirm those very suspicious, but we now believe it to be true. The pods have created a vast network beneath the Amazon Forest and are starting to bleed the life from it."

"Wait a tick. *Bleed?* Some undiscovered Jovian byproduct causing decay is one thing, but you're implying *intent*."

"Not intent, exactly. I've no idea if there's true intelligence—or anything *we* would recognize as intelligence—within those pods, but the beings that have arrived on our planet have to sustain themselves somehow. It's nature's most basic law."

"Yes, but to suggest that they're bleeding us seems like a bit of a stretch, doesn't it?"

In answer to this, David stepped up to the third microscope and motioned to it.

Sean stared at it, a feeling of dread blooming within him. He stepped closer, leaned down, and stared into the eyepiece, the aches in his body now all but forgotten. Within he saw a similar slide of pollen tubes, but in the center was a very different cluster of cells. These were unlike anything Sean had ever seen. They were oddly shaped, with a strange ochre color and spicules reaching out from the walls of each cell. This microscope, unlike the other two, clearly had a quinta essentia filter in the lens arrangement. Sean could tell from the bright chromatic aberrations present, in the interior of the cells especially. It was one of David's greatest contributions to the world of science, made and shared freely twenty years ago, well before Sean had started working with him. But this was very different than the ones Sean was familiar with. When he'd worked with David fifteen years ago, they'd been forced to capture images on daguerrotype plates, a process that—depending on how busy the university's development labs were—took a day or two from exposure to viewable image.

This was an incredible breakthrough. The lens allowed him to see the fifth element itself with the *naked eye* as it moved through the aether.

David had proven without a doubt—shortly after the creation of lenses like the one being used here—not merely that quinta essentia could be viewed and measured, but that it pooled within all living things. It did, in fact, run throughout the entire universe, but where there was life, quinta essentia thrived. No one knew if it was created or if—the amount of quinta essentia being constant—it was merely drawn *toward* life, but experiment after experiment proved that life of any kind would accrete more of the fifth element as it grew.

And here, for the first time known to man, was one form of life drawing quinta essentia from another. The study of the elements was still a relatively new science, but nothing like this had ever been seen before. It had never even been considered.

"This means that," Sean began. "This means… . Does it happen to *all* life? Animals? Insects? Sea life?"

David nodded soberly. "Lower life forms—*less complex* life forms—are apparently more susceptible than animals and humans. Bacterial life in the Amazon is being decimated. We have more evidence that worms and other invertebrates are weakening, and that soon they'll be dying in greater and greater numbers. And after that, it will start to affect *us*." He paused for effect. "If it hasn't already …"

"Why the Amazon?"

"Because life there is so vital. If the Jovians can sense the fifth element, then it stands to reason the haulms would have been drawn there."

Sean shook his head. This was all so much to digest. "You're talking about complete destruction, the loss of all life on Earth."

"I am. It's coming, Sean, and sooner than we know."

"Then we go to the Royal Society. We tell them of your findings."

"I would, but my history with them, Sean… . After what happened with the two of us, they wouldn't trust anything I offered up to them." Sean opened his mouth to object, but David raised his hand and talked over him. "They'd open up a commission. They'd study the phenomenon."

"As is proper."

"Under normal circumstances I'd agree with you, but you know what will happen. They'll examine every single thing I've done. They'll insist on an expedition of their own making be sent to South America. They'll demand they be allowed to make their own fluorite lenses, and none of them can make the kind I have here. They're years behind me. All of them. But that wouldn't stop them from demanding to know *how* they're made, to know the *process*. They'd make their own, and they'd test *those*. And even then, even if all their findings were to corroborate what you and I already know to be true, there would be some that would claim that the potential effects aren't as serious as we imagine, that the pods may, in fact, be benevolent, that they're transforming the world for the better."

"We could disprove that easily enough."

"Yes, given time. But what we're talking about is *years* of effort. I fear we have only months to do something about this, perhaps only weeks."

"Then what are you suggesting?"

"There may be a way to reach them, to speak to them on another level."

Sean shook his head, completely confused. "How can anyone *speak* to the pods? We've tried everything."

David frowned. "We've hardly scratched the surface. There could be any number of ways to communicate with them."

"Which would take years on its own."

"That would be true if we didn't already have clues." David seemed to gather himself. "Our experiment, Sean. When we—when *you*—touched that basic plane of existence, I believe we were completely successful in our goals."

"Successful?" Sean shook his arms, his muscles aching from the effort now that he'd been relatively idle for so long. "I was *ruined*, David! My life was ruined! How can you call that successful?"

"Whatever might have happened to you—and know that I will regret that to my dying day—you cannot deny that you were able to submerse yourself in quinta essentia. For a time, as our models predicted, you *were* quinta essentia."

Understanding began to dawn on Sean. "You want me to do it again."

"There's no one else who can."

"Then *you* do it."

His face turned melancholy at this. "I wish I could. But I can't. Not yet, in any case. I have to take measurements. I have to refine the process."

"Then find someone else to volunteer for your bloody mad

schemes!"

"I can't do that, either. For all we know, there's something specific about you, your makeup, that allowed you to complete the transition."

Sean stepped up to David until they were almost chest-to-chest. "Do you have any idea the sort of life I've had since that day?"

"I can only imagine, Sean, and I'm—"

Sean poked him in the chest. "Truly sorry… . Yes, I've heard it before. There hasn't been a single day, not even after the Royal Society built this damned ligature for me, that I haven't thought about killing myself. The pain is *constant*, running through every part of me like fire I can never rid myself of, not truly. You can't know how that scratches away at the mind. It grates constantly, tearing me down until I'm raw from it! Maddened!"

David tried to speak again, but Sean shoved him backward so hard that he fell with a satisfying crash and skidded along the well-worn floorboards.

"You said all would be well, and then the experiment failed. I could have swallowed that. I might have gone on with something approaching a clear conscience, but you *abandoned* me! You claimed I'd done it on my own, that I'd *stolen* your research to claim the glory of being the first to touch quinta essentia!"

David looked up at him from the floor, his eyes, his face, filled with shame. It was unlike anything Sean had seen, even in the aftermath of their failed experiment. "Why didn't you give me up, Sean?"

Sean tightened his hands into fists until they shook from it. "Because you were *brilliant*! You *are* brilliant. You have the kind of mind that comes along once a century. Once a *millennium*. You were going to do so much. So very much. Who was I to deny that to humanity? Who was I to claim that you couldn't continue your work?"

David shrugged, pushing his spectacles back into place. "They found out anyway."

They had. Of course they had. David had been stripped of rank and all the credentials granted by the University. Sean had been working toward his degree, using the money David could spare to pay him, hoping to earn his degree, become a Doctor Elementalis like David, but that had all changed after the accident. Afterwards, he could worry only about his body, about keeping it alive until the doctors from the Royal Society came up with something, anything, to help him, and even then, he would have a long way to go to repair the damage he and David had caused to his career. No matter that they'd eventually found David guilty of gross negligence in the pursuit of science. They hadn't absolved Sean from his part in it.

After standing and adjusting his shirt, David stared Sean in the eye. "This is the world we're talking about here, Sean. Not you and me. Not the Society. But everyone. Life on Earth."

Sean felt consumed. He felt betrayed all over again. "I could die, David. Or are you going to give me assurances again?"

"No, you're all too right. You could die, Sean. And there's more. In a way, I believe the two of us are responsible for this entire series of events."

"Responsible?" Sean felt confused. Angry. He wanted to run. He wanted to use his enhanced muscles to punish David for what he'd done, make him feel what *he* felt every day.

"I'm surprised you haven't pieced it together yet. Our experiment. Fifteen years ago, we touched the very fabric of quinta essentia." His eyes seemed to bore into Sean's. "A mere two years before the haulms arrived."

"Two years," Sean said, ready to argue, but his mind was already racing through the calculations. Theories abounded about how quickly one might travel through space using elemental drives, but David himself—shortly before he'd been discredited—had put a new one forth: a way to travel by distorting and drawing upon the warp and woof of quinta essentia. According to David's calculation, two years and ten days, roughly, was by a strange twist of probability the time it would take to travel from one world to nearly any other. Quinta essentia's pull, converse to popular opinion in the science community, was stronger as the distance increased, which led to a tethering effect that might allow a starship—or an extraterrestrial being—to draw itself from one planet in the universe to another.

He thought back from the date they'd run the experiment to the first recorded sighting of the haulms. Two years and seventeen days. A mere six days off from David's calculation. How could he have missed it?

He knew why, of course. He had still been in the thick of his rehabilitation then. The University had been furious, but many were concerned about their liability, so to make things look as though they were being magnanimous, they offered Sean a chance to receive their first set of human ligature. He'd accepted, for it meant a chance at life—*some* sort of life—however painful it might be. While he'd been there recuperating in the hospital, he'd hardly seen a single haulm—a few from the small window of his room, a few more from the place he was forced to exercise his muscles with the newly installed ligature, so the arrival of the Jovians, and whatever relationship they might have had to his experiment, simply hadn't been on his mind.

But now the link was undeniable. Six days was certainly a reasonable time for the Jovians to mobilize and launch the haulm seeds toward Earth. They were parasites, then. Creatures poised like spiders on a web, waiting for the telltale signs of planets that were not only capable of storing quinta essentia, but had advanced to the point that there would be an abundance, enough for them to travel there, to revitalize themselves, perhaps reproduce, and then begin the process all over again.

He might have felt burdened by this new information—he should have—but the truth was this was incredibly freeing. To know that he might have the ability to help gave him hope and a sense of purpose that had been nearly snuffed out by their past failure. And David was right. Whatever success they'd achieved last time might have had everything to do with Sean himself. If he denied David's request, there was no telling whether it would work for anyone else, or, even if it did work, how long it would take to perfect.

He had to do it. Not for David—certainly not for David—but for everyone else. For Therese. For his family. For the world.

"Where do we begin?" Sean asked.

David's smile was slow in coming. He waved to the corner of the large open space, where a set of stairs led down. "In the basement, Sean. We can begin right now."

* * *

In the basement of the factory was a set of equipment, clearly well cared for, that warred with the dark wooden rafters and uneven stone walls. Vats of glass containing a glowing amber liquid could have provided much of the light, but there were lamps of quinta incendia placed all around, their shaded points of light burning bright sapphire blue.

Sean stepped into the padded leather seat within a complex set of mechanical arms and lenses and tubes, and when he was comfortable, Vidnas, David's assistant, secured him into it using triple-thick leather straps. As usual, David had thought well ahead. Sean's ligature was strong, and they couldn't risk him ripping his way out of them during the experiment itself.

Vidnas, his brown, almond-shaped turban a match for his expressive eyes, paused near Sean's side. He smiled, his dark moustache and beard accentuating nearly perfect teeth. "Are you feeling well, sir?"

No. Sean *wasn't* feeling well, not now that he was so near a return to the experiment that had devoured his future. He couldn't keep the strange feelings of emptiness from his mind, the feelings of utter loss and loneliness.

"Feeling as well as I ever will," Sean replied.

Vidnas patted his shoulder and moved to the set of metal stands nearby. Each stand held an armature with a set of lenses that would, when David gave the signal, be situated in a spherical formation around Sean's head.

"Ready?" David said.

"Give Therese the letter, won't you? If anything goes wrong?" He might have told her himself, but she would never have allowed him to come here and submit himself to this. She'd kill him first.

"Of course I will."

"And tell her I love her?"

"Of course."

Sean nodded. "Then I'm ready."

With that, Vidnas and David began moving the lenses into place. They adjusted the clamps and telescoping rods so that the armatures rested at the proper angles and positions. Each of the armatures held twenty five lenses with watertight jars clamped to their backs. The jars were fed by tubes connected to a series of pipes that would be filled from the glowing vats of quinta integra, an extremely difficult-to-stabilize mixture of the four basic elements: incendia, aeris, terra, and unda.

As each set of lenses was moved carefully into place, Sean's heart began beating harder and harder. His breath came rapid as a frightened hare.

"You're about to hyperventilate," David said as he glanced over. "Breathe deeper. From the stomach, remember?"

Sean did, and slowly the entire chromatic apparatus was maneuvered into place around him. Outside the sphere, Sean saw segmented visions of Vidnas and David moving about, making final preparations.

And then, at last, David gripped the valve that would begin the process. "Last chance," he said with a melancholy smile.

Sean couldn't help himself. He laughed. It was the exact same thing David had said just before their first experiment.

"Into the great beyond," Sean replied, an echo of his own reply from fifteen years before.

David gave him a nod and strapped a set of thick, leather-wrapped goggles around his head—another incredible advancement, for surely David had developed them to view some crucial aspect of the experiment as it happened. He nodded to Sean—looking to all the world like some alien insect—and then threw the handle of the valve. The tank levels slowly decreased as the viscous amber liquid inched through transparent pipes. Slowly but surely, the quinta integra crept toward the narrow rubber tubes. The liquid split and split again, surrounding Sean like a hydra, each serpent doubling when its head was severed.

The liquid began filling the glass jars behind the lenses, and as they did, as more and more of the ingenious lenses David and Sean had developed were backed by the quinta integra, Sean's mind began to expand.

He felt more than his own body. More than this room.

He floated free among the aether.

Became one with quinta essentia.

How beautiful. How utterly, unexplainably beautiful. A vast, endless world of chromatic shapes. He saw this place, this old abandoned shoe factory. He saw Vidnas and David and his own body. He saw the rundown factory streets and the River Wear that wound its way through Durham. He saw the university, the whole of Durham, the whole of England. He could feel Earth itself, the solar system, the Milky Way galaxy. Faster and faster it went, this expansion, until, just like the last time, he felt as though his mind were trying to encompass all of creation.

It was too much.

His mind was drifting from his body, which was exactly what had happened to him the first time they'd tried, exactly how his mind had been irreparably harmed, with its refusal to control his body as it once had.

David had told Sean about the changes he'd made to the elemental serum and the lenses themselves. In all likelihood, he'd said, the unchecked expansion should be limited, which should allow Sean to exert some amount of control.

Sean ...

He wasn't able to, though. He couldn't. And his mind continued to attenuate as it stretched outward, through and throughout the fabric of the cosmos.

Sean, can you hear me?

By all that was good, he couldn't do it. He would become lost this time. Lost for sure.

Sean, you must listen. The pods. They should be a sink for quinta essentia. They're consuming it, Sean. Look for them. Feel for them. They'll ground you.

Sean felt, only for a moment, his body tightening, heard a primal scream issuing from his throat. But then those sensations were gone, and he was alone once again. Alone with his thoughts in this endless, universal medium.

What David had said, though… . The pods.

They were a sink. Consuming quinta essentia.

No other known beings fed on the fifth element. Not directly. That simply wasn't the way the universe worked. The very fact that this natural law had once seemed so immutable, and now seemed every bit as implausible as a geocentric universe, grounded Sean. It drew him back toward his physical form and nearer to that very phenomenon.

And that's when he felt them.

The pods. The pooling of intent near him, around him, surrounding, essentially, all life on Earth. Like a subtle adjustment of a lens bringing a landscape into focus, he could sense every part of them, and now that he could, he realized how very familiar they were. He'd felt them before, in that event fifteen years ago when he'd first entered the quintessence.

How could he have forgotten it?

They had called to him then, and they were calling to him now. He felt from them a yearning, a primal urge that spanned millennia. It wasn't malicious, as his memory had somehow made it seem, but benign. He'd been so fearful of it years ago. He was *still* fearful, but not for his own sake, not any longer. He was fearful the Jovians wouldn't understand humanity, that in their curiosity they'd trample the minds they'd come to examine, or they'd decimate life on Earth even as they studied it.

His heart, David. He's going into tachycardia.

The pods were reaching in the only way they knew how. They were holding their hands out to him, ready to take him should he wish to come.

Should we continue?

A pause, and then, *Just a moment longer.*

Unlike the last time, the urge to accept their call was strong and growing stronger. He flung his mind outward, wondering what grand thing would happen.

Now, Vidnas. Shut it down.

And suddenly the feelings diminished.

He grasped for them, but they became dimmer and dimmer until—like a mote of light that had finally burned itself out—they winked from existence.

* * *

When Sean woke, it was to the sounds of clinking, like crystal goblets at a party. Had he come home? Was Therese readying for a party?

And then it all came back in a rush. David. The lab. The pods, and the way they'd called to him.

He forced his eyes to open and thought he was still in the basement of the warehouse, but when his mind cleared, he realized it wasn't Vidnas before him, but a nurse in a white hospital gown, and she wasn't cleaning the bell jars and the lenses that had surrounded him, but the set of vials the University required to refresh the liquid stored within the core of his ligature.

He felt so very weak. And his muscles, his joints, his skin, felt as though they'd been reforged improperly, leaving him more broken than before. Though he tried to stifle it, the pain brought on a weak groan that nevertheless attracted the nurse's attention.

"Are you feeling very well?"

"I'm—" Sean could barely speak, so slurred were his words. "Where's David?"

She continued about her work. "David who, sir?"

"David Lock."

She shook her head. "Never heard of him."

He stared at her. Surely David had brought him here. "How did I arrive?"

"You were found on Stockton Road, unconscious. Constable Adams found you and brought you in, and a good thing he did. Your fluid had nearly turned. Haven't you been keeping an eye on it?"

"Of course he has." Sean turned his head to find Therese standing in the doorway. She strode in to stand by the bedside. "Each morning. You can set your watch by it."

The nurse gave Therese an icy stare. "Then I'm sure I don't know why his fluid had degraded so." And with that she topped the vials and left.

As the heels of her white leather shoes clicked away, more and more of the puzzle fell into place. He'd asked David why he didn't perform the experiment on himself. *I can't,* he'd said. *Not yet, in any case. I have to take measurements. I have to refine the process.*

He had to refine the process, which implied there would be another run of the experiment. He had needed Sean. He'd said so himself—Sean was the only one who'd entered quinta essentia so far—but he'd done it so that he could perfect the parameters surrounding the experiment. Which meant that he'd planned all along to do it himself afterward. That was the only explanation for leaving Sean as he had—so that he could remain anonymous in Durham until it was too late.

Therese stared down at Sean. Her hand lifted, but then she lowered it again. She knew from experience that even holding his hand at a time like this would cause him discomfort, but Sean reached out and took her hand, squeezed it, oblivious to the pain. "We have to talk."

* * *

As Therese sat by his bedside, her eyes stared through him. Her hands were shaking. She glanced toward the cluster of clear vials hanging above Sean, the vials that had allowed him to retain some sense of normalcy in his tortured existence. The tears gathered in her eyes finally fell down along her cheeks. "I can't do it, Sean."

"Therese, I can't go on like this." He lifted his arms, the whirring of his ligature emphasized his point much more eloquently than he could with words alone. "It's worse than before."

Therese was crying freely now. "I'll *help* more. We'll hire a man to come to the house a few days a week. It won't be so bad after a while."

Sean took her hands in his. "I'm going to a better place."

"I can't… . I can't just let you go. I don't know what I'll do without you."

"You'll go on. You'll be free." Before she could speak again, he squeezed her fingers gently. "Now, Therese. There's so little time left."

She stared into his eyes for a handful of heartbeats, then another handful more. After wiping her tears away, and a short but powerful nod, she went to work. More quickly than any of the nurses could manage, she disconnected each of the feed and return tubes from his ligature. She helped him up in his bed, a veritable angel for how strong she was being, how little of his own power he needed to exert, lest he moan and the two of them were caught. She disrobed him and helped to pull on his clothes. After giving him a familiar look, asking him if he were ready to be on his own, he nodded, and then she leaned in and gave him a deep kiss.

Bliss, he thought. A more tender thing he had never felt.

She left the room, leaving the door open a crack. "Who's been tending to Sean Brannon?" Her voice was so loud the entire ward must have heard her. Some unintelligible reply came, but Therese talked over the woman. "While *you've* been ensuring the levels were correct, he was dry as a bone. Did you even see the color of his urine?" A soft reply came. "No, I've *given* him water. He's hydrated. What I want to ensure is that he manages to remain that way while I'm gone." Another mumbled reply, also cut off. "No, *I'll* be speaking to the attending physician, thank you very much!"

"Bless you," Sean said, as he slipped from the room and limped toward the stairs at the end of the hall.

* * *

Sean reached the warehouse at the end of an excruciating walk. He would normally have loosened up by now, but things were worse than ever. His knees kept wanting to lock up, and his hips and ankles burned so badly he collapsed several times. But he got up, fixated on the siren call of the pods—in some ways a distant memory, but in others the entirety of his being.

The massive, rolling door into the factory was closed but not locked. He pulled it aside and made his way down the stairs to the darkness, staggered to the doorway where the brightness of David's lab was revealed.

David was sitting where Sean had sat less than a day before, and Vidnas was putting the last of the armatures into place around his head.

"Stop!" Sean called.

"Sean?" David said, his head moving back and forth to get a clear view of him.

"You can't do this, Vidnas."

Vidnas stared between David within the sphere of chromatic lenses and Sean, clearly startled, but more than this, with a glimmer of embarrassment.

"You can't let him go," Sean went on. "You need him. The *world* needs him."

"Sean, stop it," David said. "This needs to be done."

"And I'm the one to do it." Sean kept his focus squarely on Vidnas. He spread his arms wide and strode forward. "I'm ruined, Vidnas. I am ruined, and David is whole, in mind as well as in body. Can you even conceive of what the world might lose today were he suddenly gone from it?"

Vidnas stared deeply into Sean's eyes, but before he could say anything, David began pushing apart the stands that held the lenses, at least enough that he could extricate himself from them. "Get him out, Vidnas! We have to get him out!"

"Don't listen to him," Sean said, wincing as he took a step forward, his arms still outstretched. "You cannot."

It was clear from the expression on Vidnas' face that he was considering Sean's words, but he stepped back when David strode to a nearby workbench and picked up a syringe. He filled it with a clear liquid and then began walking toward Sean.

"Don't do this, David. Let me go. Please. You owe me this much."

David's face was red, and the expression was more intense than Sean had ever seen. "*I* was the one that brought them here, Sean. Not you."

"I'm as much to blame."

"You aren't!" David's face was red. Blue veins pulsed on his forehead and along his neck. "I practically forced you into that chair. I ran that experiment and then watched you suffer and tried to pretend it was all your idea! The Jovians are here because of *my* actions, and I cannot, I will not, allow you to take my place. They're *my* responsibility."

"Responsible or not, I'm not going to let you do it."

"That, my dear friend, is no longer up to you." He strode

forward, holding the syringe high, out of Sean's grasp, while using his other hand to grab the ligature rods connected along Sean's collar bones. "I'm deeply sorry for everything that's happened to you. I was a fool, then—young and worried for my career. I should never have betrayed you."

He tried wrestling Sean to the ground, but Sean was not powerless. It caused pain, but his ligature was a beautifully designed machine. He grabbed David's shirt with one hand, grabbed the arm holding the syringe with the other. He squeezed David's arm until he cried out from the pain and dropped the syringe.

David, knowing the tide was turning, grabbed him about the waist and pushed him, knocking him off balance and sending him crashing to the ground. But this was ineffectual, too. It was only a matter of time before Sean got the upper hand. He wrestled David down to the cold floor, began crawling on top of him, all while David scrabbled uselessly at Sean's back.

Then, suddenly, he was no longer able to hold David down.

Sean's mind raced. He didn't understand until his time in the hospital came rushing back to him. How could he have been so foolish? David had reached the cluster of controls—the mind of the ligature, in essence—at the center of Sean's back. The hospital would have removed the panel that normally protected it. He hadn't thought to have Therese put it back on before leaving.

The ligature was losing strength quickly, forcing his own muscles to do more of the work, which was causing more and more pain.

David tried to rise. Sean grabbed his shirt, to hold him in place, but it was a simple matter for David to wrest his shirt free of Sean's weakened grip. He stared down at Sean with sympathetic eyes, his gaze full of regret. "I'm truly sorry, Sean."

But before he could do anything else, his eyes went wide.

Then they went cloudy, and his body fell limp.

Into the waiting arms of Vidnas.

Sean could only stare as Vidnas laid David gently down and moved to Sean's side. He rolled Sean over and did something at the open panel, and the strength to Sean's ligature suddenly returned.

"Thank you," Sean said as Vidnas helped him to his feet.

Vidnas said nothing as he helped Sean hobble his way toward the padded seat David had so recently occupied.

* * *

Sean stared up at the lenses, watched the amber liquid flow through the tubes and bifurcate over and over again until all the lenses around him were aglow.

As before, his mind began to expand, slowly at first, but then in wider and grander increments until it felt as though he'd swallowed the cosmos.

He'd come to understand quinta essentia in a way he'd never expected. It shouldn't be so surprising; he was a part of it, after all. All life was, from microbial life all the way up to advanced life forms—mammals, humans, the Jovians—and it made him wonder whether quinta essentia itself weren't some form of life. A grand, enigmatic system not understandable by him—not yet, at least—but perhaps by the Jovians. He hoped he might one day share in such knowledge. Perhaps add to it.

For that was why the pods had come. They had come to find the beings that had reached out to them. They had come to fold those into their greater consciousness. And when that was done, they would move on. There were other worlds, other forms of life they hoped to commune with, which meant they would eventually uproot; they would travel to another world, and find more. And more after that. He could feel them already, places where haulms had seeded other worlds, which were now waiting to be visited.

Like all life, the pods were evolving, slowly accreting knowledge and wonder and experience to … to do who knew what? Sean certainly had no idea, but he hoped one day he might.

With care, he drew his attention inward, back toward Earth. The collective minds of the pods became more and more clear. In fact, so did *all* life on Earth. It felt like a thing he'd always been in touch with at some level, but now, as if a light had been shone on it at last, he could sense it separate from himself.

He recognized he was merely delaying now. The pods were

calling to him. And for his part—though he was not without regrets—he knew he was ready.

And so, after one last longing glance to the world around him, he reached out.

And allowed them to lift him up.

When Comrade Ekaterina Died for the Motherland

J. R. Hargenrader

No more than a quarter of an hour had passed when Ekaterina hungered for another kill.

Red Square was on fire. Below the burning Kremlin towers, armored traction engines and steam wagons belched smoke into the overcast sky. Snow blanketed the bodies of cavalrymen and horses cut down by laser fire. At the center of the Square lay one of the deadly silver tripods, its missing leg rendering it impotent and silent. Ekaterina waited for her signal.

If the wires were correct, London and Paris had already fallen to the armies of towering tripods, and an attack on Berlin was underway. She cared little for the fate of those weak imperialistic countries, but the simple fools provoked the creatures that had slaughtered thousands of her comrades and wrought destruction across the Motherland. To think, these *inoplanetyane* had come so close to defeating the most powerful nation in the world. A chill ran down her spine. She would teach them what it meant to be an enemy of the People.

Ekaterina flexed her skeletal metal gloves and flakes of black alien blood peppered the snow at her boots. The burn on her arm stung, reminding her of the damage to her exoskeleton. Two of the four power-assist pistons in the suit's arm were severed, weakening its total strength. Beneath one of the destroyed pistons, she could make out the charred flesh of her arm and caught a whiff of burned bacon. The stomach churning smell reminded her of the horrors of Novorossiysk—she hadn't been able to eat pork since.

Fireworks exploded at the far side of the Square, filling the sky with red and white flashes that cast shadows on the carnage below. The concussions shook snow from windowsills and bodies. Ekaterina's breath puffed white in the cold air as her eyes remained fixed on the tripod. Its rectangular doors slid open and alien soldiers spilled out. She fingered the trigger loops in her gloves.

The explosions halted and the last boom echoed through the Square. A red star burst through the thick firework smoke. The long sleek Russian airship *Glasnos* had arrived, its gondola-mounted cannons and machine guns lighting up the battlefield. This was Ekaterina's signal.

She stepped forward and the compact steam engine mounted on her back hummed in response. Using the suit's increased power, she leaped down the stairway to the bronze monument of Minin and Pozharsky. Beneath the figures, Zakhar knelt behind the granite base in his arctic camo exoskeleton and peered through the wide scope of his steamrail. Ekaterina took cover at the opposite side of the monument and aimed her cannon arm's scope at the tripod. She prayed for the strength of the two Russian heroes who pushed out the Polish invaders during the Times of Trouble.

Around the perimeter of the tripod's wide saucer-like body were rudimentary fortifications made up of vehicle scraps, dead horses, men, and the tripod's dismembered leg. Aside from the white uniforms they wore, the aliens were indistinguishable from humans at this distance. Up close, they were squat, slow, and so frail they were no match in hand-to-hand combat. In the face of a Russian exoskeleton, they were mincemeat. But despite their physical weaknesses, their armies of tripods and laser technology had brought nations to their knees. Even Russia's most advanced alloys were little match for the laser fire.

The alien soldiers fired on the indomitable *Glasnos*, light from the laser fire pulsing in flashes. None of the soldiers faced Ekaterina and Zakhar. The plan had worked. She fingered the comm loops in her glove to acknowledge her readiness. An affirmative beeped in her ear.

Zakhar left the granite base and Ekaterina followed him to a nearby steam wagon that continued to burn. Snow pelted her goggles and the cold wind created by the exoskeleton's speed stung her bare cheeks. Three alien soldiers turned from the

Glasnos. Lasers pulsed past Ekaterina, vaporizing the falling snow into steam. Zakhar reached the wagon and ducked down. Ekaterina fired her cannon arm, then ducked next to him. Between the metal plates in the back of the wagon, she could see, and smell, the charred bodies of trapped soldiers.

Zakhar knelt to the side of the blackened wagon and aimed the long flat rifle. A short cable led from the rifle, beneath his arm, and around his side to the engine at his back. He pulled the trigger. The concussion rocked the snow and debris before them. Even at this range the high velocity projectile ripped the alien apart, leaving behind a black mist where it once stood.

Ekaterina scanned the field as Zakhar's steambullets cracked the air. She keyed a message. "Overturned traction engine at one o'clock. Fifty meters."

"Acknowledged."

They waited for a pause in the laser fire. Zakhar moved out from cover while Ekaterina fired her cannon across the front of the aliens' forward fortifications. A series of small explosions sent concrete and dust into the air. The laser fire ceased. Out of the corner of her eye, she saw Zakhar take cover behind the traction engine.

"We've got this," Zakhar signaled. She could see the smile beneath his black leather goggles. She imagined the confidence in his voice, the smirk with a day's growth of stubble. Like Minin and Pozharsky, they would push these invaders out.

"You're Minin. I'll be Pozharsky."

"*Nyet*," he signaled. "My full beard is better than his."

She laughed and ducked back, ready for the sound of Zakhar's covering fire to make her move.

"Hold," Zakhar signaled.

Ekaterina crouched. Laser fire pulsed over the wagon and the heat warmed her face. The *Glasnos*' great turbines reverberated off the Kremlin walls as the massive airship approached. Laser fire on the ship intensified and smoke poured from one of its gondolas. "What is it?"

"Not sure," he signaled. "Power issue. Can you get a visual on my engine?"

Ekaterina backed away from the wagon to get a better angle

on Zakhar. She signaled confirmation and he turned to show her the steam engine mounted on his back. She ran through the engine parts—the tender, the steam dome, regulator, coupling rods, boiler tubes. Then her eyes found the primary boiler. A tiny jet of steam sprayed from the sphere, a sure sign the exoskeleton would experience a critical failure soon. Her heart fell. She'd have to go it alone. She signaled him about the damage.

He nodded. They stared at each other, seconds feeling like hours. His fingers moved and her earpiece beeped. "OK, let's move," he signaled.

"You can't go like that."

"It will hold," he said.

"You need to drop the engine and—"

"Only one of us has to get inside. There is no time, Kat."

She shuddered. He never used her nickname on a mission, only under the cover of darkness and between the sheets of her bed. But he was right, the *Glasnos* was making its final charge. This was their last chance.

She keyed her agreement. Zakhar gave her the position of an armored car to use for cover. He stood up and fired his steamrail.

The power-assist pistons in her exo's legs pushed her over the wagon and she ran for the car. The entrance to the tripod was a hundred meters away with just a handful of soldiers taking cover behind its charcoal metal leg. Zakhar's covering fire pinned the alien soldiers as she raced past debris and bodies and into the shadow of the tripod's wide body. She fired, then ducked behind the car. Secure in her position, she stepped out and covered Zakhar.

Enemy lasers pulsed high, then higher. Overhead, steam jets sprayed from Zakhar's feet as he fired the deadly steamrail. He landed in front of the detached tripod leg and ducked on one knee. A soldier popped up. Zakhar blasted its head off. He jumped over the tripod leg and pointed both arms at the cluster of soldiers. Jets of steam erupted from his wrists, engulfing the screaming aliens in a white cloud. The chorus was eerily human and Ekaterina tasted bile. Zakhar fired into the broiling mist, silencing the remaining screams.

The tripod doors slid open and a new group of soldiers

jumped out. Zakhar took cover and lasers pummeled the car around Ekaterina. She waited for an opening, but the new barrage of laser fire was too much. The vibrations from the *Glasnos*' engines rumbled in her chest.

"I'm pinned," she signaled.

"Me, too."

"Request covering fire. We'll move in."

Bullets rained down from above as blood and debris created a cloud around the soldiers. The *Glasnos*. It was enough of an opportunity for Ekaterina to fire.

"Hold your position and keep me covered," Zakhar said.

"What?"

"Finish the job as Pozharsky would. *Spokoynoy nochi,* Kat."

Zakhar jumped over the barricade and ran directly at the soldiers. What was he doing? Then she saw the steam spraying from his engine. The crack had expanded across the broiler and, with each step, the steam intensified. Ekaterina fired at the soldiers as fast as possible, the heat from her cannon melting the snow at her feet.

Zakhar leaped, his steam jets launching him into a perfect arc at the soldiers. Laser fire severed his arm, spinning him into a tumble. Another laser struck his chest.

The explosion blew Ekaterina off her feet as hot steam and debris sliced into her face. Her body slammed into the ground and shocks of pain shot down her arm. Windows shattered and crumbled, and shards of glass rained down over the sides of the tripod and bodies below.

Ekaterina struggled back to her feet, her wounded arm and heart burning with pain. She wiped her goggles and blood smeared over the cracked lenses. Through the ringing in her ears she could hear aliens yelling. One pointed at her while others charged out of the tripod's open doors, stepping over their fallen. A barrage of fire from above struck down the first few soldiers and halted the attack.

Ekaterina seized the opportunity to close in on the squad. She stepped over the bodies torn apart by the *Glasnos* and sought her next target. The new soldiers were bunched up and tripping over one another, either inexperienced or incompetent. In her exoskeleton, she closed the distance so fast the first alien didn't have time to raise its weapon. She blasted it with her cannon. Alien bits exploded in all directions and sprays of black goop smattered across the tripod's polished surface. Another alien swung at her with the butt of its rifle. Ekaterina deflected the blow with her metal arm. She lifted the alien by its neck and tore its head off. A nearby voice cried out in horror. She pitched the head at the screaming soldier and it toppled over in a heap. Two more cannon shots finished the remaining aliens.

She unclipped a *limonka* from her leg rack and tossed it into the tripod's open doors. Human-like voices howled in the ship, until the explosion ended them. Her steam jets carried her into the air and through the opening. She landed with a metallic thud that echoed off the tripod's silver walls. She swept the room with her cannon, searching for the next target. Her breaths were rapid and her heart pounded in her chest.

Nothing.

The room, a cargo bay, was filled with laser rifles, metal crates, and a few dead aliens whose white uniforms were drenched in black. Streaks of black blood smeared across the metallic silver floor led to the only other door at the far end of the cargo bay. She ran to the door, the exoskeleton's feet clanking and splashing in the black pools. She keyed the panel next to the door. It did not open.

Ekaterina gripped the lip of the door with one hand, her injured arm hanging loose, and pulled. The door slid a few centimeters. She pulled harder. The engine at her back hummed louder and the power in her glove and arm pistons increased. The door slid with ease.

She tossed a *limonka* through the door to the left, then another to the right. The explosions sent a jet of heat and smoke back out the door. Ahead in the hall, amid the clearing smoke, lay one mangled alien body. More black blood led to another door. Where was the counter assault?

She pulled open the next door and a laser pulsed wide. Ekaterina aimed and pulled a trigger loop. The alien collapsed in a spray of black mist. Behind it were more aliens. Dozens of them. She intuitively scanned for weapons. No. No. No. An alien jumped between her and the others. She aimed, then stopped.

The alien held its arms spread wide out. Its eyes were closed and its squat body trembled like that of a small child. It appeared to be … crying?

None of the other aliens were armed. At her feet, the black streaks of blood fanned apart to the walls where aliens were crowded on the floor and small platforms. Some were dead with gaping wounds and mouths frozen in silent screams. Others cried out in agony, their wounds covered with a green, fungus-like bandaging. The remaining moaned in pain, unaware of the situation. Two healthy aliens shielded the wounded with their bodies. It was a medical bay.

Ekaterina choked on the smell of bacon. She lowered her weapon.

* * *

Ekaterina stood at attention in front of the alien medical bay when the Grand Marshal entered the hall. The army's most senior officer wore a lightweight exoskeleton configuration that rested on the shoulders and supported a cannon and power-assist pistons for one arm. She paused to look over the black scar of a *limonka* blast. Then her eyes turned to Ekaterina.

Ekaterina saluted and the reflex sent a burning, stabbing pain down her injured arm. In the full exoskeleton she stood a good twenty centimeters taller than the Grand Marshal, yet she felt so much smaller.

The Grand Marshal saluted with a powered hand. "You have done well, Comrade Captain." A single white hair ran through the woman's jet black bun pulled tight under an *ushanka* hat. "Mother Russia has a great many soldiers, but none so exceptional as you. Your lost comrade will receive the Order of Stalin. I will see to that, personally."

Ekaterina straightened her back. Zakhar's death still felt distant and unreal. A part of her expected to pull her comm loops and receive his acknowledgement. "Thank you, Comrade Marshal." She saluted again.

A squad of soldiers dressed in clean and pressed uniforms

arrived to relieve Ekaterina. Their shiny boots squeaked on the silver floor as they took guard positions in front of the medical bay.

"Walk with me," the Grand Marshal said. She led Ekaterina down the hall. When they were out of earshot from the soldiers, the Grand Marshal lowered her voice. "What stopped you from killing the enemy? Why did you choose to … alter … my orders?"

The weight of the question gave her pause. Ekaterina wanted to say it reminded her of the tiny hospital near Novorossiysk, next to the Black Sea. Her first combat assignment as a soldier had been to prevent the Romanians from firebombing the city. There were no Minins or Pozharskys that night. Separated from her lost battalion, she had served as a triage nurse in a hospital overwhelmed by the surge of terrified casualties. Ekaterina would never forget the scores of dead, the agonizing moans of the dying, and the choking cloud of burned hair and flesh. Most of all, she would never forget the guilt she felt for failing her comrades. "I—" she said, clearing her throat.

"Speak confidently, comrade."

"I thought we might be able to gain more information from the prisoners, Comrade Marshal."

"No more thinking," she said. "When you speak to anyone from now on, you will answer with complete confidence. You will say, 'I knew that we had enough bodies to study and that our intelligence services would gain more information by interrogating live specimens.' Is that not correct?"

"Of course, comrade."

"And that is why you took these prisoners."

"Yes, comrade."

"Say it."

Ekaterina repeated the statement, her face hot from embarrassment.

"Say it as though you believe it," the Grand Marshal ordered.

Ekaterina repeated the statement again, but with an edge of coldness.

"Good. That sounds more like the Hero of Moscow—the exopilot who single-handedly captured and defeated these alien invaders."

Ekaterina straightened her shoulders. "I could not have done it without the help of Zak—"

The Grand Marshal held up her powered hand, her steel gray eyes arresting. "You were the lone exopilot who single-handedly captured and defeated the alien invaders."

"Yes." Ekaterina said. "Correct, Comrade Marshal."

"And you would agree that the mere presence of this alien filth is an insult to the memory of our fallen comrades. Would you not?"

Ekaterina glanced at the alien blood smeared across the floor. She thought of the alien who jumped in front of her to protect its own comrades. Had she been a fool to spare them? "Of course, Comrade Marshal."

"Good. When you are done here, you will need to get that arm patched up. Tell the surgeon to leave plenty of scarring. It will look better for the photographers."

"Comrade?"

"You are to be reassigned. You will be placed on a different front, a front of cameras and reporters. What you have done today will be known throughout the world. You are to be a symbol. No nation—no invader, can conquer us."

"Thank you, comrade." Ekaterina thought of Minin and Pozharsky. For the first time she wondered if their stories were also exaggerations, simplifications, and lies.

"There is a field hospital next to St. Basil's. Our press corps will meet you there in one hour for a first interview."

Ekaterina nodded.

"Now," the Grand Marshal said as she stared coldly and directly into Ekaterina's eyes. "You have leave to complete my original orders. I would hate to report to the Premier that you died in a tragic accident."

"Comrade Marshal?"

The Grand Marshal stepped back and lifted her powered arm. Beyond the iron fist and through the open door to the medical bay, Ekaterina could make out the figures of aliens tending to their wounded.

"I understand a roast pig is being prepared in your honor,"

the Grand Marshal said, smiling. “Do not keep us waiting. Mother Russia, and the world, are expecting you.”

An image of Zakhar crouching next to the monument came to mind. Those heroes had given her the strength she needed that day. Now it was her turn to inspire others and secure the future of Mother Russia. She had failed her comrades once before. She would not fail them again.

Ekaterina took a deep breath and saluted. “For the Motherland.”

The Grand Marshal nodded, a look of approval in the woman’s cold eyes. “Comrade Captain.”

Ekaterina turned down the hall and fingered the trigger loops in her gloves. She passed the soldiers standing guard and stepped into the medical bay. Human-like faces stared back at her. She raised her cannon arm and aimed.

Spokoynoy nochi, Zakhar.

A Clockwork Alien

Gini Koch

A spear flew through the air and imbedded itself into the wall by Algar's head. This meant it was stomach height for most beings, but a spear through the midsection was as bad as a spear through the cranium.

Of course, a spear was better than a laser shot. Lasers had their place. Spears, too. The throne room of the most powerful kingdom in this particular solar system wasn't really the place for either, though.

He pulled the spear out of the wall, walked over to the throne, and tossed it at the feet of the young man sitting there. "I beg your pardon?"

The current King of Alpha Four looked around. "Sorry."

"That's it? 'Sorry?' You almost kill me and you manage two syllables?" Of course, the reality was that a spear through the head probably wouldn't kill Algar. But no one else needed to know that. "Why are you throwing spears at the wall?"

"Bored. Bored, bored, bored. Did I mention, bored?"

Algar resisted the urge to heave a sigh. "Really, Your Highness? Ruling your planet and solar system is too dull for you?" It always started this way. The boredom led to the desire to explore and conquer. Algar had spent century upon century ensuring that each new king found a good channel for their boredom. A safe channel. A channel that wouldn't bring the wrong beings here.

Some royal families on other planets inbred and went strange or stupid. Alpha Four's royal family did their best to keep their bloodline fresh. But whether it was that or if the original king's curiosity about the cosmos was genetically handed down, this bloodline liked to go exploring with the intent to conquer. Only

King Reginald's father had already conquered their solar system when Reginald was just a little boy.

There were other systems, of course. Though they were quite far out in terms of this particular galaxy, there were still some options. However, Algar knew the closest neighbor wasn't really ready for visitors from afar. And going closer to the Galactic Core wasn't in Algar's best interests. And when it came down to it, the only interests that mattered, as far as Algar was concerned, were Algar's.

So traveling closer to the main galactic planets was definitely out. And traveling to Earth wasn't in anyone's best interests—too many others wandered by that lonely little rock and Earth's inhabitants just weren't ready to learn they weren't alone.

Then again, beings on Alpha Four and Earth resembled each other enough that Reginald could pass for one of them. Algar could as well. And, of course, there was more than one way to visit.

He whistled softly and his pets appeared. The Poofs were loyal and loving and, as far as the royal bloodline were concerned, came with the royal package. The first king had understood that the Poofs were on a familial loan, but Algar hadn't felt the need to share this with anyone else, the current king included.

Reginald brightened up. "Har and Ten! Come to make me happy with your fluffy purrs?" The Poofs did love the Royal Family, so, after Algar had petted them, they bounded over to Reginald, purring as requested.

At this size, the Poofs were small and fluffy, with eyes like black buttons, tiny paws, no visible ears, and no tails. When roused, they were three times bigger than Algar, and their mouths were filled with razor sharp teeth. They were excellent protection and could make the journey Algar was considering without issue. Plus they'd help keep an eye on Reginald.

"Save me from boredom," Reginald murmured to the Poofs. "Because I'm going mad."

Algar made up his mind. "Your Highness, have I explained the concept of other universes to you yet?"

Reginald nodded. "Yes. There are many, more than I can

comprehend. Some are very like ours, some are very different." He looked at Algar, and his eyes sparkled. "Are you suggesting we go to one?"

Algar closed his eyes and let his mind travel. Yes, there it was. A universe a few major occurrences away from this one. Alpha Four was the same, meaning Reginald existed in this other universe, so there would be no need for certain indoctrinations and inoculations. And Earth was different — more technologically advanced than the Earth of this universe, with people more open to the wonders of science and the cosmos.

And…there was something quite interesting going on as well. Something that would alleviate his boredom along with Reginald's.

Algar opened his eyes. "Yes. For a visit." Then he smiled, and snapped his fingers.

* * *

"Faster! Pull the main rudder to lee! Maybe we can lose them in that cloud bank to starboard!"

I so pulled. Captain Tucker wasn't given to shouting at his crew for no reason.

Going into clouds meant, among other things, that the crew on the main deck would end up wet as well as cold. But everyone had their flight suits and caps on, and all either had their goggles on or hanging around their necks. Those of us with longer hair would have wet ponytails, but that was a small price to pay to remain alive.

"Harder, Jeanette! Put your muscles into it, girl!"

"You're a lot bigger than me, and stronger, too. Why don't you take the rudder and let me steer?"

"Because you're a madwoman at the helm."

I looked behind us. Whatever it was in the sky, it wasn't made by any man—at least, not any man or woman on Earth. "I'm thinking a madwoman might be your best choice, Captain."

He cursed under his breath, but gave the order for us to switch places. "Crew, prepare for turbulence! Jeanette, on three…two…one…now!"

The captain and I both leaped for each other's places. I managed to grab the yoke before it spun out of control or dropped our nose down too far. As soon as the captain had the rudder, I pulled back, to bring our nose up, and spun the yoke to starboard while the captain kept the rudder hard to lee. The *Golden Voyager* turned quickly up and to the right and, as suggested, flew into the clouds.

It was a dangerous maneuver. The cold and wet of the clouds would dampen the silken balloons and sails, and if the air and hydrogen cooled too much, we'd be going down, whether the oddities after us shot us down or not. The deck could become slippery, meaning, official flight boots with an anti-slip tread or not, a crewman might take a spill at an inopportune time. And if there was anything in these clouds, we'd likely have no time to avoid it.

Our airmen were busy keeping the balloons filled, while the ruddermen adjusted the trim of both balloons and sails based on both what the captain and I had done and the instructions he was shouting. At least those I could see. The *Golden Voyager* was a longer boat, and the captain and I were midship.

I could have shouted the same—in fact, Captain Tucker tended to say I was the best at giving directions; at least, that's how I chose to interpret his saying I was the best loudmouth on his crew—but in tense situations, one clear voice of authority is better than many. And when I was manning either the rudder or the yoke, the Third Officer handled the repetition of the captain's orders.

One of the shipteens ran back to us. "Captain, Ex-O," Missy said breathlessly, "Mister Manning says we can't go up much higher or we'll freeze or stop breathing."

"Manning's too timid," I muttered.

Missy heard me. "Do you want us to prep for emergency situations, Ex-O?"

The captain snorted. "Miss Gunnels, have you young people not perhaps noticed what's chasing us?"

"Yes, sir, Captain. Mister Manning would like to stop running away from them and get a better look."

"Would he?" I didn't try to keep the sarcasm out of my tone.

"Is this the time Mister Manning is going to take up arms or are we again hoping to capture fascinating images for his daguerreotype, petri dishes, and microscope?"

Manning was our science officer. Honesty forced me to admit that he was the most handsome man on our crew. Quite possibly the most handsome man in the United Territories. Tall, well-muscled, and very pleasing to the eye, with thick brown hair and deep blue eyes, he could have been an Ex-O or even a captain, if he'd had the desire. He had the look, the build, the brains, and, frankly, the charisma.

But Manning didn't like to fight, and he rarely enjoyed giving orders. His interests were all in science and discovery. Which, when we weren't being pursued by things we knew not what of, was a somewhat charming trait.

In danger situations, however, Manning's desire to try to reason out what was going on tended to put me on edge. I fell far more into the "shoot your ray gun first and question the brigand later" mindset.

"Jeanette, Manning's right, and you know it. Miss Gunnels, please ensure all crew have their breathing apparatus on, though not triggered. Any not in their high altitude gear should change immediately. You and the other shipteens should cover their posts, two to a rudder, sail, or balloon."

"Yes, sir." Missy ran off and shared this order with Vrabel. Our Third Officer ensured the order to prep for higher altitude passed along to the crew, loud and clear.

As Captain and Executive Officer, we both had our high altitude gear and breathing apparatus on as a matter of course. However, on and active weren't the same thing. I wasn't ready to put in my breathing tube—the Captain and I still needed to be able to speak to each other and the crew clearly.

However, I risked taking a hand off the yoke to adjust my lenses for further distance and spectrum expansion. It was a risk I was glad I'd taken—one of our pursuers had gotten in front of us somehow and was lurking in our cloud bank.

"All hands, sails and wings in, balloons back, full steam, and hang on!" I pulled back on the yoke and our nose went up as Vrabel bellowed my orders on. The crew had already attached lifelines, when we'd first spotted our pursuers, so I had few worries that we'd lose someone overboard. I was worried we'd lose everyone by smashing into the terrifyingly odd thing in front of us.

We passed within arm's length of this other ship, so we were all treated to a closer examination. I hoped Manning was paying attention.

At least, I assumed it was a ship. It looked nothing like any ship that sailed on water or through the air.

The *Golden Voyager* was a Dragon Schooner, meaning we had a base adapted along the design of longboats from the Vikings of old, complete with decorative dragon head and tail. There were also three sets of side "dragon wings" that could extend or retract. As with the head and tail, these were lovely, but were more than decoration—they helped with lift, ballast, and balance, and they also assisted when we needed to hover. The ship's hull was three levels deep, and in addition to supplies and other cargo, we carried a crew of forty-four.

We did so because the *Golden Voyager* utilized a newer dirigible system that had sets of smaller balloons held within three larger ones, all controlled by an intricate system of ropes and pulleys. This gave us more maneuverability as well as lift capacity.

Because of our size, we also had sails, just as ships of the sea did, only ours were all jibs, not mainsails, and we had jib masts set all along the sides. When the balloons were at full, the dragon wings were extended to catch the upward air currents, and the sails were all out catching the wind, the *Voyager* was a beautiful sight—a gleaming dragon attired in crisp white sails and crimson and azure balloons showing our United Territories colors with pride.

The ships after us were all metal, with no sails or balloons at all in evidence, and less evidence of the beauty of design. They resembled upside-down soup bowls, but each had a rounded bump on top. They spun through the air, like a top, via no mechanism I could see. Unlike our ship, they were also all enclosed, though there were many portholes.

As we passed, I saw what looked like a giant bird's head

through one of those portholes. Somehow, the creature inside and I made eye contact. I felt no kinship, and the glare I received said that the creature felt none, either.

Manning came to us at a run. "Captain, we need to stop. They're clearly more advanced than we are. We need to see if we can communicate."

"Did you see it?" Captain Tucker asked, in almost a whisper. "It looked so … alien."

"I believe the best communication will be a shot off their bow. We can aim for that glittery bump."

Manning shook his head. "Now's not the time for aggression, Miss Thompson. Now is the time to show that humanity is ready to face the greater universe."

"Oh, could be, could be," a sardonic voice said from behind me, before I could mention, yet again, that Manning was supposed to call me Ex-O. "On the other hand, it might be the time to show that humanity is the nasty, vicious piece of work it really is.

* * *

I risked a look over my shoulder. Sure enough, our passengers were disobeying direct orders and, instead of remaining in their quarters, were standing behind me.

Sir Reginald was a man who gave Manning a good run for the money in the looks department, only he had long blond hair and was on the rangy side. He was royalty from Europe, or at least that's what his manservant, Al, had told us when they'd booked passage on the *Golden Voyager* six weeks prior. They'd paid in pure gold, so we hadn't asked for proof of a heraldic seal or birth records.

Al was also handsome, very muscular, with dark, wavy hair, though he was about half the size of Sir Reginald. Frankly, he was half the size of me.

"Why aren't you two below decks as ordered?"

"Turbulence was terrible, Miss Thompson," Sir Reginald said, shooting me a rakish grin. He was a passenger. He was allowed to call me Miss Thompson. Him being charming had nothing to do with it.

Manning could take a lesson from Sir Reginald. At one time I'd fancied the idea that Manning and I might, one day, match up. But unless courtly reserve, an inability to acknowledge my rank, and the desire to share all his knowledge with me at any reasonable opportunity were Manning's way of showing interest, I'd accepted that unless I was a specimen for a Petri dish, I wasn't someone Manning wanted to spend the rest of his life with.

But I was the Ex-O of the finest ship in the United Territories fleet, and if all Manning and I would be were fellow officers, then that would continue to be enough. Besides, the man drove me crazy.

Captain Tucker shook his head. "Jeanette's right, Sir Reginald. It's not safe for the two of you to be on deck right now."

"I'm more interested in why Mister Gar is urging us to violence, not diplomacy," Manning said. "Though I'm sure Doctor Parker has something for your weak stomach, Sir Reginald." I'd spent the last six weeks with the strong impression that Manning didn't like Sir Reginald. Had no idea why—as passengers went, Sir Reginald and Al had been charming, helpful, and entertaining. If all passengers were like them, we'd have had to add another level to the ship.

Two little furry heads peeped up out of Sir Reginald's pockets. Al had said they were Guinea Cats, but he'd only said this after Manning had shared that he'd yet to set foot in New Guinea. Har and Ten looked nothing like real cats, but they were soft, loving, and adorable. And they, like Sir Reginald and Al, didn't belong here.

Al shrugged. "Yes, I am. Why will become clear to you soon."

"I believe Miss Thompson and our Captain both want you two below decks, however," Manning shared. "Upcoming events or no."

"What our Science Officer said." One day, perhaps the man would use my title. Today didn't seem to be that day, and since we had terrifying things to deal with, I chose to, once again, let

Manning's lack of protocol slide. "And while I'm sure Mister Manning doesn't agree with Al, I must admit, the creature I saw in that ship, if it is a ship, didn't give off the air of universal brotherhood."

"It's a ship," Al said. "All six of them are ships."

"There are six?" Captain Tucker asked. "I've only spotted four."

"I've seen the six Al saw, Captain. And I say again, they don't bode well for us."

We crested the cloud bank and, as if to give punctuation, or concurrence, to my statements and thoughts, another one of these alien ships was waiting for us. It fired a blast from its edge.

On the positive, the shot seemed to be a warning one. On the negative, it still hit. Not one of the balloons or sails, but one of the crew. A very vital one of the crew.

* * *

"Captain down!" I bellowed as loudly as I could, as Captain Tucker collapsed into Manning's arms. "Doctor to the bridge! Sir Reginald, you're closest—man the rudder! All hands, sails in, wings out, balloons held—we're going to all stop!"

Sir Reginald did as requested—he was, thankfully, easily as strong as Manning, and an all stop required strength, particularly on the rudder. The rest of the crew obeyed as well, and, while Vrabel—who had impressive lungs which she was quite expert at using—shouted along my request for our good doctor and all the rest of my orders, the rest of us brought the *Golden Voyager* to a hover.

Our ship's doctor was excellent, probably the best doctor in the air, but one look told me that Dr. Parker would be too late.

Still, she came running, medical bag in hand. "What did those devils hit him with?" she asked as Manning laid the captain down on the deck.

"I have no idea," I admitted.

Captain Tucker's eyes were glassy as Dr. Parker ripped his shirt open. We all gasped. The captain's chest had a perfect hole through it, easily an inch in diameter. There wasn't as much blood as I'd have expected—the wound looked cauterized. Vicious and mortal, but not nearly as messy as it could be.

Dr. Parker put her fingers to the Captain's throat, then looked up at me. "He's gone. There's nothing I can even try, not with that hole in him." Her voice shook. "There's no … heart left for me to try to restart."

"Third Officer, to the bridge!"

Vrabel raced over. "Ex-O, orders to shoot these bastards?"

"I appreciate your enthusiasm, Elizabeth, but that shot was far too accurate. They shot the captain to show us that they can hit anything on our ship they want to." And kill any and all of us easily, but I didn't add that aloud. The expressions on those I could see shared that they'd all come to the same conclusion anyway.

"That's right," Al said. He sounded impressed. I chose not to allow this to flatter me. "They took out the person in command."

"You're captain now," Dr. Parker said, making Al's accurate observation just a little more chilling.

"Technically, I suppose." I wasn't afraid of dying. But succession hadn't been a thought in any of our heads an hour ago. Now, the man I'd sworn my allegiance to years ago when I was just a shipteen was dead in front of me, and I'd been able to do nothing to protect or save him. He'd saved me—ultimately, he'd saved every one of us on his crew at some point during the War. We'd all lost our leader and the man who was like our father. I'd never wanted to destroy anything as much as I wanted to destroy these alien things floating around us.

"No, you are," Manning agreed, bringing me sharply back to reality. "Protocol is quite clear on this point—if the captain is incapacitated, then the Executive Officer takes command. In the case of … the death of a captain, then the Ex-O retains command." He cleared his throat. "I believe surrender may be in order … Captain."

"Mister Manning, don't take this the wrong way, but if we're all feeling that we're going to follow protocol and I'm now the captain, my first act isn't going to be to surrender to these alien creatures." I turned to Vrabel before Manning could reply. "Elizabeth, you're now Ex-O. Who do you recommend for Third

Officer?"

"Carswell, Captain Thompson," she replied without hesitation. "Edward's the most prepared of our junior officers. Shall I call him to the bridge?"

"Call all the crew to the bridge, please, Elizabeth. As your last act as Third Officer."

While Vrabel bellowed for all hands, I checked on Sir Reginald. He was doing a fine job keeping us in hover, which isn't as simple as it sounds. "Do you need relief?" I asked him.

"No, Captain, not at all. Use me in any way you need. And, may I express my condolences on your loss?"

"Thank you." I stepped closer to him. "Are you sure you don't want to go below decks at this time?" I asked in a low voice.

"No," he replied in kind. "Despite how I may appear to you, I'm from a line of warriors. Al and I are with you, all the way."

Manning cleared his throat. "Captain, the crew are assembled."

I turned back to see Manning giving Sir Reginald a stony look. However, I had a crew to calm. Manning's personality issue with Sir Reginald would have to wait for later.

I addressed the crew. "We've been attacked by what, as of right now, we must assume are alien invaders of some kind. They've drawn first blood, and, unfortunately, Captain Tucker was in their line of fire. I'm sorry to say that we've lost him."

Most of our crew were young. Dr. Parker was the eldest among us, and she was the ripe old age of thirty-two. However, the war within the Greater Americas had only ended two years ago, and even our youngest shipteen had served for the United Territories in some way. So this wasn't the first time any of us had experienced violent death. But it didn't lessen the blow. No matter how many times, death was always the unwelcome visitor.

However, not as unwelcome as those whose strange ships now surrounded us.

"We must assume we are, as of this moment, at war. Unless there are objections, I will be taking over as Captain. At war or not, now is the time to say if you feel someone else is better qualified to captain the *Golden Voyager*."

The crew looked at each other. Missy raised her hand. "I think I speak for all of us. There's no one we'd rather follow than you … Captain Thompson." The rest of the crew nodded.

I allowed myself to feel the warmth of this moment. But only for a moment. "Thank you. I shall endeavor to do my best, as all good Captains should."

"We will serve as all people good and true must do," the crew replied in unison.

Our wartime succession ceremony now completed, I officially promoted Vrabel to Ex-O and Carswell to Third Officer. Carswell had no sooner accepted than Manning nudged me.

"We are surrounded," he said quietly. "I would expect we'll be boarded shortly." He took my elbow and gently turned me around.

There was a golden, glowing light flowing from one of the alien ships. It hit our aft deck and I waited for it to burn a hole in the *Golden Voyager* as they'd put a hole into Captain Tucker.

But instead, three figures floated down through the light. The light disappeared and we took our first look at these creatures.

My initial impression was correct—they were bird-people. They were short and stocky with heads that looked something like a humanoid version of an eagle, with an extra large lower jaw. Unlike most birds, their eyes were more centered, though those eyes were, as many birds' are, quite beady and very non-human. I cocked my head. From another angle, they looked like something else vaguely familiar. Something else that didn't like us.

"Dinosaurs," Manning said in an excited whisper.

"Ah, that's it." They resembled the drawings I'd seen of the mighty Tyrannosaurus-Rex, only they were to that giant lizard as Al was to Manning. Their bodies were completely hidden by flowing white robes, so I was unable to determine if their bodies were also like the T-Rex, but I did spot six large talons sticking out from under each robe. The talons were painted with designs I didn't recognize.

Feathers stuck out of the sleeves of their robes. Whether this meant they had wings for arms, or were covered with feathers, or something else, I had no guess.

One of the three stepped forward. "I am K'tano. This is Ast'ria and this Riol." It indicated the others who nodded curtly at the mention of their names. "We are the Z'porrah. Our planet is far away, at the galactic core. We have come to teach you the ways of peace."

Heard someone snort behind me even as Manning drew his breath in with excitement and the crew gasped. From where the sound of the snort came from, I assumed it was from Al. I shared his reaction.

"I don't find your murdering of our captain to be a peaceful act," I said, as I stepped forward as well. "We call that an act of war. Especially when perpetrated by an alien race as their first act upon meeting us."

"You are a backwater planet, peopled with violent, hairless apes. You only understand strength. We are strong. And we are stronger than you."

"Maybe so, and I'll choose to ignore your insults and not share that you look like dinosaur birds, but your statements again don't sound peaceful. I'd like to know how you chose us, this ship, as your first point of attack and what you plan to do to bring about peace for all."

"You were nearest."

"Ah. So it's just luck." Bad luck, to be sure, but still, random chance. What would happen next was dependent upon the luck of an alien race's draw. I didn't like our odds.

The Z'porrah nodded. "You will surrender, and we will usher in an age of peace. Or you will not surrender and you will all die. You have fifteen minutes of your time to choose." It stepped back to rejoin its fellows. The light shown down from the ship, and the Z'porrah flew back up and inside.

"An age of peace," Manning said longingly. "Wouldn't it be lovely?"

"If it were true, yes."

"Peace can be overrated," Al said.

I turned to him. "You know something. More than you've told us. You knew what these were before they even attacked us. I'd like some answers, and some honesty." I looked at the supposed Guinea Cats peering out of Sir Reginald's pocket. They looked like no animals I'd ever seen—as with the Z'porrah there were similarities to Earth animals, but no exact match. And as with the Z'porrah, I now didn't think these animals were from around here. "The real truth, Al Gar. If that's even your real name."

Al's eyes twinkled. "Oh, it's my real name. And the truth depends greatly upon whose viewpoint you choose to share. The Z'porrah firmly feel they'll bring peace. And they will."

To his great credit, Manning didn't immediately demand we capitulate. "How will this peace be achieved?" he asked.

Al didn't speak. "Tell them," Sir Reginald said strongly. "I know you know. Tell them the truth."

"As you wish. They will offer you things—enslavement and war or pretty words and useful things. If you pick as others have, you'll have a couple hundred years of peace and prosperity."

"That sounds good," Manning said. "I presume you're about to explain how this is far too good to be true?"

"I am. After you've destroyed all weapons and any plans for how to create them, and after all your warriors are dead and the desire to fight is bred out of you, then the Z'porrah will be back, in greater numbers. They'll overtake and enslave the Earth, and turn all creatures on it into subservient beings, if you're lucky. If not, they'll just wipe out all animal life and seed it with their own people."

We were all quiet for a few moments. "And if we fight?" I asked finally.

Al shrugged. "They'll destroy your ship and you'll all die."

"What will happen to the future generations?" Manning asked.

"Ah, now that *is* the good question. If the *Golden Voyager* goes down fighting, the rest of the United Territories will join together and fight these invaders. They won't win. However, the rest of the Americas will join in, and then the rest of the world. The war will go on for years. When it's done, Earth will be a planet devoted to war and every being on it will be clear that there are stronger enemies out there who could arrive at any time, without warning, and attack a merchant ship peacefully traveling."

Part of me wondered if Al was making this all up. But in my soul I knew that he'd looked into the possible futures somehow, and had told us what would come to be. I knew my choice.

I turned to the crew. "This is not my decision alone to make. My choice is to remain with the *Golden Voyager* and fight these invaders, even though it means we'll join Captain Tucker in the afterlife much sooner. But each of you has an equal vote in this."

The crew was quiet. Then Manning spoke. "Those who support our Captain's decision to fight now and save the future of mankind, raise your hands." His was the first hand in the air.

The rest of the crew raised their hands. None hesitated.

"I'm proud to lead all of you," I said, trying to ignore the lump in my throat. "Even if it will potentially be the shortest command in history."

Sir Reginald and Al were having a quiet but vehement discussion. Sir Reginald seemed to win. "Captain, if I may speak with you for a moment?" he asked. "In private?"

"Why not? I believe we have five or so minutes left of our allotted fifteen."

We went to the far aft of the ship. One of the Z'porrah ships hovered close by, the others at the fore, starboard, and lee sides, with one above us and, as I craned my neck over the side to see, one below. We were utterly surrounded.

"Captain … Jeanette … there is another way." Sir Reginald took my hand. "We've misled you—Al and I both are not from this planet. Or this universe."

After discovering we were at the start of an alien invasion, this was unsurprising. "I knew they weren't Guinea Cats."

Sir Reginald chuckled. "No. They're called Poofs. And they're what I want to speak of." He put his hand into his pocket and pulled out the Poofs. But instead of two, there were four, two of them smaller. "The Poofs are androgynous and mate when a royal wedding of my people is at hand."

"Oh? Were we taking you to your bride?" Another reason to despise these Z'porrah, as if I'd needed one.

He gave me an odd look. "No. I am not betrothed. Yet. I was hoping…" He took a deep breath. "I was hoping that you would accept my suit. I can take you away from all this."

I was dumbstruck, but managed not to let my jaw drop. "Al doesn't approve, does he?" was all I managed to say.

"He approves of you but not of my taking you with me."

A throat cleared behind us. "Excuse me," Manning said stiffly. "I would like a word with Miss Thompson, too. Right now."

I could remind him to call me Captain, but why bother at this time? "I'll just be a moment," I said to Sir Reginald, as Manning led me to another part of the aft deck.

"He asked you to marry him?" Manning asked, voice and manner still stiff.

"He did, in fact."

"And your reply?"

"What business of it is yours?" I looked up at him, surprised by his presumption.

To see that he looked stricken. "Will he save you from this?"

"Yes, supposedly. How—"

"There are no such things as Guinea Cats. I've researched it. And there are other oddities. I believe Sir Reginald and Al Gar are aliens, just as these Z'porrah are. Though clearly more as we are and, one presumes, not our enemies." He cleared his throat again. "Since he can save you, I will … not speak my mind."

"No, speak it. Because I have no idea why you pulled me aside other than to warn me of something Sir Reginald had just admitted."

"I … I wanted to …" Manning looked panicked, then resigned. Then sad. He looked down. "I wanted to tell you something, and ask you something. Neither matter any more."

"She didn't say yes," Al said. "I'd suspect she won't, either, if you'd just manage a coherent sentence."

"I requested privacy," Manning said, demeanor back to stiff.

"And you've botched having it." Al shook his head. "Tell the girl or she'll never know. And she deserves to know, doesn't she? So she makes the choice of her own free will."

"I deserve to know what?"

Manning shook his head and spun on his heel. Only Missy was there, blocking him. "Tell her," she urged. "She's not aware, but all the rest of us know. Please, Mister Manning. Tell her."

"By all that's holy, tell me what?"

Manning turned back, pulled me to him, and kissed me. Quite passionately. It was probably un-captain-like, but I found it impossible not to respond in kind. He ended the kiss slowly. "I love you, Miss Thompson."

"Oh. That's why you don't use my title."

He smiled. "It is. I was hoping it would show you that …"

"That you have no clue about proper military order, nor any clear idea of how to woo a woman? It did." His face fell and I felt badly. I leaned up and kissed him again. "It's alright, Nicholas. And, I believe, for the all of one minute we'll have left, that you can call me Jeanette."

"I now pronounce you husband and wife," Al said. "It's official, at least as official as you want it to be."

"Under the circumstances," Manning said with a small smile, "I'll accept it as extremely official."

"I as well."

Sir Reginald sighed behind me. "She would make a wonderful queen."

I turned to him. "Could you take the crew? Wherever you were going to take me? Get them to safety, spare them all of this?"

"What of you?" Al asked.

"The captain goes down with the ship."

Manning took my hand. "You will not go alone."

"No," Missy said. "None of us will leave, Captain. We're with you 'til the end."

"All of you?" Al asked. "Of your own free will?"

Vrabel had joined us and she nodded. "Doctor Parker and I took a vote. The crew, to a person, is committed to following the Captain's course."

"You two had best leave, however you're able," I told our passengers. "Thank you for helping."

Sir Reginald didn't look happy. "That wasn't helping," he muttered. "Not like we could."

"There are rules, lad," Al said.

"Hang the rules," Sir Reginald snapped. "If we can't help,

why bother to come? Why spend weeks with these people, get attached to them, fall in love with them, to leave them to this fate?"

"The fate is necessary," Al said. "This Earth must be made ready." He looked around. "It's a lovely ship."

"It is," I agreed.

"Not suitable for space travel, though."

"No. We're not there yet. Soon, we hope."

"Sooner than you think." Then Al snapped his fingers.

* * *

We were in a ship, as strange as anything the Z'porrah were in, but still, more familiar, more human. I could see some of the *Golden Voyager* in this ship. Which was good and proper.

Unlike the *Golden Voyager*, this ship was fully enclosed, and made of metal, its design more like a bullet or a dirigible than our regal flying ship. It possessed seven decks in addition to the machinery deck, with spacious living quarters, at least as compared to what we were used to, an impressive weapons locker, and some even more impressive cannons and lasers on the ship itself. An advanced propulsion system that was set up to be self-replicating, so that running out of fuel was close to impossible. Which was important, since this ship was made to go into space. Deep into space.

We were above the Z'porrah ships. I was fairly sure they couldn't see us. They were too busy destroying the *Golden Voyager*.

As I watched our beautiful ship fall slowly out of the sky, I focused on what Al was telling us. "… and you cannot come back to Earth. All on the planet must know and believe that you're dead."

"What about those with families?" I heard someone ask, and realized it was my own voice.

"If you're doing this you can do that, too," Sir Reginald said firmly.

Al shrugged. "They'll need the genetic material." He snapped his fingers and all the immediate families of those who still had them appeared. Manning and I were alone—neither of us had anyone left on Earth. But now we had each other. Manning took my hand and squeezed it gently.

"Why can't we return?" Vrabel asked Al. "What you told us makes it sound like Earth will need our help."

He shook his head. "You're providing the impetus for Earth's survival. And you'll be the ambassadors of your race and your planet."

"Why aren't we more … upset?" Manning asked Al. "All that's happened is so fantastic … I'd expect to be suggesting that Doctor Parker sedate most of the crew. And yet, we're all calm, and so are the family members you just snapped here out of nothing."

"Distress isn't what you need right now. Action is."

"Then thank you, again, for whatever you did to our brains to make all of this comprehensible," Manning said. "And to keep us calm and accepting. I think."

"That was simple, and none of your minds have been harmed. The knowledge I gave you is why you're all calm—you understand, at a deeper level than any of you can realize consciously—exactly what's happened."

"But?" I asked. "Because there sounds like a 'but' must be about to follow."

Al nodded. "But you have the hard work ahead of you. Preparing the greater cosmos for the arrival of Earth onto the galactic stage. Staying alive out in space without my being around to help. Surviving. Putting technological knowledge and the clear understanding of events into all your minds was nothing compared to this."

The *Golden Voyager* was now out of sight. "Can we destroy these Z'porrah ships and still have Earth join together?"

"No," Al said. "However, the command ship is the one directly under us. And it might be good to show that the *Golden Voyager* fought back before being defeated."

I went to the bridge, Vrabel, and Manning coming with me. Dr. Parker was already there, as were Carswell, who was now in charge of Weapons, and Missy, who I'd promoted to Navigator, since, on this kind of ship, the Captain couldn't perform that function.

"I've examined all supplies, Captain," Dr. Parker said. "We should be self-sustaining for at least a decade, and I can create medical supplies as needed."

"Excellent, Lori, thank you." I seated myself, Vrabel in the chair to my right, Manning to my left. "Elizabeth, Edward, let's test out the weapons system, shall we?"

* * *

"I wish she'd have come with me," Reginald said. "Now my heart is broken and I'll never see her again."

"It's all for the best," Algar said. It was. More for the best than Reginald would ever know. At least the Reginald in this universe. "They're a good couple—her bravery, his caution, their combined intelligence. If I had to break the rules, they were worth breaking them for."

"But you've done one other thing right, Algar. I never want to leave this system again. I can't risk meeting someone else like Jeanette and having to leave her behind."

He patted Reginald's knee. "Don't worry. You won't have to."

"Thank you, though," Reginald said. "For saving them. I still love her and, despite him winning, I like him as well. I just wish they weren't alone."

Algar patted Har and Ten. "Don't worry, lad. I left them something that will help them. For at least as long as their line lasts."

* * *

Somewhere during the time when we fired and the Z'porrah ship blew up, Al and Sir Reginald left us. Dr. Parker had checked the entire ship, just to be sure, but she confirmed that they were gone. And we hadn't even said goodbye. Or thank you.

"Do you think we'll really be able to survive all the unknown we're heading for?" I asked Manning as I had Missy set a course for the nearest star to ours. Alpha Centauri was our first destination. Per the information Al had given us, we'd be there in about a year, give or take.

Manning took my hand and put the two little Poofs into it. "Yes. As long as we're all together, we'll never be defeated."

"Then let's head the *Brave Voyager* out into the cosmos and see what comes, shall we, Mister Manning?"

"Absolutely, Missus Manning. Absolutely."

Heart of the Empire

Jason Palmatier

The pistons that had replaced Admiral von Trite's heart rose and fell with a soft *hiss-gush, hiss-gush,* playing peek-a-boo behind his rigid shoulders. A light smoke swirled up from his stack, no more than would curl from a fine walnut pipe, tingeing the air with the acrid smell of coal-fire. He glared at the crisp parchment in his hand, twisting his magnificent mustache between thumb and forefinger as he read.

"Admiral?"

Von Trite's frown deepened and he glanced up at his oldest, dearest friend and confidant, Dr. Titus Jenson.

"What does it say, sir?" Dr. Jenson leaned forward, squinting through his thick spectacles.

Von Trite grunted, looked down at the letter and cleared his throat. When he spoke, his voice boomed, still full of command in this, his fifty-seventh year.

"Sir. Your offer of aid to the Crown in these trying times is most appreciated. As we endeavor to throw back the relentless invader that has beset us, it is a great comfort to Her Majesty to know that such an honored and dear friend holds her safety close to his heart. However, at this time Her Majesty feels that the best hope for the Empire lies in the courage and arms of the magnificent Gendarme Elektrièni. Her Majesty beseeches you, her most beloved Royal Explorer, to seek safety in the underground of our dear capital while our newly armed company defends her."

"I … I see." Dr. Jenson paused, not quite sure what to say. The steam-powered heart he had designed for his friend had slowed the Admiral some, but it had not reduced his temper. He braced himself for the venting that was sure to come from such a curt letter of dismissal.

The Admiral slowly shook his head.

"'Close to his heart' indeed," von Trite mused. A distant explosion rumbled Dr. Jenson's teacup on its saucer and knocked a shrunken head from its stand in one of von Trite's glass curio cases. "Forty-three years, Titus." The great clock atop the mantel bonged loudly, a hiss of steam shooting from the side nozzle that regulated pressure from the house boiler. "Forty-three years of service to the crown on the highest of high seas, in the darkest of dark jungles."

Dr. Jenson swallowed, nodding his head, fortifying himself for the verbal onslaught that was surely imminent. But instead, the Admiral's face fell slack and his arm dropped onto the desk. His magnificent, mustachioed head sagged forward. Dr. Jenson startled, then reached out for the small pile of coal at the corner of von Trite's desk. But he caught himself, fingertips inches from the ornate silver charger that the black char sat upon. Nothing set the Admiral off more than feeding his hopper for him.

"Sir." Dr. Jenson cleared his throat. "Sir!"

Von Trite blinked, looking up groggily.

"Your fire, sir. It's low."

Von Trite squinted, confused, then blinked in understanding. He flopped his arm forward, worked a nugget of coal from the pile, and laboriously lifted it into the hopper over his left shoulder. It clattered down to sit atop the firebox door until von Trite weakly twisted the spring-loaded door handle on his left side.

The coal fell in and ignited. The pace of the shining pistons on his back quickened. Blood surged through the fine glass sight tubes that ran across the back of his neck. Slowly the fog cleared from the Admiral's eyes. He pulled in one deep breath, then two. Presently he resumed talking, his mind ramping up along with his boiler's pressure.

"I blocked an assassin's bullet for her with my own heart, Titus, and this ..." von Trite tossed the paper onto his dark mahogany desk. "This is how she repays me? Telling me to hide in the underground like a rat? A rat!"

Dr. Jenson flinched at von Trite's vehemence. If the Queen

only knew how much the old Admiral still loved her, she would let him throw himself at the invaders in a vain but glorious attempt to defend her. But she did know. That was the problem. She didn't want him to die because she loved him too.

When von Trite had knelt before her, dashing, young, cocksure, asking for a grant to map the Antarctic for crown and country, she had gazed down at him with fixed fascination, smitten from the get-go. Dr. Jenson had watched von Trite lock eyes with her, challenging her to say no and wooing her to say yes, all at the same time. It had been magnificent. Classic von Trite. But all of that steadfast love had now brought about this stalemate of the heart. Her Majesty would not risk von Trite in battle, and von Trite would not sally forth without Her Majesty's approval.

The Admiral shoved himself to his feet, sweat beading his brow. Dr. Jenson attempted to curtail the inevitable. "I know, sir. But she only means the best. These …" he waved his hand at the ceiling, "Kappa Cygni invaders, or what have you, are very dangerous. Not a single one has been felled by her majesty's forces."

"Not even by the 'Gendarme Elektrièni?'" The Admiral spat the Queen's prized brigade's name out like rancid olives.

"Well, they have been held in reserve until now …"

"Bah!" The Admiral shook his head in disgust. "The upstarts. What have they got over the *Morgan*? Eh? What have they got with their light poppers and crackle makers? A fancy show? A glowing exposition piece? They still need the steam, Titus! They still need the fire and the water to make their contraptions work. They still need the steam!"

"I know, sir."

The Admiral settled back, waving his hand. His specially crafted great chair, with cutouts for the boiler and engine on his back, creaked in protest. The centrifugal governor whirred, the bar arms flattening out to slow down the inflow of steam to his pistons, keeping them from over-speeding and throwing a rod. Dr. Jenson swallowed and tried to calm his nerves. It looked like the storm had passed for the moment.

The room shook to another rumble, this time closer and

longer lived, followed by a muted volley of rifle shots. The great steam clock gushed again, releasing excess pressure. Dr. Jenson jumped. He turned and glared at the clock. "Now what would make it do that again so soon …"

Running footsteps in the hall interrupted his musing. A loud knock sounded at the door.

"Come," Admiral von Trite bellowed.

The door flew open, revealing a royal messenger out of breath and smeared with soot.

"Tesla's weapons have failed!"

The Admiral and Dr. Jenson frowned in confusion.

"The Gendarme Elektrièni have fled from the streets in disarray! The invaders are closing in on the palace unimpeded. The Queen beseeches you for aid, sir!"

The Admiral stared. The great steam clock ticked out four distinct seconds. The Admiral rose slowly to his feet, knuckles resting atop his desk.

"Tell Her Majesty that she shall have it."

The messenger sagged in relief and bowed, then turned and fled back down the grand hallway. Dr. Jenson turned to the Admiral with a look of shock.

"But sir! How? The *Morgan* will never be ready in time."

Von Trite said nothing. Instead he walked stiffly over to a grand curio of solid oak and turned the key to its stained glass door. From within he withdrew a small, black walnut chest garnished with gold leaf. He raised the lid and looked over to Dr. Jenson, whose eyes flew wide in recognition.

"Battle Coal!" Dr. Jenson cried.

The Admiral nodded. Dredged from the shallows off the coast of Cuba, the coal had fired the great ship *Morgan* into full battle frenzy for two years, burning hot and fierce, letting them run on a quarter bunker load. They flew over the seas, blasting, boarding and ramming with glee. They sank Russian and pirate ships with ease, sealing the Admiral's name in sea lore before their supply ran out. Dr. Jenson had thought none had survived.

"But that's not enough to fire the *Morgan* …" Dr. Jenson began.

The Admiral gave his friend a knowing half-smile. "Ah,

Titus. It's not going to fire the *Morgan*. It's going to fire me." Von Trite picked a small jet-black piece from the chest and tossed it into his hopper, firebox door already open. The coal rattled down and exploded into flames, burning bright blue tinged with deep purple. The pistons on his back bucked hard, ratcheting up to an as yet unseen level. Dr. Jenson gasped.

"Sir, you must be careful! You will exceed your governor limits and shut down your boiler!"

The Admiral flared his eyes, the flames of the coal seeming to burn within them. He stretched his back with a crack and two pops then reached over his shoulder and yanked the madly spinning governor off, slamming it onto the desk. "Now we can't have that, can we Titus? There's an empire to save!" Von Trite dumped the remaining coal into a small sack and shoved it into his jacket pocket. "To the *Morgan*!"

The Admiral brushed past his stunned friend, snatched his greatcoat and hat from the wall, and strode down the wide hallway, picking up steam with every step. Dr. Jenson stammered, and followed as fast as his stiff legs would allow. The Admiral pounded down the servant's staircase while settling the hat of the Admiralty overtop his thinning hair.

As he raced to follow, Dr. Jenson called out, "But the *Morgan*'s boilers, sir! And the crew!"

Dr. Jenson emerged in the echoing dampness of the basement and stopped dead in his tracks, gaping in amazement.

The *Morgan* sat plumbed to the house, as she had for the last ten years, her great boilers powering the clocks and gadgets and heating the rooms, but now her hull sat in the Thames, instead of in the hoist frame above it. And her decks swarmed with men, ratcheting, wrenching, oiling. Her boilers seethed at battle pressure, needles just below the red arc that would trigger an emergency blow.

"That's why the clock blew so soon!" Dr. Jenson exclaimed. The Admiral could always smell a fight coming. He must have sent the cabin boy to round up the men. And they had all come, every last one of them. Come for the fight, for the adventure, for the Admiral.

Von Trite shouted to Tawny, a shirtless old sailor in jaunty blue, who heaved on a massive four foot wrench to close the outflow steam valve to the house. A shout went up from the men as the *Morgan*'s pressure gauges wobbled a hair's breadth further up, grazing the red line. Then three other sailors, all weathered and old, hauled on a sleeve nut two feet around and the *Morgan* slipped free of the house plumbing, drifting in the choppy Thames.

"Spin the paddles, lads, bring the pressure down!" The Admiral's face glowed with youth and vigor, the call of adventure dashing the years away, pulling Dr. Jenson along with it. The doctor sprang forward from the slippery stone floor, forgetting his age, and landed on the *Morgan*'s deck with sure feet.

"That's it Titus! Just as when we were lads on the storming Indian Sea! Ha ha!"

The six great paddle wheels of the *Morgan* began to turn, dipping in the water, their massive gears rotating on immaculately maintained spindles. The steam engines that powered them huffed and chugged, echoing like thunder from the damp stone walls.

"Get 'em moving boys, full power! We have a Queen to save and a cur to fight!" The crew cheered as they threw off the last moorings and secured the last ropes. It was time for battle.

The Admiral took hold of a worn peg of the rudder wheel from the helmsman. "I'll steer her, my lad. It's been too long since I've guided her fury with my own hands."

The helmsman stood in shock for a moment, then nodded and backed away. The crew paused at the sight of their great commander at the wheel, smiles spreading across their faces. This is the way it had been in the old days, the way it should be. Von Trite at the helm, high station be damned, steering them towards victory in their greatest time of need.

Dr. Jenson disappeared below but returned quickly, the two dozen lenses on his multi-monocle headpiece giving him the appearance of an exotic bird. He flipped down a telescoping one and adjusted it, saying "I would like to get a look at one of the invaders, if possible, Admiral."

"I have been told that will not be a problem, Titus."

The *Morgan* churned the rank waters of the Thames into frothy brown as it emerged from the imposing stone foundation of von Trite's manse. Her sharp prow clove the water with predatory glee, forged iron ram jutting forth. Gray smoke billowed from her main firebox stack at the center of the ship, lesser columns of dirty brown drifted up from the smaller stacks fore and aft; three fire boxes, feeding three engines, turning six massive paddle wheels in a puffing, chugging, click-clacking frenzy. The gunnery crews swarmed over the three swiveling cannon on her foredeck. The main deck sat idle, bereft of any armament due to the high arcs of the paddle wheels to either side. But the high captain's deck at the rear held a single swivel mount, empty for the time being. Von Trite stood at the wheel before it, surveying the chaos of the city around him.

Threadbare Londoners bellowed and ran, clutching children, gripping sacks of precious belongings. They glanced over their shoulders in fear, terrified of pursuit. Fires burned and smoke rolled, blotting out the drab façades of row houses, turning the streets into a hazy confusion filled with muffled shouts. Horses reared, carts overturned and shots rang out.

And above it all floated the orbs, eerily silent, slowly moving, infused with red and orange with hints of yellow that glowed dully against the roofs of the buildings. Twine-like tethers sprouted from the orbs' sides, hanging slack save for the last few feet near the ground. There each tether attached to a skeletal automaton about the size of a man but with a spinning gyroscope for a heart. The automatons' thin limbs and delicate bodies moved with unpracticed jerks and wobbly steps, like babes just learning to walk. They peered in doorways and windows, explored alleys and culverts as far as their tethers would allow, searching, investigating.

Von Trite frowned. His crew stared in wonder. Dr. Jenson simply stood with his mouth hanging open, monocle forgotten. It was a sight to behold.

"I have your guns, sir!" Mr. Mitchell, von Trite's second in command, puffed up from below decks, red in the face, the eight foot barrel of von Trite's mahogany stocked trophy taker, Ulysses, crushing his shoulder. Von Trite's eyes lit up at the sight of the great gun. Dr. Jenson grabbed a peg of the wheel so von Trite could assist Mr. Mitchell in hefting Ulysses onto the captain's deck swivel mount. Once done Mr. Mitchell pulled a radiantly bejeweled black powder pistol from his belt and handed it over, worn palm-grip first.

"Ah Maude, it has been too long," von Trite said as he held the ancient pistol. "Are you ready for a fight, my girl? I know I am!" Von Trite growled in anticipation and slid Maude into his belt.

"Sir, the orbs are tethered to something in the sky!" Dr. Jenson pointed heavenward, hand shaking slightly. Von Trite followed his friend's direction and noted that each orb sported a single large tether at its top that swooped up into the solid London overcast. Von Trite counted over three dozen before giving up and barking orders.

"Cedric!"

"Sir!" The burly dark-skinned man responded from the foredeck.

"Load the eighteens with solid shot. We're going ashore."

"Yes, sir!" Cedric turned and shouted orders to his gunnery crews while von Trite hauled the wheel over, pointing the *Morgan*'s prow directly at the chaos at the water's edge.

The great iron ship steamed full ahead. Von Trite stood steadfast and bow-legged on her captain's deck, wind whipping his greatcoat and coal smoke swirling about his head. The stone wall of the riverbank rushed at them. Von Trite did not slow. Dr. Jenson flipped up his monocles, scrunched his face and clutched the railing. The rest of the crew grabbed hold of something solid and held fast. Von Trite heaved a five-foot-long lever from the railing to the floor just as the point of the *Morgan*'s ram scrapped the stone of the river wall.

Steam rushed into great pneumatic struts, dropping the *Morgan*'s paddle wheels eight feet straight down and raising the hull skyward with stomach turning force. Her forward paddles clawed their way up onto the shore with a tremendous jolt and the middle and aft wheels followed. And just like that the *Morgan* rolled down Wellington Street, water streaming off her hull and cobblestones crunching beneath her wheels. Londoners dove for cover, horses shrieked and flashed the whites of their eyes at her approach, but the orbs and automatons did not spare a glance.

"All hands, fire at will!"

The eighteens roared with long-silenced fury, lobbing massive iron balls at the automaton invaders closest to them. The guns recoiled against curled springs and popped back into position, ready to accept the next charge of powder and round of shot. Von Trite's blood blazed in his veins, the old adventuring fire flaring after years of neglect. He drew a breath to bellow in triumph but a bizarre sight knocked the wind from him

"My God, sir, did you see that!" Dr. Jenson gasped.

"Yes I did, Titus."

The solid iron shot of the *Morgan*'s eighteen pound guns had flown true towards the invaders, but had suddenly diverted a Queen's yard before them, swooped around in a half circle and continued on their way.

"The shot went around them, like it was traversing one of Gauss's magnetic fields!"

"Hmm …" Von Trite twisted his mustache, eyes narrowing in thought until he noticed the fast approaching buildings ahead and yanked two levers to turn onto Strand. The prow gouged the Lyceum Theatre's side, showering the street with stone and iron window fittings just as the eighteens roared again.

Boom, boom, boom!

One shot flew low, blasting a hole in the street and flinging chunks of cobblestones into a group of invaders who were furiously pawing through coal spilled from an overturned cart. Three automatons fell to pieces, their spinning gyroscopic hearts knocked from them by the stone shards. The others paused, faceless heads rising to look at their fallen comrades and then turning to stare blankly at the *Morgan*.

Cedric berated the gun crew who had missed with curses and blasphemes that would normally have warmed von Trite's heart, but as the automatons slipped from view the Admiral could only stare in thought at what he had witnessed, his keen eyes mere slits.

"Cedric!" von Trite bellowed.

"Yes, sir!"

"Fire at the ground before the invaders. Give them a taste of shattered earth."

Cedric's frown at the thought of missing on purpose was brief, but unmistakable, yet he shouted back with hardly a pause, "Yes, sir!"

"Mr. Martin!"

"Sir!"

"Bring me my chest of shot."

Mr. Martin pulled an ornate chest from a heavily weathered cabinet bolted to the back railing. He opened it to reveal dozens of round shot, hand-shaped from exotic elements collected from every worldly continent and numerous uncharted islands. Von Trite gave them a shrewd glance then lifted his chin to his selection. "Load the Stone of Constantinople and pack it tight."

"Yes, sir."

"The invaders are closing on the palace!" Dr. Jenson pointed down the narrow confines of Charles Street to the sprawling park beyond, one eye huge in a new monocle lens.

Six orbs floated across the green pastures of St. James's Park, the automatons tethered to them slogging through the lake, some completely submerged. Von Trite steered for Parliament Street then heaved back hard on the starboard lever to bring the *Morgan* around onto Great George Street and finally Birdcage Walk.

Screech-Boom! The London gloom lit up to a tremendous thunderclap. Dr. Jenson gaped, pointing in front of Buckingham Palace at a line of crackling, sparking barrels spun by furiously pumping steam engines. In front of each barrel, connected by a thick bundle of exposed wire, stood a team of men holding a large, flat sheet of metal with sparks dancing across its face. A bolt leapt from one sheet, streaking out to strike a group of automatons before terminating on another flat sheet of metal staked at the other end of the park.

"Tesla cannons!" Dr. Jenson shouted with glee.

But the bolts from the cannons passed around each individual automaton just as the iron shot had, leaving them untouched. Von Trite scoffed.

"A lot of good they do, they already have to out-flank the

enemy to use them!" Von Trite pointed to the staked metal sheets. "Cannon there would be better!"

Just as von Trite spoke, a volley of cannon and musket shots rang out from behind the Tesla canons on the raised stairs of Buckingham Palace. The metal shots slid around the same invisible spheres and continued on their way, leaving the automatons untouched.

"Hmpf," von Trite commented. He wheeled the *Morgan* around, plowing her hull through the wrought iron fence that enclosed the park. The *Morgan* burst forth onto the rolling lawn just as the gathering automatons stomped firmly into a long, straight line. The automatons' arms rose into the air and dropped in unison.

Bwaaaa! A massive, concussive sound wave leapt from them, knocking the riflemen on the steps of the palace to the ground and throwing the Tesla cannons and field artillery into haphazard piles. Men moaned, steam engines shrieked to a halt and the Tesla cannons popped, sizzled and fell silent.

"What in God's name!" Mr. Mitchell cried, clutching his ears.

"Ack!" Dr. Jenson stumbled sideways, falling to his knees with one hand on the railing.

Von Trite winced, feeling his glass sight tubes vibrate to the sound, but he held course. A rakish smile spread across his face as the *Morgan* steamed straight for the end of the automatons' line, in perfect flanking position.

The wheels of the *Morgan* crushed over the first automaton, riding up its invisible field onto the field of the one beside it. The glowing orb to which both automatons were tethered suddenly flared, shrinking as it did so, until it abruptly winked out, revealing a silvery metallic sphere. The *Morgan* dropped straight down, crushing the two automatons flat then chewed through the remaining eight automatons as they staggered feebly under the dragging weight of their own severed tethers.

The remaining automatons watched, arms raised to the sky, in a stunned stupor, then suddenly broke ranks as the *Morgan*'s paddle wheels rode up over the next group.

"Fire at will!" von Trite bellowed hoarsely.

Mayhem reigned. Automatons fell like pigeons at a social shoot, crumbling from gyroscope hits, spinning away with broken limbs from glancing blows, collapsing over shattered legs to lie clawing at the ground. The *Morgan* dropped down, squashing another half dozen automatons flat. The men roared in bloodless lust, the recovering Tesla gunners and troops on the steps joining in, cheering them on as the crew bashed and bullied their way through the park.

But von Trite suddenly staggered, catching himself on the iron rail. He let out a pained breath and lay his hand against his chest, where his heart should have been. He felt the bag of Battle Coal resting there.

He reached under his coat, searching for the appropriately sized nugget and tossed it over his shoulder into his hopper. The fire door opened and closed. Smoke poured from his stack, clean and shimmery as the nugget ignited.

And at that instant an unearthly wail tore the air, rippling the drifting smoke, causing the men to crouch and cover their ears. Every automaton in sight stood stock still, pointing at von Trite and emitting a screech that drilled into skulls like whirling diamonds.

Four automatons leapt onto the deck of the *Morgan*, but found themselves hovering three feet above it, their invisible fields repulsed by the iron. Von Trite bellowed, "Boarders on deck! Send 'em overboard!"

Cutlass and daggers slid out and swung high, but bounced harmlessly from the automaton's invisible spheres.

"Your billy clubs, lads! Use something of the simple earth! Wood or stone!"

The crew complied, leaping for their foes. But only two made it close enough to bash at flailing shins. The others found themselves yanked backwards by the metal adornments they wore, rings or necklaces or nosepieces that the automatons' protective spheres did not allow to pass. But two sailors were enough. The automatons tumbled overboard, save for one that fell to pieces after a savage poke to its gyroscope heart.

"That's it boys! Give them the old heave-ho!" Von Trite yanked levers again, clipping a fleeing automaton with the prow.

With a short booming report an eighteen-inch gun blasted apart the last remaining automaton with a skillful miss. The orbs, their tethers dangling empty and flaccid, floated back up into the clouds, lighting them up from the inside before fading completely away.

"We've bested them, Titus! They are fleeing!" von Trite shouted with triumphant glee.

But Dr. Jenson did not hear his friend. He had scrambled forward as soon as the decks had been cleared and knelt in front of the pile of automaton bones, his hands hovering an inch from them, afraid to touch.

"Titus!"

Dr. Jenson looked up, microscope monocle already in place. "We must get these below and study them, sir. They are invaluable to science and to our cause!"

Von Trite smiled at the earnest look on his friend's face. "Of course, my friend. Take them below. I will call you if I see anything of note."

Dr. Jenson grabbed an empty gunny sack and carefully slid the pieces inside, then disappeared below with the sack clutched to his chest. Von Trite smiled after him then turned as Cedric pointed to the palace and shouted.

"The Queen! The Queen!"

The crew knelt, heads bowed.

Her Highness stood on the balcony that overlooked the park, a royal aide pleading beside her, gesturing back inside. But she ignored him, standing statuesque in all black, still mourning her late husband some thirteen years gone. The gaze she laid upon the *Morgan* and the man at its helm held emotions so tightly balled together that they formed an even, impenetrable sphere.

Von Trite's engine faltered then hissed in recovery as he saw her. He stood for a moment, simply looking at her. Though saddened by years of loneliness, with her hair pulled back in a severe bun, she was still the woman he had cast eyes upon forty years ago and instantly loved. Her power radiated from her even more now, stately and stoic. No hint remained of the smile she had discreetly covered with a fan when he had asked for a ship to spread the glory of the empire to the southern seas. But he still loved her, and the imagined life they could have had exploring the world together lingered in his still-keen mind. He hefted the steering levers about and made straight for her.

The *Morgan* huffed and chugged to a stop broadside to the balcony and even with its height. Von Trite stepped over to the railing.

"Your Majesty." He bowed low, removing his hat with smooth grace.

"Admiral von Trite," she said curtly, her mouth severe. "You have bested the enemy?"

"I have broken their forces here, Your Highness. Many more remain in the city."

The Queen looked past him at the numerous tethers that still hung from the clouds. They wove among the streets, no longer pausing to inspect or investigate, but instead marching steadfastly towards the very place where she stood.

"Can you defeat so many?"

Von Trite straightened and gave a roguish smile. "Have I ever failed you before?"

The Queen's steady gaze fell full upon him. He did not flinch, only raised one bushy eyebrow in challenge. His pistons chugged along, each hiss and gush a reminder of his devotion to her, of the sacrifices he had made for her. The Queen's lips pressed tighter.

"No."

Von Trite smiled broadly, pleased. He settled his hat back upon his head. "Then with Your Highness's permission, I would like to take the fight to the enemy."

The Queen paused, seeming unable to speak. Her eyes lost focus, gazing beyond him. Von Trite could see the turmoil within them, the push and pull of her desire to keep him from harm versus the desperate needs of the Empire. And for the briefest moment he wondered if her love for him would trump reason even in this darkest of hours. But when she finally looked at him again, with eyes at once pained and resolute, he knew he had won.

"Admiral von Trite, you are granted free rein to drive the invaders from the city. All of the assets of the Empire are at your disposal. Spare nothing to protect it."

Admiral von Trite bowed his head to hide his broad smile. "As The Queen wishes." He turned and looked at the determined, soot-smeared faces of his men. His pistons lugged under the weight of pride and camaraderie he felt for them. None better had ever lived and none better would ever live again.

"Mr. Martin!" he shouted. "Release the globe sails and fire them full. If the enemy wishes a fight then a fight they shall have!"

"Hoo-rah!" the crew roared. Coal-grimed hands gripped massive levers, cranking them down, setting the teeth of a dozen cogs in motion. The cogs wound great flat springs that pushed against the outer plates of the *Morgan*'s hull, straining the bolts that held the iron plates fast. The great ship creaked and moaned as von Trite steered it towards the closest approaching orb, his eyes on the tether that attached to it and disappeared up into the clouds. Then, with a bang that drove shockwaves up his shins, the entire hull blew away, littering the ground with massive slabs of four inch thick wrought iron, leaving nothing but exposed decks jutting from the massive central keel.

"Sir!" Dr. Jenson's voice warbled from the trumpet-flared end of a tube that curved up out of the steam control panel. "I am performing delicate investigations! Did you have to remove the hull?"

Von Trite gave a knowing half smile, imagining his friend hunched over his desk in his cluttered stateroom which now lacked an outer wall. "Yes, Titus. I felt the *Morgan* should stretch her wings."

A pop and hiss sounded. Burgeoning bladders of brown stitched canvas rolled from the exposed under-decks, flopping out then floating up as they filled with red hot air shunted from the *Morgan*'s furiously stoked fireboxes. As the ropes that held the dirigible balloons fast to the *Morgan* tightened von Trite unlatched a bright red lever and hauled it flat against the deck, pinning it with his foot.

With a clank, the exposed decks of the *Morgan* lifted from the paddle wheel chassis. The *Morgan* rose into the air, a skeleton of a ship, buoyed by sixteen massive balloons. Steam jetted from a dozen aft nozzles, shoving the *Morgan* along while periodic puffs on either side of her prow adjusted her course.

"Admiral!" Dr. Jenson's voice bellowed from the tube in excitement. "There are no fasteners to hold the invader's pieces together. They appear to be held together by some invisible force. A Gaussian field? Perhaps that is why they fall apart when their gyroscopic heart is removed."

"Fascinating, Titus," von Trite replied, only half listening. The London overcast enveloped the *Morgan* as it rose. The crew tightened their grip on their billy clubs and glanced nervously about.

"Fog, lads, fog. Nothing more, nothing less. We've seen thicker, in rougher seas …" von Trite's voice trailed off as they broke through to clear sky. White tendrils of mist clung to the *Morgan*'s sides and rolled from her decks. Von Trite shielded his eyes against the sun-blazed cloud tops then slowly dropped his hand, stunned.

An indescribably massive orb floated above the clouds, burning bright orange as it soaked in the sunlight. Over a hundred tethers sprouted from it, snaking down into the cloud layer, all of them wriggling oddly, coiling themselves up tight against the mother orb. Von Trite's awe morphed into a hard scowl as he realized what the tethers' movement meant.

"No time to waste, lads. They are reeling them in. We'll have company soon and no earth to throw at them." Von Trite pushed a double set of levers full forward and steam shrieked from the aft nozzles. The crew grabbed for handholds as the *Morgan* surged forward, balloons creaking as they dragged to catch up.

"There! Beneath it. That's where we'll land." Von Trite pointed at delicate scaffolding that hung from the bottom of the great orb, almost hidden completely by the coiling tethers that surrounded it. At the center of the scaffolding spun a massive gyroscope, its three rings flashing around two flat bisecting slabs of shining metal, one vertical and one horizontal.

"Hold fast, men!" Von Trite fired steam to port, swinging the prow to one side of a retracting tether. The port side balloons bobbled and bounced off the tether's side. Exposed deck edges scraped it with a tremendous screech.

Dr. Jenson's voice cracked from below in annoyance. "Bah! I dropped my pick! Can't we hold still for one moment? I'm trying to pry open the heart of the invader!"

Von Trite frowned, concentrating on navigating the thickening forest of tethers. "Crowded skies, Titus. Crowded skies. Keep working."

A tether thumped off the bow, sparks flying as the *Morgan* scrapped down it. Men fell, slid across the deck, some barely catching hold at the far rail. Von Trite set his jaw, squashing the stomach churning thought of losing one of his dear crew over the side. He gushed steam to bring the ship around, using the tether as a pivot point, then grunted in relief as the crew regained their feet and re-manned their stations. The ship broke free into the empty space between the tethers and the bisecting planes, sailing fast.

But at that moment the first automatons punched through the clouds, dangling from their orbs which blazed brightly at the touch of the sun. They whipped past the *Morgan* in their ascent to the mother orb.

Von Trite growled and cut the heat to the balloons. The *Morgan* stopped rising. He steered directly for the middle of the bisecting slabs of metal.

Thunk! An automaton landed on the deck, feet firmly planted on the wrought iron. The men turned. Von Trite frowned, wondering why the automaton did not hover above it, helpless.

"Repel boarders!" he bellowed as he drew Maude from his belt and aimed. *Crack!* Maude's shot whistled briefly, struck the automaton in the gyro and crumbled it to pieces. Von Trite's frown deepened but he yelled, "They're fighting bare knuckled now, lads! Give 'em the cutlass and the shot!" The crew roared in return, pulling blades from barrels and grabbing for muskets even as a dozen more automatons plopped down on the deck. The men set about their work tackling, slashing, head butting and bowling over, each one a brawling, adventuring sailor at heart, glad to have another go at it.

Von Trite shoved Maude back into his belt and peered ahead, noting a gap at the very center of the bisecting planes.

"Titus!"

Silence.

"Titus!"

A metallic tinkling emanated from the tube followed by a grunt of victory. "There! Got it!"

"Titus!"

"What is that? My word!"

Clang! The *Morgan* jerked to a halt.

The crew tumbled forward, falling into their foes, rolling into the outer railing. Von Trite fell into the stand that held the steam levers, ribs crunching painfully, steam engine coughing, missing three strokes. The *Morgan* shuddered, trying to move forward, its bow crumpled on thin air, grating against it, getting turned aside.

Choked sounds emanated from the voice tube, as if Dr. Jenson were trying desperately to speak but could not produce the words.

For von Trite the world wavered, contracting then expanding as he drew breath with his shattered ribs. He blinked slowly, near delirium, and wondered at the sight of an irregular black mass hovering in a gap at the intersection of the metal slabs, two hundred yards away. He squinted then pulled forth his mariner's spyglass with a grimace and a hitched breath. Von Trite stared for a moment, mind reeling through the implications of what he saw, then he grunted and let the spyglass fall. He looked down at the main deck, eyes on the glowing sight-windows of the firebox doors. He nodded in understanding and shoved himself backwards, towards Ulysses.

Dr. Jenson staggered up the canted steps from the lower decks, clutching his stomach, trying to regain the breath that had been knocked from him. He croaked out two words, "Martmortimer, don't!"

Von Trite grabbed the stock of Ulysses and swung it around. He turned to Dr. Jenson with a deadly serious look. Dr. Jenson froze and clutched something to his chest.

"What have you discovered, Titus?" von Trite asked.

Dr. Jenson swallowed and opened his hand, revealing the purple-black chunk of coal von Trite knew he had pulled from the captured automaton's gyroscope sphere. "Battle Coal, sir! Except, it … it is alive! Look!" Dr. Jenson shoved the chunk of coal into von Trite's hand and held his largest magnifying monocle over it. Minute glimmers suffused the coal's surface, ebbing and flowing, reaching up as if searching for the inner edge of the sphere that had encased it.

Von Trite could feel the warmth of it even through his calloused hands, the pulsing of it, the life. He spoke without looking up.

"And what of it?"

"And what of … ? But don't you see Martmortimer! The Kappa Cygni invaders, they are Battle Coal. Living Battle Coal! And they've come for their lost brethren!"

"Their lost brethren." Von Trite could feel the small bag of coal beneath his coat, pressing into his chest where his heart should have been. "The brethren we burned in our fireboxes, Titus? The ones that burn in mine as we speak?"

"I …" Dr. Jenson paused, unsure of his friend's meaning, of his flat tone.

"What will they do when they've deduced what we've done? What will their temperament be, their actions?" von Trite continued.

"I, I don't know, sir."

"Nor do I. But I do know my duty, Titus: to preserve the Empire, to protect the Queen." Von Trite lifted the chunk of coal in his hand, looking out at his crew who watched him; at the automatons that stood next to them, equally enthralled but with a tension in their stance von Trite could feel like a blade in his gut. "I cannot place either in jeopardy with a gamble on good will." Von Trite looked back to his friend, the steam engine on his back giving out a sluggish sigh, its pressure gauge falling fast.

Dr. Jenson's mouth hung open in shock. He began to stammer a reply. But von Trite spoke with a tired sigh.

"Anyway, old friend, I think my fires need a little stoking." Von Trite threw the chunk of coal over his shoulder, into his hopper and twisted the firebox door knob.

Purple-blue flames erupted. The automatons pointed and shrieked. Von Trite spun and snugged the butt of Ulysses to his shoulder, sighting down the long barrel at the distant chunk of coal at the nexus of the slabs. *Boom!* Ulysses' stone shot flew true, blasting the coal from its position like a billiard ball, shattering it in the process. The great orb flared, sending a bright orange pulse down the tethers to the smaller orbs that then passed it down into the hearts of the automatons. *Whoosh!* The spheres at the automatons' hearts shot up the tethers, passed through their parent orbs and continued up into the great orb above, disappearing into its heart.

And then everything fell apart.

Automatons collapsed into piles at the feet of the stunned crew, their tethers bursting from their backs and from the orbs they had attached to in great sprays of light. The massive tethers that connected the smaller orbs to the great one above blew apart, showering the *Morgan* with large chunks of debris, sending sailors diving for cover. The bisecting planes groaned ponderously and began separating, falling lazily earthward. Von Trite retook the helm, the steam engine on his back pumping furiously under full, ungoverned pressure. Balloons tore and gushed air. The *Morgan* listed, spiraling down as von Trite growled, clutching his side, struggling to steer the great ship out from under the rain of debris.

The decks shuddered, debris slamming down, bending the railing, smashing the fore steam engine's guide arm, which screeched and groaned and sheared in two. Von Trite gritted his teeth and heaved levers, shut valves, shunted steam. A chunk of tether took off his hat, slashed his cheek and ripped three buttons from his coat. He scrunched an eye at the burning cut and dumped more steam to port. A full length of tether slammed onto the deck, buckling it, sending sheared-off bolts whistling through his mustache. He twitched his lip and put full steam to the aft nozzles.

The *Morgan* spiraled down, bursting from the bottom of the clouds, trailing smoke and mist and iron as her decks gave way. Von Trite aimed her for the open space of St. James Park, sweat rolling from his brow, pink froth tingeing his mustache. The *Morgan*'s prow slammed into the earth, digging up a great furrow, screeching and groaning as it slid to a halt a mere foot from the balcony of Buckingham Palace. Her remaining engines, warped by the buckling of the deck, shrieked and froze, blowing out solder joints and sleeve connectors in a hissing billow of steam. Silence fell save for the white-noise bleed-off of pressure and the thumping of great chunks of tether onto the earth.

Titus pulled himself from the deck, spectacles askew, monocle lenses cracked and scuffed. Von Trite threw two more levers, venting the last of the steam from the *Morgan*'s boilers and shuttering her fireboxes. He counted his crew as they pulled themselves from the deck, his heart rising with their rising numbers. He flicked sweat from his brow and turned to find the Queen arriving, out of breath, flanked by horrified advisors, staring at him in disbelief.

"You are still alive, Admiral?" she gasped.

Von Trite cleared his throat, attempting to stand tall despite his broken ribs. "Yes."

"The enemy is defeated?"

"They are."

"And the Empire is secure?"

"It is."

The Queen shook her head, gazing out at the battered city as the remaining tether pieces crashed down onto it. After a moment of stunned reflection she spoke. "You are a magnificent man, Martmortimer."

Von Trite beamed, his eyes lighting up and the remains of his mustache twitching in delight. "I have always endeavored to impress My Queen."

She turned to him, eyes round with wonder. "Consider your endeavor successful."

Von Trite smiled broadly, a singular warmth spreading through him. He felt no need to reply, choosing instead to bask in the glow of her appreciation. It was not the love he had sought in his youth, but it somehow satisfied him more than he could describe.

"But now you have lost your ship …" she said.

Von Trite looked over the sagging remains of the *Morgan*, her bent smokestacks, her mangled engines, her bruised and bleeding crew. She was little more than a pile of steaming iron ready for the scrap heap. But he felt no sadness for her. "I think it the only fitting end for so fine a ship: to die in glory, protecting the heart of the empire."

Von Trite did not take his eyes off the Queen. "And saving the city was important too, of course," he added.

The Queen looked back at him sharply, a matronly frown on her face. But von Trite gave her a roguish grin, eyes alight with mischief, and her frown melted into a sour smile.

"You never give up, do you Martmortimer?"

Von Trite shook his head. "I find failure does not become me."

The Queen shook her head, fighting it a moment longer, then threw her head back and laughed; deep and long and genuine.

* * *

Dr. Jenson tightened von Trite's rib wrappings with an unnecessarily rough tug, smiling with satisfaction at the grunt of pain it elicited.

"Gah! Are you going to stay mad at me forever, Titus?"

Dr. Jenson harrumphed, tying a knot to keep the bindings in place. "Not forever. You'll die sooner or later."

"Bah! What more could I have done?"

Dr. Jenson pressed his lips together, speaking sharply. "What more? Negotiated a ceasefire! Brokered peace! Who knows what we could have learned!"

Von Trite shook his head. "In another time, Titus, in another place. But not here, not now. The risks were too great, the situation too grim."

Dr. Jenson shook his head, unwilling to give up on what could have been. But eventually he sighed. "You are probably right, old friend, but I wish it were not so."

"As do I. But we must deal with what is …"

"Not what is supposed to be. I know."

Von Trite nodded, smiling at his friend's patronizing tone. He settled his head back and closed his eyes. "Besides, you forgot to check my coat pocket."

Dr. Jenson frowned, but as he pulled the sack of Battle Coal from von Trite's tattered great coat his eyes lit up. He dumped the contents out and stared with stark fascination at the impassive lumps in his hand. Von Trite peeked at him from the corner of his almost-closed eyes.

“Take them, Titus. Do with them what you will. Perhaps that upstart Tesla can aid you in bringing life back to them. As for me, I’ve got a full firebox, a pounding head and a need for a long, well-earned nap.”

The Red Queen and the White

C.B. Pratt

Despite the strides that had been made in exploring the forsaken places of the world, even with the efforts of mankind to fill every available niche, regardless of the wonders of modern communication—heliograph, aerograph, and sonic-tubes—when the first sky-ship appeared, no one knew of it for weeks.

A Bedouin ushering his family across an otherwise empty quadrant of the Sahara first reported it to the French Army outpost at Ain-Salah. Another week passed before the commander sent a party out with the insistent Bedouin. A stringer for the *New York Times* went along looking for local color. A devotee of *Alice Through the Looking Glass*, he dubbed what he saw The White Queen.

"A large shining wing reflecting the white sands below and the pitiless sun above, all who see it are struck dumb in wonder. One can only find oneself in that reflection by jumping up and down, waving your arms, or otherwise attempting to make oneself larger than life. Slowly it dawns upon me that this Earth, the purported Jewel in God's Eye, is not so alone in that as we have ever believed."

My father, department chief of the *New York Times*' Foreign Bureau, crossed out the last sentence with a firm stroke of his pen. "Old Danvers sounds frightened to death," he commented. "Still, there's no excuse for blasphemy."

Home from Massachusetts Institute of Technology for the end of term holiday, I'd come in for our traditional Father-Daughter luncheon. As usual, his "I'll be ready in a moment" had turned into thirty minutes of "just one more thing." On more than one past occasion, luncheon had been taken at quarter-to-six in an otherwise deserted restaurant.

"Is the story true?" I asked.

"With Danvers, one never knows. He landed a masterful scoop once when the Russian prince was murdered in Cairo, revealing a secret treaty. On the other hand, he's much too willing to believe all the native jibber-jabber he hears, which is why he's still just a stringer. We haven't forgotten his report of the Great White Ape."

Father dropped his voice. "Plus I fear he is not very steady in other ways." Translated, that meant either drink or women.

"Will you run the story?"

"Yes, of course," he said, marking it for publication. "Now to luncheon!"

Delmonico's glistened with gilding and crystal, all against a background of red plush. The crowded tables had the usual proportion of businessmen, lunching ladies, and stage performers. Father, gratifyingly, was recognized by persons from all walks of life.

I waited until the coffee had been poured and his single cigar of the day lit before broaching the subject I'd intended to discuss all along. He was chattering merrily on about whom he intended to invite to my graduation the following spring. "Definitely Aunt Ermy, don't you think?"

"She's been predicting since freshman year that my brains would never take the strain of so much education."

"All the more reason to invite her. Though she thinks even Boston is too uncivilized a place for a New Yorker."

"Well, perhaps she won't have to travel quite that far. I'm planning to transfer to Columbia."

"Columbia? I thought you loved Cambridge?"

"I did. I do. It's been a wonderful experience. But I have an opportunity to study with a great professor here. My Alchemy master recommended me."

"Another alchemical professor? Lead into gold, eh?"

Everyone makes that joke to alchemical students, sometimes repeatedly. "No, transmutation of materials isn't until senior year. Besides, I'm changing from alchemy. Dr. Brock has made a life-long study of Franklin's Theory."

"Franklin's Theory," he said musingly. Then he sat up

straight. "You don't mean electricity?" I nodded. "But that's dangerous, child! It killed Franklin stone-dead in the blink of an eye."

"Yes, but we know what he did wrong now."

"You've discussed this with your mother, I take it."

"She's delighted. She never liked my going all the way to Boston."

"Then I suppose you've already settled the matter between you and my permission is unnecessary."

"But appreciated," I said brightly.

Early the next morning, I set out, ostensibly to search for an apartment. Mother had it in her head that I'd live at home in my old room. She gave way eventually, provided my brother went along when I inspected apartments. Rob was only seventeen, but as the star forward on his high school football team, he was big and strong. He was living for the day he'd be on the starting line for Harvard or Bowdoin.

Once we were trundling along in the Stanley, he nudged me. "You've already picked out an apartment, eh, sis? Somewhere around Harring Place?" He chuckled at my surprise, a deep, warm sound. "Dad's not the only one with reporting instincts. I, too, have my sources."

He was no fool, despite being a bit spoiled. The two infants who had followed me into this world had each died within months. Rob had survived a sickly babyhood. Reason enough to spoil him. Add a roguish charm that had been prompting illicit sweets from cooks, parlor maids and maiden ladies since he was in his pram and he was able to drift through life on a smile and a wink.

Later, as we walked in the park, he brought up the story from the Sahara. It had run on page 14, between a story on the new Arizona copper boom and an ad for elastic-sided boots.

"By Jingo, imagine if it were true! It's like something out of a Boy's Own Paper. I just wish I could go and see for myself."

"Father said the reporter isn't very reliable."

"Still … just imagine what we could learn!"

The Letters to the Editor for the next several days were divided between Rob's level of excitement and sharply expressed opinions that the *Times* had sunk to the level of the yellowest of journalism.

Though my position at the college didn't start until the fall semester, I found myself drawn to the lab every day. Dr. Brook, a woman with a delicate elegance many a debutante lacked, merely smiled understandingly and put me to work with those dozen or so others who were irresistibly drawn to electricity. I had no attention to spare for wild tales of alien craft.

Six days later, the Red Queen took up position just north of the Faroe Islands, about four hundred miles off the coast of Iceland. This time, there was no delay in reporting. It could be seen, like the arc of the sun above the horizon, from Iceland, Norway and the north of Scotland.

Almost at once, steamers full of tourists began heading out for a closer look, beating even the navies of several nations. The *London Times* shared their reporting with the *New York Times* until, by bribing a cruiser captain to go farther than recommended and by tearing off the superstructure to feed the boilers, one of our reporters reached the site.

Sending heliographs on that beautiful spring day was easy. Until the sky lit up with a crackling fire that blinded the relay station operator and could be seen as a flashing light on the horizon as far away as Newfoundland and Labrador in the West and Germany and Lithuania in the East. How it looked to our reporter is unknown, except that it was likely the last thing he ever saw in this world.

The horrible bolts of lightning continued to flash for almost two hours. When they ceased, a three-mile wide vein of destruction ran straight as a ruler for almost thirty-five hundred miles, between the Sahara and the North Sea. It became known as The Line. Scotland, England, France and Spain, Morocco and communities around the Bay of Oran suffered the most complete devastation. Fires burned in every street. Forests had become conflagrations which spread beyond The Line. Many months passed before anyone attempted to estimate accurately the numbers of the dead.

Infants in cradles, women at their sewing, men in the pubs, schoolchildren at play, birds wild and domesticated, even the rats in the sewers, died between one instant and the next. The British lost a fifth of their royal family. In Spain, a medical convention held by an ill-fate on the track of The Line meant that an eighth of their nation's medical staff was wiped out. An American battleship sailing through the Mediterranean drifted onto shore with a crew dead at their stations.

The next day, again, for two hours out of every four, the lightning flashed and burned through the sky by daylight and moonlight. The smell of ozone was unbearable anywhere near The Line. The outpost at Ain-Salah reported through Danvers that the White Queen was both receiving and sending these powerful bolts in a violent battle with the nemesis over the water. The ships that dared to go close to the Red Queen reported the same actions.

The first I knew of the devastation of The Line came when I arrived at the lab that morning. Dr. Brook stood at the blackboard, writing out formulae. Her audience was not undergrads and coeds but stern men with square shoulders set off by epaulettes stiff with gold. She introduced me. They told me tersely what had happened. I had to sit down, head to my knees. The most decorated of them all brought me a paper cup of water. I apologized for my weakness.

"Never mind, Miss Lyle," General Cotman said. "When they told me, I had to lie down."

"They had to revive me with brandy," said the glittering one in blue.

"Well, hand it over, George."

So we all had some in paper cups, the wax lining peeling off to float in the brandy. They resumed the discussion I'd interrupted. The military wanted to know, immediately, what kind and level of power they were to anticipate. Similar meetings were underway in Chicago, Austin, the University of Los Angeles, and anywhere else a scientist or alchemist had spent any time at all on an obscure study.

"Naturally, gentlemen, without proper measurements, it is difficult to analyze these events comprehensively," Dr. Brook began. "There are sure to be more reports coming in. I ask you to ensure that I and my national colleagues see whatever information you receive from whatever source."

"Absolutely guaranteed," General Cotman promised. "I speak for President Armstrong when I say this. I met with him this morning."

Dr. Brook returned to the board, attempting to show in simple terms the mysteries we spent our days trying to unravel for ourselves. Like my father, all they really knew was that electrical force had killed one of our young nation's most promising minds a hundred years previously and caused the disaster at the Paris Exhibition of 1868. Now it had slaughtered millions.

"What I wonder is," I said, into an appalled silence, "why here? Why Earth? There are at least six unpopulated planets just in this solar system. Why come to Earth to fight their battles?"

"Why shouldn't they?" General Cotman asked. "They may be intelligent but as far from us as we are from ants. Why have they come here to fight, young lady? Why should they go elsewhere? We can't stop 'em or tell 'em to vamoose. Did anyone ask the ants at Gettysburg if they'd mind if we fought a battle where they lived?"

For the next three weeks, Dr. Brook and her assistants labored to solve the tiniest piece of the puzzle before us. We learned that the Red Queen tended to float higher above the water than the White did above the sand. But we didn't know what made it hover. We estimated the mass, the length, the volume of the ships, and the capacity of the bolts thrown, seeking the one fact that would open our understanding. Always at the back of our minds was the horrible cost of The Line.

General Cotman or his aides called upon us every day but we had no answers. Our counterparts, including now Russian and Chinese experts, showed no greater results.

Our task was made no easier when fewer students and adjunct professors came to work each day. Even those I'd taken for the most enthusiastic and dedicated were failing to appear at the lab. When they did come, they hardly worked at all. Some slept at their desks, others stood about talking idly. They spent their nights at parties that continued until dawn or they wandered aimlessly about the town in search of yet another party. No one seemed to care any more about the Queens.

Then, one day, no one came. I finished my formula and put away my equipment, the coils and the wire. I told Dr. Brook that I'd return shortly. She nodded, smiling her far-away smile. As I looked back, I saw her nipping from a small silver flask. She caught my eye. Hollowly, she said, "Toothache."

The last person to abandon her studies had been Anna Clary, a quiet girl from Brooklyn. She'd been there yesterday. I'd see to it that she'd be there tomorrow if I had to drag her by the hair. I felt invincible in my cloak of scientific righteousness.

I heard her apartment before I saw it. Though the morning was far advanced, the numerous persons at her apartment were all attired in at least the remnants of evening wear. I recognized several of my fellow students, at least two of whom were drunk. The girls only giggled at my severe glance.

Anna wasn't there; neither were either of her roommates. I refused a breakfast of caviar, melting ice cream, and French onion soup and went to search for the next student on my list.

This one, David McArmish, was at his home, not far from my apartment. The door stood open. A gathering was in progress there as well. He wore a bedsheet, toga-fashion. A chaplet of vine leaves sat askew on his flaxen head.

"Why aren't you at the lab?" I demanded as if I had a right.

He poured a glass of rich red wine. "What's the point? We aren't going to learn anything new. Have we advanced one inch beyond where we started?"

"But today we might …"

"Ah, today's breakthrough or tomorrow's. No, no, my dear girl. Some say the Queens are our punishment for our sins. But what sins? I've never committed any before today. Yesterday? Recently. I could pray but I'd rather get drunk. To imminent demise!" He drank.

"So why not indulge ourselves?" I asked scornfully. "Throw ourselves into sin and spiritual waste. Do all the things we've been warned against all our lives?"

"Yes. Exactly."

I took the glass from his hand and tossed off the dregs. I knew in my heart that he was right. No one could predict what the Queens would do or when. They might leave as suddenly as they came or move over another area creating another Line in their battle. We, the human race, were helpless and doomed.

I remember little of the next several weeks. Despair burned like a drug in our veins. Nor was it the only drug to be had. Pharmacies reported break-ins in record numbers, strychnine and other poisons stolen as often as cocaine. Liquor stores couldn't keep glass in their windows. Gambling halls, brothels, and bars did a roaring trade among every age and sex.

Life for me became a traveling circus. I saw my brother and his cronies once or twice, never to speak to, only in passing. We all started to paint our faces, men and women both, to conceal or emphasize the ravages of our brutal, senseless new life. Some died of alcohol poisoning, overdoses, or wild rages that became murder. We hardly acknowledged their deaths as the bacchanal rolled on.

One afternoon, red-stained sunset light filling my apartment, I awoke alone in my own bed. I had no recollection of how I got there. Someone was knocking on the door. I stepped over a few sleeping strangers, still entwined in temporary passion on my floor. I'd fallen asleep wearing someone else's black evening gown, ripped at the shoulder and smelling of beer.

"I heard you come in," my landlady said. "So I took the liberty of bringing up this note."

The respectable creature I'd rented from was now as frowsy and red-eyed as any Bowery Madame, as I was myself. But she still looked at me with mingled pity and disgust. "I thought you was such a nice girl, being one of them scientists and all."

"No nice girls now," I said. "No scientists either. And no answer."

The note came from my mother's doctor. "Mrs. Lyle is quite ill and asks to see you if you can spare the time from your studies."

I threw cold water on the strangers and boiled myself in the tub. Unearthing a clean shirtwaist and skirt, I fancied that I at least looked decent. But my straw hat, once charming, only emphasized the hollows in my cheeks and the black marks under my eyes. I resisted the urge to stop into a 24-hour bar for a steadying sip.

I walked to my parent's home. The summer's heat had come to New York, like a sticky net that I dragged behind me, collecting emotional garbage and dead spirits. I paused in a pocket-sized park to be sick. I felt more myself afterwards.

My mother's priest was with her but only for comfort, not for anything dire. I, at a loss in the home of my childhood, sought for comfort in the attic nursery. I couldn't look at the dolls, slumped in attitudes too reminiscent of my recent decadent life. I turned instead to the desk under the window, where Rob and I had first learned our letters and numbers. An ornate iron-work shelf held my earliest scientific books, still in alphabetical order. Anderson's *Multiples of Mathematics*. Bocault's *The Story of Steam*. Riviere's *First Principles of Alchemy*. I toyed with the old ebony ruler with which Miss Pontifex, our governess, had often threatened but never struck.

Every schoolchild knows how Archimedes discovered the principle of displacement while lounging in his bath. I'd always had doubts about it. Experimentation, elimination, examination—these lead to discovery, not some sudden flash of insight.

Yet I was blinded in that instant by an insight so profound that I threw the ruler on the desk and covered my eyes with both hands. But the inner illumination could not be blocked out. It burned like phosphorus, like magnesium, like colloidal copper. It burned away the last of my despondency, even as cleansing fire destroys an infestation of some disease.

"First principles," I gasped. Somewhere recently I'd learned a low-class fast-paced shuffling tap step and I did it now, my feet clattering over the boards.

"What the devil is all this row?" My brother, his eyes as hollow as the walking dead's, flung open the door.

"First principles!" I laughed, grabbing his hands to have him dance with me.

"You're on the hop, here?" he demanded, surprisingly shocked considering all I'd seen and heard of his activities.

"Neither mad, drunk, nor high, dear brother."

"Then what the devil … ?" His dull eyes brightened as if he'd downed a gallon of black coffee. "You've got it. Have you got it?"

"I don't know. Maybe. Listen, what kind of shape are you in right now?"

"Nothing a quick gin and quinine won't fix."

"No, you mustn't…"

"Preaching propriety? After what I saw you up to…"

"We're not going to talk about that. Not now. Not ever."

"It's a deal."

We solemnly shook hands. "Listen, remember something for me, can you? My head's going to burst. Remember just one thing."

"What?"

"Not a battle but a battery. Go dress and come with me but keep repeating it. Don't forget. Not a battle but a battery. Please, don't forget."

I sat at the desk and searched for paper, finding none. The ink in the pot had dried up and the only pen I found had a broken nib. I rang vigorously for the maid, demanding pencil and paper. The butler brought it, true to his training, showing no alarm at my wild looks. The paper was a single scented sheet and the pencil a pretty sky-blue.

I wrote a note to my mother and stole the pencil. We found an omnibus going in the right direction. I scribbled on my cuffs, Rob's cuffs, and would have started on strangers' linen if some kind soul hadn't handed me the *Times* to write in the margins. Thus I learned that the White Queen had moved from the Sahara to the Gobi Desert. No word yet on whether the Red Queen would match her sister's movements. I alone knew that she would do so soon and had a notion where she'd wind up.

Our first stop was Dr. Brook's. I left Rob to sober her by fair means or foul. I raided her dusty desk for paper. Formulae and images flowed from my hand like water from a fountain. Rob's methods opened the doctor's eyes; my scribblings completed her cure.

Dr. Brook communicated with the uniforms, bidding them to meet us at the lab. The generals and the admirals arrived simultaneously with the Press, who'd been alerted when Mother had shown my note to Father. Military decorum was forgotten as they all shouted more or less the same questions. Rob ushered the Press into a separate room easily enough, having known most of them since childhood.

Whatever doubts anyone had—and there were many—were resolved when the Red Queen moved over the Continent and settled over the cold Antarctic Ocean not far from Tierra del Fuego precisely as I had predicted. The projected line from one Queen to the next threw the Far East into frenzy. Massive evacuations began from the major population centers of Pekin and Tianjin as well as Jeju Island off the coast of Korea and the southernmost tip of Japan. A great many areas, especially in China, had little communication with the outside world. It sounds callous to say that we only lost a million people when the New Line fired, but we had surmised that twenty million at least would perish.

The key to my plan was the recent copper boom in Arizona. The United States' government stepped in to commandeer the entire production. Surprisingly, though resistance had been expected, there was none. Mine owners from the largest industrial producers to the smallest single-man operations stepped forward. Mr. Pullman and Mr. Rockefeller offered their extensive railroad holdings. Massive amounts of ore and smelted metal began to pour into factories.

I traveled to new factories in Chicago, to converted yarn mills in Massachusetts, to Brooklyn and Hoboken. I felt awestruck that a few words and symbols from my mind had led to all this industry. It was a measure, I suppose, of humanity's desperation that they'd seized upon the only hope offered.

Only to Rob, my companion on these tours, did I dare express my own doubts. I can never forget his kindness during that dark time. People would tell me many times a day that they prayed for our success. I prayed, too, the prayer of the slide-rule, an abacus my rosary. Rob alone could tell me to put them away to eat, to sleep.

The Net was finally ready eight weeks after the Queens had shifted location. The journey to the Gobi by ship, train and mule was arduous, filled with anxiety, not just for me but for all who participated. Tensions grew tight. Tempers were exacerbated.

Not even photographs prepared us for the sickening yet graceful geometry of the White Queen. It brought home to the emotions with appalling force that we were fighting something not of our world. Some of our people, the most courageous and intelligent force ever assembled, broke into anguished tears at the sight. They were replaced in the airships by anyone who could bring themselves to board. Rob, who was to have gone with me, took another's place. His carefree wave as the ship lifted its portion of the vast copper net remains with me to this day.

The fleet rose slowly, steadily advancing, hunters stealthily approaching their prey. Every moment had been plotted by the leading aeronauts of six countries. The Net, fused from thousands of pieces of thin copper wire, glowed like sunlit silk as we approached the huge White Queen. From instant to instant, we expected a counter-attack.

As gently as if setting a bridal veil on the head of an adored daughter, we draped the Queen with my creation. Then we fled.

When the flares began, sending immense charges of pure energy to the Red Queen so far away, some of the dirigibles that had taken the North-East side did not get clear in time. Their gas-bags exploded. Yet their fiery sacrifices went all but unseen in the sun-flare of the White Queen administering her own execution.

The combination of two metals created a power surge that, instead of being sent to the Red Queen and thence to whomever or whatever had sent the machines to Earth, drove inward, destroying delicate mechanisms, frying the ship alive. The ship twisted and groaned in her agony.

She plummeted into the ground, sending forth a shock-wave that buffeted our ships, shaking us to pieces, sending others to follow the White Queen to destruction. My own vessel suffered in that way. I only drove the bone of my left arm through the skin while others died.

Reports came eventually that the Red Queen remained steady above the ocean. Salvage operations were discussed almost immediately. But before the effort could begin, the Queen sank late one stormy night. The water where she lies is too deep and cold for any mortal to retrieve it. She may be there still if the corrosion of the salt-water has not eaten her away.

The White Queen became a scientific anthill. Colleagues have studied it intensively for thirty years and may study it for a hundred more without understanding all they see.

The cost of Victory came high. Medals for the living; monuments for the rest.

Honors poured in for me from every nation. I deserved none of it. Had I fought the malaise that dragged us all down, perhaps I would have saved many lives. That thought has haunted me continually, keeping me from enjoying any of the praise I received.

General Cotman appeared one day. "Why not come work for me? We think electricity has potential."

"As a weapon?"

"Of course."

"Thank you, no. I'm returning to Cambridge, to resume my work on alchemical principles." Since then we have made considerable strides toward unlocking atomic structure which, at least, has little likelihood of becoming a destructive force.

Mankind began to rebuild what had been destroyed, though it was long before London or Pekin regained their stature. Our parents returned to their lives, their works, their God, faces newly lined but hearts filled with renewed hope. Our younger brothers and sisters soon forgot the bitter and dreadful events of that spring, summer, and fall.

Many have told the story of those days. At first, they emphasized the heroics, the willing sacrifices. Only one writer dared to tell the truth. His book, *We, the Stained*, received only a small print-run and even then failed. No one wanted to remember how we'd defeated one enemy but had surrendered to despair. Only now has my brother's book been recognized as a classic.

When Rob drank himself to death, I started attending church again at my mother's request. But I stopped when she passed on. We stained ones do not speak of our pasts, even among ourselves. We recognize each other and pass on without a nod, knowing that memory alone never dies.

The Wizard of Woodrow Park

Jean Marie Ward

It started with a bang. Really. A shiny red, open-chassis aircar struck the curb at the corner of First and Main, and its right front tire exploded.

Further down the block, in front of the Main Street display windows of Teil's Dry Goods, a tall, rangy man wearing a leather vest and a white shirt with rolled-up sleeves whirled at the sound. He dropped smoothly into a shooter's crouch. But instead of pulling a gun, he clenched his right fist, and sighted down the length of his arm.

The gesture activated the controls of the camouflaged, vambrace-style weapons unit attached to Aviann Special Agent Hreaak Meekram's forearm. Shielded from the early morning glare by the broad brim of his brown felt hat, he scanned the firing display superimposed on his vision. The crosshairs locked on the spot where the driver's canvas cap met the leather strap of his goggles. The target automatically recalibrated as the roofless aircar juddered over the sidewalk.

Hreaak yanked his arm back. What was he thinking? His mission was a search-and-rescue, not an assassination. The goal was not killing anybody, especially not a native. Blasted human suit—wearing one always made him edgy.

At least he wasn't the only one who reached for his gun. But he was the only one with an invisible weapon, so he was the one getting the fish eye from the other pedestrians. He straightened, stretched his lips in the harmless smile he'd practiced, and pretended not to notice the way a passing matron flicked her skirts out of his personal space.

The brass air tanks mounted behind the driver's seat clanked as the right side of the car dropped from the sidewalk to the street. The vehicle wobbled, unbalanced by its ruptured wheel. The driver shimmied the steering rod to compensate. When that didn't work, he grabbed the horn.

DAH-dum, it blared. DAH-dum.

Across the street, a horse harnessed to a delivery van trumpeted in counterpoint. It reared in its traces. Spooked, the aircar driver bucked in his perch. He pulled the steering rod hard to the right. The car veered. The lantern hook on its prow shot toward Hreaak.

He leapt clear the same instant someone screamed, "Look out!"

The driver heaved left. The car shook. Squealed. Swerved. The smell of burnt rubber momentarily overwhelmed the reek of aging produce, horse sweat, and dung trapped between the brick and frame buildings of the street. Then the car lurched into its designated traffic lane and rattled up Main with all the grace of a three-legged Farrentak after a four-day bender.

Hreaak exhaled a long breath. His pulse slowed to what humans considered normal, but aftershocks of adrenaline still sparked along his nerves. Maybe he should've shot the moron, or at least disabled the car.

A short, teenaged girl hopped off Teil's front step. Hands on her hips, she shouted after the car: "There ought to be a law—no driving until you know how!"

Hreaak flinched. The girl could've given screaming lessons to eagles. All the way across Second Street, the aircar driver hunched defensively. But her voice didn't startle Hreaak as much as her outfit. Her ruffled gingham blouse was tucked into a pair of khaki twill trousers identical to his own. A ball-shaped leather helmet dangled from one arm.

That was wrong. According to Kleaax's Preliminary Lexicon of New Dominion Territories' Language and Mores, gender roles in the town of Woodrow Park typified the rigid distinctions of an early industrial society. Admittedly, Kleaax's intel was seventeen years out of date, but it shouldn't have mattered. Hreaak had completed enough missions among primitive cultures to know their mores simply didn't change that fast. The women of Kleaax's New Dominion Territories shouldn't be wearing trousers for another two generations, much less engaging in activities that required a helmet. The people on the street should've been pelting the girl with rotten fruit, not encouraging her with shouts of "That's right!" and "You tell him, Genny!"

Good thing he'd disabled his automatic surface-to-ship uplink as soon as he landed his stratoflyer. Since arriving in town, he'd seen enough cultural and technological anomalies—aircars in a coal-based society, electric streetlights, industrial-sized P'lod coils—to have every desk jockey in the Aerie calling for military intervention. Hreaak wasn't about to let that happen, not until he figured out what was going on and how it was connected to the disappearance of Weevirril Kleaax.

"You know, that's not a bad idea," Genny continued at a more conversational volume. "They make us go to school for reading and math. Why not driving?"

A muffled grunt drew Hreaak's attention to the sidewalk on the other side of the entrance. A pair of scuffed work boots attached to denim-trousered legs protruded from a collapsed sandwich board advertising Teil's summer prices.

"Shiro," Genny gasped, "are you hurt?"

"Umm." The voice was male and surprisingly deep.

The girl lunged for the sign. Air hissed through her teeth as she strained to lift the metal-framed placards.

Aviann agents were held to the same strict Allied Planets Consortium non-intervention standards as embedded anthropologists and other scientific observers. But no matter what body you stuffed him in, Hreaak wasn't a churl.

"I got this," he said.

The deep voice belonged to a boy no older than Genny. Unlike her, Shiro was tall for his age and, from the size of his hands and feet, still growing. He wore a white-collared gray shirt and red suspenders consistent with the images in Kleaax. But in the context of Woodrow Park, his straight black hair, the ochre tint of his complexion, and the shape of his dark brown eyes looked far more alien than the straw-colored hair and craggy features currently attached to Hreaak.

Yet another anomaly. Kleaax hadn't mentioned anyone of Shiro's ancestry in the Territories. The boy had obviously been around long enough for the town to accept him and Genny as a couple. The girl fluttered around him in a classic display of courtship behavior, and passersby only smiled.

"Is anything broken?" she warbled. "Should I get a doctor?"

"Genny, I'm fine. Just give me a minute."

Despite the differences in their voices, the teenagers shared the same accent. Linguistic analysis confirmed they were born locally. Since it took a generation to integrate immigrant populations into comparable industrial societies, Shiro's family must have lived in Woodrow Park at least thirty years. Why hadn't Kleaax mentioned them in his reports?

Answering that question was worth drawing out the conversation. Hreaak did a quick scan of the boy's vitals.

"Nothing's broken," he said. His internal translators supplied the appropriate idiom from the Lexicon. He hoped it still applied. "He just had the wind knocked out of him."

"Then why isn't he getting up?" Genny demanded.

"Because you're standing too close. I might knock you over by accident."

Her eyebrows lifted. "You'd rather do it on purpose?"

Hreaak bit back a smile. The kid was embarrassed enough already. But he couldn't stop his too mobile human lips from twitching as he helped Shiro to his feet.

Shiro flushed to his ear tips. "Give me a break. I'm still growing into my feet," he growled. His color deepened. "Sorry. That came out rude. Thanks for your help, mister. The sign weighed more than I thought."

He extended his right hand, presumably to be shaken. Kleaax claimed the locals shook hands for everything from greetings to thanks. Hreaak clasped the boy's callused palm.

It was a mistake. Hreaak's weapons unit was virtually indestructible and, like all AP cybernetic interfaces designed for field use, keyed to its host. It couldn't be disabled without priming the release with a sample of his DNA. Its camouflage field, on the other hand, was a mist of carefully balanced illusion. It was never meant to withstand the enthusiastic pumping of an over-compensating adolescent who didn't know his own strength.

The unit's projected image of tanned forearm buzzed and

vanished. Hreaak hoped Genny didn't scream when she saw the vambrace. The nearest local equivalent was a convict's shackle.

"Wow," Shiro said. Without letting go of Hreaak's hand, he angled his arm for a better view. "I've never seen a prosthetic like this. Feels heavy. What's it made of? Is there a reason for the de—"

He stopped mid-word, staring at the cover to the unit's stunner port. Sweat beaded his hairline. His fear hormones spiked, sharp enough to smell, no additional sensors required.

Nobody reacted like that to a stunner cap unless they'd seen a stunner in action. The only other person on the planet with that kind of technology was the embedded anthropologist Hreaak had been sent to find. Had Kleaax been forced to use his defense unit, or had he done so voluntarily? Crap. Hreaak might be forced to call in the military now. A flashback to the last "planetary rectification" he'd witnessed dried the spit in his throat.

Genny pressed the back of her hand to her forehead and groaned dramatically. "Oh, no, not a new prosthetic! I'll never get my steamcycle lesson now. We'll be here all day."

Shiro jerked his hands away from the device. He hissed, "Genny."

Hreaak rubbed his arm. The unit had become such a part of him, he seldom thought about its weight. He asked mildly, "You interested in prosthetics?"

"Interested?" Genny chortled. "You'll be lucky if he doesn't try to take it apart while it's still on your arm. Shiro's nuts for anything mechanical. Has been since he was a kid. Now he's the youngest assistant engineer in the history of Kleaax Industries. He's worked on some of their biggest projects ever."

"K-K-Kleaax?" Hreaak stuttered. "Weevirril Kleaax? It can't be!"

"Only Kleaax in Woodrow Park. Well, unless you count the missus, but May Belle still uses her maiden name for business reasons. Then there're the kids, but they all kept their father's name, even though Mr. Kleaax adopted them ages ago."

"Genny! Stop!" Shiro grabbed her arm and towed her toward the store. "We've got to get inside. Now!"

Genny started to protest. His expression changed her mind.

Hurriedly unlocking the door, she muttered, "What's going on?"

"Close the …" The door clicked shut behind them.

Not that they were in any danger from Hreaak. He was too busy imitating the impact site of an extinction class meteor.

Weevirril Kleaax, Avinar's favorite missing anthropologist, was alive and well seventeen years after his last transmission from Woodrow Park. He'd started a manufacturing company, hired engineers, and showed at least one of them his defense unit. Then he started a nest—with humans, no less.

But that wasn't enough for Weevirril Kleaax. Oh, no. The misbegotten son of a live-birth lizard did it all under his legal name, a name unique to their home world, Avinar! Every brain cell and enhancement in Hreaak's skull spluttered with the potential consequences. For this world. For Avinar. For the entire Allied Planets Consortium …

The bustard must have lost his feathered mind!

Or else he was laying the groundwork for an insanity defense.

Either way, he had to be stopped, and the damage reversed. Ideally without military intervention. The humans had done nothing to deserve a planet-wide cataclysm of remotely triggered "natural" disasters. As for Kleaax himself, Hreaak would ensure he never saw the inside of a courtroom. Let the Aerie honor his ashes. What they didn't know wouldn't hurt anyone else.

Hreaak had to find him before he could kill him. The quickest way would be to tail the boy. The planet lacked any real-time communications system beyond a few telegraph wires. If Shiro wanted to warn his boss, he'd have to go in person. Unfortunately, the range of Hreaak's internal sensors extended no further than the alley behind the store. Trailing Shiro the organic way would be impossible. The town offered too many places to hide, and despite his enhancements, Hreaak's vision in the ape suit was no better than human.

But Genny had given him a better idea. Hreaak lifted his gaze to the stout, mushroom-shaped P'lod coils crowning the hill directly west of town. Anything named Kleaax Industries would need a lot of power. In the absence of a developed power grid, P'lod coils would be the ideal source. His star cruiser's sensors had noted the presence of manufacturing facilities near the generators. If Kleaax wasn't there, someone at the power station would know where to find him. It might take a while to locate the right someone. The factories' main shift wouldn't begin for the local equivalent of an hour. But it wouldn't take long.

A canvas-hooded steamcar with a towering boiler mounted over the rear axle eased to a halt in front of the Second Street Bank. Hreaak considered stealing it for as long as it took the driver to set the brake. By that point a blue-suited policeman had appeared at the intersection and begun directing the non-existent traffic.

With a mental shrug, Hreaak headed west on Second Street. He doubted Shiro's steamcycle ran any faster than a horse, and the hill wasn't far. It wasn't as if Kleaax possessed any meaningful defenses to prepare. To prevent technological contamination, the Council of Academies limited an embedded anthropologist's field kit to his library/communications pad, DNA-specific prophylactics and healing agents, and a single, underpowered stunner. The irony wasn't lost on Hreaak.

After a dozen blocks the town's gardens gave way to hillside farms. The day grew hotter as he climbed, and he was glad he'd brought a hat. The slope had been cleared of trees. The planet's fierce yellow sun hammered the dusty road and the cornfields spreading from its shoulders.

His march slowed to a walk. Towering, silk-crested stalks hemmed the road, their ranks so vast and dense as to appear limitless. Their sugary perfume crashed into his lizard brain. He forgot the awkwardness of his heavy human limbs, the way his unaccustomed clothes chafed his tender featherless skin and the itchy, gamy sweat collecting under his simulated leather vest.

Whooping like a deranged Hooparan, he plunged into the corn and broke off the largest ear within reach. He shredded the husk with both hands, not waiting to pick out the silk before sinking his blunt human teeth into the honeyed kernels. The nectar dribbled down the sides of his mouth, gluing bits of the silk to his chin. He didn't care. He would gnaw the cob bare and suck the memory of its juices from the strands. It had been generations since the leached soil of Avinar had produced anything so magnificent.

Was this how Kleaax turned rogue?

The thought shook him to the cells of his Aviann core. He clenched his teeth against the craving to take even one more bite, and forced himself to run the obvious scans. The soil's composition, like the planet's eminently breathable air, wasn't that different from ancient Aviann baselines. His unit detected no unmanageable pathogens. The genetic structure of the corn itself was close to its Aviann counterpart. If it weren't physically impossible, they could've been hybrids of the same root stock.

Avinar had been looking for granary planets since the days of Hreaak's grandparents. Why hadn't Kleaax mentioned this in his Lexicon or the twelve standard years of reports he filed before dropping off the scope? He could've been a real, stupendously wealthy hero without breaking a single law.

The wheezy chucka-chucka of a tiny steam engine roused Hreaak from his daze. Using the cornstalks as cover, he peered down the road. A motorized bicycle huffed up the hill. Wisps of water vapor clouded the road in its wake. A leather-helmeted figure hunched over the handlebars like a jockey in a native horserace. As the cyclist drew closer, Hreaak recognized Shiro's gray shirt and red suspenders.

How did Shiro wind up behind him? He probably had trouble convincing Genny to forego her steamcycle lesson. Not that Hreaak was complaining. A hatchling could follow Shiro's vapor trail.

The chase ended at a two-story clapboard building with a peaked roof. The building's pillared porch overlooked a small parking area at the end of a graveled drive. Another open-chassis aircar, this one black, nosed a porch-side hitching post. On the ground beside it lay Shiro's steamcycle.

Two, tiny, round-headed dogs with bulging eyes lounged on the porch. As Hreaak approached, they jumped to their feet, barking and bouncing in place. Hreaak shook his head. Dogs. What did humans see in them?

At least these two were smart enough to get out of his way. Three strides later they bolted through small flaps cut into the building's double front doors. Switching to heat vision, he watched their yellow-orange thermal images scoot toward a humanoid shape his sensors identified as an aging, artificially generated human suit. A much younger, native-grown body darted to the back of the room.

Hreaak punched the doors. By the time they scraped across the rubber entrance mat, his sensors had mapped the interior. Illuminated by bare windows and simple electrified chandeliers, the space extended to the rear of the building. Glass jars packed the tall shelves between the windows. A row of tables ran along each side of the room. One table boasted a miniature P'lod generator. Others were furnished with sinks and canisters of gas. More rubber mats covered the floor behind the tables, but the floor in the center of the room was bare.

The back wall featured an electromagnetic shielding cage, an outside door, and a set of stairs. Shiro must have thought he was hidden behind a collection of crates under the table nearest the stairs. He could stay there as long as he didn't try anything. Hreaak would prefer not to shoot around gas.

The old rogue sat behind the center table on the left. Despite the enormity of his crimes, Hreaak couldn't suppress a reluctant tug of sympathy. Human suits aged poorly. Kleaax's hair had thinned to cottony wisps drifting over a liver-spotted scalp. His skin, originally the warm light brown of milky coffee, looked drab and peaked. Deep wrinkles scored his forehead and trailed from the corners of his gray moustache. The inverted triangle of his upper body had sagged into a pyramidal paunch. Despite the season, he was buttoned to his chins in a high-collared shirt, vest, and gray wool frockcoat. Hreaak didn't know how the anthropologist could stand to wear so much clothing in this heat.

Was it fear? Kleaax's pulse stuttered, despite the pugnacious jut of his jowls.

"Go away," he boomed. "The lab doesn't open 'til nine."

Hreaak stepped into the center of the room and activated the mandatory holographic IDs. "Weevirril Kleaax, on behalf of Avinar and the Consortium of Allied Planets …"

"Avinar? Avinar!" Kleaax pulled a pince-nez from his coat pocket and peered at the projected display. The thick lenses made it difficult to tell, but his eyes seemed to brighten. He jumped to his feet. “Well, it’s about time! Where’s my money?”

“Your what?” Hreaak asked.

“My twenty-nine standard years and three months’ back pay, that’s what! And you’d better not have forgotten the interest. My contract with the Council of Academies calls for full hazard pay with a non-delivery bonus of five percent compounded annually. And that’s before you add in royalties from the Lexicon.

“Uh uh uh, don’t try to tell me it wasn’t published.” He wagged a knobby forefinger at Hreaak. “I didn’t finish my dissertation yesterday, you know. Those old clucks in Galactic Field Studies tried to pull that with my master’s thesis. They didn’t succeed then, and you won’t succeed now. If it hadn’t been published, you wouldn’t be standing there dressed like a two-bit desperado, now would you?”

“Yes. No. I mean …”

Hreaak closed his mouth. Kleaax had gone from terrified to excited in a matter of heartbeats. His readings showed none of the usual signs of deception, either. Given everything he’d done, did the old coot really expect the Council to send him a windfall?

“Let’s start over.”

“You can start over as many times as you want, you still owe me …” Kleaax rifled a stack of papers on his work table. A significant number tumbled to the floor. The dogs shot out from under the desk and joined Shiro behind the crates. Hreaak activated his weapons array.

“You owe me … Ah, here it is!” Kleaax triumphantly hoisted a collection of slats Hreaak’s implants identified as a slide rule. Kleaax shifted the slats, aligning the markings until the results elicited a satisfied grunt. “Just as I thought, the Council owes me eight million, six hundred thousand, forty-three feddeks and change. Or it did as of three months ago. But for tax purposes, we might as well call it eight-point-six. It would take more than a week to work out the taxes on a slide rule, and my time is money.”

Hreaak shook his head, trying to clear it. He wondered if sniffing all that corn had affected his wits. The number twenty-nine rattled around his brain like it was important.

Something happened in this sector twenty-nine standard

years ago, something buried in the data he uploaded for this mission. Multiple lines of coded information streamed past his mind's eye. There! Despite his ingrained Aviann stoicism, he was tempted to throw up his hands. He settled for shutting off the holograms and shifting his array to standby.

"The Consortium collective mining the system's exo-planets automated its operations twenty-nine years ago."

"What's that got to do with the price of eggs?" Kleaax demanded.

"The transition disrupted your pay string."

"So? My reports got through. If they didn't, you wouldn't be here, speaking the lingo like a native, now would you?"

Hreaak's stomach knotted around the corn he shouldn't have eaten. "Did you complain through proper channels?"

"Of course I did. What kind of capon do you take me for?"

Hreaak refused to answer that. There were all those criminal charges to consider. "For the record, could you tell me what steps you took to correct the problem?"

Kleaax scratched a ragged patch of white skin under his ear. "It's been a long time, and I don't keep my field notes here. But I followed all the steps in the manual. I wrote Departmental Finance. When that didn't work, I petitioned the Department Chair, then the Academies' Bursar, and the Council Deans. Toward the end there, I may have fired off a … less than polite message—or two—to my Aerie Representative." His embarrassed grimace showed how far those missives deviated from Aviann standards of decorum. "You don't think that'll affect my pension, do you?"

"Trust me, that's the least of your worries." As they talked, Hreaak tracked Kleaax's data streams through time. Everything was perfect up to the point when the exo-post's last living employee exited the station. "I understand why you finished the Lexicon. It was a matter of survival. But why did you keep filing reports for twelve years when you weren't getting paid?"

"It takes ten standard years for the courts to declare someone dead. Since I was dealing with the Council and an exo-post, I figured I'd give it an extra couple years to be on the safe side." Kleaax ducked his human head in a disconcertingly Aviann expression of discomfort. "I kept hoping someone would answer, but it was like flipping stones at a black hole. I got receipt notices, but nobody answered my messages, even when I attached those, ahem, letters I mentioned."

They never answered the messages, because the Department Chair of Galactic Field Studies never saw them. The Chair's gatekeeper program automatically stripped everything that wasn't an anthropological observation.

Which didn't mean records of Kleaax's communications didn't exist. Buried in the records Hreaak had uploaded—which constituted only a tiny part of the Council's hard-protected archives—was enough information to topple the sitting Deans and compromise the senior members of the Aerie's Social Sciences Committee. Whether or not they knew about the situation wouldn't matter. They should've known one of their most honored scientists had been cut loose on a planet where gun duels were a spectator sport. Killing Kleaax now would trigger an automatic investigation of his records and a search for heirs, turning the case into a galactic scandal and magnifying the political fall-out by a factor of five. So much for the easy way out of this mess.

Something of his frustration must've registered on his too expressive primate face. Kleaax's readings spiked.

He said, "You didn't come to pay me, did you?"

"No, the Aerie assigned me to investigate your disappearance."

"Took them long enough. They were probably hoping to find proof I was dead. That way their friends in the department would own all the rights to my work instead of just half." His face grayed and his pulse raced. "They, ah, didn't send you to…" He jerked his thumb across his throat.

"Not part of my brief," Hreaak answered.

As a Special Agent of the Aerie, Hreaak was charged with protecting Avinar's interests and terminating all threats. He had killed for the greater good. But the more he learned about this case, the more he started seeing Kleaax as a victim instead of a villain—abandoned by his Academy, marooned among humans for thirty long years. The nature of Hreaak's work meant he lived his life as an outsider. His job came with a star cruiser and a stratoflyer. He could always get away. Kleaax was dropped here. He had no way off this rock. No wonder he ran mad.

"The important thing is I found you. I'm going to bring you home."

Kleaax retreated as if from a bad smell. "Oh no you aren't."

"You can't seriously believe the Council is out to get you. You're a Hero of Science. You'll be a celebrity, as well as rich. Better yet, you'll get your feathers back."

"Feathers!" Kleaax blew a wet sound through his lips. "What good would feathers do me? At my age, all they'd do is molt."

Hreaak heard a clatter from the vicinity of the stairs. He couldn't tell if it was Shiro or the dogs.

"If the Aerie wants to honor me, all they have to do is send a little of the money they owe me, preferably in gold," Kleaax continued. "There's nothing for me on Avinar. After thirty years, I wouldn't recognize the place. It's not like anyone's pining for me, either. It took them seventeen years to notice I was gone. Here, people care about me. They depend on me. You know they call me a wizard?" He hooked his thumbs in his vest pocket and grinned so wide Hreaak could see the steel bridge where his upper right molars should've been. "The Wizard of Woodrow Park—that's me."

"There's no such thing as magic," Hreaak said. "There is, however, a Consortium-wide mandate known as the Uniform Non-Intervention Pact of Standard Year 4614."

Kleaax's eyebrows pulled together, multiplying the creases on his forehead. Could the author of the Lexicon, and the founder of a major manufacturing operation, really be so dense?

Another rattle issued from Shiro's hiding place. Behind his thick lenses, Kleaax's gaze slithered toward the sound.

"Old floors," he said. "They creak in the summer."

"Not like that, they don't," Hreaak replied. "Shiro, come out where I can see you."

The dogs whined. Shiro stilled like prey gone to ground.

"You know your boss isn't human, right? That's just a body he wears. His real face has a beak for rending flesh."

The boy gasped.

"You bustard," Kleaax swore. "Why'd you have to scare him like that?"

"He needs to be scared. Under Consortium law, he's an accessory to the crimes of a galactic felon who contaminated an entire world with his dangerous alien technology."

"I did nothing of the sort," Kleaax said. "I couldn't work outside this planet's existing technology if I wanted to. The manufacturing base wouldn't support it."

"That excuse won't fly. An Allied Planets' scientific observer—regardless of origin or discipline—is prohibited from entrepreneurial operations in any field related to industry, technology, manufacturing …" In the space between words, he heard another click.

"Shiro!" he barked. "Get out here. Now!"

"Do as he says." Kleaax's big bass voice shook slightly. He cared for the boy. In addition to his stressed vocal chords, his readings registered a sharp increase in the hormones associated with nurturing in primates. "Don't hurt him," he pleaded. "Please."

"Don't beg," Shiro said. Slowly, sullenly, he rose to his feet. He edged sideways across the floor. "It won't do any good. Whoever this guy is, he's not your friend. He's been questioning you like a lawyer this whole time. He's setting you up to take a fall."

Hreaak tasted bile. The charge cut too close to the truth. He rasped, "Move away from the cage, Shiro. Keep your hands where I can see them."

"Do you want me to dance, too?"

Kleaax's breath hitched.

Hreaak almost smiled. "Not when you're still growing into your feet."

That drew his eyes to the oversized extremities in question and the wire running out from under the boy's trouser leg.

"Banzai!" Shiro shouted. He ripped the end of the cord from his pocket.

Hreaak fired. The charge lifted Shiro off his feet. He dropped to the floor. The dogs erupted from under the table. Snarling, they threw themselves between Hreaak and the boy.

At the same time, a swarm of toy-sized rotorcraft erupted from Shiro's former refuge. They fanned across the center of the room, too fast and too many to risk shooting with so much gas around. They attacked an instant later. Sharp blades notched the sides of Hreaak's right hand and sliced into his shoulder. He slammed them from the air with his vambrace and his hat. He stomped them to scrap.

By the time the dogs stopped barking and the last of the rotors lay shattered on the floor, Hreaak's right sleeve and the front placket of his shirt were shredded and red. Blood seeped from a cut on his cheek, filling his nostrils with a meaty tang. His breath labored from exertion and pain. He trained his weapons array on the large, yellow-orange thermal blot huddled behind the table nearest the metal cage.

"If you think you can activate an electromagnetic shield before I fry your chicken ass, you've got another think coming."

Kleaax's upraised hands preceded him from behind the desk. "You killed Shiro," he spat.

"I stunned him. I'll have to mind-wipe him unless we can fix this mess."

Kleaax's eyebrows pushed his wrinkles to his topmost tuft of hair. "You wouldn't."

"I wouldn't enjoy it. But I would. Under Consortium law, you're both dangerous criminals. The courts won't care that you lost your livelihood to a data glitch. The only things they'll care about are P'lod coils, anachronistic aircars, premature electrification, and all those signs out there reading 'Kleaax Industries: Home of the Invention Factory'." He fought the urge to howl like one of those wretched dogs. He could've finessed almost anything else, but he couldn't erase those damned signs from his optical data banks. "Of all the stupid things to do, why'd you have to start a business?"

"I had a family to support!"

"They're apes," Hreaak said brutally. "Nesting with them—also a crime under the Pact."

"What about denying me the means to survive? Isn't that a crime? Who's going to be punished for that?"

"Nobody." Hreaak hated it, but he couldn't do anything

about it. The universe might be infinite, but as the guardian of Aerie interests in this sector, his options for averting a miscarriage of justice were limited.

"Believe it or not, Kleaax, I'm trying to help you. There's only one way you can prevent the authorities from turning you into an organ farm. You're going to dust off your communications pad and write another report, a copy of which I will personally deliver to the Aerie. You're going to tell them you've spent the past seventeen years preparing a turn-key granary world for entry into the Aviann Commonwealth."

"I will not!" Kleaax exploded. "This is a protected planet!"

"Were you born a moron, or was that your human suit talking? The planet lost its status as an anthropological theme park the minute you got into the invention business and changed the course of its technological development."

"That's ridiculous. Ninety percent of our products are nothing more than improved versions of things that were already out there. The only reason the Pact and the rest of those non-intervention laws exist is to preserve the status quo. Avinar and everyone else break them all the time."

Privately Hreaak agreed with him, but he was too professional to admit it. He was also too professional to continue indulging in these simian fits of sentiment. They were undermining his effectiveness and interfering with the job.

Kleaax took a deep breath and braced his hands on the table. "We're arguing about the wrong things. The point isn't the laws; it's the principle behind them. What's best for a developing world? It isn't colonization. I've devoted my life to studying these things, and the records are appalling. Colonization is a death sentence to indigenous peoples. Between conflict, disease and societal stress, we're talking catastrophic population collapse. There could be a ninety-eight percent die-off in the first generation alone."

"A survival rate of two percent is better than none at all," Hreaak said. "Besides, isn't it hypocritical to talk about the evils of colonization when you're living in a territory, which according to your own Lexicon, was colonized less than four generations ago?"

"It's their planet!"

"In Avinar's sector of influence. Our exo-post is still here."

Hreaak's scanners measured every blip and flutter of the anthropologist's bodily functions. But he found himself wishing he could see the old Aviann's eyes. Something was happening behind those distorting lenses. He could read it in the set of Kleaax's jaw, and smell it in the sudden flowering of his shaving lotion. The pulse in Kleaax's human suit sped, then steadied, like an antique internal combustion engine revving for action.

"And when was the last time anyone checked up on us?" Amusement rumbled through the words, like the echo of laughter in a subterranean cavern. "How long do you think it'll take before someone comes looking for you?"

They'd retrieve his cruiser and his stratoflyer. Hreaak himself was expendable. He'd always accepted that fact the same way he'd accepted the weight of his vambrace.

"Special agents have a lower life expectancy than space marines in a plasma fight," Kleaax continued. "I ran the stats for a class. Less than twenty percent survive to claim their pensions. Your bosses expect you to die on the job. They count on it."

Hreaak hefted his weapons unit. "Is that supposed to be a threat?"

Kleaax shook his head. Hreaak dropped his guard for a milli-instant, and the old man roared: "Gorge, Brunhilda, attack!"

The dogs took off like someone ignited their farts. Hreaak knocked one aside. But the other clamped its jaws on his left hand. Instinctively, he pulled away. His arm exploded in agony.

The dog hung on, lips curled back from a wired steel jaw. Growling, it heaved its small body from side to side. Its metal teeth ground deeper, sundering the bones inside his palm. His hat dropped from fingers no longer able to grasp. The battle yodel of the other dog thundered in his ears.

He couldn't think through the pain and the noise. He raised his vambrace to shoot, and barely stopped himself in time. He smacked the dog with the side of his fist.

It dropped, yelping, and scuttled out of sight. Meanwhile, the second dog had regained its feet. Its hind legs danced in preparation to jump.

"Don't," Hreaak said.

The dog whimpered and dropped to a squat. Urine poured from between its legs. And poured. And poured.

Stupefied by the pain of his shredded hand, all Hreaak could do was stare. Basic anatomy dictated the amount of urine an animal produced was determined by the size of its bladder, which was, of necessity, proportional to its mass. But apparently nobody had told the dog. According to the calculations spooling through his brain, the dog—which weighed about as much as a small chicken—had just pissed half its body weight. And it was still peeing. The urine gushed across the floor, splashing Hreaak's boots, soaking the floor beneath them, and swamping what was left of his senses with its rank smell.

A sharp crackle and the hum of machinery drew his attention back to Kleaax. The anthropologist stood next to the tabletop P'lod generator. Searing white sparks arced between the domed poles. Smoke-colored goggles shielded Kleaax's eyes from the glare, but the static discharge pulled his sparse hair into a ball of fluff. In keeping with his delusions of wizardry, he held a crystal wand in his right hand.

Hreaak's head felt too heavy for his neck. He'd taken plasma burns that hurt less than his mangled hand. He was bleeding from a dozen cuts, and he was standing in pee. He was the one with the weapons unit. Why was he the one bleeding and standing in pee?

He still had a job to do. He primed his weapons array for a hip shot.

"Weevirril Kleaax, this is your last chance. It doesn't have to end like this."

The old fool laughed. "That's the smartest thing you've said all day. Stay here. This is a whole new world. The past doesn't exist. You can be anybody. Do anything. Nobody's going to come looking for you. If they did they might have to pay you."

The fingers of Hreaak's right hand curved.

"Uh uh uh," Kleaax warned. The tip of his wand quivered no more than the width of a barbule above the sizzling white sparks. "You might be fast, but no human body is as fast as lightning. All I have to do is twitch."

And Hreaak was standing, surrounded by broken steel toys,

in a liquid conductor with less resistance than water.

He kicked one of the rotors at Kleaax's smug face and raced to the rubber mat by the doors. He spun on his heel. Raised his arm.

Something round and hard jabbed the base of his skull. His sensors screamed warnings he didn't need. Steel. Oil. Gun.

The back door burst inward. Genny stormed through the opening, sighting over a short-barreled shotgun pointed at the bloody center of his chest. The void of space was warmer than her gray eyes. Her aim never wavered as she marched to Shiro's side.

Hreaak could've taken her. He could've taken the human behind him. But he didn't need his sensors or the analytics attached to his weapons array to know he'd never take both.

"Sweetums," a nasal female voice brayed at the back of his head, "is this man bothering you?"

"Bellissima!" Kleaax caroled. "And little Genny, on the spot as always."

"Sorry it took us so long. I was changing a tire when Genny showed up. Some fool blew his wheel on a curb. What's wrong with Shiro?"

The dogs yapped excitedly from their respective retreats. Kleaax turned off the generator and pushed the goggles to the top of his head. "He's had a nasty shock. He'll wake up in a few minutes."

Genny didn't blink.

Hreaak should've been scheming, calculating, planning. Instead, he was floored by an unexpected sense of relief. He was relieved to be stopped. Relieved to be divested of agency. Relieved the only blood on his hands was his own.

"What do you want me to do about him?" the woman asked. The pressure on Hreaak's skull increased infinitesimally, as if she needed to make a point.

"Just keep him still, May Belle."

Kleaax wet a white handkerchief in the closest sink and bustled out from behind the tables. He moved with surprising grace for a human of his age and bulk.

Hreaak's breathing slowed from force of habit. If Kleaax

fouled Genny's shot, he could disarm the woman behind him in an instant.

But Kleaax was too canny for that. Holding his wand in one hand and the wet handkerchief in the other, he sidled out the door and reappeared on Hreaak's right. Tsk-ing softly, he dabbed the blood off Hreaak's shoulder.

With a mental start, Hreaak realized their human suits were the same height. In fact, if you looked past the ravages of age and wear, and the cosmetic choices of complexion, feature and hair, their bodies were identical. They could've been printed from the same template, stamped from the same mold. Was it coincidence or a symptom of some deeper flaw—a shared compulsion that sent them chasing across the outstretched wings of the galaxy? In the name of Avinar. But it wasn't for Avinar. Not really. To be honest—and a man with a gun to his head owed it to himself to be honest—he'd never once in all his missions used his cruiser to go home. Was the old man with his spectacles and spotted flesh, his unhealthy frame and illicit nest, a portent of his own future?

Would it be so bad?

Inside his human suit, Hreaak's soul itched.

Kleaax waited. His gaze held neither challenge nor censure. Hreaak's right arm sagged against his side, the burden of his vambrace almost too heavy to bear.

Maybe that's why he didn't resist when Kleaax smeared the blood-soaked handkerchief across the plates of his weapons unit. All AP cybernetic interfaces designed for field use were keyed to their host's DNA. Kleaax knew. He'd been in the field for thirty years.

"Be careful, hon," his nest-mate May Belle said. "This fella strikes me as a desperate character."

"I suppose he is," Kleaax agreed.

He rubbed the crystal wand over his wool sleeve and jabbed the point into the unobtrusive slot on the underside of the vambrace. A shock of electricity jolted up Hreaak's arm. The weapons control panel vanished from view.

"But it's nothing we can't handle"—the weight of Hreaak's vambrace dropped from his arm into Kleaax's open hand—"together."

Of War and Wings

Tansy Rayner Roberts

Fire. The sky is on fire, and your wings don't work.

You twist and turn, struggling to soar up beyond the billowing clouds of smoke and steam, as so many soldiers do.

Your throat chokes on the smell of polished brass and burnt flesh, and you can't fly any more. Your metal wings buckle under you, and the harness slips uncomfortably.

No, you should not have come here, into this.

You are seventeen.

You know how to dance, and make polite conversation. Your needlework is exceptional, and you are at least competent at the piano, if called upon to play a piece.

You do not know how to do this.

And yet, when the blazing, impossible lanterns of the alien ship blast full in your face, and it bears down upon you, in that moment you know exactly what to do.

Your musket fires, as if some other soldier has laid his hands over yours. You fall back, tossed helplessly through the sky by the ricochet.

But the alien falls faster.

Your first kill.

His ship bursts into flame as it hits the ground, and that is when you know that this is, after all, where you are supposed to be.

* * *

Three angels alight from the train at Paddington Station, their bronze wings pulled back tightly so as not to get caught in the folding doors. They walk along the platform, one of them limping, until they reach the long queue for shelter and food.

Angels are always given preference—whether that be a sleeping pallet in the stairways and corridors of one of London's many underground stations, or a larger serving of rations. Still, these three show no tendency to swagger or throw their weight around. One of them even takes a bar of chocolate out of her pocket and offers it to the children clustered nearby.

The children divide the chocolate and scoff it down in a few moments of greedy delight, but not one of them takes their eyes off the gleaming bronze of the angel wings.

"Pease porridge again," says Madge, unhooking her tin plate from her combat belt in anticipation. "I told you Paddington never has anything but pease porridge. I heard a rumor of roast pork at King's Cross."

"There are always rumors of roast pork," Daisy says with a sigh. "I don't believe there's a pig been killed in this country in two months or more. Unless by the enemy."

"Perhaps the enemy have eaten all the eggs, too," says Peg.

The three of them have been flying together for six months, give or take, which makes them veterans in this war that has seen so many shot down over London's skies. All three were christened Margaret, and they have been friends so long that it barely matters at all that Madge was once a lady's maid, Daisy a milliner, and Peg the daughter of a Viscount.

When their turn comes around, they each receive a large ladleful of pease porridge on their tin plates, and a slice of some sort of pudding.

"Is it Jam Roly Poly?" asks Daisy, prodding the slice with vague interest.

"The currants are too close together," says Madge, giving it a sniff. "It's plum pudding, I reckon, or as close as they can get to it."

"Criminy," says Peg. "Is it Christmas already? I promised Aunt Ermentine in my last letter I'd try to get away for it. I suppose it's too late now."

"The enemy don't care about carols and church and all that," says Madge.

"Neither do I, much," says Daisy, who rather likes to shock

the other two when she gets half a chance.

The three of them select a spot on one of the abandoned platforms to lay out their bedrolls for the night, and to enjoy what warmth their meager supper has to offer them.

"They said it would all be over by Christmas," says Madge. "Didn't they?"

"I expect that's just the sort of thing one says," says Peg. She takes a bite of plum pudding before her pease, thinking how shocked Aunt Violet would be at all this—rubbing shoulders with girls of the lower orders, and then to top it all off, eating her pudding before her main.

"What are we to say now?" sighs Daisy, releasing the harness that holds her bronze wings in place. They clank and clatter as they fall on to the hard station floor. "It will all be over by Easter? That hardly has the same ring to it, and St Valentine's is too close to be realistic."

"I don't know about that," says Madge, wolfing her pudding down. "Reckon there won't be enough of us left by Valentine's to worry about it."

This is no good. They have a whole two hours to rest and recover before their next shift in the sky, and if they grow despondent now, they will be wrecked by then.

"It could be worse," Peg says lightly. "The Season starts in a few weeks. Why, I could be preparing myself for debutante balls and being presented to the Queen as we speak."

The other two look at her, and laugh. It's hard for them to imagine her in froth and finery. Peg cut her hair off weeks ago, to stop it tangling in the wings, and her face is never clean. The London sky is almost as filthy as the London streets, and the ships of the enemy give off such wretched clouds of grit and smoke that you can never entirely scrub it off your skin.

"How did you convince those high and mighty aunts of yours to let you play angel with the rest of us drabs?" asks Daisy. She's light-hearted, but there is genuine curiosity in her voice. They've never talked about this.

"I didn't," says Peg. "Aunt Violet—she's the worst of them—took me to the Alexandria to be kitted for my coming out. Silks and muslins, all that rot. Did you ever go to the

Alexandria?"

The other two girls nod and smile. You can't help but smile when you think of the Alexandria.

"My Sidney always wanted to work there," says Madge. "He applied eight times, for their armoring and weapons department. They said he was good, but the list was so long, of blacksmiths and leatherworkers who wanted to work for them. He never made it."

"My gran took me for tea there, when I was little," says Daisy wistfully. "I'd never been anywhere so posh as that tea room. Tiny cakes the size of sugar lumps, and sandwiches thin as embroidery silks."

The Alexandria was the first and most beautiful shopping arcade in England, all wrought iron and glasswork on the outside and the most exquisite shops and boutiques on the inside. Peg was eight years old when it first opened in Kensington, and even the dread aunts could not fault it for class and style.

"The Alexandria sold the best of everything," Peg says. "So of course we went. The Paris fashions would be just in, Aunt Violet said, and Aunt Alice was planning my wedding trousseau in anticipation. But when we arrived, we were greeted at the door with a polite question. 'Is it for the Season, or for higher purpose?' I realized then, standing there, how wrong it was to plan for dances and tea parties and conversation when there was a war going on over our heads."

"I bet your aunts loved that," says Daisy. "Silly old cats. Even with so many men dead, and so many gals like us wearing wings, you're still more likely to meet a husband in the services. What kind of man could you catch at the Season this year? Cowards and criminals."

"You're right, of course," says Peg softly. She is not thinking of the imaginary Baronets that her aunts had dreamed up for her. She is thinking of Arabella Dray, the Steel Eagle, who flew more raids against the enemy than any other angel since this war began. Peg was her wingman three times over, last October, and they talked of so many things in between sorties.

Dead now, Arabella. Shot down over Whitehall. Garlanded with every posthumous honor that the Queen had to pin upon her corpse. Before her last flight, Arabella kissed Peggy in the shadow of St Paul's Cathedral. It wasn't a kiss of chums, but a kiss of sweethearts. Such a precious thing a kiss could be, so fragile and barely lasting a moment. The world changed after that, irretrievably, and Peg has no idea how to change it back.

"So you ran away?" says Madge.

"Sneaked off, while Aunt Violet was talking to the proprietress about French lace. They were making custom armor not fifteen feet away, across the other side of the arcade. I'd heard the clang of anvil while they were measuring my stays."

The other two girls grin at that, their hands brushing over the bronze and leather of their own armor. Only six months ago, Society though it was inappropriate for a respectable young lady to walk down a street unaccompanied. Now they can go anywhere, and be met with a salute and an approving nod. The armor isn't an aberration. It is a revolution.

Women have wings now, and a war to fight.

* * *

Hyde Park is on fire. There are flames and smoke everywhere. You are still in the air, borne aloft by your powerful bronze-and-workings wings, ready to destroy the enemy.

But there is no enemy, just smoke and fog and other angels, flocking around you.

"A retreat!" you hear screamed across the sky. "Is it a retreat?"

The thought that it might be over chokes you up, but you know better than to cling to that sort of hope.

It has been two Christmases now, and the only shock is that London is still here, that there is anything of London left. You have seen the Alexandria Arcade from the air, the most beautiful place you knew, and it is twisted, damaged, parts of it blown apart. The wrought iron railings have burst free like so many spider's legs, unraveling across the wide pavement of the King's Road.

You are eighteen years old, and killing aliens is what you do.

As the clouds part, revealing a phalanx of ships in attack

formation, you soar towards them, musket at the ready, yelling like a fishwife for every angel in the sky to join you.

This is it. This time, you will not make it out alive.

And yet …

Your wings are strong, and your armor is tough. As you fall into the haze of smoke that is the city below, you can be satisfied that you take half a dozen of the bastards with you.

* * *

Christopher Robin dreams of angels: beautiful creatures in pantaloons and bronze armor. The strength and power of their wings make them more than a match for the Fleet.

He (he is the closest approximation, and yet remains a poor translation) did not expect to find angels here in this wasteland planet of primitive industry. Something has gone terribly wrong, somewhere along the way.

Christopher Robin misses his ship, much as he might miss an arm or a leg now that he has got used to this many-limbed body that was chosen to match the natives of this world. She (in the absence of pronouns which mean other and the same simultaneously) was destroyed in the air, and it was only a last minute ejection bubble that allowed Christopher to survive the fall.

He should be fine with his suit for protection, until help arrives to recall him safely to the Fleet. His suit is a thin filmy layer of artificial fabric with the computing power of a city and the strategic ability of a War Cabinet. It has, however, stopped talking to him, which is something of a problem. He is not even certain if his call for help has been heard.

It has been three days, which suggests that he is on his own.

Sheltering in the ruins of a city structure, he has had time to contemplate everything that has happened since his Fleet first began their occupation of Earth. He has had time even to sleep, though this is a disturbing experience because of the dreams. He has shot down thirteen of the glorious bronze-winged angels since his shift began, four months of this world's calendar ago. It is a good record, something of which he can be proud when he returns to his hive.

Why, then, does he feel so wretched about it? Why does he dream of these shining men and women with their beautiful, primitive wings, in those moments before the lasers from his ship tore them apart?

Why does he dream at all? It is a new symptom, one that Christopher Robin might never have known about before this planet wormed its way inside his head.

He has built himself a nest in part of a bomb-blasted shopping complex, tearing up the remains of the various long and impractical dress tunics he found here, in order to be snug and warm.

The air of this city is distressingly thick with smoke, coal dust, and steam, which makes it painful to breathe. Christopher Robin misses his hive, the warm cleanness of his lungs and the close presence of his husbands.

He is hungry, but has not yet been able to identify which of the produce items in each of the surviving pods of this structure are food as opposed to artifacts, ornaments, clothing, and so on. It is all far too difficult, without his suit to translate the world to him. He is hungry, and too frightened to eat in case he poisons himself and dies.

He sleeps again, and wakes to find a creature from his dreams standing over him.

The angel, armored in blackened bronze and leather, smelling of battle, stands over him with a long weapon pointed at his torso. She is magnificent, her wings spread out to frame her warrior's shape. "My name is Lieutenant Peggy Danvers," she says in a steady voice. "And you, sir, are a prisoner of war."

* * *

Peg has lost so much. So many friends, so many potential futures. Daisy was shot down earlier tonight, and Peg could not find her body. She might have made it, but who can say? No word from Madge.

Peg is tired. Tired and worn out, and even with all the losses she has endured, nothing has made her angrier than the destruction of the Alexandria Arcade. This one, perfect place loomed so large in her childhood. The aliens have taken everything good from her now, everything that mattered.

She has one of them now, in her power. She wonders how badly she is going to misuse that power.

The alien is small and slight. He looks like a paler, bluer version of a twelve year old boy. They look human, but not quite, not enough to feel real. There's a disconnect to them, an otherness she cannot quite explain. His uniform is a pathetically thin layer of cloth. Do his generals not even allow them to be armored against the enemy?

He is humble and quiet, which is what Peg wants as she collects her thoughts. They walk along the remains of the covered walkway in silence, heading for the food hall. There may be some supplies in the kitchens, something to stave off the hunger that gnaws at her stomach. She can't think when she is so very, very hungry.

"What is your name?" she asks him as they pause to step over rubble and climb under some fallen beams. She never lowers her musket, not for a second.

"Christopher Robin," says the alien.

Peg hesitates at that. "Christopher?" Such a normal-sounding name.

"It's from a book of your culture that hasn't been written yet. They issued us new names to aid communication between our species."

"To aid communication?" Peg says, incredulous. "When have you tried to talk to us? When have you done anything but raid and shoot and kill?"

Christopher Robin gives a small, plaintive shrug. He looks wretchedly vulnerable. It upsets her that she might have to shoot something that looks like a child.

"What is your real name?" she demands.

Christopher Robin gives a series of chitters and numbers which string together into nothing that will ever make sense.

"Stop," she says, interrupting him. "I don't care. Stop making that noise."

They make their way towards the food hall in silence.

* * *

There is glass everywhere. The food hall once had a magnificent domed glass ceiling, when Peg was Little Miss Margaret Alice Teasdale, and came here with her aunts for tea. She remembers looking up, marveling at how the dome looked like a clear summer sky on one side, and a star-filled night sky on the other. Day and night, both at once. The ceiling of the Alexandra Arcade food hall won architectural awards for its magnificence.

Now it is dust and shards on the floor, and a few spiky corners of glass still clinging up there to the metal framework. It makes Peg want to cry, but she has not drunk any water in eight hours and there are no tears in her body. *Rubble and sawdust, that's all you're made of now, Peggy girl.*

She is hurt. She hasn't admitted to herself yet how badly hurt she is inside. There may be bleeding, but she hasn't taken off her armor to check.

The armor is all that's holding her together at this point, and besides, she's not altogether sure she would be capable of removing it.

"Come on," she says abruptly. This alien creature has torn her world apart. The least he can do is help her open a few doors.

It's hard to believe that there will be anything left. The destruction of the Alexandria was days ago, maybe weeks. Peg has already seen evidence of looting back in the main arcade. Armor and silks, weapons and chemises—all stolen. She likes to think that the gowns have gone to women who might appreciate them, but they have probably been torn into strips for bandages, or chewed into fuel for the making of more armor, more wings.

This looks promising, though. There are marks all over the kitchen door as if someone has taken both a mallet and a hacksaw to it, and yet the lock holds fast. The contents might yet be secure, and yet Peg has no mallet or hacksaw, and how is she to do anything but place her hands plaintively over the rough, damaged surface, and wish?

The alien comes up beside her, his head barely reaching her shoulder. He places his palms on the door as well.

"It won't work," says Peggy, holding back the tears. So tired, so hungry. "The lock's too good. It kept everyone out." She has her musket, but little ammunition left, and a shot would bring snoopers and looters. She does not have the strength to fight a mob for food.

Christopher Robin reaches into the door, his fingers passing through the substance like an aunt running a piece of fine dress silk over her critical hands. The lock on the door goes, "click."

And just like that, Peggy is in Paradise. Perhaps Paradise should not smell quite so much like curdled cream, but there is real unspoiled food here too, a whole ham in the larder, several smoked fish, faded fruit, hardened white bread. She finds crumbly cakes that have escaped a patina of mold, and eats them, one after the other, until her stomach rebels.

Tea. The kitchen is rich in dried tea, she could drink cup after cup if she could only boil water. When her hands stop shaking, she might be able to find a way to light the stove.

Giddy with it all, she leans against the wall and watches the alien's own methodical search. He finds a cupboard of boxed biscuits, and jar after jar of fine pickles, jam and oily fish. So many provisions.

He does not eat, though, and she wonders why he did not break into this treasure trove long before she got here. Did he not know it was here? Does he not eat food?

Finally, the alien turns and passes her a beautiful, satin-lined box. Inside, she finds an assortment of Harrods chocolates, hand-rolled and perfect, and it is impossible now to hold back the tears.

Daisy and Madge would have squealed and squabbled over the chocolates, but she can barely stand to put one in her mouth. After everything else today, it is too much.

* * *

Christopher Robin climbs the iron frame that he can see once held a domed ceiling of colored glass over this hall. He swings easily across the melted, damaged fronds of metal, scrambling up high so that he can see the battle.

He has cowered enough.

The damp fog of the city is closing in, but he has a good

view of the Fleet, streaking in their glowing saucers across the gray and darkening sky.

Perched up here, so close and yet so far away from his unit, he feels very alone. So many supplies behind the door below, and yet with his suit malfunctioning, he still cannot tell what would be safe for him to eat. It is no signifier that some of the food was evidently right and proper for the angel Lieutenantpeggydanvers, as what is good for her might be poison for his biology.

Better to eat nothing at all.

There are so few angels left in the sky. Is this the end, then? Is the battle phase nearly over? Can the occupation truly begin, once the last of the resistance is stamped out?

Christopher Robin does not enjoy fog and he wonders not for the first time why the Fleet were ordered here, to invade this particular city, when he is certain there are warmer zones on this world.

He hears a whir of steam-powered wings, and the angel Lieutenantpeggydanvers steps up through the air beneath him, holding a vessel in each hand. She rises above Christopher Robin and then lowers herself gracefully to perch upon the twisted metal framework, as he is doing. She hands him one of the vessels, which is warm to the touch and full of a swirling fog all of its own.

"This must be the last battle," she says. "Your fleet has all but won."

He does not, will not, apologize. Not with this cup in his hands that might be a peace offering and could very well destroy him from the inside out. It smells enticing and strange, and his stomachs twist for craving it.

The angel lets out a long sigh, as if she has been holding it in for months or years. "I don't care any more," she says, and drinks a long draught from her warm cup before closing her eyes. It is not a safe place to sleep, and yet her wings and armor seem fused to the metal of the ruined dome. She does not fall.

As the evening draws dark, a new sound of steam and bronze gears fills the air, a cranking and a wheezing. Christopher Robin watches, quite amazed, as a brand new fleet of humans rises into the sky from somewhere near the building he has identified on maps as Buckingham Palace.

Angel ships, brand new, made of the same stuff as angels and their armor, all bronze and leather and steam. They make a slow swooping sound as they take to the sky against the saucers, wings flapping, cannons at the ready.

A great hissing boom fills the air, and then another. Cannons roar, and the twisted railings shudder beneath Christopher Robin. One by one, as he watches, the perfect silver saucers of his Fleet are blown to pieces in clouds of steam and rubble.

One, and another, and another, and then the final twelve, and then only six, and then every single one until nothing remains of the occupation force but a sparkling, acrid smoke even now disappearing into the London fog.

Even if he could fix his suit, there is no one to call for help now. His hive is too far away. They will assume that he has been blasted apart like the others.

This has happened before, on other worlds. The destruction of one Fleet is a sign that the Hives must look elsewhere for conquest. There will not be another sent here. No rescue, then. No hope of return. Nothing left.

Christopher Robin drinks the tea. What has he left to lose? It does not poison him, though it is less of a comfort than he imagined it would be, now that it has grown cold. Still, it is good. It is something.

When he reaches over to brush the angel awake, she is cold too.

"I don't know what to do now," he whispers to her. She has no answer for him.

The steam-and-bronze ships of the angels retreat in ungainly victory, leaving no trace of the invaders in the air behind them. Finally, the sky is empty. Christopher Robin keeps watching long after there is nothing more to see.

Airship Down: A Sound and Fury Adventure

Gail Z. Martin & Larry N. Martin

"Three orbs at three o'clock, over the Homestead Works." Mitch Storm's voice carried over the hum of the dirigible's engines.

"I see them." Jacob Drangosavich leaned over to speak to the airship pilot, who veered their craft like a black ghost over the Monongahela River. "Get in close," he said to the pilot. "I want to get as close to the sons of bitches as we can."

"They match the description of what they sent us out to find," Mitch replied. "Too far away to see detail. Is the camera working?"

Jacob checked over the camera controls. The Department had outfitted the airship with the best new, secret technology the folks in Rochester could come up with, small cameras that ran on a remote switch, something the agents could operate from the bridge of their airship. "They're set, if they work," he sighed.

"And there go the lights," Mitch said, pointing. As if on cue, the Edison lights that illuminated Carnegie Steel's flagship factory dimmed to brown, flickering out several times before struggling back to their original glow.

"Same as the other times," Jacob said, scribbling in his journal with a Waterman safety pen and still managing to get ink on his fingers.

Mitch sighed and shook his head. "I don't know why you bother," he said, resignation coloring his voice. "No one will be able to read that chicken scratch."

"I will," Jacob replied. "You think it's bad in English; even my mother can't read my Croatian."

"Sir," the pilot, Captain Nowak said. "The lights are moving."

Mitch and Jacob dropped their banter and scrambled back to

the observation window. "Keep them in view," Mitch ordered. "Don't lose them." Dark-haired and dark-eyed with a five o'clock shadow that showed up at three, Mitch Storm looked like what an adventure-book illustrator would come up with for an army captain and sharpshooter. Mitch was a few inches shorter than Jacob, but what he lacked in height he made up for in attitude. He had a pugilist's build, all-muscle, and a gleam in his eyes that promised mischief.

"I'm on it," Nowak replied. He was a good ten years older than either Storm or Drangosavich, with a little gray starting to show in his brown hair around the temples. To Jacob's eye, Nowak looked more like he belonged at the prow of one of the river barges than high in an airship. He had the rumpled, lived-in look of a man who has spent his life in one cramped ship or another, either on the Oder River in his native Poland, or navigating the traffic on one of New Pittsburgh's famed three rivers. Instead, a stint in the Navy had landed him in the nascent airship corps, and the Department had snapped him up for their own uses.

The airship's engines whined as Nowak increased the power, steering their ship above the black ribbon that was the mighty Monongahela River, or as New Pittsburgh locals liked to call it, the Mon. Behind them, the Monongahela and the Allegheny Rivers joined to become the powerful Ohio, which in turn found its way into the Mississippi. Beneath them, the burn-off flares from the Jones and Laughlin steel mill on the south banks of the river reflected off thick clouds of coal smoke from factories that churned out coke and steel around the clock.

"What'd that reporter say it looked like?" Mitch asked. "Hell with the lid off? He got that right."

Their airship, the *Onyx Shadow*, glided above the city. From here, the Mon seemed to be illuminated by torchlight, as up and down the river Mitch and Jacob could see the tall flare stacks of one massive steel mill after another.

"Have a care to give those flames a wide berth, or we'll have big trouble," Mitch warned.

"Don't worry. I've got them in my sights," Nowak assured them.

"The orbs are moving faster," Mitch said. "Keep after them!"

Jacob looked down, and then thought better of it, gripping the railing white-knuckled. "I hate flying," he muttered. The river bank slipped by rapidly beneath the airship with its rail lines and mill towns, as barges chugged downriver without a care about the excitement in the skies above.

Jacob pushed a stray lock of dark blond hair out of his eyes. He didn't like his hair as short as regulations called for, or nearly as short as Mitch preferred to keep his. With a long thin face and pale blue eyes, Jacob was well aware he looked like the majority of Eastern European immigrants who had flocked to the manufacturing cities of the Northeast to work in the factories of America. The same slight accent that occasionally prompted a dour look from the Brass made him fit right in among the mill hunks and factory workers, as did his ability to speak several Slavic languages like a native. Like those mill workers, Jacob was tall and broad-shouldered, and hard work had put muscles on his lean frame. He seldom started fights, but often finished them.

Nowak maneuvered the *Onyx Shadow* through the ever-present smoke. Visibility from the airship's small bridge waxed and waned, and Jacob fingered his St. Blaise medal, certain they would plow into one of the high brick smokestacks or the steep hillsides that sloped down to the river. The experimental airship moved at top speed, faster than any of the commercial or private dirigibles, thanks to the Department's top-secret technology and design. It was even faster than the *Flying Scotsman* locomotive in its best race. That didn't bear dwelling on, in Jacob's opinion.

"They're damn fast," Nowak said, leaning forward as if it would help the airship gain momentum.

"Can you keep up?" Mitch urged. Jacob had seen that light in his partner's eyes before, usually just before the two of them created a calamity that tended to include explosions and which required lengthy explanations to their superiors.

"I can try," Nowak said, his expression set in grim resolve. "We're still working out the bugs. Not completely sure yet what this baby can do."

"Do it." Mitch moved as far forward as the airship bridge allowed, staring at the flying orbs as if willpower alone would narrow the gap.

"They're heading upriver, like as not toward the Edgar Thomson Works," Nowak said as he managed the instruments and checked the gauges. Their reconnaissance ship held a crew of five, including Mitch and Jacob. Compared to the bigger zeppelins, the *Onyx Shadow* was fast, light, and classified, using a combination of rotorcraft and a much smaller gas envelope than the typical airships.

"I've got 'er opened wide up," Nowak said. "With a little luck and a tailwind, we'll keep them in sight."

Jacob was torn between heady exhilaration and sheer terror, a common feeling when he and Mitch were in the field. The bridge was humming from the sound of the straining engines, and without feeling or hearing the sound of the wind whistling by them, a glance down made Jacob think that the moving scenery far below them was nothing more than scenes from a praxinoscope projection.

"We're gaining on them," Mitch said, with the same raw competitiveness that had made him the Department's top crack shot three years in a row. He held a portable version of the airship's cameras and had it pressed against the glass, muttering as he tried to hold it still enough to get a shot of the glowing orbs that danced through the sky.

"I can't hold this speed forever," Nowak snapped. "This airship wasn't tested for this. It's fragile."

"Just a little longer," Mitch said, never taking his eyes off the orbs. "We've nearly got them."

Jacob could hear the airship's engines protesting. "Mitch, this isn't a train. Push a locomotive too hard and you stop rolling. Push this too far and we fall out of the sky. Those rotors need to spin to keep us in the air."

"Almost there," Mitch said, in a tone that let Jacob know that Mitch hadn't heard a word he or Novak had said.

The orbs dipped and swirled toward the massive Thomson Works mill, moving fast. They aligned over top of the mill, and the factory lights and all the street lamps dimmed and flickered, casting the Braddock riverside into near-darkness before the power came back.

"There they go again!" Mitch said, carefully snapping another picture as the orbs began to move again.

Nowak opened his mouth to protest, but before he could say anything, there were two loud bangs from the direction of the engines.

"Abandon ship!" a man's panicked voice shouted from the speaking tube on the bridge. "Repeat, engines failing, rotors two and three both down, abandon ship!"

"Not again," Jacob muttered.

Mitch grabbed his parachute and tossed chutes to Jacob and Nowak. He strapped his on almost without looking, then made sure he secured his precious camera inside his leather jacket before heading to the emergency hatch. Jacob grabbed his journal and shoved it into his jacket and zipped it up.

"*Wariat*! You're insane," Nowak shouted. "You're bloody insane!"

"Get ready to jump," Mitch said as if he had not even noticed Nowak's outburst. He yanked open the emergency hatch, and cold wind ripped through the bridge, scattering papers and howling in their ears. The airship was no longer level, slowly sinking towards the river as the two remaining rotors fought gravity. Nowak struggled with the controls, trying to slow the airship's rate of descent and level it out as much as possible for everyone to clear safely.

"Come on!" Mitch said, grabbing the pilot by the arm and shoving him toward the hatch. "Jump!"

Nowak had the same training Mitch and Jacob had taken, but Jacob bet that the pilot hadn't needed to use his as often. He went out the hatch pale with terror.

"Jacob—jump!" Mitch shouted, holding tightly to the railing to keep from being pulled out of the airship.

"*Magarac*," Jacob muttered under his breath, not bothering to translate. He had called his partner a jackass often enough that Mitch knew at least one word in Croatian. He dove from the hatch, counted silently and pulled the cord, feeling his heart in his throat until the black silk billowed into the sky above him. To his left, he spotted the two men from the engine room, gliding down with their parachutes. He saw Mitch a little ways over, his dark clothes nearly invisible against the night sky, but his face alight with the thrill of the jump.

The *Onyx Shadow* nosed toward the river, its engines sputtering and three of its rotors now in flames. They had dimmed its running lights to avoid notice, but even so, it would be difficult to imagine that no one was going to notice a large flaming object falling out of the sky and into the swift waters of the Mon. Once or twice, this kind of thing could be explained away with tales of weather balloons or atmospheric disturbances. Too often, and they'd have to call in help to clean things up. Jacob sighed. He should have known the night was going to end this way.

Jacob brought his chute down on a barren strip of land by the railway, not far from where Nowak and Mitch had landed. They wrapped up their chutes, weighted them with rocks and sank them in the river. Jacob shook his head. He had way too much experience with this sort of thing.

Nowak, still cursing in Polish, had gone in search of his crewmen. Mitch already had his camera out. "Come on," he said. "We'll track them on foot."

Jacob opened his mouth to argue and shut it again with a sigh of resignation. There was no reasoning with Mitch when he was like this. The best he could do was to try and keep the damage to a minimum, if it wasn't already too late for that. Mitch could explain it to the higher-ups. He always did.

"Damn." Mitch struggled to the top of the embankment, where he had a good view of the massive steel mill. The orbs were gone.

Jacob removed a cigar from his pocket and lit it. "Put that out!" Mitch said. "Someone will see us."

Jacob shrugged and shoved his hands into his wrinkled canvas jacket. "See what?" he said out of one side of his mouth. "Two jokers walking by the river? We sent the chutes to the bottom, along with the airship. Tomorrow, a barge with no markings will come along and dredge this area, and take out some odd-shaped thing under a tarpaulin. Colonel Falken will hand us our asses when he finds out, you'll sweet-talk our way out of it, we'll end up on probation—again—and next week, just to let us know they're annoyed, they'll send us out to the Rockies to find that big furry guy—again."

"I thought we made a deal with him that we'd leave him alone if he didn't bother the railroad workers?" Mitch said, looking genuinely confused.

Jacob took a drag on his stogie and sent the smoke in Mitch's direction just to watch him cough and swat the air. "Right now, I'm going down to Birmingham since we're on the south side of the river and get some decent pierogies," he said. He said it the way the locals did, "sah side."

"And a beer?" Mitch asked with a knowingly raised eyebrow.

Jacob grinned. "This is New Pittsburgh. A shot-and-a-beer. Iron City." He took another puff. "See how many people are talking about strange doings over the Mon," he said, and his accent, usually nearly non-existent, grew more and more Slavic. "Need to know how much damage control is needed. Before we stir up more."

"You don't care what I'm going to do?" Mitch retorted.

"Nope," Jacob said. "Because you're going to hang around here and get some pictures, telling everyone you're a newspaper man. Then tomorrow, you're going to wake me up early and drag me out to Tesla-Westinghouse to see if that boy-genius had anything to do with the orbs," Jacob added, his gravelly voice carrying even though he did not turn his head.

"You're angry about the crash," Mitch said. Jacob shrugged and kept on walking.

Mitch jammed his hands in his pockets and glared at him. "Who insisted on having parachutes on the airship?" He said. "Me, that's who."

"And who made us need to use the parachutes?" Jacob replied drily. "You, that's who. See you at the house, Mitch. If I win a few hands of cards, I might bring you a bucket of beer." With that, he sauntered off down the riverside.

At first, he could hear Mitch fuming behind him, but it was all for show. He and Mitch had been partners since the Johnson County Wars out West, only back then, they were green recruits, still wet behind the ears, newly signed up for the adventure of being in the U.S. Cavalry. He took another long drag from his stogie and let it out slow. *Adventure. That's what they called it. Nearly got our asses shot off. Still have some lead in my leg from that one.*

By the time Jacob reached the safe house in Shadyside, it was after midnight. The lights were out, and no one responded to his quiet knock. Jacob picked the lock and let himself in, then crept up the back stairs.

"About time you got back," Mitch said. He had hooded the room's only lamp so that it could not be seen burning from the street. "I waited to send our report until you came back."

On the table in front of him sat a clockwork carrier pigeon. It was a mechanical marvel, designed with the ability to fly long distances and return to its home base just like its living counterpart. What set the Department's "pigeon" apart was the hidden compartment on its steel back into which small objects could be placed.

"I developed the pictures we shot earlier," Mitch said. "Got in a good photo or two. I had to make them small to fit the bird, but it's enough to give Falken an idea of what we're seeing." Mitch stared at the photos for a few minutes before maneuvering them into the hidden compartment. On the table nearby lay a mobile telegraph switch, and Jacob saw a wire snaking out of the window to the pole outside.

"I think we need to show these to the *wunderkind* over at Tesla-Westinghouse. You printed extras, right?" Jacob asked.

"Yup," Mitch said. "Oh, and Falken telegraphed. We're on probation—again."

Jacob muttered under his breath in Croatian. "I hear Idaho is lovely this time of year. We might as well buy a cabin."

"Not a bad idea," Mitch replied. He turned off the light, opened a window and released the clockwork bird into the night sky with the sound of the rustle of brass wings.

* * *

Jacob groaned as sunlight streamed through the window, hitting him full in the face. "Get up, lazy ass!" Mitch's voice sounded far too chipper given the late night they had put in. "The carriage is coming for us. I brought up a cup of coffee and a roll for you, but you need to get dressed."

Jacob had barely pulled on his clothing and gulped his coffee before the driver arrived. He grabbed the roll, biting off chunks as he followed Mitch down the steep steps. "No cross words from Mrs. Hanson about last night?" he asked with a mouthful of bread.

Mitch chuckled. "She's got nothing to complain about. The Department paid to patch up the holes from the last time. You can hardly see where the fire was."

Hans, their driver, waited with the carriage in the street, a second cowled man beside him. Hans had his cap pulled low over his face, shading his features. Most people wouldn't look twice at a carriage driver, but if they did, one glance would have made it clear he had been modified.

Half his face was metal, with a mechanical eye and exposed gears—results of a bad explosion a few years back. Likewise his companion kept his visage equally hidden. Hans was still obviously human, but the second man was clearly a mechanical, one of the latest generation of Werkmen the Department had begun to deploy. They were loyal, trustworthy, did exactly as ordered, and they did not require hazard pay.

"Hello, Hans," Jacob said as he and Mitch climbed into the open carriage door.

Hans nodded curtly. "Good day, sir," he replied, with the odd whirring and clicking that accompanied his voice when he spoke.

"Tesla-Westinghouse—you know the way," Mitch said when they were settled.

"Very good, sir," Hans replied, climbing back up into the driver's seat beside the guard.

The carriage wound through the crowded New Pittsburgh streets. Jacob glanced out the window. Most of the damage of the Conflagration of 1868 and the Great Pittsburgh Flood of 1869 had been repaired, although the devastation had changed the city's destiny forever, especially after the Quake of 1872. The catastrophes had leveled buildings, changed the topography, opened up rich natural resources and made or destroyed fortunes. And for once, the Department hadn't had a thing to do with it.

"You really think *Wunderkind* can help with the orbs?" Jacob asked, drawing himself out of his thoughts.

Mitch grinned. "If he doesn't, he can figure out how to get what we need. He's as good as his reputation—maybe even better."

The carriage brought them across the Monongahela to Wilmerding, where the main Tesla-Westinghouse labs were housed. The carriage pulled up to "The Castle," the elaborate, turreted Renaissance Revival/Romanesque building that housed the company headquarters. A fire two years ago had leveled the structure, and the rebuilding not only restored the grand structure but added a new set of secret laboratories beneath it.

"Stay with the carriage, Hans," Mitch said as he and Jacob disembarked. "Keep your ears open—I'll transmit if we need you."

Mitch and Jacob each wore a wide-banded "watch" that was one of the Department's latest toys, since it included among its many functions a short-range Morse transmitter. The receiver was concealed in a rather large lapel pin. Jacob had no reason to expect danger, but he had grown accustomed to being surprised.

Mitch flashed his Department badge at the agent on duty. "Hi, Grace," he said with a grin and a wink.

Special Agent Grace Palmatier gave him a coolly appraising glance. "Captain Storm," she replied. "And Captain Drangosavich. Nice to see you again. Please try to leave the building—and our vehicles—intact, this time. Your last visit was expensive."

Mitch gave her his best "aw shucks" look, but she shook her head and Jacob chuckled. "I think she's got you figured out, Mitch," Jacob said as they took the stairs to the basement, then entered the left elevator, where Lars, another Werkman, was dressed as an elevator operator.

"Good day, sirs," Lars said with mechanical stiffness.

"Minus three," Mitch said. "We're expected."

"Very good, sirs." The elevator buttons only showed the upper levels. Lars flipped a switch, revealing a secret control panel, with the subterranean levels that were home to Tesla-Westinghouse's confidential and experimental projects.

When the doors opened, a tall, skinny young man in a lab coat was waiting for them. A mop of straight, sandy brown hair fell into his eyes, over wire-rimmed glasses that appeared to be smudged. "*Wunderkind*," otherwise known as Adam Farber, stood several inches taller than either Jacob or Mitch but looked as if he skipped regular meals. He was gawky and rail-thin, all of maybe twenty-two years old, and one of the most brilliant inventors on the Eastern seaboard.

"Come on back," Adam said, dispensing with formalities. "Coffee?" He was as twitchy as a squirrel, making Jacob think the man had probably consumed more than enough caffeine, even though the morning was still young.

"No thanks," Mitch replied. "But we're hoping you can help us with a new project."

Adam poured another cup of black coffee for himself and took a seat at a cluttered table, gesturing for Mitch and Jacob to join him. "What do you make of these?" Mitch asked, laying out several photographs of the orbs.

"Who wants to know—and why?" Adam asked. His eyes suddenly appeared much older, wary from the time he had already spent navigating the push and pull of competing powers who wanted to ransack his intellect for their own purposes.

Mitch rolled his eyes. "The Department of Supernatural Investigations—who else? We chased these damned things up the Mon last night, lost one of our new recon airships doing it. We think they're behind the power failures, and I thought there was an off chance you might know something about them."

Adam studied his coffee for a moment, then grabbed a pastry and took a few bites. "We don't know for sure," he said with a full mouth. "No government is claiming them and we haven't had direct contact. We refer to them as 'the visitors.'"

He paused to swallow and wash the pastry down with more coffee. "They showed up right after the first time I tested one of my larger inventions," he said. "Highly classified. Works on Mr. Tesla's designs for something that could shoot a beam of energy a long distance." He grimaced. "It may have gone a bit farther than we originally thought."

"Meaning that you shot something off into space like an invitation to a family reunion and some long-lost galactic cousins showed up?" Mitch asked incredulously.

"I wouldn't have put it that way, but that's the basic idea." Adam shrugged. "Could be a coincidence." He paused. "Then again, big power-drains happen when the 'ships' are sighted."

"So they're sucking up the power from the biggest factories and using it for fuel?" Mitch pressed.

Adam shrugged. "Maybe. Just conjecture."

"If you see them again, and they're hostile, Colonel Falken said I could give you these." Adam opened a small metal box to reveal several odd clockwork cartridges, about the same size as a shotgun shell. "They attach to whatever they hit and you can track them using this controller." He indicated a large piece of equipment.

Mitch regarded Adam skeptically. "Come on. You're holding out on us."

Adam grimaced. "Sorry, that's as much as I can tell you—classified."

Mitch looked like he was going to say something Jacob would regret. "Thanks for your time," Jacob said quickly, grabbing Mitch by the arm and taking the cartridges and the controller. "We're due for a meeting with Falken. Keep up the good work."

Mitch kept silent until they were back in the carriage. "Well, that was interesting," he said. "I hate it when he pulls out the 'classified' card—hell, we're the ones who are supposed to keep secrets."

* * *

"Well if it isn't *Sturm und Drang*, the sound and fury boys," Colonel Kurt Falken said as Mitch and Jacob entered his office. "I noticed that your message omitted the loss of *another* prototype recon airship." He paused. "Good thing Captain Nowak makes a *complete* report.

"Of all the dimwitted, reckless, irresponsible things you have ever done, losing the *Onyx Shadow* has got to be the worst yet." Falken's glare could melt ice. "I can't bury this," he ranted. "That airship cost as much as a private railcar—maybe two. I've already had a telegram from HQ wanting a report. And do you know what I had to report to them? That you burned and sank their goddamn airship!".

Mitch wasn't having any of it. "Farber says any other details on the orbs are classified. Is that true?"

Falken muttered a curse. "Sit down. That's an order, Storm. You too, Drangosavich."

"We damn near pitched into the river going after those orbs. Do we keep chasing them?" Jacob asked.

"Absolutely," Falken replied. "I'm not convinced these orbs are alien—at least, not alien from space. There's some unrest going on in Europe. They could be using these orbs to test our responses, maybe even keep us under surveillance." He glared at them. "I got you a new ship. Ironically enough, it's the *Phoenix*. I want this one returned in working order. I mean it, Storm. If there's a scratch, I'll have you and Drangosavich working off the cost of repairs in Leavenworth, so help me God."

"I'm counting on the two of you to figure it out." He thrust the mechanical carrier pigeon at Jacob. "Without too much additional damage. Now get out."

The door shut loudly behind them. "Damn, that was more painful than usual." Mitch said in a sulk. "Ok, ok, show's over. Go back to work." Mitch added loudly, looking around the large office where everyone was staring open-mouthed at the two agents.

"I feel like my flesh has been flayed from my body," Jacob muttered. "I told you there'd be hell to pay. Probation again." Jacob groaned.

"Look at the bright side. We got a new ship and we're still on the case!" Mitch encouraged.

"One toe out of line and we're investigating Bigfoot again."

Mitch grinned. "Not this time. We're on the right track. We'll head back out to the Thomson works. If the pattern runs true, they'll be back," he said with confidence as he and Jacob climbed back in the carriage.

* * *

A few hours later, after darkness fell, Mitch and Jacob stood outside the rear door of the rooming house, and Jacob shook his head. "Where the hell did you get those things?"

Mitch grinned, resting his hand with pride on one of the two steam bikes outfitted with brass boilers, unusual tubes and a dangerous looking mechanism right behind the rider's seat. "It's a velocipede," Mitch said. "With some modifications courtesy of *Wunderkind*."

Jacob eyed the unwieldy contraptions. "Are you sure Adam isn't just trying to kill you?"

Mitch slapped him on the shoulder. "So little faith. They run on water, they're small enough to slip around traffic, and at top speed, they move as fast as a horse at full canter."

Jacob paled. "Why not just get horses? They run on water, too."

Mitch rolled his eyes. "Horses get spooked around machinery, and there's no telling how they'd react around the orbs." His steam-cycle had two leather saddlebags strapped on the back, from which Mitch produced a pair of unlikely-looking guns.

"Here. Take this."

Jacob grimaced. "More presents from *Wunderkind*?"

Mitch grinned. "I told you, he likes us." Mitch held up the gun. "Adam's been experimenting with elastic materials. Think of these as new-model harpoons." The grip and trigger resembled that of a large handgun, while in the front, an iron grappling hook was connected to a length of strange-looking braided rope. The rope was coiled on one side of each of their bikes, attached to the top of the grappling hook, which had an iron shank that disappeared into the barrel of the gun.

"Didn't know we were chasing whales," Jacob observed.

"Big, glowing sky-whales," Mitch replied, excitement alight in his eyes. "Orbs, my friend."

"Let me get this straight," Jacob said. "You want to ride over there on these contraptions, chase down the orbs, and then harpoon them?"

"Yep."

"And then what? Are you going to hang on while they take you into outer space?"

Mitch sighed. "The cords are heavy elastic—another one of *Wunderkind*'s new inventions for us to try. Weshoot one hook into the ground, the other into the orbs, and the orbs go nowhere. Then we figure out how to take them down."

Jacob gave him a skeptical look, but Mitch was already swinging one leg over the velocipede and gave it a kick. The engine started up with an awful racket that drew glares from the neighbors and more than a few curious stares.

So much for covert operations, dammit. Jacob thought. Mitch was already speeding toward the street before Jacob had gotten his bike started, then he drew a deep breath, kicked the starter, and sputtered off behind Mitch.

Night traffic was light. Their steam bikes spooked cart horses as Mitch and Jacob sped across bridges and down New Pittsburgh's nearly deserted streets, heading for the Edgar Thomson Works. Jacob cursed under his breath whenever the bikes hit brick streets, jarring unmercifully with the thinly padded bike seats. Mitch was undeterred, and kept the bike's regulator full-open, forcing Jacob to do the same to keep up.

They thundered over the West Braddock Bridge, a narrow trolley bridge that was the only way over to the far side of the Mon for miles, except for the railroad trestle Port Perry Bridge just below the steelworks. The steam bikes clattered over the bridge's wooden bed, and Jacob was convinced his teeth were going to rattle out of his head.

"I think they'll hear us coming," Jacob groused.

"I slipped the night guard a couple of bills," Mitch replied, ignoring Jacob. "Enough to guarantee he'll keep their goons off us." He looked up at the night sky. "Now we just wait for visitors."

Coal smoke billowed from the stacks, and the gas flares lit the night without a need for moonlight. The Edgar Thomson ran all day and all night. Mitch and Jacob stayed in the shadows, still astride their steam bikes, watching.

"You got the tracker?" Jacob asked.

Mitch nodded, patting the pocket of his jacket. "Loaded it into a Very Pistol. That way I can shoot with one hand and keep the bike on the road with the other." He dug into his saddle bag and handed a second Very Pistol to Jacob. "That leaves us a couple more devices for later, if we need them."

If we survive, Jacob added silently.

Just after two in the morning, three dancing lights dropped toward the mill. "Get them!" Mitch shouted, gunning his bike to life. He and Jacob roared from their hiding place, surprising a couple of tired workers who leaped out of the way with shouted curses.

Jacob hunched low over his bike, as much to help him hang on as to increase his speed, as Mitch veered crazily in and out of open spaces in the cluttered mill yard, swerving around piles of steel bars and concrete blocks, weaving past wagons and hand carts.

The cold air stung Jacob's face. The orbs seemed closer than ever tonight. They hung like rogue stars over the mill, and Mitch skidded to a stop, pulling his Very Pistol. Jacob did the same, and they fired nearly in unison. Two tracking devices soared into the night sky. Mitch's shot fell short, but Jacob's hit and stuck.

"They're onto us!" Mitch said as the orbs rose and began to retreat. "After them!"

The steel mill lot was not designed for racing. Twice, Jacob nearly spun out on gravel. Mitch was determined to follow the orbs by the most direct path, which meant cutting through the train yards next to the mill

"Watch out!" Jacob shouted as men rolled a car onto a siding just at Mitch veered in that direction at top speed.

Mitch gunned the bike and made for the narrowing gap between the moving car and the rest of the parked train. Workmen gestured and shouted, then threw themselves out of the way. Mitch's bike shot through the gap just before the couplings were close enough to touch. Jacob veered right, taking advantage of the irate workmen's distraction to hurtle past. He gritted his teeth as the bike crossed a set of tracks, sure he would lose his manhood to the hard seat. Mitch was ahead of him, his bike streaking down the center pavement between a narrow-gauge set of tracks.

"Of all the pig-headed, stupid, dare-devil stunts—" Jacob muttered as he tried to coax a bit more life from his overtaxed bike.

They were heading away from the heart of the mill complex, out into the far reaches of the vast train yard, filled with cars waiting to be unloaded or loaded. It was a dangerous place to walk, let alone flying through it at top speed. Not that such a thought would hold Mitch back in the slightest, Jacob knew.

"Hey! You're not supposed to be here!" Two mill guards came running. Whoever Mitch paid off obviously hadn't gotten the word to everyone. The guards took up positions, firing their revolvers at the two speeding figures.

One bullet grazed Jacob's left arm, and he made a sharp turn to the right, pushing the bike to its limit as he veered to one side and then the other. Three more shots whizzed by, too close for comfort.

Alarms sounded, and across the darkened mill yard, searchlights began to light up the sky, flooding the area nearest the main buildings with light. Jacob dared a glance toward the tall light towers along the riverbank, braced for them to blind him at any second, waiting for a bullet to take him in the back.

The mill's guards ran after them, shooting as they went, following the bikes through the maze of equipment and materials.

Smoke stung Jacob's eyes and his back ached from hunching forward. Other parts, not mentionable in polite company, were going to be sore for a while, too. Shots fired overhead, far too close for comfort. Jacob longed for goggles as he tried to keep Mitch's dark, darting form in sight. Above them, the orbs glowed brightly, like stars fallen too close to Earth.

"No, no, no, no!" Jacob muttered as the orbs changed direction, heading out over the Monongahela River. Mitch never slowed down, taking a sharp turn to the right and zooming after his quarry across the trains-only Port Perry Bridge. The wooden bridge bed felt like a washboard under the steam bike's tires. The guards did not stop until they reached the edge of the bridge, firing off more shots, the muzzles of their guns sparking in the night.

Beneath Mitch and Jacob, the dark waters of the Mon slid past, deep and swift. Barges slipped beneath the bridge, heedless of the drama unfolding overhead. Up and down the river, gas flares blazed high in the sky from the mills along both sides, and in the distance, Jacob could hear the whistle of a freight train. The nighttime glory that was the sprawling city of New Pittsburgh spread before them.

The train whistle sounded again, closer now. Jacob swallowed hard, glancing behind him and trying to make out whether there was movement on the tracks that ran alongside the river on both banks. Trains ran all day and night in New Pittsburgh, and the tracks to the mills were among the busiest in the bustling industrial city. The eerie, lonesome sound of train whistles echoed from the steep hillsides, but to Jacob's ear, the howl was definitely closer.

Halfway across, too far to turn back even if there weren't armed men waiting for them. Mitch was focused on the orbs, dodging and weaving overhead. Mitch put on a burst of speed, trying to close the gap with the closest orb, his "harpoon" already in hand. Swearing mightily, Jacob readied his own harpoon-gun, wondering if the grappling hook could possibly find purchase in whatever the glittering orbs were made of.

He caught up to Mitch, who had stopped his bike in the center of the bridge. Mitch had tied off the end of his elastic rope to one of the main bridge supports, and just as Jacob pulled alongside, Mitch raised the gun and fired. The grappling hook sailed into the night sky, and to Jacob's astonishment, he heard a clang as metal tore into metal. The line uncoiled fast as the orb headed away.

The train whistle sounded again, much closer. This time, a blinding light accompanied it, down at the far end of the bridge, rapidly growing closer.

"Mitch! Train!" Jacob shouted, too terrified to be angry. The bridge shook with the might of the steam locomotive that hurtled toward them, closing the distance with every second. The rhythm of the pistons was a death knell. Even if going back didn't mean a chest full of lead, their steam bikes could never outrun the train. Jacob eyed the dark water beneath them, a drop of at least fifty feet into the icy current.

"You've got your gun?" Mitch asked, eyeing the train.

"Here." Jacob shoved the gun to his partner. *There won't be enough left of me for Last Rites,* Jacob thought as the train thundered closer.

"Give it to me, and let me drive!" Mitch shouted, climbing onto the bike in front of Jacob. Since death was inevitable, Jacob didn't feel like arguing. Mitch handed him the back end of the second elastic rope.

"Tie this around us. Hurry." And with that, Mitch kicked the bike to life, riding straight for the oncoming train.

Soldiers keep moving when the brain freezes in terror. Jacob's training took over, and he wound the end of the rope around their chests, under their arms, knotting it securely. *It won't matter. There won't be enough left of us to identify.*

Behind them, the orb Mitch had hooked with his shot strained against the rope, pulling it tight, jerking the orb back and down.

"Here. We. Go!" Mitch shouted.

The train was close enough for Jacob to read the manufacturer's plate on the front. He heard the second harpoon gun discharge, then Mitch tore the steam bike to the right, hitting the rail at full speed and vaulting over the side. They were falling in darkness, toward the pitiless waters of the Mon River. Mitch kicked the bike away from them. Sheer panic made them hang on to each other like drowning men.

Overhead, the train hurtled past, as the orb gave a mechanical shriek and fell out of the sky, colliding with the train's engine. An explosion rent the night as the train and the orb became a massive fireball, thundering toward calamity when the freight train reached the rail yard.

Jacob was muttering the words of the Hail Mary as they plummeted. Mitch was bellowing the tune of a drinking song. Five feet above the inky waters, the elastic rope caught with a force Jacob thought would rip his arms off. Caught—and held.

He had only an instant to process not-dying before the elastic jerked them back into the air, then dropped them again so close to the water that Jacob might have been able to touch the rippling surface had he been head-down and not holding on for dear life to his partner, who had just as tight a death grip in return.

Five times they bounced, as overhead, the sound of ripping metal and the screams of panicked men filled the air. A series of bone-jarring crashes told Jacob that the train had missed its turn, and its cars were piling up near where the guards had squeezed off their last shots.

Finally, their momentum spent, the elastic rope left them dangling in the cold night air.

"I hate you," Jacob said.

"Wouldn't have it any other way," Mitch said. His wide grin and the light in his eyes told Jacob that Mitch had enjoyed the evening far too much.

"Now what?"

Mitch whipped a knife out of a sheath at his belt and severed the cord before Jacob could protest. They dropped like stones into the cold water, fighting the current to make it to the opposite shore.

Jacob sputtered as he pulled himself out of the river and onto the bank. "That's the second time you've nearly drowned me in as many days," Jacob growled, wringing the water from his sodden clothing.

"We're alive."

Jacob glared at him. "We lost the bikes."

Mitch shrugged. "Adam knew it was a risk when he gave them to us." He grinned. "Come on. Let's get back to the room. I think one of the trackers stuck."

"We just crashed a freight train into the Edgar Thomson Works," Jacob pointed out, holding onto his anger because it was his last, slipping link to sanity. "They shoot saboteurs for less!"

Mitch started walking. "Good thing, then, that we're on the other side of the river, huh?"

* * *

Not enough remained of the wrecked train or the orb that collided with it to find any trace of the tracking device. Disguised in stolen police uniforms, Jacob and Mitch heard the railroad inspector exclaim over the unusually hot fire from the explosion, and had gotten close enough to the wreckage to assure that nothing of the orb had survived.

Late the next night, Jacob watched from the ground as Mitch climbed to the top of the tallest brick smokestack towering over the Jones and Laughlin steel mill. They had left the car down the road, and Hans and the Werkman were taking opposite circuits, roaming the night to make sure they did not get disturbed.

The guard at the gate had appreciated the beer Jacob had brought him, until his eyes had rolled back in his head and he had slumped to the floor of his gatehouse. Once he awoke, he'd have a nasty headache, but no memory of how he had gotten there and no lasting after-effects.

The muted tapping of Morse Code sounded close to Jacob's ear from the receiver on his coat collar. Mitch was in place. Jacob chewed his unlit cigar, wishing he was sitting in Mirko's Bar, drinking beer and smoking his stogie down to the stub.

Jacob maneuvered himself into position. He was next to the main power line coming into the plant, and he had tapped in with one of the Department's gadgets so that he could watch any fluctuations in the electricity and send a warning to Mitch. Up on the tower, Mitch had a shotgun ready, loaded not with bullets, but with a gadget of his own making. The Very Pistol shot from the other night had hit but not stuck, leaving them with no tracking information to show for their trouble.

The dial in Jacob's hand spun wildly. *This is it*, Jacob thought, chomping down on his cigar. He tapped out "go" on his wrist piece, signaling Mitch to be ready to shoot. He looked up, but he couldn't see Mitch against the darkness.

Overhead, two orbs danced against the night sky as the mill's lights dimmed until they were almost dark.

Jacob heard the crack of the shotgun. A heartbeat later, an explosion rocked the ground. Fire blossomed where the orbs had been. Jacob thought he saw a shadow fall from the tower. The shockwave shattered windows in the mill, spraying the area with broken glass. The explosion rocked the ground and made the steel roof groan. Its force sent Jacob sprawling, and for a heart-stopping moment, he thought he saw the tall brick tower sway before the whole world went dark and silent. Slowly the sound returned. He heard alarm bells clamoring, and men shouting, whistles shrieking and footsteps pounding closer. The mill was dark but his eyes were now adjusting to the moonlight.

If we get caught, they'll assume we're saboteurs and the Department will probably let us hang, Jacob thought.

"You need to get out of here now, sir." Hans had come up behind Jacob without a sound.

"Not without Mitch," Jacob said. "He was up on that tower, but I don't know how he could have kept his hold with that blast."

"Werkman is retrieving him. I'll keep watch." Hans usually went to great lengths to hide his adaptations but now, his clockwork additions propelled him across the short distance to the tower faster than any Olympic sprinter. Jacob saw Hans connect with the Werkman as they circled the tower, then the Werkman went up the tower like a mechanical spider, scaling it without a living being's regard for pain or fatigue. Jacob squinted, trying to follow his movement, but it was too dark. He had seen a shadowy figure fall when the explosion hit, and his gut clenched. The tower was far too high for anyone to survive a drop like that.

"You there! Stop!" A guard shouted in heavily-accented English.

"I just came out to take a piss," Jacob said in Polish, before he clocked the guard with a roundhouse punch. "Sorry about that," he added under his breath.

"Run!" Hans yelled. "We've got him." Jacob glimpsed that the Werkman carried a body in his arms and his throat tightened.

"Get Mitch to the carriage," Jacob ordered. "We've got to see what kind of debris that thing left behind. I've got false papers, just in case. I'll be fine. Go!"

Hans and the Werkman melted into the darkness with the faint hum and click of gears. Jacob dragged the unfortunate guard into the shadows, and lit his cigar.

"Stop or I'll shoot!" The speaker wore a guard's uniform, but the voice sounded like it had barely reached puberty.

"Will you now, lad?" Jacob replied, his voice heavy with an

Irish brogue. "Don't make more trouble for yourself than you're already in with the Inspector." At that, Jacob flashed the badge in his pocket.

"Pinkertons, Special Agent Cavanaugh," he snapped. "And put that damn gun down, boy, before I shoot it out of your hand."

"There was an explosion … Anarchists …" The young guard was pale with fright and the gun in his grip trembled so hard Jacob feared he might get shot by accident.

"The gun," Jacob ordered. "Put it down, lad. I'm on your side, and I'm here to help."

The guard lowered the gun but seemed rooted to his spot. "Come with me," Jacob said, puffing on his cigar and striding toward the darkened mill. In the moonlight, he could see the millworkers standing in small groups, talking in hushed voices in a babble of languages from across Europe's poorer nations.

"What did you see?" Jacob asked briskly. Between the guard's fright over the explosion and his terror of being in trouble with the Inspector, the young man nearly fell over himself to clear the way for Jacob and maneuver them through the onlookers with official prerogative.

"I was walking my rounds, sir, and I saw those damned orbs in the sky, the ones that show up before the lights dim," the guard replied, his voice reedy and tremulous.

"And then?" Jacob snapped, knowing that the more he kept the guard off-balance, the less likely it was for the man to question his authority.

"I thought I heard a shot, and then the sky lit up and I got knocked flat on my ass," the guard replied. "Sir."

"You heard a shot?" Jacob countered. "Are you sure? Could it have been a weather balloon popping?"

The guard looked doubtful and scared. "Maybe. I guess so, sir."

Jacob nodded. "I thought so," he said, and let out a string of curses. "Damned government Weather Service. Send those flimsy balloons up to look for storms and they drift loose and something like this happens." He gestured with his cigar. "Your boss should send in a bill to the government for all the lost production time, that's what he ought to do," he grumbled.

"What are we looking for, sir?" the guard asked as Jacob began to stride up and down along the side of the building nearest the blast. He could see where a section of the sheet metal in the roof had bowed with the force, and several of the air vents on the roof peak canted to the side. Shards of glass littered the ground.

"Bits of weather balloon, strange pieces of metal, anything that doesn't belong," Jacob replied tersely. "Find some, and you'll be a hero for your boss. I imagine with proof like that—after the Pinkertons validate it, of course—he wouldn't have any trouble at all getting damages back from the government."

Jacob tried to hold off the thoughts that crowded into his mind. *Mitch wasn't moving. He must have fallen. Dammit! He's dead and the least I can do is get the goods on whatever it was that put off that blast. Damn.*

Near the base of the brick tower, Jacob spotted a spent shotgun shell and pocketed it before his helper could see. But nowhere were other debris in evidence, other than the obvious damage to the steel mill. No canvas skin for an airship or a weather balloon, no bits of metal from the engine or frame, nothing that seemed odd, out of place or even slightly alien in any sense of the word.

"How could they just vanish like that without leaving debris?" the young guard wondered aloud.

Jacob puffed on his cigar. "That's the thing with these weather balloons nowadays, built so flimsy that it probably burned up completely in that fireball." He gave the boy a look. "Be glad it wasn't one of those big airships raining fiery bits down on everyone."

He made a show of scribbling in an otherwise empty notebook, then snapped the pad shut and slipped it into his pocket. "Looks like we're done here. I'll file a report and make sure I put in a good word for you," he said. "You've been a good lad, maybe there's a promotion in it for you."

"Thank you, sir. Kind of you, sir. Is there anything else I can do to help, sir?" the young guard asked, looking like a hungry puppy, eager to please.

Jacob gave a curt shake of his head. "No, I think I've got everything I need. If they find something, make sure your boss knows to send it in for a claim to the government. You deserve to be compensated."

"I will, sir. Thank you, sir."

As they had talked, Jacob had maneuvered them back along the building until they were near the fence. "That's it then." He paused. "You'd better go see what's going on," he said, pointing along the back of the mill, far removed from where the rest of the action was. "I just saw a man in a supervisor's hat waving to you."

The young guard peered into the shadows, but saw nothing. "Go on," Jacob urged. "You don't want to keep him waiting. I can find my way out." He waited until the guard had turned the corner before he headed off at a brisk walk for the hole in the fence they had used to enter. There was enough commotion near the front of the plant that Jacob's exit went unnoticed, and he soon made his way back to where Hans and the Werkman had hidden the carriage.

"I was about to come looking for you, sir," Hans informed him.

"I'm here," Jacob said. His mood had soured considerably on the walk, now that the reality of what happened had sunk in. *Falken will have my head, and I don't care. I lost a good partner. Those are hard to come by. What a stupid way to die.*

"Tell him to get his *dupa* in the carriage so we can get going." Mitch's voice was strained but there was no mistaking the speaker.

Jacob climbed in, utterly bewildered. Mitch sat on the other side of the compartment, stiffly positioned against the cushions. One eye was well on its way to swelling closed and his shoulder looked oddly askew. Mitch's clothes were torn and from his shallow breathing, Jacob guessed he had cracked a couple of ribs. "What the hell?" Jacob said as Hans got the carriage in motion.

Mitch's eyes widened in pain as the carriage bumped down the rutted access road, and he went pale. "You don't happen to have a flask on you, do you?" he asked, his voice thin.

Jacob chuckled and pulled one from his boot. He cranked off the cap and handed it across. Mitch took a hearty swig. "I saw you fall," Jacob said, still reeling from the turn of events.

Mitch let out a ragged breath. "I did. But I'd used a safety cable—my father built some bridges in his time and it was something he always did in high places. I figured the recoil might put me off balance—never figured on blowing the damn thing up." He gave a chuckle that sounded as if it hurt.

"The Werkman found me dangling and unconscious. I swung when I fell and hit the side of the tower hard enough to knock me out and break a few bones. He and Hans got me down."

"Damn, you gave me a scare," Jacob admitted.

"Me, too," Mitch replied. "Did you find anything?"

Jacob shook his head. "Just your shell casing, which I've got. No other debris, which there should have been if it had been an airship."

"Check the instruments, sir," Hans said. Mitch pointed to a bulky receiver on the seat next to Jacob

"What do you—" Mitch started to say, but gasped in pain at the effort and fell back, looking as if he were going to pass out.

"I'll have a look." Jacob waved Mitch silent and took over. It was a rare turn of events, and usually happened only when Mitch was bleeding.

"The tracker appears to have connected with its target," Jacob mused. "And it's headed East, toward the ocean."

"Told you!" Mitch's exultation was dimmed considerably by his broken ribs.

"But this can't be right. It's moving too fast—and rising quickly." Jacob shook his head, staring at the rapidly fluctuating dial. "I don't know of any experimental craft that can go that fast or that high—wait!" He gently jiggled the indicator, and then looked up, mystified. "It's gone. The dials are all at zero."

"So what was it?" Mitch asked between gritted teeth. "European spies? Or Farber's 'visitors?'"

Jacob was still staring at the indicators as if they might suddenly reveal the answer, but they remained lifeless. "I don't know," he said quietly.

He opened his flask, took a swig, and passed it to Mitch. "Let's get you to a doctor," Jacob added, leaning forward to give instructions to Hans. He settled into his seat. "We need to get you patched up. Because I bet they'll be back. Especially now that you've shot down two of them."

"And how do we write up this one for the Department?" Mitch wheezed.

"Like always. Supernatural phenomenon, source unknown …"

Steamsuit

David J. Fortier

"E.J. Barlowe, Inventor Extraordinaire?" The man's voice was rich and deep.

Emily spun around and nearly answered before remembering her façade. Her heart raced from her near mistake. No proper woman in London would be, or could be, an inventor. As far as everyone knew, the actor she'd hired to make public presentations was E.J. Barlowe, and she was simply his assistant.

The man standing in front of her wore an expensive black suit and glistening top hat, but his plain metal pocket watch avoided ostentatiousness. The unconventional cane handle, shaped like a bird beak, provided a touch of unique style to the conservative attire. Not a lord, though certainly a man of importance.

A second man in black with no hat or cane hovered outside the back stairs of her long workshop wagon. Through the flickering gap in the curtain a third man, broad shouldered with thick mustache, stood watch on stage near her latest invention—the steamsuit. Who were these men and what was going on?

Emily drew on the dim-witted voice she used to play the assistant, and let her nervousness affect her tone, "Mr. Barlowe is not here right now, sir. Would you like to leave a card?"

"I'm not here to see Mr. Driscol, your actor," the gentleman said with no hint of amusement. "I'm here to see you Miss Barlowe. But where are my manners? Mr. Richard Smythe." He removed his hat and bowed low, as if addressing a lady from lesser nobility.

If he knew who she was and knew where she came from …

Emily hesitated, her fingers covered in grease. She would have wiped them on her smudged gray overalls or the stained green apron, but there was no clean place left to wipe. Reluctantly, she extended her hand. He gently held her fingers, and she tensed, still uncertain as to his motives. His lips didn't touch her skin, appropriate given their unfamiliarity. When he released her hand, she breathed a little easier and assumed a tone her mother would have approved of: "And where do you come calling from, Mr. Smythe?"

"I am not permitted to say, exactly." He casually wiped the grease on a pocket handkerchief as if nothing had happened. "Though, I am in Her Majesty's service."

What did a secret branch of the government want? Emily's throat tightened.

For a moment, she considered bolting, but realized they were probably not here to apprehend her. They wouldn't care about the overdue bills for her mother's sick care, and hiring an actor to play E. J. Barlowe while posing as his assistant might be worth a constable, but not three of Her Majesty's finest.

"No doubt, you are aware of the large obstruction hovering over the Thames west of London, beyond the town of Reading."

"I am, Mr. Smythe, when I first heard of it, I freed myself of previous engagements and travelled with haste to investigate. By the time I arrived, Reading had been evacuated and all paths forward were blocked by soldiers. My time, wasted. And for what? To observe this 'obstruction' from so far away that I could only learn it looks like a thick-seated bar stool with four legs. The soldiers called it a water treatment device." She scoffed. "If you wanted to clean up the Thames, you would place it near London. I don't buy it, and I don't think anybody else does either."

"Indeed," Smythe replied. "That's been our cover story from day one for lack of better ideas. It's an alien craft that arrived from the northwest two weeks ago. Initially, we sent out some of our finest translators and communicators in an attempt to contact the craft. They failed. Her Majesty's navy has tried to board the vessel, and were attacked by four appendages, much like giant octopus tentacles. Guns and mortars couldn't damage the craft and several sailors died in that confrontation." Mr. Smythe's voice choked up, but he quickly regained his composure. "Our divers learned that two legs are sucking clean water in upstream, while two other legs are pumping out some kind of dark-blue sludge downstream. They collected a sample and it's highly toxic. Within days, the divers suffered convulsions and strange growths before going into a coma."

"What do you need of me, Mr. Smythe?"

"One of our airships has seen the top of the alien craft. There are hatches that open up at regular intervals, emitting a mist of some kind. We believe your knowledge of steam power and pumps would help us gain access and stop the pollution before it reaches London. I can't provide details now. We've been instructed to bring you and your possessions to a secret location to discuss the particulars."

Emily felt mildly abashed at her tirade, as it seemed keeping her away had been for her own protection. Still, if they had been less pig-headed at Reading or she more insistent, she could have helped learn about the toxic material and possibly helped the divers avoid injury. Since Emily's mother had fallen ill from contaminated water, Emily's studies and inventions had become more environmentally focused.

Emily's mind raced. There was also the prospect of an alien ship, filled with new technology.

"Very well, Mr. Smythe. Let me pack my things."

* * *

Emily crossed the small wooden stage to her steamsuit, which looked like nothing more than a rusty, old suit of plate armor with a metal backpack. The suit had been designed to help workers with heavy, dangerous labor, though she'd yet to find a buyer. She cranked the mini-bellows on the pack and waited for the internal boiler to heat the water to steam. The suit hissed and clanged as the metal pipes that ran along the outside of the legs and arms filled.

Smythe's man nodded in a polite business sort of way, but that didn't stop a chill from running up her spine. Their story sounded plausible, but she didn't know their true intentions. She opened the modified front of the suit like a grandfather clock and stepped inside before adjusting the straps on the internal framing.

Her worry melted away, encased in her steam-powered suit of armor.

After a few minutes, the first pistons released with small audible click and she used the steamsuit to move the trashcrusher and rest of her heavy inventions inside the mobile workshop, a feat that would have taken several grown men. Then she raised the stage and secured the safety locks on all the hatches, protecting her investments. Lastly, she walked the steamsuit back inside and hesitated, not wanting to leave its safety and security.

But she needed to do this, to prevent further pollution and illness to the people of London, and maybe help discover a way of helping the divers.

Resolved to do her part despite the unknown, Emily unstrapped the steamsuit and exited through the back door. With everything secured, she fired up the workshop boiler, which powered Trotter, her mechanical horse. Using the control box on the reins, she steered Trotter through south London, anxiously following Mr. Smythe, who rode horseback. His men trailed her. After winding through a labyrinth of turns toward the docks, they reached a decrepit red brick warehouse, where a man with Smythe's build leaned on a carriage house door.

Emily shut Trotter down with the control box and secretly kicked the master switch by her feet, effectively making the horse a quarter ton of immovable steel and coal. She couldn't shake the feeling that this wasn't going to turn out well.

"Could you bring your steamsuit inside?" Smythe asked.

The steamsuit? His request felt peculiar, though Emily didn't mind the security it offered. Once again she donned her steamsuit and followed Smythe down an old stone staircase to an underground boat launch, where water from the Thames sloshed against blackened stone. Several low-profile steamships with Her Majesty's Navy insignia bobbed in the water, some appearing damaged. Her armored footsteps echoed as they passed a pair of thick-necked men guarding open double doors to a bright room lit by several gas-lamps.

The room was no more than twenty yards square, lined on two walls with tables cluttered with familiar brackets and hoses, greasy rags, and various tools. The room resembled her workshop, only less organized. An elderly man with gray hair and spectacles was discussing something with several other men nearly half his age, all older than Emily. His voice trailed off with her arrival, hand gesturing to a compression pack on one of four steamsuits.

Emily's latest creation.

Crafted in secret.

Driscol, that damnable shady actor. She should never have trusted him.

"You've stolen my steamsuit," her voice echoed from within her helm. She hurriedly started unstrapping herself, while addressing Smythe directly. "Did Driscol at least get paid well?"

"I assure you, Miss Barlowe, we're only borrowing it," Smythe said. "And if all goes well, we will pay for use of your designs, enough to cover your debts and more."

Emily pushed her way out of the armor and hurried forward to inspect the suit the men had been discussing.

"Gentlemen, this is the aforementioned E.J. Barlowe, inventor of the steamsuit." All the men seemed shocked that she was a woman, a testament to her widespread promotion in London. "Miss Barlowe, this is Robert Johns, lead engineer and his team of technicians."

Smythe shuffled along beside her. "We would have let you in on this sooner, but we had to keep the suits a secret. There are Members of Parliament who believe the aliens are benevolent and we cannot fully disclose the danger of the toxic material without causing widespread panic. Please believe me when I say that I wanted to be up front about this, Miss Barlowe.

"Miss Barlowe?"

Emily had heard what he had said, but it didn't change what they had done. She buried her fuming anger with curiosity about the new suits. Unlike hers, which was made of heavy, pitted steel and pig-iron piping, these suits were made from a thinner, polished steel and copper pipes. These suits would be lighter and stronger than anything she could have made.

"Miss Barlowe?" Smythe repeated.

She checked connections and fittings, pressure gauges and pumps, noticing problems.

"Let me guess. They're overheating," Emily said to Mr. Johns.

The elder scientist smiled like a grandfather, while the younger men stared at her with condescending glares.

"And the left arm loses power."

One of the men nodded reluctantly, a thin man who stood next to Mr. Johns and seemed to be feeding off his elder's body language.

"And you're blowing couplings on the pressure pack right before—

"You haven't had any blow up on you?" Emily's shoulders tensed and stomach knotted in fear. "Nobody's been hurt, have they?"

Mr. Johns stepped forward, "Yes, we've lost a friend because of an explosion and a few more have been injured. Could you explain how you so accurately described the problems we're having?"

"I'm sorry. I really am," Emily said, chest feeling heavy. "Yes, I can tell you why you're having problems. Because Smythe stole plans for the old version, before I made adjustments to stop overheating."

"You can fix this," Smythe said. It could have been a question, but sounded more like confirmation.

"I can, but to what end? How is my invention going to be of any use?"

"We're going to equip four men in steamsuits, then drop them from an airship on the alien craft so they can get inside and stop the aliens. But we have to hurry. Even by closing the locks between Reading and London, by our calculations, if we don't stop the craft within a week there will be too much toxins in the Thames. It will flow downstream and contaminate our drinking water and much of London's population will be affected."

"We'll be hard pressed, but with the help of your people I can do it," Emily promised.

She knew Smythe wasn't telling her everything. Her suits would grant great strength, and protect the wearer from harm, but it didn't explain how they intended to use the suits to stop the aliens. She trusted the answers would come in time, once she had proven herself.

* * *

Three days passed and the team worked frantically with Emily to reverse the packs, reinstall hoses, adjust couplings and modify the suits to prevent overheating. Two suits eventually worked, but the others still overheated regularly.

Late in the evening on the fourth day, hungry and exhausted, Emily found the problem with the third suit: a weak pressure valve inside the compression pack that needed to be replaced. She built one, working into the night and the next morning and had the third suit ready come morning on the fifth day. But it wouldn't be enough. There was no way their fourth suit would be ready in time.

"Does it have to be these four?" she asked, glancing around the room.

Smythe's his eyes lit up. "Any four will do."

After topping off the water and firing up her suit, she checked it over with the team. They made adjustments so it would fit one of the sailors, who was clearly larger than Emily. Satisfied that she had done all she could, Emily followed the entourage up to the roof.

There she watched the arrival of the largest airship she had ever seen.

* * *

The *Queen Mary* approached, growing with every minute and looking to blot out the bleak sky above London with her bronze and gunmetal frame. The cabin beneath could have housed a battalion of soldiers or heavy machinery, larger than Emily's wagon. The airship docked with the smooth precision of an experienced pilot, resting close enough to the building's retaining wall to hop across without effort. Emily waited for the ramp to lower.

Smythe gestured for her to precede him, and they entered into the loading bay and watched as four sailors wearing steamsuits carried two large racks up the ramp. Within each swayed a large green cylinder labeled with explosive warnings. They strapped the two bombs against the wall and then returned for two more.

It all became clear. They were not going inside to stop the aliens from discharging poison into the Thames, they were going to load the alien craft full of explosives and blow it to smithereens. She bit her lip.

Emily didn't know much about bombs, but if these had to be loaded onto an oversized airship with her steamsuits, they clearly were bigger than anything used before. But wouldn't this spew the toxins into the river and potentially all across the English countryside? What if the toxins were still dangerous when airborne?

"Why such large explosives?" she demanded.

"Of course you noticed," he said, sighing. "I expected you to. We calculated that an explosion of this magnitude will vaporize the toxins that the craft is carrying. Anything short of this might only scatter the toxins to the four winds. I'm sorry we didn't tell you, but we can't let word get out of the attack."

"So you need four steamsuits to lower four bombs inside the alien craft. What are the risks of an explosion that size?"

"As with any problem of this enormity, there are side risks. Not all of the toxins may be destroyed. Those camped outside of Reading and the surrounding towns may be affected by the blast. But fewer will be harmed than if we allow the ship to continue polluting the Thames."

Emily knew nothing she could say would make a difference. Smythe's team would throw away a huge opportunity to gain knowledge and technology by destroying the aliens outright. There could be an abundance of things to be learned: where the alien craft came from, how it was powered, and what the toxins were. Too impatient—or perhaps too frightened—to find a peaceful solution, they would react with mindless violence, destroying what they did not understand.

Fools.

With a heavy rumble and a rhythmic thumping, the *Queen Mary* lurched skyward, groaning like a lazy ox. It was truly amazing that the behemoth could fly and Emily pondered the scientific principles that made air travel possible. It helped distract her, but not for long. The four sailors powered down their suits to conserve resources and stepped out of them for the flight.

The trip north of Reading, where the alien craft was gobbling up the Thames and dumping out poison, was scheduled to take two hours. Enough time for Emily to busy herself, checking gauges and connections and reloading the coal and water for each suit so that they would have full strength.

* * *

A terrible screech of metal grinding on metal vibrated down to Emily's bones. She looked away from the empty suit she was prepping. Mechanical failure? No. Something else. The grating continued, louder from her side of the airship.

Through a port window she witnessed a mass of dark metal sway through the air like a giant octopus tentacle—toward the *Queen Mary*.

Her heart raced. They were flying too low.

Emily grabbed a bench with both hands just as the tentacle hit the hull of the airship.

One second she was in a confined area, full of sailors, steamsuits, and armaments. Then metal tore as easily as wet paper. The next second, the front of the cabin had been replaced with sky, clear and blue and so very open.

Without a pilot, the *Queen Mary* lurched forward, imbalanced, swaying violently from side to side in stomach-churning motions as people and gear fell into the emptiness.

The tentacle retreated.

"Emily!" Smythe shouted from the floor, holding onto the edge of the opening.

She started to rise, still clutching the bench.

"The parachutes."

Right.

Bracing herself against the airship's sway, she quickly unfastened the straps holding a bundle of parachutes, letting some spill free and throwing others toward the crew who were clinging to parts of the cabin. A pair slid down the deck toward Smythe, who let go of the deck with one hand and struggled to loop his arm through a strap.

Just then, one of the explosive racks tore itself loose with an ear-piercing whine and skimmed down the deck toward Smythe.

"Look out!" Emily shouted over the howling wind and grating metal.

Smythe quickly switched hands, but before he could fasten the front buckle, the approaching rack forced him out into the open air.

Emily stared at the destruction, mouth agape. Three sailors and two of the suits were gone. One sailor, who must have been near his suit, was strapping in and powering up. He clipped a thick metal cable to the suit and nodded to Emily.

Emily squeezed the coarse fabric of the parachute in her hand, frozen. This was their only chance to stop the aliens from polluting their water. She imagined people getting sick from the toxins, growths appearing on their faces and arms, their bodies going into shock and a coma. Worse than her mother, who lay in bed nursed daily by a stranger. She had to do something, and now.

There was still one suit left: hers. And a support cable swung nearby.

She let the parachute fall and grabbed the dangling cable. Then, pushing off from the hull with both legs, she swung over to her suit. In seconds, she had both legs in place and locked in. It was too big at the moment, but that was the least of her worries. She fired up the compressor and fastened the support cable to the frame, then started shortening the legs.

The tentacle hit again, this time she heard a gush of air escape like a deflating balloon as the *Queen Mary* tipped and started descending. The top of the alien craft hovered below. She licked her dry lips.

They were running out of time. She cranked the chest and waist straps, pinching whatever tools still hid in her apron to her body. No time for comfort.

"Release!" the sailor shouted and they each hit their locks. Both winches whined as the metal cables spooled out, bouncing them across the deck and out through the opening toward the flaming front end of the airship. Emily choked on the smoke.

Then they were falling. Fast. Too fast. The *Queen Mary* wasn't supposed to be descending with them.

"Unhook on impact!" the sailor shouted.

With a series of echoing clangs, her steamsuit landed on the alien craft and only being strapped in tight kept her legs from buckling. She fell to one side, arms slipping within the suit for purchase, banging around inside. Something snapped and her left hand felt as though she held a hot coal. She lay there on her back, watching the *Queen Mary* descend, flames leaping from the front where the hydrogen was escaping.

Metal clanged, getting louder. Footsteps. The sailor hovered over her, partially eclipsing the spectacle above, unhooking the cables and dragging Emily toward the center of the alien craft. They weren't going to make it; the *Queen Mary* was too enormous. Emily squinted, not wanting to watch, but unable to look away.

Then a second tentacle slammed into the airship like a child swatting an oblong balloon.

The *Queen Mary* collapsed, the air suddenly becoming thin. Then the gigantic ship of brass and steel exploded first in a bright orange hydrogen fireball, then a secondary blue-tinged explosion that tore off the end of the tentacle. It was beautiful and dreadful at the same time.

Flaming bits of the *Queen Mary* rained down around them. The stubby tentacle flailed and smoldered, billowing black smoke.

"We must get inside, quickly. But your arm—"

"I can still function using my steamsuit, though it will bloody hurt. But what can we do? We have no explosives." Her arm felt like it was going to burn up, pain shooting up into her shoulder and neck.

The sailor unlatched his hand, slid it free from his suit and started cinching her arms in tight. "We don't need explosives. You're E.J. Barlowe, Inventor Extraordinaire." He smiled. "I'm William Parsons, but you can call me Fish. I'll get us inside and you can stop them from dropping that toxic stuff. Agreed?"

Maybe if she could figure out the alien pump systems, she could disable, or even reverse them. “Very well, Fish,” she said, gritting her teeth against the pain. “Let’s get inside.”

He slid his hand back into his suit and used it effortlessly to help her up.

A series of panels lifted from the top of the craft, releasing colored mist. The ones that Smythe had mentioned. Fish ran to one just as it closed and started pulling up. It wouldn’t budge, even with the suit. It opened again, emitting a foul stench worse than the rotting vegetables and feces of a London alley.

“Get back.”

They scrambled away from the vent, coughing, eyes watering.

Fish shook a fist. “That was supposed to be our way in.”

“Not unless we’re climbing down into a tank of toxic sludge.” Emily ignored her pain and considered their problem. The ship was similar to a giant tank with hoses on either end, somehow draining the liquid from one side and filling from the other. Presumably they would have to keep the water and sludge separate, so there would need to be a divider to prevent them from mixing. That meant separate containers, and on the side where the water was being pumped in, air would have to be vented.

Water couldn’t fill the entire ship. Or could it? There had to be controls and mechanics, kept dry to operate. When Trotter sprung a leak, she had to find it quickly before it damaged his compression systems. Surely the same principles held true here.

“We need to find the controls. They should be in a space between the water tank and the outer hull.” It was a guess at best, but she tried to project confidence. “Maybe near the legs that are sucking up water on the north side.”

They scrambled across debris to reach the far side. To the north, a flailing tentacle swung angrily about, defending the legs on either side. Emily wondered if it could sense their presence, or if they were too small to be considered a threat.

“What about this?” Fish asked, forcing a release vent farther open above the leg.

The tentacle stopped, poising to strike.

"Inside!" she shouted.

Fish leapt inside and reached out to help her clamber in. Emily banged her arm awkwardly on the edge of the opening, tears welling up in her eyes.

The tentacle slammed the hatch shut behind them with finality, but they were in.

* * *

Emily and Fish climbed down between the solid outer hull and a smoky glasslike barrier that housed the water, using awkwardly-angled support posts as a makeshift ladder. Every movement sent vibrations shooting up Emily's arm and into her chest.

They stopped for a quick rest on the crossbars like children in a tree. Emily adjusted the waist cinch on her suit to check her apron to see what tools still remained. Not much. A small wrench, a few clamps, a screwdriver, and a hose coupling. Things she would use to make repairs or minor modifications. Nothing that would likely work on the alien technology. She rearranged her tools so they would not be crushed against her and re-tightened her steamsuit.

After at least an hour, maybe longer, they reached what seemed to be the bottom because the hull leveled out below them. Fish rapped on the smoky glass or whatever it was that held the water away from the hull.

"Bloody thick," he said, testing the barrier. "Strong too."

Emily said nothing, gritting back the numbing pain.

But he was right. The sheer pressure from the water had to be enormous. She wondered what kind of clear material could withstand that kind of pressure and if it could be manufactured in London.

A dozen creatures swam almost lazily to the glass where Fish had knocked. They were about four feet long and shaped like salamanders. Some were deep green with yellow spots, others black with orange spots. The cluster parted for a larger red one, which swam to the forefront.

Its head glowed faintly through what seemed like translucent skin. Emily felt suddenly lightheaded. Only the sturdy design of her steamsuit kept her standing. Her vision blurred, and Fish and the salamanders faded away, replaced by visions of muck.

Everywhere, the brown sludge covered the land, toxic fumes rising from slimy filth and brackish water. There were no buildings or cities, and the place didn't appear to be Earth. Not exactly. Salamanders climbed out of the water to plop down on the putrid shores, excreting slimy liquid from bulges in their skin. A deep green one approached a red spotted one and nudged it with a wet snout. The spotted one didn't move. They appeared sick, perhaps poisoned. Emily wanted to help them, to somehow make them better.

Then a craft appeared above them, on four legs, much like the one that Emily and Fish had climbed into. A ramp lowered and fresh water trickled down the ramp, beckoning the salamanders aboard.

The ones that could move freely climbed the ramp to face a tank of clean water. There, a red, glowing being transformed into a salamander and swam in the water. The salamanders climbed the smoky wall, and dove inside. Relief washed over Emily so strongly that her arm even felt better.

Then there was a sense of movement, passing through space and time. The salamanders multiplied. The water darkened and then lightened. The tank had been reduced in size, cramping them, making them sick again. All the while the red glowing one swam among them, healing some, feeding others. Eventually the light in the glowing one dimmed.

Then the vision faded.

"Miss Barlowe?"

Before Emily could respond, the red salamander changed several times into various creatures she'd never seen before, finally to something resembling a human, and then changing back to a salamander. It pulsed briefly and she sensed a feeling of hope and the expectation of a continued journey.

"These creatures escaped a dying world, saved by this red one, which isn't really one of them. They're trying to refill their ship with water, to stay alive longer, on a journey to find a new home."

"How?" Fish shook his head. "Even if it's true, it doesn't

change our mission, does it?"

Emily stared at the sickly creatures. Her chest ached for them. They only needed the clean water to survive. But then, so did the people of London, who depended on the Thames. How could she decide? This wasn't her place. She wasn't the Queen, or the Prime Minister, or even a Member of Parliament. She wasn't even responsible for any pets.

It didn't matter how much fresh water the ship needed, there was plenty enough for both the aliens and humans. But the toxic sludge was a different issue. Emily couldn't let people get sick the way the salamanders had on their world.

"You'll have to stop dropping the sludge," she said.

The red one flared.

"Fish, we need to find controls, switches, anything that looks like it can be toggled on and off. There has to be a way to stop the sludge."

He nodded and they began searching behind pipes and prying off panels. They found thin wires, a metallic web of crystals, and a panel that was radiating heat through the metal of the ship. Despite the dampness in the ship, here she started sweating. Still, there were no levers or switches. No controls.

Circling back, Emily caught sight of the red glowing one again. This time, the smoky wall of the tank flickered on the inside. Perhaps the alien manipulated the ship from within the water.

"We're stuck, Fish," she gestured to the creature. "It controls everything from inside. We would have to get in the tank to stop the sludge. We might as well just make a hole in the bottom and jump out."

"Except we'd drown in the suits," he said. "We'll have to leave them behind."

The idea made Emily's stomach churn. She'd rather destroy the steamsuits than leave them in the alien craft. But to destroy them, she'd have to undo the improvements she'd made.

That was it.

"If I reverse the super compressors on the packs back to the old design, the suits will overheat. If we were to set them on the highest power output and close the valves, when they explode they may do enough damage to stop the pumps or at least damage pipes." Even just damaging the pipes might buy the government enough time for another attempt.

"Good plan, but we only have two suits and there are four pipes."

"We stop the sludge. One suit per pipe."

Fish shook his head. "The bombs were supposed to incinerate that stuff. People are going to get sick."

Right.

They had to incinerate all the sludge, but how? She didn't know anything about the alien technology. Maybe the mechanisms of the alien craft could overheat like the suits. But even if they could, that would mean the aliens…

Emily's throat thickened and she felt a heavy weight growing on her shoulders. This wasn't a decision she could take lightly. These creatures had fought so hard to survive, travelled who knows how far, and she was going to wipe them out for the good of her people.

There had to be another way.

If they damaged the ship without destroying it, it might just crash to shore and leak more toxins. Or maybe it would fly away and trail toxins all over England. The possibilities were dreadful. Any option other than incinerating the toxins wasn't acceptable. Who knows how much damage the sludge had already caused?

Damn them. If only the aliens had responded peacefully when first contacted, maybe they could have worked together to find a solution. She stormed back to the warm panel and tore it free. Heat and blinding yellow light radiated out from inside a short tunnel to a bright room. She had to squint to look inside. She heard a deep, reverberating hum. She recognized that sound.

Power.

Inside the room, a glowing amber crystal atop a pedestal radiated heat. She tried to touch it, but an invisible force flickered and repelled her hand. Anything worthy of such protection must be important.

"We'll set them up in here."

Silence. He wasn't behind her.

"Fish!"

"Coming," he called, entering the tunnel. "What's the plan, Miss Barlowe?"

"We set the suits to overheat and lean them against the pedestal. Hopefully they do enough damage to set the ship and its contents aflame." Fish was already stepping out of his suit. Emily started to do the same, but stopped. If she used the strength of her suit to modify his, she wouldn't need tools. She loosened the straps holding her legs and broken arm, but kept the suit on. Feeling blood flow back into the limb more freely only made her head swim. She kept her good arm in the suit.

With the strength of her suit's gauntlet, she hoisted Fish's suit easily, leaned it on the pedestal, and crushed the hoses and valves leading out of the pack. Far more potent, and dangerous.

She stepped out of her suit and with his help leaned it against the pedestal. Then, donning one arm from his suit, she clamped down on her suit's pack. A tear formed in her eye and her chest tightened. Her greatest creation, meant to aid mankind, turned into a fearsome weapon.

She cranked the dials on both suits to full power. The super compressors banged and whirled as they boiled water. It was going to be quite the end.

"Let's go," Fish said, tugging on her arm.

"Go where?" she asked. Without the suits, they were trapped.

"I pried open a hatch to escape from."

She allowed herself to be led back through the tunnel. It was considerably cooler outside the room and Emily wiped her brow. Fish led her to a piece of bent metal and a small opening, barely big enough for him. The Thames sloshed below, beckoning them.

"You first," she said.

Fish crouched over the opening, then stopped, a blank stare on his face. Over his shoulder, Emily could see the lead salamander's head pulsing red. It must be communicating with him as it had earlier with Emily.

"Fish, we must hurry."

He didn't respond and was blocking the exit.

"Fish hurry, please."

Hissing whistled from inside the tunnel.

"Fish! William!"

Fish's eyes lit for a brief moment. He dropped through the hole and into the open air. Emily followed even as she was overcome by a mix of anger and sadness from the salamander.

The water's surface rushed toward her. She took a deep breath right before she made contact and plunged into the icy depths of the Thames, her arm flaring in pain.

From under water, she saw the alien craft explode in a fiery white ball brighter than the sun. She held her breath and kicked, trying to make the surface. Pain from her arm radiated through her entire body, nearly forcing her to scream. She surfaced, coughing and hacking.

She sputtered, sucking air, legs kicking to stay afloat while her arm throbbed. Then a strong arm reached around her and held her head out of the water.

Fingers of Steam, Veins of Gold

Brad Hafford

The following is a series of letters recently found in the attic of a derelict house in Tennessee. They tell an intriguing tale of the Steam Age, when automatons were primitive and humans were hardened to their environment. Addressed to a Miss Sally Chalmers of Knoxville, they were sent by her brother, Edward, who details his travels to the Klondike in pursuit of gold. Of great relevance to historians, some of the details are understandable only in light of later events, particularly the Interplanetary War.

* * *

Seattle, Washington
February 17, 1898

Dearest Sally,

Got your letters when I arrived in Seattle. Hope Pa is feeling better. Sounds like the Doc took good care of him. I know the two of you will be fine, and I'll bring back so much gold, we'll be set for life. Just you wait.

Lots of folks up here, all trying to get passage up coast to Alaska. Dirigible is booked up full for three months. Don't even go inland over the mountains, neither. Too much wind. Them that fly still got to take the trail, just like us poor folks. Wouldn't it be great to take a trip in the sky, though? See the world from up on high, like an angel looking down? One day, Sally, you and me and Pa, we'll up and fly around the world. You'll be the angel up there. Just you wait.

I got me a ticket on a third-class steamer headed out next week. Got supplies too. Jonas carries most of it so far, but from what I hear, I got to get a whole lot more. Mounties don't let you cross the border with less than 1,000 lbs per man. Jonas won't need no food, but I got to keep his boiler working and that takes wood, the way we built him. Remember that Sally? You and me, building a steam-butler? Seems ages ago. I think he misses you.

I'm thinking of converting him to coal. He'll get more heat for less weight of fuel and still be able to use wood in a pinch. Got to strengthen the boiler, though. I met an engineer who says he can help me. Name's Mike Radigan. Funny looking little guy with a flat nose like it been broke a couple times, but he's nice enough.

I'll drop this in the mail on the way to Radigan's shop.

Your Loving brother,
Edward

* * *

Dyea, Alaska
March 21, 1898

Dearest Sally,

This here country ain't like nothing you ever did see. Mountains keep getting taller the farther we go. Sheer sides dropping straight to sea, ice floating along in places. It's damn cold.

Radigan joined me, seeing how strong Jonas were and all. We converted him to coal and added a pressure drill for one of his arms. You wouldn't recognize old Jonas now, Sis. He's a regular mining machine.

It's good to have Radigan for company, but damned if he don't cheat at cards. Maybe he'll make us some money here in Dyea. Lots of saloons and gambling houses here. Seems every building is one or t'other. And folk's is paying for everything in gold dust. Prices so high I don't know as we can get our supplies. We got near 700 lbs each, but a ways to go. I got tobacco enough for the trip, but there's a 50 cent duty on it across the line. Maybe I'll sell it here, give up the habit.

More people here even than I expected. Me and Radigan is just two in a sea of hundreds arriving every day, all of them set on winning their fortune. All of us'll hit the trail to the river, then wait out the ice so as we can continue in boats to Dawson. Keep note of that, Sally. My address'll be Dawson City, North West Territories.

For now I get mail at Dyea, Alaska. Sad I ain't got a letter in the week or so I been here. Maybe you been sending to Seattle still. Don't do that no more, Sally. There's people will bring letters to me on the trail, but it costs a fair bit.

Yukoners is saying it's mighty rough out there, but I reckon Jonas can get us through. Some folks got steam-horses and laugh at our Jonas. But we'll show them Sally. We'll show them.

Love to Pa.
Edward

* * *

Chilikoot Trail
March 29, 1898

Dearest Sally,

We got our sleds on the trail now. Climbing all the while. It's mighty cold. Radigan's got the sniffles but I'm hanging in there as good as I can. We pull our gear a ways, rest a bit, fuel up Jonas, and do it again. I been cooking for us nights, beans and potatoes and such. We're doing pretty good as far as requirements to cross over into the Yukon. But fuel for Jonas adds at least another 1,000 lbs. He can't pull more than one sled at a time, so me and Radigan pull at one. It's mighty tough going.

It's funny watching those what thought they was clever bringing steam-horses up here. They ain't no good on the mountain. Higher and steeper we get, more they bog down or slip. I welded spikes on Jonas' feet so as he sets in and moves forward. Uses his weight to push toward the mountain 'stead of back against his rump. Steam-horses just fall back. One slid down near a thousand feet, crashing into sleds along the way. Fellas was arguing all day about who owed what.

Most folks is calling this place Scrap Heap Trail nowadays. Bunches of dead mechanicals out here in ditches, rusting metal sticking out of fresh snow like old bones. Raiders take what they can, a steam graveyard picked clean by vultures, then dusted over again with clean white. Seen the carcass of a steam-butler today. His head and steam-vent top-hat were all broke and bent, body gutted of gears, boiler gone. He had an enamel face like the one you done up for Jonas, but not as nice. And now it were all smashed and spidered. Don't want to see Jonas like that.

Candle's short so I'll stop for now.

* * *

Chilikoot Pass
April 1

Been the worst April Fools. Some folks is trying to lighten the mood, but this here climb ain't no joke. We're up past 5,000 feet in a never ending line. Jonas' gears can pull the tackle but he can't walk the sled at this angle. We're just trying to make it to the summit like everybody else, but you got to wait for the fella in front of you to step up afore you can move.

Worse, there's a storm raging. Getting colder and lots more wind pulling up old snow, mixing it with new. We got as far up this damn mountain as we could afore we braced for it. Summit can't be far, but damned if you can see it in this weather. We'll be in all day tomorrow I reckon. I'm in the tent now writing by a candle that's flicking like crazy. Just wanted to say that me and Jonas miss you. Still ain't heard from you and it's a damn sight lonely out here even though there's hundreds of us on this here mountain.

* * *

April 3

There's been a terrible landslide, Sally. Snow, ice, and rocks coming down like nobody's business. Covered all the lower pass and all the hundreds climbing. I reckon you might read about it in the papers, so want you to know I'm safe. Radigan and Jonas too. We just peaked the summit not hours afore the snow give out. I hurt my knee pretty good, though. Tackle broke just as our last sled mounted the top and the chain took my leg out from under me. Ain't nothing compared to what those poor saps below suffered not six hours later. Radigan rigged up a brace for me out of two pieces of sled runner. It ain't no easy task walking like this, but it's a damn sight better than being dead.

I set Jonas to helping dig folks out here near the top. Least they ain't more than a few feet buried. Even so, I seen three dead already. Hope I never have to see suffering like that again in all my days. A few others we got out alive. One, a kid, can't be more than 16, was climbing with his Pa. Can't find his Pa nowhere now. Makes me wonder how you and our Pa are doing.

I'll hand this letter off as soon as I find somebody going back to town. God help all those caught under the snow. And God look out for you and Pa. Me, I just got to keep pushing on.

Your Loving brother,
Edward

* * *

Lake Linderman
May 25, 1898

Dearest Sally,

Last night we saw a fire in the sky. A real, honest-to-God trail of fire right across the stars, bright as day. Made a screeching sound too, like cannon shot straining against the wind. Lots of folks is saying it's a sign, like what led the Wise Men. Either God is showing us where to go or punishing those what are already there.

For near three weeks we been building rafts and waiting on the river to thaw. Then we set out for Dawson, shooting rapids right along with chunks of ice as big as Jonas. It were mighty rough and plenty of folks ended up in the icy water. Rapids toss you about like nobody's business. We got through most, but in the end, Jonas come off the raft. We had him tied on, but he's mighty heavy and damned if the ropes didn't break. He went under and his fire went out, steam exploding off the cold river. Radigan and me spent the next two days dragging him out and drying him. Without his coal fire melting the freeze around us it's a damn sight colder. And if he can't start up again, our hopes of mining is pretty much gone. I'll get him fixed though. Don't you worry none.

My knee never did heal up right, but Radigan added gears to the brace and it works as good as you might think. Like a mechanical leg, but no steam power. Hurts like all hell, though. And all of us is getting testy, worried about staking our claims. They done hung two fellas here in Lake Linderman for stealing. At least they got the law. We ain't had to unpack our guns yet.

Write and let me know how things is back home. I see folks coming through with mail from time to time, but still none from you. I'll just keep writing no matter what. Honest to God, Sally, I'm here for you and Pa, not for me. I'm mighty sorry for leaving you and all, but it were the only way I could see as to get money enough to make it all right. I know I'm gone for a long time, but you always been the level-headed one and me all running off. I promise as I'll be back with lots of gold and it'll all be better.

Your Loving Brother,
Edward

* * *

Dawson City, N.W.T.
June 9, 1898

Dearest Sally,

Got your letter dated March 12. It were addressed to Seattle but one fella brung it to me here for a pretty penny. I was sore glad to get it, but mighty sad at the news it brung. I didn't know it were that bad. Hope he didn't suffer none too much.

I'm sore tempted to come home, but I can't quit now. And I been too long gone anyways. Pa'd understand. He never cottoned to a quitter. Hope you understand, too, Sally. I'll strike gold. Then I'll buy the nicest tombstone in the whole cemetery for our Pa.

We brought Jonas in like the rest of our cargo, leaving him cold and tied on the boat. Don't like seeing him like that, like he's dead. Don't want to think of Pa like that neither. I come to think of Jonas as one of the family, like I know you done from the beginning. But his boiler cracked and we had to get him to Dawson for repairs. Didn't have no money, and prices is mighty steep. Radigan made some gambling wins and I got the proper tools to repair Jonas myself. He's running pretty good again, steaming out his hat just as afore. One fella offered me good money for him once he seen him working. But I can't sell him, and 'sides, he's our ticket to striking real gold.

That fiery streak we saw a couple hundred miles out sure as everything come down right near here. Struck the central Klondike fields, near the top of the dome about 50 miles from Dawson. Some right crazy stories about that place being told now. They say folks what gets near ends up mad or dead. Some sort of electrics that makes a blue haze in the twilight, or so they say. Since nobody goes up there, I reckon it's where I got to go. I come too far to get scared now. And everything else is already staked out. If I can successfully dig into the dome, maybe I'll hit the mother lode. And with Jonas' help, I reckon I can do it.

Radigan met a fella playing cards who says he knows that area right good. Name's Davies, an old codger who's drunk as a skunk most of the time. Had no place to stay so he come out to our camp after Radigan took all his money. We give him some coffee and stew and he starts telling us stories. Been in the Klondike more than a year now and damned if he ain't seen everything. Swears he used to be a physician, so we call him Doc Davies. Not sure as we can trust what he says, what with all the whiskey he's put away, but he reckons that dome is where all the gold done welled up from within the earth and what the sourdoughs is getting out of the fields below is just small potatoes. Says he'll show us where to stake a claim.

By the time I write again, we'll be rich. Then I'll make it all up to you Sally. Can't bring Pa back, but we'll do it up right for him.

Edward

* * *

CRD Claim
July 1, 1898

Dearest Sally,

We got our claim but not sure as I'm happy about the way we got it. Strange things is happening. I didn't believe the stories about electrics I heard in Dawson, but some nights I swear the whole top of the mountain lights up, makes your tent go all green-blue and there's a crackling in the air makes your small hairs stand up. T'other night I went out to see it, and damn sorry I did. Shouldn't have seen whatever it were I seen. God's punishing me for it, or for leaving you and Pa. Probably both.

Not sure as I believe it myself, Sally, and I were there and got the scars to show for it. I heard something, something akin to that screeching in the sky we heard afore, only higher pitch still. I climb up the dome as far as I can, clouds gathering round as they shouldn't in June, and I swear a big metal ball were up there, half sticking out the mountain, glowing blue-white as the spring waters we used to jump in when we was kids. The whistling got louder and something sparked off the ball. Not sure as there were anybody really there but a shadow grew like a man and next thing I know another spark, a stabbing pain in my eye, and I'm falling.

Radigan found me next morning, leg brace bent double and my eye all burnt away, even the eyelid. Lucky Doc Davies were mostly sober and remembering some of his learning so as he could tend to me. Radigan climbed up the dome and swears there weren't no metal ball. He's seen the blue haze, though, and my eye got to say something happened. Some say I burnt it out with a stogie, too drunk to remember. Others that I got to welding on Jonas in my sleep, fell over and burnt out my eye. But that just ain't so.

It's been a week or more since, and it still hurts something awful. But Doc Davies says it burned clean and no other damage. Didn't lose no blood nor nothing like that. I can see out t'other eye good enough, I guess. Me and Radigan fixed the leg brace, but the fall done my leg real bad and Doc figures I'll have to wear it the rest of my life.

Most folks'd give up by now, but I ain't most folks. That gold got to be here, Sally. Just got to be. If it ain't, my whole trip were for naught. God can keep punishing me if he wants, but I ain't quitting.

Jonas been cutting through permafrost like nobody's business. Now he cuts direct into the side of this dome sticking out from the Klondike basin like a thumb. If there's gold, we'll find it sure enough. Radigan reckons somebody's trying to scare us away from it. I don't know, but we're keeping watch all the same. Unpacked our guns and expecting sure we might have to use them. Radigan's got the biggest shotgun you ever did see. Sure looks funny sitting there with a gun almost bigger than he is.

Don't worry about me, Sally. I know I'm talking some fright into you, and maybe I shouldn't tell you all that I been writing. I'm doing fine 'spite of all the hurting I've been through. You know me, Sis, I can take a beating. Just you tend to you, but let me know how things is. I'm damn sore curious. Ain't got a letter since that one in Dawson.

Even if you can't forgive me for leaving, I'm going to take care of you. I swear to it, Sally.

Your loving Brother,
Edward

* * *

Dawson City N.W.T.
July 10 1898

Dearest Sally,

I come into town today just for Church. Praying forgiveness

for all my wrongs and hoping the Good Lord will take me back into his graces. Most important, I got to tell you that we done it. We struck gold!

It were just a glitter in the wall, but damn sure a vein that goes deeper and bigger still. I'm praying to the Lord for more. It's mighty hard working the mine, even with Jonas holding his own against the mountain. Had a minor cave-in t'other day, but lucky for us Jonas held most of the tunnel stable. Now we got to brace the roof the deeper we go and it gets mighty hot in that small hole, what with Jonas' steam and all. He runs through coal faster than we eat, even with Doc Davies' mouth to feed too. Damn tough keeping Doc in whiskey, though.

Met a mighty strange man in Church today. He were all smart in his white shirt and pressed trousers. Nobody that clean round here. I right took him for the angel Gabriel at first. He come up to me after the service to ask if I were the fella digging on the dome. I seen gold in his eyes, but not the way you see it in most folks round here. It weren't the desire, but near the sparkling stuff itself. 'Stead of saying, "What's it to you?" I just said, "Sure am."

Turns out he's some sort of Lawman. Got a funny way of talking. All proper like. Says he "wants to know about the incident with my eye." I tell him the story, after a belt of rye round the saloon, knowing he weren't going to believe. But he don't doubt none.

I wear a patch over the eye now. Radigan says he can engineer a kind of loop, a monocle thing that the Doc can set in the socket. Maybe even get me some sight if the nerve's still working. Best to make it out of gold, since that'll set all right with the skin.

God bless and keep you, Sally. You're my only sister and my link to a better place. The gold is here, I just got to get it out of the mine and I'll be home afore you know it.

Edward

* * *

CRD Claim
July 30 1898

Dearest Sally,

I feel a might better these days. My leg's still hurting, mind you, but my head's not bad. Can't see all that good, and hard to tell how far away things is, but it don't hurt none. Best thing is we're getting gold out of this here mine. Not as much as I like, and it'll take time afore I can get enough to come home, but for now it's enough so as we can keep buying bracing materials and coal.

Our picks and shovels is sometimes getting all magnetic and sticking to Jonas with a mighty clank. Doc Davies says it's acause we're getting under the earth's skin, like lancing its boil, and down here there's things we don't understand, magnetics running like blood maybe. 'Course, he's still hitting the whiskey pretty hard. He couldn't fix my eyesight, but he set the monocle loop Radigan made pretty good. We're having a lens ground down to slot inside, but since Doc can't find a way to make my eye nerve work without no eyeball, it ain't going to do no good. Meanwhile, I slot a half dollar in there real nice. Damned if I don't look funnier than Radigan these days. All of us is haggard and worn like hobos, but we'll be rich soon enough. Just you wait.

That there Lawman come around t'other day. Damn near got hisself shot, seeing as he come in pretty late and we was drawing straws for first watch. I took the shift and stayed up talking to him. I swear he were as clean as the first day I met him, even though he must have walked through all the muck round these here creeks. And his hair's all in place even when he takes off his hat.

I ask his name and damned if he don't say "Forty-three." I tell him that's a strange name but he don't say nothing. Maybe it's a badge number or some such. I reckon I'll still call him Gabriel. He tells me he ain't found no "culprit" yet. Funny word that, some sort of legal-speak meaning crooked folk. He says he'll be round the dome a good deal, looking at the scene where it all happened. I guess there ain't no harm in that, but Radigan don't trust the fella. Thinks he's snooping round our gold mine, figuring we're about to hit it big.

I offer him a swig of whiskey but he don't take none. We play a hand of cards and then he look at my eye apiece. I ask him if he's a physician and he says no but he might can help. Takes out a cold metal stick and rolls it round my eyehole. There's a light from somewhere and that's when Radigan come in to take over the watch. Gabriel says his goodbyes and after he's gone Radigan tells me again that he don't trust him. Thinks he's getting direct to my brain through my missing eye. Radigan don't much seem to trust me these days neither.

Still waiting for a letter from you Sally. I ain't going to stop writing even if you ain't writing me. I'm going to keep believing it's just the mail not getting here. I got to believe that.

Your Loving Brother,
Edward

* * *

CRD Claim
August 19 1898

Dearest Sally,

Gold still coming, but never enough. Ain't hit the giant pot Doc Davies says is under this here boil of a dome but we get more every day. Doc and Radigan been arguing about how much each of us gets. I reckon I deserve most since it's Jonas as doing the heavy work. You and me built him, Sally. You deserve a second share, even if Jonas hisself don't need one.

I don't much like the way Radigan is acting these days. Doc seems happy enough, long as he got his drink, but he might just up and run off with the gold if you ask me. Got to keep an eye on both of them, but I only got one eye. One real eye. My other ain't truly working, but damned if that Lawman Gabriel didn't come through on his promise. He come round again and used that metal stick, sparkling like a lightning bug this time. Made my tongue twitch when he run it round the gold monocle. Smelled like frying pig fat for a second, but it didn't hurt none. He slots the big lens back in and then fits a movable one on a tiny swing arm. I ask if he's an engineer and he says no.

At first nothing happens, but after a few days, I can see a haze of things, movement and swirling colors. When I swing the smaller lens in front, damned if I can't make out shapes of people, all red and glowing, even at night. It's amazing strange. Hard to get used to, but it's better than being half blind. Now I got almost more moving parts than Jonas. Hope he ain't jealous.

Magnetics still acting up from time to time, and Radigan says it only happens when Gabriel's around. Funny enough, seems to be true. Sure is a strange coincidence.

Got to get back to work. That gold ain't going to mine itself. I'll be home afore you know it and we'll be richer than you ever did dream.

Edward

* * *

Dawson City
September 10 1898

Dearest Sally,

Ain't had much time to write lately. I don't much trust t'others, so I been watching them close. More gold we get, more I been thinking they done stashed extra away so as we can't split it up proper. Even though we get more and more, it all seems to go to buying supplies and we ain't got none to spend on ourselves. At least I ain't got none.

'Course, we spent a good deal fixing Jonas up after the last cave-in. Almost lost him for sure. Magnetics went all crazy and he flung up to the ceiling, all 800 lbs of him, along with wheelbarrows and picks and such. Took out the bracings and rock come down all around. Lucky for us it were only Jonas down deep. Spent the next week digging him out. He were too beat up for me and Radigan to fix, so we hauled him here to Dawson.

Other folks is taking to our methods now. They got drills bigger than Jonas and they dig tunnels on the mountain below. Guess they ain't scared no more. But maybe all that extra drilling is causing the electrics to get stronger. Radigan still blames Lawman Gabriel.

Gabriel did stop by our claim to check on my eye and to tell us he still ain't caught the fellas what done the damage. I reckon if it were a fella, he's long gone, but Gabriel thinks there's more than one and still here. We seen most nobody on watch these long nights, so I can't see as he's right. Radigan says he followed Gabriel when he left, followed him right up the mountain. Swears he started doing something up there akin to drilling, set up some sort of machine like a big gun that pushed a beam of light down into the mountain. I think he's just worried the Lawman will find his stash of gold and tell me about it.

I got better at using my new eye over the past few weeks and damned if Gabriel don't look different than everybody else. Jonas is big bright red, while most folks is just dark orange, but Gabriel is purple-blue if anything and hard to see in the dark. It's got me a touch worried. Still, I don't reckon as Gabriel is after my gold, so I probably got to worry more about those what likely is.

Edward

* * *

CRD Claim
October 20 1898

Dearest Sally,

Winter settling in the Klondike. Has it been more than a month since I wrote? I can't keep track of time no more and reckon you might not even read these here letters. But I promised I'd keep writing, so I will.

We hauled gold out of this here claim, that's for sure, but I can't say as I'm all that proud of it now. Sad news to report,

Sally, but I reckon you ought to hear it. We been working so hard and pushing Jonas so much, well, we lost him. Both him and the Doc. We fixed up Jonas real good last month in Dawson, put twice the horse power in his steam engine and built up his drill, so as to compete with the other tunnelers. But the image of Jonas' face haunts me now, Sally. The face you painted up so nice changed over these months. Enamel chipped through, showing hard metal, rusting in most places. He'd grown wicked—or we had. We put him back in the mine and we was feeding his boiler constant. Running all day and all night. Just for a few nuggets of gold. Got so as I couldn't swing the small lens over my eye since it showed nothing but bright red. Ain't real sight in that eye, but some kind of heat sight. Shows hotter stuff brighter and redder. And it got real hot down there what with Jonas' fire and all. Looked like the pit of Hell. Couldn't breathe none for the smoke and steam, neither, but we just wouldn't stop. And poor Doc Davies, he were just unlucky to be the deepest right then. We work that position in short shifts and there he were, no more sober than usual I reckon, so maybe he didn't feel much. Could have been any of us.

You'd think as we'd learn our lesson when Jonas' boiler explodes, killing the Doc and sealing off our mine for good. But Radigan and me, we just fell to bickering about who were to blame. Radigan were middle in the tunnel, so I done accused him of causing the explosion, though I ain't proud of that now. He got problems but he wouldn't blow up the mine, nor kill Doc neither. He says there were lightning down there, electric sparks and the magnetics going crazy. Blames Gabriel, says he must have been up the mountain doing that drilling with light again. Gabriel did try to come round t'other day, but Radigan threatened him with that big old shotgun of his, so he left. We checked with the Northwest Mounted and they don't know who this fella is. After apiece, I'm agreeing with Radigan. Gabriel ain't no angel.

Now we're hunting us a lying Lawman.

* * *

October 23 1898

Pray for me, Sally.

Gabriel is dead.

Me and Radigan found him all right, atop the mountain just as Radigan reckoned. And that mountain were going crazy, all blue and sparking like that night I done lost my eye. Metal ball were sticking out the mountain again and damned if Gabriel don't have some sort of machine in his hand. Look like a gun bigger than Radigan's, only it were dull black with glittering dots. There were a low humming noise all round, and this time every hair on my head is sticking up, near pushing my hat off. I get my extra lens down so as I can see better against the blue electric glow. Reds stand out from people. But not Gabriel. Not the ball neither.

Radigan shouts at Gabriel and levels his shotgun. I got my rifle aimed in on him too. Not sure as he can hear us over the noise. He's looking only at the ball, and it's growing metal spikes off its surface as we watch. Other folks is climbing the mountain round us, noise and lightning sure bringing them from below.

Radigan yells out again. This time Gabriel turns. Don't know whether he were pointing his gun or not, but Radigan don't waste no time. He pulls both barrels full into Gabriel's chest. Rips a big hole right through that crisp white shirt. Throws his body against the metal ball and he staggers like a drunken Doc Davies. He ain't wearing a hat, and none of his hair standing up neither. And his purple-blue is starting to fade even as glowing orange people surround him.

He turns back to the ball and does something with his gun. A spark come off one of them spikes and hits a fella next to me. Damned if he don't go all stiff and every bit of red go out of him. It's like he turns to charcoal in an instant. I reach out for him and he crumbles, Sally. Crumbles into black dust in my hand.

That's when another fella shoots Gabriel full on.

Radigan's been getting everybody fired up about this Lawman what ain't a Lawman, and I reckon seeing him next to something as can't be explained, something that done killed a man, give them the notion to put more lead into him. I couldn't as pull my trigger, though. He just weren't threatening as far as I could see. He were doing something with the metal ball, and that may have been the cause of our troubles, but I don't know as he were responsible for it. I think maybe he were trying to stop it.

This time, the Lawman falls, his legs took out from beneath him. And that ball glows bright, right then, red coming in quick and the whole mountain rumbling. None of us can stay on our feet, and good thing too, as the sparks fly off them metal spikes like crazy and might have taken us all dead if we was standing. The ball come free from the mountain and shoots off to the stars.

Radigan were first to get up. He puts another shell in his shotgun. But Gabriel ain't moving. A hole ripped through him so big, nobody could survive. I go take the shotgun from Radigan. Terrible strange, looking at Gabriel. He ain't got no blood. Shirt blackened from powder, but instead of guts, just glittering strings. Wires and bits of metal. And damned if most of it ain't gold. Machine pieces the likes of which I ain't never seen is in there, some glowing a little, dying hearts maybe. This here fella were some kind of Jonas—built up to look like a man but weren't a man. Can't prove it now, though, as there ain't nothing left of poor Gabriel. 'Stead of wondering how a fella could build a mechanical like this, Radigan and the other folks as were up there fell immediate to ripping out the wires when they seen they was gold. Bickering about who gets what. Nothing else matters round here.

Well, I ain't for it no more. I'm on the trail back home. Going overland to Edmonton as near as I can and I'll be home soon. I'm terrible sorry I ain't got us rich, Sally, but we got to forget about the gold. The price is just too damned high.

Always Your Loving Brother,
Edward

* * *

Historic records show that the addressee, Sally Chalmers, died of Typhoid Fever in early May, 1898, not long after losing her father. Of Edward himself, no further documentation exists.

Heart of Clockwork

S.C. Butler

Like watermelon seeds from the mouths of spitting children, a hundred Jovian saucers burst from a hundred dimpling puckers across the dome of the African sky. The saucers paused, adjusting to the sudden change in pressure, then whirled down toward the dreadnoughts assembled to meet them a thousand meters above Stanley Pool.

The helmsman of the *Goshawk* swung the wheel hard to port. Captain Jean Leguin grabbed a handful of rigging to brace himself. In perfect synchronicity, the Great Congo Air Fleet came about like a vast herd of elephants to meet the enemy head on.

"Lieutenant!" As he spoke, Jean looked back at the great fans whirling high atop Leopoldville's lofty towers.

Crossthwaite snapped forward. "Sir!"

"Check the droplines one last time, if you please. We want no misfires, today, not with the Queen in the gallery."

Grinning, Crossthwaite glanced back at the towers as well. His ginger mustache lifted, revealing the large gap in his front teeth. Pity, that. A sign of beauty among the natives, but not at all what a young European lady looked for in a husband.

The crunch of the flagship's first broadside signaled the start of the engagement. The fleets remained several kilometers apart. A rolling barrage from the *Aeolian*'s sister ships followed. Alas, the *Goshawk* was only Devonshire class, not Antwerp, and her guns remained silent. Her mission was to maintain the outer edge of the formation. All the same, the beat of her engines and the thrum of the wind in her rigging disappeared beneath the capital ships' massive roar, doubly loud as they fired from both port and starboard batteries to maintain stability. Billows of black smoke obscured the sun.

The Jovians answered with a rattling volley of their own. But at that range their frozen sulfide bullets melted into drizzle far from their intended targets.

"Bloody gasbags," Crossthwaite cursed. "Take away their poison gas, and they turn toothless as old women. No European would ever fight like that."

"Steady, lieutenant." Jean did not disagree with the man, but he did not want him anticipating an easy victory. "Paris and London are hollow shells because of those tactics. They fight well enough in their armored mansuits."

But not that well at a distance. Which was why the saucers closed on the GCAF as quickly as possible. The dreadnoughts' cannons were most effective firing looping shots from a distance. Attempting to hit the flat saucers head-on was nearly impossible.

The barrage had already knocked dozens of Jovians from the sky. They crashed into the pool with geysering splashes. The rest thrust forward on horizontal jets, unable to make as much speed as the GCAF because they needed to employ their vertical jets to maintain altitude.

Midshipmen Garret-Swynge monkeyed over the side from his observation post beneath the gondola. "Captain" he declared, so excited he almost forgot to salute. "An enemy ship has broken free of their formation!"

Jean followed the midshipman's pointing finger. One of the Jovians was falling away from its fellows like a stone. At a height of perhaps a hundred meters it stopped its descent and arrowed for the riverbank.

The *Goshawk* was the only ship close enough to catch her.

"Corpsman!" Jean barked. "Bleed gas! Helmsman! Hard to starboard! Everyone else, batten down!"

The helmsman's brawny arms bulged beneath his matelot as he strained against the wheel. Slowly the deck canted as the propellers bit at the new vector. The ship's nose nudged downward. Five degrees. Twenty. Beneath Jean's feet, the deck shuddered. The rigging sang as the wind swung into their faces. With one hand on the for'ard tumpline, Jean grabbed the engine room speaking tube with the other. "Damn it, Sparks! We need every ounce of steam you have! Don't let a little five knot breeze shut us down!"

The roar of the engines was too loud to make out Sparks' salty reply.

The ship turned. Now the *Goshawk* was chasing the Jovian. Jean pulled out the heavy gold pocket watch his grandfather had given him before he died, and used the second hand to measure the ship's speed against the landmarks below. Even with the wind mostly in the *Goshawk*'s face, her powerful steam engines had her closing the gap between the two craft at a rapid clip.

The saucer headed toward a reed-filled lagoon. Crocodiles slithered off sandbars, ducking the spray kicked up by the Jovian's jets. A small herd of hippopotami snorted, then vanished completely underwater when the *Goshawk*'s shadow crossed their broad backs.

They caught the Jovian craft thirty meters from shore. Before that, however, Jean had already climbed into the for'ard rigging with four khat-chewing marines. Never make anyone do something you were unwilling to do yourself, was his firm belief, whether tapping rubber trees or leading an aerial boarding party. Natives or airmen, they were all human.

Which the Jovians definitely were not.

He clipped a line to his harness, climbed to the top of the port railing, and, brandishing his swagger stick, cried, "For Queen. And planet!"

The marines answered with a lusty cheer, and followed him over the side. Jean felt a moment's thrill as he fell free the first dozen feet before applying pressure to his descender. The safeties caught with a slight tug on the harness, then the winches freed and he dropped again.

His boots hit the saucer's deck with a metallic clang.

"Hookup!" Jean commanded, unclipping his tether. "Now!"

The Jovians were nothing if not predictable. Already the saucer had started to spin. Like clockwork, Jean and the rest of the squad roped themselves together in both pentagonal and star-shaped patterns, then braced themselves around the small bump that marked the center of the saucer's gently sloping deck.

The saucer accelerated. Jean felt the stress in his thighs. The craft accelerated more. A moment's giddy dizziness threatened to overwhelm him, but he swallowed it manfully down. Focusing on the stable faces of the men around him, and not the whirling land and sky, he kept his nausea at bay.

The saucer twirled madly for several minutes before the Jovians accepted the fact that their tactic had failed and allowed the ship to slow. Unsnapping the lines, Jean and his men readied themselves for the next act in the Jovians' predictable strategy.

"Nine o'clock!" shouted Beckwith.

A hatch flipped open behind the marine between Beckwith and Jean, striking the marine just behind the knee. As Smythe-Smith toppled, Jean pulled out his revolver, and fired off a quick shot. The round pinged inside the opening, but the only thing that emerged was a thick black hose.

"Masks!" Jean shouted. He slipped on his custom Hermes Icarus-13 just as the nozzle began to dance about the deck spraying its deadly gas. Like natives in ibogi ecstasy, the marines hopped back and forth trying to keep out of its way. Their gasmasks might keep the sulfuric acid out of their lungs and eyes, but, given more than a couple minutes' exposure, it would start to eat through their clothing.

The squad hustled downwind. At the same moment, a second hatch opened, and a Jovian in a heavily armored mansuit clambered out. Two more followed close behind. Jean's first shot clattered off the lead creature's breastplate, but Sergeant Manleywale's was better placed, catching a jointed knee. The mansuit exploded in a burst of greaves and goo. The sticky spray temporarily hid the two Jovians behind it, but not the bullets hammering from their machine pistols. Manleywale went down as the squad dove for the deck. Jean rolled behind the slight protection of the open hatch, fearing the spray of sulfide bullets, deadly at such close range, much more than the spitting hose.

Around him, the squad returned fire. Though the wind had dissipated the aspirated Jovian, the spray from the poison hose still provided the others with exceptional cover. The snipers in the *Goshawk* were unable to see them through the hissing fog.

Jean seized the hose with both hands and wrestled it to the side. The cloud lifted off the Jovians. The sound of rifles popping from above followed swiftly.

A cry from his left told Jean that a second marine had been hit. But the snipers on the *Goshawk* were making their mark. Another Jovian exploded, and a third. The deck was secure.

With Beckwith's help, Jean wrestled the hose back down the hatch. His hands dripped with acid; his leather gloves steamed. Quickly stripping them off, he tossed them over the side. There was no point trying to pursue the Jovians into their craft. Not when the pressure inside was worse than the bottom of the ocean, and poisonous to boot.

Jean looked to his men. Smythe-Smith was down with what looked like a wound to the thigh. Manleywale, however, was not moving.

The second squad joined them in a chorus of clangs. Sergeant Remi reported to Jean with a crisp salute, while his marines began unfurling the canvas wraps. "Carry on, Sergeant," Jean ordered wearily. Then he and Beckwith strapped Manleywale and Smythe-Smith into the gurneys the *Goshawk* had lowered, and called for them to be lifted away.

The second squad wrapped their sailcloth around a third of the saucer. Someday the Jovians would build aethercraft with thrusters on top and bottom, but, until they did, the saucers were at the mercy of any boarding party. Cover enough bottom thrusters, and the craft unbalanced immediately.

In less than a minute, they had the wrap in position. Jean checked to make sure everyone was buckled to one of the dozen lines dangling from the *Goshawk*, then signaled for the men to cinch the great leather straps that pulled the canvas tight. As they did so, the craft instantly tilted sideways, and shot toward the great river below.

Jean and the hippos watched it fall. Just before it hit the water, he thought he saw one of the hatches open and something slither out.

"Did you see that?" he asked Beckwith, dangling on a line beside him, as the lagoon fountained.

"See what, sir?"

"Something fled the ship just before it struck."

"Sorry, sir. I was checking our harness and didn't see a thing."

High above, the few surviving Jovian ships disappeared back up into the sky. Black smoke soiled the swirling wind, but the battle was a complete rout. Leopoldville, the last lonely citadel still standing against the Jovian invaders, had survived unscathed once more.

* * *

The Queen herself attended the victory ball three days later. And everyone else, including the American ambassador. The ambassador's daughter, however, Jean did not see until he went into the gardens for a cigar.

It was a lovely night. Several of the lower fans had been switched from aerial poison defense back to their original climate function, and the surrounding jungle's heat and humidity were beaten back by their circling blades. The rooftop gardens blazed with light, every gas line in the city diverted to the entertainment. The breeze from the great fans hummed through the lush green of the rooftop plantings—date palms and bananas, lime and lemon trees, hibiscus and jasmine—and all the flowering riot of the tropics carefully tamed and tended by native gardeners disciplined to European techniques. On the roof of the Governor's Palace, an orchestra played the latest waltzes.

"Hello, Johnny. Are you looking for me?"

A soft hand settled on Jean's arm. Only one person in all Leopoldville called him Johnny, which partly pleased him, but mostly irritated him beyond bearing.

He bowed politely. "Good evening, Miss Randolph. I suppose I should not be surprised to find you out in the gardens unescorted."

Jenny Randolph laughed lightly. She was the most beautiful woman in Leopoldville, and the most impossible. Change her just the slightest bit and Jean—and every other young officer in Leopoldville—would be desperately in love with her. Her auburn hair crowned her head simply, without jewelry or ribbons, though her lavender gown was straight from pre-war Paris. Her shoulders gleamed alabaster in the gaslight. If only her ideas, and her country's, had been less radical.

She swept the ostrich feather she was carrying thoughtfully along the underside of her chin. "You know I don't care about that sort of thing, Johnny. No one in the United States does."

"You will excuse me, Miss Randolph, if I decline to talk politics with you."

Her hazel eyes softened. "I'm sorry, Johnny. Jean. I did not mean to offend you. You and your family are well known for your kindnesses to the natives. I hear you even have a school."

He answered her quizzing honestly. "It is our duty to help the Africans better themselves any way we can. It is not their fault they are not European. But this is not the time to be distracting ourselves with the burden of our social responsibilities. We are at war, Miss Randolph. At war with a species that desires only our enslavement or extermination. If you were not American you would understand that. Your cities have not been destroyed."

"But that's just it." Jenny's eyes brightened. Whatever her faults, there was no meanness or insincerity in Jenny Randolph. She was a true descendant of the Abolitionists. And how close had they come to destroying their country because of their principles?

"The Jovians have no intention of overthrowing anything, Jean. They know they can't live here. They only want to trade with us. That's why the United States has gotten along so well with them. We support free trade. Europe prefers colonies, which is why you think the Jovians want to colonize you. But they don't."

"Nations do not sack each other's cities in the name of free trade," Jean declared.

"Tell that to Peking."

"You Americans took what you could in that war."

"Yes. But now that we are potentially on the other side, we know better."

Jean shook his head. "I am sorry, Miss Randolph. You and I simply do not see the matter in the same way at all. London, Brussels, Paris, all three are smoking ruins because of the filthy poison the Jovians rained down on them from the sky. You Americans are fools to trust them. What have they given you in return for your iron and gold? Their technology? Of course not, just as Europe has never shared its technology with Africa or the East. Now that your country has allied with them in so cowardly a manner, all that stands between the Jovians and Earth is the handful of us fighting them here in Africa. Thanks to the abundant gas that powers our turbines," Jean pointed up toward the great blades windmilling overhead, "and the GCAF, they have not been able to conquer the planet completely. We remain a threat, but the minute we are gone, mark my words, you will wish you were one of the natives on my family's plantation."

Jenny drew herself up stiffly. She started to say something, changed her mind, and said something else. "I would rather be dead."

"And I would rather be alive. That is the difference between us."

"A wide gulf. On second thought, Johnny, I'm not sorry I offended you at all. If you will excuse me."

Pulling her shawl closer against her shoulders, Jenny ventured deeper into the garden. Given her extreme pacifism, Jean wondered why she had attended the victory ball at all.

He left in the other direction, but the vagaries of the garden paths brought him circling back to the same place several minutes later. Jenny had also returned, but this time she was speaking intimately to a man who stood with his back to Jean. Realizing she was having an assignation, Jean pivoted away.

Something thumped softly behind him, followed by a rustling in the bougainvillea. His stomach tensed. Fearing the worst, he turned around, only to be further surprised when he saw Jenny on the path, but not the man.

A Jovian in an unarmored mansuit emerged from the flowers.

"Did you get the key?" Jenny asked.

The Jovian displayed something in his mitten-like hand.

Jenny nodded briskly, and the two of them marched away.

Jean was dumbfounded. It was one thing to treat with the Jovians, but quite something else to conspire with them. He remembered the Jovian he thought he had seen escaping from the saucer over Stanley Pool. He had not imagined it. There was a Jovian on the ground, and Jenny Randolph was helping him.

He considered calling for help, but the orchestra had launched into a boisterous polka, and no one was close enough to hear him. His only choice was pursuit.

Passing the bougainvillea, he spotted a foot sticking out from under the flowers. Jenny and her mansuited companion turned a corner and disappeared, but there were few branches off the path they had taken, and Jean was confident he could catch them before they went too far.

The man groaned as Jean pulled him out of the shrubbery. Trevor Thorne-Hopping? What on earth? Thorne-Hopping did little beyond dine at his club and talk rubbish about the war. And then Jean remembered that Thorne-Hopping's father was Thomas Thorne-Hopping, a planter best known for his mistreatment of the natives before the enactment of the Anti-Cruelty statutes. Thorne-Hopping had insinuated himself well enough with the government to be declared Interior Minister at the start of the war. And the Interior Minister was in charge of the fans.

They were heading to the works! He was sure of it. Thomas Thorne-Hopping doted on his son. It would be a simple matter for Trevor to trick him out of a key. That had to be what Jenny and the Jovian were after. Once inside the Clockworks, they could shut down the fans. And once the fans were shut down, Leopoldville would be as exposed to the Jovian's poison rain as London and Paris had been.

Leaving Thorne-Hopping to recover on his own, Jean hurried after Jenny and the Jovian.

He found them climbing into a hot air balloon tethered to a mooring cleat on the far side of the garden. Like some grotesque parody of a gentleman, the Jovian handed Jenny into the basket, then followed. The basket sank swiftly under their weight, allowing Jean to climb onto the top of the balloon easily, without being seen. He twined his arms and legs securely through the netting as the burner roared to life in the basket below.

The balloon rose. Jean had first learned aeronautics on his father's plantation in a balloon just like it. A simple craft, with a gas tank to fuel both the burner and the small propeller. As long as they encountered no stiff winds, Jenny would be able to guide the craft anywhere she wanted.

At first they only ascended. The fans of Leopoldville sucked them upwards. A western breeze pushed them towards the Governor's Palace, which meant that Jean no longer needed to worry about informing the authorities. They would see what was happening themselves the moment the balloon passed overhead. Taking out his grandfather's pocket watch, he estimated their airspeed at approximately three knots.

The burner shut off. The propeller kicked on. The balloon's course swung several points north, toward the central tower. Did Jenny actually intend to fly them straight into the heart of the fans? Granted, there was enough room for a small balloon to pass between them—if the turbulence did not make navigable flight impossible. Jean would never have dreamed of flying through such a gauntlet, no matter how small the balloon, and he was one of the best pilots in the GCAF.

He was impressed by Jenny's nerve.

But why head toward the central tower? The central tower emerged from the roof of the Interior Ministry, the most heavily guarded building in the world. Surely the key Jenny had procured from Thorne-Hopping unlocked one of the works' less conspicuous entrances. One that did not require threading the needle through an alley of veritable typhoons.

The balloon soared over the Governor's Palace. Below it, the entire cotillion—orchestra, footmen, dancers—stared skyward in slack-jawed wonder.

Jean's attention shifted to the whump-whump of the spinning blades as they approached the first fan. He tightened his grip on the rigging as the vortex sucked in the balloon like a cork on a raging stream. He tossed and turned, swayed and swung, as the winds swapped the balloon from fan to fan. Down, then up, then up, and down again. His ankles ripped loose from the netting and his legs swung free, whipping back and forth with every gust and gyration. He was certain he was going to fall, then the balloon found a spot of relative calm and he was able to resecure his grip.

A blade sliced through a single strand of netting as the balloon slid under the last fan. Rifles popped, only this time the Jovians were not the targets. Pale smoke puffed from the rifles of the Queen's Guard as they shot at the balloon from the roof of the

Governor's Palace. Men in evening dress gesticulated wildly. Women fainted.

The central tower loomed ahead. Great fans thundered above and below, but Jenny was bringing them in between both as steady as you please. The tower's glass siding blinked gold and black as the lower blades sliced through the rooftop's gleam. Jean guessed they were going to miss the tower by at least five meters, until a grapple, presumably thrown by the Jovian, arced out from the basket. A perfect shot, the iron hook caught the rungs of a ladder that climbed the tower's side. The balloon, still rising, pulled taut on the line before it hit the upper fan.

Jean peered around the balloon's edge as Jenny and the Jovian climbed onto the ladder. The Jovian carried a large carpetbag hooked over his shoulder. Jenny had changed out of her ball gown into a leather flying jacket and the heavy dark blue cotton trousers that were all the rage with miners. Her gorgeous hair was tucked practically inside a leather flying cap, a revolver holstered at her hip.

Descending, they soon reached a small door. Jenny unlocked it with a key. The Jovian entered first, but, before following, Jenny pulled the revolver from her holster, and pointed it at the balloon.

"Well, Johnny, since the fans didn't brush you off, I guess you can come down now. If you don't, I'll shoot the balloon."

Sheepishly, he climbed down. Though a woman, she was an American, and he did not doubt she was an expert shot. And even if he did manage to wrest the revolver from her, he doubted he could overpower the Jovian as well.

"How long have you known?" he asked as he squeezed through the door.

"The balloon was significantly heavier than it should have been when we took off."

"And you knew it was me because?"

"Who else could it be? You were the last person to see me before Trevor. I should have known you'd follow me. You've had a thing for me since the day we met."

Jean swallowed his reply. No sense giving Jenny the satisfaction of knowing she was getting under his skin. And even if he had been attracted to her once, that could never be the case now that she had shown herself to be a traitoress to the entire world.

The inside of the tower was a lattice of iron similar to the Crystal Palace and *la tour Eiffel* Already the cables of the maintenance lift that filled the space hummed, gears clanking loudly in their housing overhead. Far below, massive engines thumped and steamed.

The lift arrived. The Jovian entered first. Jenny gestured with her revolver, indicating that Jean should follow. He closed the lift gate behind her and, again at her direction, hit the button that switched the car to manual.

"Where to?" he inquired, his hand on the drive lever.

"The bottom."

"You'll never get away with it, you know." Jean's stomach lurched as the lift jerked into a rapid descent. "A company of marines are probably sealing off the building right now."

"This lift goes straight to the works."

"Where you hope to do what, exactly?"

"Really, Johnny." Jenny pointed at the carpetbag. "Even you aren't so naïve as to think our bag is filled with coconuts."

"It hardly contains enough explosive to destroy the entire works."

"Perhaps we don't need explosives to do what needs to be done."

Once again a look came into her face that suggested she was about to say something she thought was important.

"You know," she said. "It's probably better you're here. Now I won't be the only witness."

"Only witness to what?"

"The proof of everything I've said. About how the world will be better off with the Jovians in charge than it ever could be with us."

Jean shook his head in disbelief. "You are mad, do you know that? Absolutely mad."

"As you'll be, once I show you what Trevor showed me. He actually believed it would make me think well of him."

The lift slowed as it reached the bottom. Jean hoped to find a squad of soldiers with bayonets at the ready on the other side of the door when they finally came to rest, but the corridor was unfortunately empty.

The Jovian exited the carriage first, followed by Jean, with Jenny and her American revolver last.

They stood on an iron catwalk at the top of a vast cavern. Smoke and steam billowed around them, concealing whatever lay below. It was hot, too, and as humid as the jungle. Jenny removed her flying cap, her hair already frizzing. In five minutes, they would all be soaked to the skin.

An enormous piston swung out of the smoke, passing bare centimeters from Jean's face before disappearing back into the steam. Far above, the fans whirled through another turn.

The catwalk followed the wall around the pit in a series of long descents. Further catwalks extended into the heart of the cavern, their destinations hidden by the seething tumult. The deeper the three of them went, the more cacophonous the cavern grew, and the more frequently they spotted the great belts and wheels, boilers and drive shafts of the works. It grew hotter, too. Jets of steam, some of them almost scalding, arced uncomfortably across their path. Jean felt as if he had plunged fully clothed into a bath. From the brief glances he got of Jenny whenever he looked over his shoulder, he could tell she was drenched as well. Her clothes clung to her revealingly and, had the circumstances been different, he would have admired her figure very much.

He hoped he would not have to kill her as well as the Jovian, when it came time to stop them.

They saw no one through the entire descent. Jean knew there were workmen everywhere—the need for power from the works was constant, which meant the need for supervision and maintenance of the machinery was constant, too. But whatever mechanics were about, they remained at their duty stations rather than wandering the stairs.

At the bottom, the passage branched both left and right. Arming himself with a revolver from the carpetbag, the Jovian disappeared along the left hand way. Jean descended the last few steps, and discovered a row of ragged natives sitting in a line along the far wall, their hands and feet manacled to a heavy chain. None of them looked up as Jean appeared out the darkness, but sat coughing in the dim light of an oil lamp guttering on the wall.

"What in the name of God?"

He looked up as the Jovian reappeared. A man materialized from the other direction. Although he was dressed in the greasy coveralls of a mechanic, he carried a rifle slung over his shoulder, and a heavy truncheon at his belt.

Jenny's revolver boomed. The overseer collapsed, the chambered bullet that had been readied for Jean killing the overseer instead. Jean felt little regret at the man's murder. If he was in charge of the poor souls chained along the wall, he deserved no less. But what in the name of all that was holy was going on? The worst excesses of the Congo had been put to a stop when Jean was a child, due in no small part to the efforts of his mother and father, and other like-minded reformers.

"Do you still believe the Jovians could be any worse than this?" Jenny gestured grimly toward the prisoners. Gunpowder smeared her face, her auburn hair streaking her cheeks in long strands.

Jean could not answer. There had to be an explanation, but he had no idea what it was. Even after the death of the overseer, the chained men and women kept their eyes averted from the Europeans.

He spoke to the closest ones, asking where they were from. But they answered neither his French, nor his Bantu, nor his Swahili.

"Don't waste your time," Jenny said. "They're not from around here. You passed your laws, but did you really think that people capable of cutting off a man's hand for not meeting his daily rubber quota would pay attention to them? Especially after they found such a profoundly more powerful way to use people?"

"What are you talking about? These people's situation is grotesque, but I do not see how they are being used. This isn't a mine, and there's no rubber plantation down here, either."

"You'll see," she said, and waved him forward.

She led Jean and the Jovian up a narrow stair to what looked exactly like an observation deck above a large operating theater in a European medical college. A rapidly spinning rod stretched from one side of the theater to the other, its middle a five foot long copper cocoon swathed in a thin haze of pale blue fire. On the far side of the room, white-jacketed scientists faced a wall of gauges and heavy switches, meters, and speaking tubes, their backs to the humming rod.

The air smelled like lightning and burnt pig.

The spinning mechanism slowed. The pale blue fire snapped off. Jean noticed a shriveled blob at one end of the copper coil. A workman with a macabre sense of humor appeared to have painted a caricature on it. Bright white teeth inside a skinless jaw. Blackened, eyeless sockets.

He retched. Champagne and bile puddled his shoes.

"It's human!" he gasped.

"Was human." The anger in Jenny's eyes was almost violent enough to spark her explosion.

He wiped his hand across his mouth. "But why?"

"To power Leopoldville. Did you really think it was all natural gas?" She looked back at the charred, shriveled corpse being removed from its copper cocoon.

The Jovian opened the carpetbag. From it he began removing and screwing together several pieces of shiny pipe. Though his mitten hands moved clumsily, he assembled his apparatus expertly.

Jenny touched the Jovian's translucent arm. "Wait for the next one," she told him. "I want Jean to see how it's done. So he knows."

The Jovian nodded, and continued his work.

"They'll be changing armatures soon," she said to Jean.

"Armatures?"

Disgust dripped from Jenny's voice. "That's what Dr. Kurtz calls these poor people once he's connected them to the works. That blue light is an aetheric field. By spinning a human artificially stimulated with khat and ibigo within that field, aetheric current of the same sort the Jovians use to power their ships across space is generated. That poor man down there, and two more in rooms like this one, generate enough aetheric energy to power the entire city. And of course the fans. Now do you understand why I have to do this?"

He understood. And he wished with all his heart that Jenny had made her discovery after the war with the Jovians was won.

The mechanics left the theater with their blackened burden. An armed overseer entered, leading a shackled woman. A white-jacketed scientist followed.

Jean recognized the man's pince-nez and trim goatee. "Why, that's Dr. Kurtz! He cured my mother's last bout of malaria."

"Yes," Jenny sneered. "Africa's foremost man of medicine."

Jean shuddered, remembering how he had paid the man in South African gold sovereigns, and shaken his hand as well.

The new victim could have been any of the women he had seen in the hall. She did not struggle as the overseer led her to a small bench in the center of the room. But when Dr. Kurtz approached with an enormous syringe, she screamed. The overseer cuffed her; Jean gripped the railing tightly to keep from vaulting over the wall to her rescue. Horrible though it was, one woman's pain was more than offset by the need to stop Jenny and the Jovian.

Dr. Kurtz plunged the hypodermic into the woman's neck. Her body went stiff. Her eyes rolled until only the whites showed. Removing her chains, the overseer slid her feet first into the coil.

The blue fire reappeared as the mechanism began to spin. The woman screamed. Sheets of tiny lightning leapt from flame to coil. The woman's face turned red, then yellow, and finally white before disappearing in a blur of speed.

Jean's skin crawled. For a moment, she had looked just like his mother.

"Now," Jenny told the Jovian.

Assembled, the Jovian's weapon looked like an ancient fowling piece crossed with a sextant. As he raised it to his shoulder, the sextant began to rotate. Slowly at first, then faster and faster. A spot of pale blue fire appeared in the spinning center.

With a single kick, Jean knocked the weapon from the Jovian's hands, and reached for Jenny's revolver. Rather than grab it from her, he aimed it toward the Jovian while it was still in her hand. The revolver fired, but the shot missed, and then the three of them were wrestling for control.

Jean grabbed for the alien's weapon. A powerful hand closed around his ankle, and pulled him back. Twisting around, he kicked his free foot at the Jovian's chin. The Jovian's head jerked agreeably, and his grip on Jean's ankle loosened enough for Jean to slip free.

Jenny raised her revolver. Jean danced back behind the Jovian. Jenny shouted for the Jovian to move aside. The Jovian picked up his own revolver from the floor. Jean grabbed its spongy arms and pulled. Employing the baritsu techniques he had learned in London before the war, he rolled backward, caught the Jovian in the stomach with his feet, and kicked him over the low wall. But the Jovian grabbed Jean's arms as he flew over Jean's head, and the two of them plunged to the operating theater floor.

The Jovian landed first. His revolver skittered away. His body gave slightly as Jean landed on top of him, like a tightly packed pillow, enough so that Jean did not have the wind knocked out of him. The Jovian, of course, contained no wind. Or bones. And though he got up slowly, it was no slower than usual.

Unfortunately, he was between Jean and the revolver.

"You!" Jean shouted at the armed overseer, who was gaping in the middle of the floor. He pointed at the Jovian. "Shoot him! He wants to destroy the works!"

The guard stared dumbly. Dr. Kurtz and the rest of the scientists reacted no better. Judging the armed overseer to be his most immediate danger, the Jovian picked up his revolver with cool aplomb, and shot the man through the head.

The guard's rifle clattered to the floor. Jean rushed the Jovian once more. His kick caught the Jovian in mid-turn, but this time the Jovian was ready for him, and knocked him away with a swipe of his arm. Jean landed on the floor with a loud crunch. His grandfather's watch fell out of his pocket, smashed to pieces. Shards of glass and a hook of jagged spring gleamed.

The Jovian stepped forward, and aimed his revolver at point-blank range. Jean twisted away desperately.

The Jovian's foot came down heavily on the broken watch.

With a loud whoosh, the mansuit rocketed crookedly into the air. The Jovian's insides foamed from the pierced foot. Smashing into the aetheric fire, the mansuit disintegreated. Jean covered his face against the toxic explosion, and collapsed to the floor.

"Are you all right?"

Jean looked up. Jenny was leaning over the wall, her voice oddly gentle.

"Potentially," he answered. His hands stung horribly.

"If you can walk, you'd better get out of there."

"I am in no hurry."

"Suit yourself. I'm going to fire the Jovian weapon. I don't know what effect it will have on you if you're too close."

"What?" He looked at her dazedly. The Jovian was aspirated. Why would she use the weapon now?

"The Jovians told me how it works. It will send an overload through the entire clockwork, destroying it utterly. I don't know if you'll even be safe up here with me, but it has to be safer than where you are now."

Jean looked at the mechanism humming in the center of the room. Wisps of smoke plumed above the woman's horribly spinning face. The smell of ozone and searing flesh had returned. What had been done to this poor woman—and who knew how many others?—was horrible. As vile as anything any human had ever done. But what would happen to humanity if the works were destroyed?

"You cannot," he said weakly.

"Excuse me?" Jenny's eyebrows rose.

He found the last of his strength. "I said you cannot. Not now. We have seen it. We know the evil that is being done here. Those responsible will be brought to justice. But you cannot do this now. The Jovian fleet is probably hovering over Leopoldville at this very moment, waiting for the fans to stop. It will be a massacre every bit as bad as what we have committed against the Africans."

"No, it won't." Jenny's gentle mood vanished. Her eyes glittered, hard as steam and iron. "This massacre will be deserved."

She shouldered the alien weapon.

"You don't have to do this," he pleaded. "The Jovians will take over the entire world."

"Better them than us, if this is the best we can do with it."

Laying her cheek on the barrel, Jenny aimed and fired. A spark of jagged lightning, blue and gold and red, streaked across the room.

The world exploded.

Lady Antheia's Guide to Horticultural Warfare

Seanan McGuire

1.

"I sometimes think it would have been better had my first encounter with humanity been a man, and not a woman of low station with no family to mourn her. Better for who, I cannot say."

—from *Lady Antheia's Guide to Horticultural Warfare*, first printing.

* * *

It is customary to begin one's memoirs at birth. As I was not "born" in the gross mammalian sense, I shall begin instead at a more logical point in time. To wit:

I was borne to Earth on cosmic winds, falling through chance and the grace of the heavens to root in the soil of Notting Hill. There I grew rapidly to adult stature, devoured a lady's maid who had the misfortune to come too close to my tendrils, and assumed her form. It was a discourteous way to introduce myself to the human species, but I must beg forgiveness: my kind are not precisely well-mannered when we first bud, and must be taught proper behavior before we can be trusted in polite society.

As servants are rarely found with skin the color of young watercress and hair the color of mature nettles, I presented quite a curiosity when I staggered through the doors of the house which previously employed the now-devoured lady's maid. I was still in the process of absorbing her memories, and had discovered the directions to her place of employment without acquiring the context that would have allowed me to understand that returning there might be bad for my chances of continued survival. Indeed, I was not the only seed to fall to Earth that day. I was simply the only one fortunate enough to eat a lady's maid whose mistress was sister to a man of science—Sir Arthur Blackwood, botanist in the service of Her Majesty, the Queen of England.

Where most men would have looked upon my vibrantly green face and seen a monster, Sir Blackwood saw a miracle in the making: something entirely new to present to Queen Alice, who was so very fond of novelty. Alice had been raised a princess, with no hope of the throne, only to find herself elevated and her engagement to the Grand Duke of Hesse cancelled after an ill-timed smallpox outbreak left her the heir to the British Empire. God save the Queen.

I was presented to Queen Alice on my third day of adult growth, after my mind had finished processing the linguistic and behavioral data harvested from the unfortunate lady's maid. I was able to curtsey and offer a polite greeting to Her Majesty.

She was charmed, of course. Who wouldn't be? I was a very well-mannered sapling, and have only grown into my graces as I bloomed and cultivated my better nature. Jill Lane—the lady's maid I have spoken of—was a great help. She had in her an endless eagerness to please, and I often returned to her deep well of knowledge and propriety as I navigated the echelons of British society. But ah, I am getting ahead of myself.

How vividly I recall that first day in the Queen's presence, me still unsteady on the bifurcated stems of my legs, Jill's voice still reedy and uncertain in my mind. Queen Alice looked me up and down and then turned her attention to Sir Blackwood.

"Does your green girl have a name?" she asked.

"She came before us with nothing but her pretty face," he said. "I have taken the liberty of calling her 'Antheia,' after the goddess of flowers and floral garlands."

The Queen had smiled. That was all it took to seal my fate within the Empire—for you see, after that, I was a favorite of the Queen, and a novelty unlike any other. That made me the toast of every great house in Britain, opening endless doors, and the manners I borrowed from dear Jill opened still more, until some spoke, half-jesting, of my successful invasion of the nation. They called me their flowering princess, representative of some savage fairy race that dwelt beneath the hills of Ireland, and oh, how they laughed at the idea that I could represent their downfall.

How they laughed.

2.

"It is important that we record the last days of the Planet Earth in their own languages, for these languages contain the concepts with which the meat-based life forms of that world were most familiar. They could no more express the delight of fresh sun falling upon their roots than an unbonded pod could explain the intricacies of a lady's undergarments. By preserving the manners and culture of the planet in this way, we can better understand them and, should we ever encounter another such species, we can bring about an even swifter and more efficient conquest."

—from *Lady Antheia's Guide to Horticultural Warfare*, first printing.

* * *

It was a Thursday afternoon when the advance scouts broke through the upper reaches of Earth's atmosphere, announcing their arrival with the usual chromatic displays in the thermosphere. The lights drew attention across the globe, stargazers and young romantics alike clustering in the fields as they strained to watch these strange and heretofore undocumented rainbows of the night. I was less interested in the phenomenon, naturally; I have always done better during the daylight hours, and the things I do in open fields are better not shared with those of delicate mammalian sensibilities. I was seated in the parlor at home, working on my needlepoint and snacking from a tray of cunning little sandwiches, when Sir Blackwood burst into the room, his hair mussed and his jacket askew.

"Antheia!" he cried. "Why are you here, and not out on the veranda with the guests? They're asking about you."

"I have no interest in watching the excited collision of

atoms," I said, tugging another loop of thread carefully through the muslin. A fine cabbage rose was taking form under my fingers—some of my best work, if I did say so myself. "The colors will be there with or without me to watch them, and besides, it was time for my tea. You *do* prefer that I continue to take my meals in private, do you not?"

Arthur blanched. It had taken the household some time to adjust to my predilection for eating only raw animal flesh and drinking only fresh blood. Sir Arthur's sister, Julia, had adjusted rather faster than he had—she'd already known I was a beast, as evidenced by the fact that I had eaten her lady's maid. Dear, sweet Arthur had devoted his life to the study of plants, and even the fact that I was not the first flesh-eater he had encountered had not prepared him for the notion that one day he might meet a flower who could smile and curtsey and request a hot bowl of pig's blood for her supper.

"Yes, but the lights—"

"Are better left to those who can appreciate them." I reached for a sandwich. The delightful smell of raw, fresh-sliced beef addressed my nose. "Really, I thought your sister had banned you from her stargazing party. Something about the noises coming from the basement?"

"I don't understand why she gets so upset," he said, dropping into the seat on the other side of my sewing table with a loud thump. He automatically reached for my plate of sandwiches, and looked offended when I smacked his hand with my needlepoint frame. Rubbing his fingers, he continued, "My steam-powered sun will make us richer than she can imagine."

"You see, that is her trouble: she suffers from a shortage of imagination, and as such, cannot see where a loud, clanking clockwork machine could possibly improve her life." I took a dainty nibble from my sandwich. "Remember, she forbade poor Jill to use *any* modern machinery in maintaining the house."

Arthur blanched again. He enjoyed being reminded that I'd eaten Jill even less than he enjoyed being reminded of the rest of my diet. "Julia is a traditional soul, that's all," he mumbled.

"We live in an age of wonders," I said. "The fact that she cannot embrace them is a shame. The fact that she can stand on her veranda marveling over a scientific curiosity while forbidding the pursuit of more concrete sciences is a sham. I will never understand how you can tolerate her willful interference with your business, Arthur."

"She'll wed eventually. One of her hulking suitors will make an honest woman of her, and she'll have no more grounds to interfere." Arthur looked wistfully at my sandwiches, but didn't stretch out his hand again. "What do you think of these lights?"

"Natural atmospheric distortion, of no more interest than any of the other things one sees in the sky." I nibbled my sandwich, swallowed, and added, "Excepting, of course, Her Majesty's airship, which is a wonder and a blessing and is in no way an eyesore that blocks the sunlight from reaching my roses."

Arthur laughed. "I swear your tongue gets sharper every year, Antheia."

"What good is a rose that has no thorns?" I smiled, pleased when his cheeks reddened in reply. Blood-based circulatory systems are such traitorous things, betraying the emotions of their owners even as they struggle to keep them alive. "I presume you have some motive for asking these questions, apart from the pleasure of my company?"

"I was speaking with Lord Harrington of the Royal Astronomical Society about the lights," said Arthur, carefully. "I thought he might have something interesting to offer on the topic, and in fact, he did. He said similar lights—similar in color and design, although less grandiose in scope—were seen in various locations around the world some six years ago."

"Is that so?" I asked politely, before taking another nibble of my sandwich. The bread, made specially from bone meal and ground fish scales, was deliciously nourishing. I kept my eyes on Arthur, waiting for him to finish his explanation with the inevitable and begin the next phrase in our little dance.

I had been waiting for so long, and as ever, Arthur did not disappoint. "The lights were last seen on the night before you appeared," he said. "Antheia, I have always assumed, in some vague way, that you were one of the fairy-folk of legend, escaped from beneath the hill and come to grace us with your presence. Fairy-folk have sometimes been said to be green of skin, you see.

But now I come to wonder … did you come from beneath the Earth? Did you come from the Earth at all?"

I smiled dazzlingly, showing him my teeth in parody of the primate grimace that he and his sister wore so often, and to such good effect. Jill had taught me my manners properly, you see: no deportment coach could have been better than my own internal lady's maid. "I never claimed a terrestrial origin, you know. I simply felt that such matters were better left behind us than discussed in polite company."

"Antheia …" Arthur frowned, his brows furrowing together as he looked at me with such gravity as to make my breath catch in my chest. "These lights. Are they more of your people?"

"Oh, no," I said blithely. He began to relax. "If this were merely more of my people, you would need only to lock up your lady's maids and gentleman's companions long enough to let them take their human forms from the less desirable levels of society—or at least from the parts of society where the people would be less dearly missed. This is the invasion."

His mouth fell open. He stared at me, shocked into silence, as I set my sandwich aside, picked up my teacup, and took a dainty sip of its bloody contents. He continued to stare. I put the cup down, folded my hands in my lap, and offered him a tight-lipped smile.

"I'm sorry," I said. "I thought you knew."

3.

"As with so many worlds, Earth's dominant life forms were mammalian: hot-blooded, quick to anger and to passion, and unwilling to pace their lives to the rhythm of the world around them. This allowed for some incredible leaps forward of technology and science, and we should work to retain these streaks of stubborn inventiveness and, dare I say, emotional engagement, within our own cultivars. They may serve useful, after all, even if they did not serve the human race with particular efficacy."

—from *Lady Antheia's Guide to Horticultural Warfare*, first printing.

* * *

Julia and her friends had watched disdainfully as Arthur bundled me out of the house and into the waiting steam-powered carriage below, as if the method of our conveyance somehow rendered us low-class and common. I spared a smile and a waggle of my fingers for Julia, who glared and turned her face away. Then I was in the carriage next to Arthur, and we were being carried into the night, with the rainbow blaze of ships piercing the atmosphere dancing in the sky above us.

"I have already sent a telegram to Lord Harrington, asking him to be prepared for us," said Arthur, watching out the window as if he expected my brethren to be stalking the streets already. "He'll want to know everything you can tell him about this 'invasion.' No detail is too small. We're all going to need to do our part to beat these blighters back!"

"Well, what about the ray guns atop the palace and the Royal Observatory?" I asked. "Won't they automatically take aim at anything larger than Her Majesty's airship that enters England's skies?"

"Yes, and we can take comfort in that, but—and please don't take this as a criticism of your fair self, my dear, you have never been anything but a blessing to my house—they didn't shoot *you* down, and that leads me to worry about the strength of our aerial defense net." Arthur looked at me solemnly. "Are you positive that this is an invasion? Couldn't it be a simple atmospheric disturbance?"

"I am not positive, as I have been on this planet and in this form for six years, and that does rather limit one's communications with one's fellows," I said. "That aside, six years is roughly the time needed to travel here from the nearest habitable star, if said travel is undertaken in faster than light seed-ships."

Arthur's mouth fell open. "F-faster than light? But that's beyond the reaches of modern science. Why, even Professor O'Malley's moon-ship only traveled at a rate of seventeen thousand miles an hour. Light is—"

"Light is a far faster beast," I said agreeably. "I am sorry. I thought you knew."

It was a bald-faced lie, and not the first I had told him during our acquaintanceship. *Lying is wrong, miss,* said Jill's small, stern voice.

Ah, but the lies are coming to an end, and sometimes things which are wrong are also comforting, I told her. *Now hush, be still. I have a scientist to attend to.*

"Faster than light travel would be a discovery great enough to put the British Empire ahead of the rest of the world forever," said Arthur. "You *must* discuss this with Lord Harrington."

"I will, if you bid me, but I am no engineer." I refolded my hands in my lap. "I've never seen the drives, nor do I understand the physics behind them."

Arthur frowned like he was seeing me for the first time. "So you remember yourself before you were—" He waved a hand, indicating my form in a most ungentlemanly manner. "This?"

"You mean, do I remember my existence before I consumed Julia's lady's maid?" I asked, baldly. If he was going to forsake manners for expediency, then I saw no reason not to do the same. "Yes, and no. My seed was coaxed from a cutting of a specific cultivated line. I have never been anything but what I am: I was a seed, and then I was a sprout, and then I was the Lady Antheia, who has very much enjoyed your hospitality over these past six years. The line from which I was grown, however, is a strain of diplomats and explorers. All the seeds that came to this world with me were of that same strain." Had any of them managed to sprout, I would have had siblings all across the globe—but alas, more and more, I had come to believe that I alone had found welcoming soil.

"A...diplomat?" Arthur blinked at me as our carriage rattled to a stop, presumably in front of our destination. "But the first thing you did was eat my sister's maid."

"I am aware," I said primly, gathering my skirts as I waited for the doors to slide open on their well-oiled tracks. "But I was sorry afterward, which is the very definition of diplomacy."

Arthur didn't have an answer to that.

4.

"Being only a cultivar of our greatest diplomat, the honorable and merciful Rooted in Many Soils, I cannot possibly know what it is to have conquered more than one world. I have offered my genetic material back to the trunk which grew me, and my experiences will be preserved for future generations, as is only right and just. Still, I know enough of what my parent and original experienced during their own explorations to know that the conquest of Earth was entirely unique, and extremely common, all at the same time. But then, this is always the way when we encounter a sapient race: they are all different, and they are all sadly, tragically the same. Meat is not capable of much variance."

—from *Lady Antheia's Guide to Horticultural Warfare*, first printing.

* * *

Lord Harrington was a walking mountain of a man, tall and broad-chested, with a ruddy complexion that spoke of much blood pumping very close to the surface. He always made me hungry in a faintly embarrassing way; it's rude to stare at a man and think of how much his blood would do to nourish your vines.

"Arthur," he greeted, in his booming voice, before turning his attention on me. "And the Lady Antheia, who appears to be the woman of the hour, if what Arthur tells me is true. Do you know what's causing the lights in the sky?"

He knew the answer: I could hear it in his tone. I politely inclined my head, not quite looking at him, and asked, "How long ago did your telescope begin picking out the ships in the auroras?"

"Perhaps half an hour; no more," he said. "I never trusted you."

"I know." I raised my head. "I did not press the issue. It seemed more sporting to allow you your little rebellion, rather than charming it out of you. Sportsmanship is not a uniquely human trait, you know. Very little is unique about any world, although they all assume themselves to be."

Lord Harrington's lips peeled back from his teeth as he drew the gun from his belt and pointed it at the spot where my heart would have been, had I possessed such an inconvenient thing. "Lady Antheia, by my authority as a Peer of the Crown, I place you under arrest for treason to the British Empire."

"Oh, lovely." I clapped my hands. "That is *fantastic* news, because you see, as the diplomatic ambassador of the … .well, there isn't a term in English that's quite right for what we are, because we've never encountered English before, and thus far I'm the only one who speaks it, so let us say, the Vegetable Empire? As the diplomatic ambassador of the Vegetable Empire, I refuse to be arrested, but I'm happy to be taken before your Queen, as it seems the invasion is about to properly begin."

As if on a timer, the guns atop the observatory fired, their steam-fueled chambers expelling rays of hot light that seared across the sky. Several seed ships would be destroyed in this barrage; it was natural. They didn't yet know to make themselves smaller, and would learn only through those losses. Those which survived the initial wave of gunfire would split into multiple vessels, and continue their implacable descent. I couldn't mourn for the dead of this wave. They would only be seeds, after all, and of no more consequence than a promise, always intended to be broken.

The guns fired again. And so, in the din, did Lord Harrington. His aim was true: the ray gun hit me squarely in the chest, burning a hole in both my favorite bodice and the bright green skin below, until it was possible to look through me to the room beyond. Arthur cried out. I looked down, considering the wreckage of what had been my sternum.

"Oh, I *do* wish you hadn't done that," I sighed, my voice rendered weak and reedy by the damage to my lungs.

And then I lunged.

Lord Harrington had always treated me as a strange sort of pet, a harmless trinket to be either studied or ignored, depending on his mood. To learn that he had mistrusted my intentions all that time was almost a relief, as it meant that he was not *quite* as stupid as I had assumed. Still, like most men of science, he believed only in the evidence of his eyes, and what his eyes saw when he looked at me was a woman. Green of skin and hair, yes, but apart from that? In every other regard? I was the very flower of English womanhood, with my curves trained to the corset's embrace and my skirts hanging full and demure down past my ankles. Why, had it not been for my face, and for the narrow band of skin between top of glove and bottom of sleeve, he could easily have forgotten my vegetable origins, as so many others had tried to do. Poor man. What he did not consider was that skirts can conceal more than legs.

He jerked backward as my hands found his throat, my thorn-sharp nails piercing the skin beneath his jaw and finding purchase there, the tiny barbs that lined them making it nigh-impossible to pull me free without killing him in the process. Lord Harrington pressed his gun against my stomach, firing again; much of my midsection joined my chest in nonexistence before I could wrap a vine around the ray gun's muzzle and rip it from his hands, hurling it away. As I did that, the creeper vines and long, thick roots I normally kept concealed—as a proper British woman would, had she found herself burdened with such things—emerged from beneath my skirt and wrapped tight around him, binding him in place.

Arthur was shouting behind me. I knew that civility meant responding to him, or at least begging his pardon, but my injuries were too great; Lord Harrington might not have known my anatomy, but he had done a remarkably good job of reducing my overall mass. So I committed the unforgiveable sin of ignoring my friend and patron as I drove my roots into the body of his colleague, linking them into his circulatory system.

His blood tasted of fine wine and excellent breeding. Perhaps there was something to be said for the aristocracy after all.

It only took me a few moments to drain the life and fluids from Lord Harrington's body. I leaned back, glancing down, and was pleased to see that new growth had covered the holes in my chest and stomach, replacing the gaping holes with smooth, if somewhat indecent, green skin. It was paler than the rest of me, but the patchwork effect that it created was not unpleasant, and would be mostly covered by my clothing under normal circumstances. I pulled my roots from the husk of Lord Harrington, unwinding my creeper vines until he remained upright solely thanks to the nails which remained wedged in his throat. I yanked them free, and he fell with a hollow rattle, like a dried-out old seed pod.

"Well. That was uncivil of him," I said, smoothing my skirt with the heels of my hands as I pulled all the pieces of me back into their proper places. "Arthur, dear, I don't suppose I might borrow your jacket? I am quite underdressed, thanks to the holes your friend saw fit to shoot into my clothing."

"You killed him." Arthur's voice was as bloodless as his colleague. "Antheia … how could you?"

"The mechanisms of it were easy, and do not really require explanation," I said, turning to face him. It was no real surprise to find that he had retrieved Lord Harrington's ray gun, and was aiming it at me. His hands were shaking. There was no way he would pull the trigger. "As to why I would do so, well. He shot me. Twice. You cannot blame me for protecting myself against a man who was so clearly determined to end my life."

"But you … but you …"

"Did nothing you were not already aware I had the potential to do, Arthur." I took a step toward him, chin up, eyes fixed on his. "We met shortly after I devoured dear Jill. You remember? You knew I had this in me. If I am a monster, then you are the man who nurtured me, and saw to it that I had good soil in which to grow. I am your fault as much as anyone else's."

He whimpered. Just once, like a child.

He's frightened, miss, said Jill.

He has reason to be. Now hush, I replied, and reached out to take the gun, gently, from Arthur's hands. That was the moment when everything could have gone wrong: when the human race could have started truly fighting back, instead of simply lashing out against an enemy it did not understand. I was leaving myself vulnerable to attack—a foolish thing to do, more suited to a hot-blooded meat creature than to a diplomat of the Vegetable Empire, but ah. I did harbor some affection for the man. I might even have loved him, in my way, had my purpose on his world not been so antithetical to the very notion. So I left my throat unguarded, giving him the opportunity to deliver a killing blow.

He didn't. Then the gun was in my hand, barrel still warm from the two shots Lord Harrington had delivered to my body, and Arthur's eyes were beginning to overflow with salty tears. I reached out, quite improperly, and brushed them away with a sweep of my thumb. My skin drank the moisture eagerly.

"Come now, stop your crying," I said. "It's time we went to see the Queen."

The great guns atop the Observatory shuddered and fired again, blasting more of my people out of the sky, and Arthur wept.

5.

"It is not that the idea of invasion was incomprehensible to the humans: a simple visit to the breeding pens will expose the curious to dozens of pre-conquest humans who have no trouble accepting the reality of their situation. They were always prepared for the idea that an enemy might try their borders. No, the incomprehensibility came when they were defeated. The sun was said never to set on the British Empire. I am sure there are some who still cannot understand how they could have been so very wrong."

—from *Lady Antheia's Guide to Horticultural Warfare*, first printing.

* * *

London was in a panic. The streets were thronged with would-be defenders of the Crown, their ray guns and small sonic cannons clutched in sweaty hands and aimed toward the distant sky. Some of the buildings we passed were already aflame, no doubt ignited by falling debris. I schooled my expression into one of mild dismay as I gazed out the carriage windows on the spreading chaos. My people had not yet fired a single gun, nor killed a single head of state—Lord Harrington being far too close to common to count. All this was the humans' own doing.

"You were always going to rip it all down by yourselves you

know," I said conversationally, glad that our carriage was a clever conveyance of steam and gears, and not a thing driven by a living human who might have understood the meaning of my words. "That's what meat does, when it gets control of a world. It devours itself, and then it goes looking for something else to eat. We're simply shortcutting the process."

"I thought you were my friend." Arthur's voice was dull, lacking its usual fascination with the world. A pity. I hadn't intended to break him. "I took you in. Supported you. *Cared* for you."

"Yes, and believe me, your assistance in gaining the access I needed to higher society is appreciated." I allowed one of my climber vines to uncurl from around my leg, extending it to brush against Arthur's cheek. He might not recognize the affection in the gesture, but that was of no matter. My days of pretending to humanity were coming to a blessed end. "This will be much less painful, thanks to you."

"I have betrayed my Queen and my country."

"No, darling, no. Betrayal implies intent. You have simply allowed something dangerous to flourish in your garden. A weed among roses, although that's a terribly common metaphor, don't you think? More like a rose among cabbages, all things considered." I allowed the curtain to fall back across the window. "I have grown healthy in the fertile soil you afforded me, and now it's time for me to bloom. Me, and all my brothers and sisters."

"Why?"

"Well, I don't know. Why did your British Empire see fit to colonize so much of the planet? Superior force of arms was definitely a factor, and a misguided faith in your own sense of morality. 'For Queen and country' and all of that lovely jingoistic nonsense. But that's all petals, isn't it? Pretty blooms to hide the thorns. You did it for two reasons." I leaned closer, smiling. He paled as he met my eyes.

Now miss, it's not polite to taunt a man by knowing things he doesn't, chided Jill.

No, but it's certainly enjoyable, I replied. Aloud, I said, "The places you took had things you wanted. Resources. Tea and cinnamon and precious metals and girls no one would ever debase themselves by marrying, but whom every British gentleman was happy to deflower. That's the first reason you did what you did, and that's the first reason we do what we do."

Arthur swallowed hard before whispering, "What's the second reason?"

I leaned closer still, watching my reflection expand to fill the reflective surfaces of his eyes. Such a wonderful biological invention, the eye. Functional *and* delicious. "Because we can."

Arthur turned his face away. I sighed, leaning back into my own seat.

"Really, Arthur, I wish you wouldn't be that way. I'm only acting according to my nature. Isn't that what you've told me every time one of your countrymen leered at your sister or called me a savage jungle girl? Me, who has never even *seen* a jungle, who originated in a hothouse that spanned a world? 'They are only acting according to their nature.' Those were *your* words. Why is it correct when they do it, and so fearsome when I do?"

"You killed a man."

"He shot me. Twice, might I add. I think he quite deserved what became of him."

Arthur's eyes snapped open. "That does not *matter*," he snarled. "You are not judge, nor jury, nor executioner!"

"No, dear: I am none of those things. I am the vanguard of an invading army, and that means your laws no longer apply to me." I shrugged. "If we fail—and we will not fail—I'll be tried for treason and imprisoned until the Queen can find a suitably gruesome means of execution. If that happens, be sure they put me in a prison with large windows, or I won't live long enough for you to kill me. If we succeed, your laws will be permanently suspended, and cannot be used against me. The things we do tonight are crimes of war. They are not things for which we can be punished in the court of law."

"Britain will not lose."

I sighed. "Oh, my sweet, foolish mammal of a man, it already has. It just doesn't know it yet."

The conveyance rattled to a halt behind the palace, near one of the many entrances used to bring in those who were better than servants, but less than noblemen. There was a soft sighing sound as the springs relaxed, allowing our carriage to sink lower to the ground. I stood, smoothing the wreckage of my skirts with my hands.

"We've arrived," I said. "Do I look ready for an audience with the Queen?"

Arthur merely glared.

"Don't be tedious, Arthur; it's not polite." I opened the carriage door, stepping into the London night.

The air, which would normally have smelled of burning gas and the wood fires used to stoke the steam engines of those too poor to afford solar paneling, smelled like sap and petrichor and electrical discharge. And blood, of course. The streets would be red come morning, painted carnival bright with the lives of those who had built this country. I hesitated a bare moment before kicking off my shoes and allowing the small root surfaces packed into my toes to taste the earth between the cobblestones. Ah, yes; the taste of home. It was falling to the planet's surface with every barrage of laser fire and steam-powered bullets that ripped apart the sky. Our ships were designed to serve more than one purpose, after all, and with every one that fell, the Earth became a little more suited to our needs.

Footsteps behind me telegraphed Arthur's emergence from the carriage. I turned to see him standing in front of the door, backlit by the rainbow and ray gun colored sky. It turned his skin a dozen shifting rainbow shades, from milky pale to carmine, and he was beautiful. I wondered if he would ever understand how beautiful he was. I wasn't sure he'd have the time.

"Come now," I said. "Walk with me."

"I am not a traitor." His voice broke on the last word.

"No. You're not. You're a man doing his duty to his Queen, and taking an ambassador to her, that she might properly negotiate surrender."

Arthur looked unsure, as well he might: I had not, after all, specified who would be surrendering, and who would be the recipient of an empire. But the habit of mannerly comportment was drilled into him, and so he simply nodded, and said, "I pray we may end this peacefully," and walked with me into the palace, while London burned behind us, and the night was radiant with alien light.

6.

"There were those who would insist that a lady's chief graces were as follows: breeding, beauty, and a blind adherence to the manners of the society in which she takes root, no matter how senseless or silly those manners may be. It was considered better to bloom beautifully and without offending anyone than to grow wanton and in healthy abundance.

"Clearly, this was a civilization cultivating itself for conquest."

—from *Lady Antheia's Guide to Horticultural Warfare*, first printing.

* * *

As I had hoped, the Queen was in her chambers. Sadly, she was there along with the Prince Consort, the Ministers of War, and a dozen other powerful men. I sighed. This would have been so much simpler had she been alone. Humans were not a hive mind in any rational way. A human alone could make reasonable decisions, come to reasonable accords. Humans in a group all seemed to believe they and they alone had the authority to speak for their species, and disputes were resolved by shouting until the loudest won. Truly, this world would be more peaceful once it was ruled by cooler vegetable minds.

All those powerful men turned at our entrance, their eyes taking in my charred, disheveled state and Arthur's pale, shocked face, and reaching the logical conclusion. "Lady Antheia, are you hurt?" asked a Minister, a round, ruddy-cheeked man whose name I had never bothered to remember.

"Not any longer, but thank you for your concern," I said. "I do apologize for the hour. I have a matter of some importance to put before the Queen."

Queen Alice finally turned, a frown on her pretty, pleasure-loving face. She had never been equipped to rule. I was here to do a favor, really. "Lady Antheia. This is most irregular."

"I know, Your Majesty." I proffered a curtsey. "I am here to thank you for your hospitality of these past few years, and request your immediate surrender to the Vegetable Empire. We have superior weaponry, and we are even now amassing the superior numbers we will need to take your world as our own. If you cede yourselves to us, we may be merciful."

And then, exactly as I had expected, all those powerful men drew their powerful weapons and shot me dead where I stood. My consciousness winked out before my body hit the floor.

7.

"Humanity, in addition to being delicious and very well designed for its environment, was constantly coming up with excuses to make war upon its own kind. If they had survived as an independent species long enough to establish the means for long distance space travel, we might have found ourselves with unwanted rivals for this galaxy's treasures. It is because of this yearning for conquest that runs so strong in the veins of most meat that I must recommend we speed up our efforts to become the only sapient life living free in known space. It is, sadly, the only way to be safe from the threat of empire."

—from *Lady Antheia's Guide to Horticultural Warfare*, first printing.

* * *

I never put my shoes back on.

That may seem like a trifling detail, but that is because few people fully understand the deeply concentrated root systems to be found on the soles of a diplomat's feet—or whatever passes for feet in the local environment. My body was destroyed, broken beyond repair, and my poor Jill broken with it. But when the Queen's men toted that unwanted seed pod away, they did not notice the small roots that had broken off in the carpet, already working their way down, down, deep into the foundations of the palace.

When we sprout, we sprout quickly, for surprise is our best weapon. Dawn came, and I rose, faceless, a pale green whisper of a thing dressed in a mockery of human form. All in silence, I moved through the chamber to the door beyond, which led to the private apartments of the Queen. She was sleeping, innocent of what was about to befall her, her husband and consort snug beside her in the bed. I did not see them, for I did not have eyes, but there are other ways of sensing such things. She did not know I was there; she presented no threat.

I ate her.

8.

"It was a small matter for our soldiers to subdue the populace, once they had seen their Queen unmasked as an alien, welcoming the invaders into Buckingham Palace with open arms. Perhaps if we had been a little less swift, there would have been time to mount a resistance…but that was not to be. As the humans once said: the Queen is dead.

"Long live the Queen."

—from *Lady Antheia's Guide to Horticultural Warfare*, first printing.

* * *

I set my quill aside, considering the words I had written. They were good words: they would do nicely, and would serve well as a guide to the next invasion of a world like Earth. The fields were rich with our seedlings, and the men of science already looked outward, considering the next path our colony ships would take.

Footsteps behind me alerted me to the approach of my husband—a human custom, yes, but one which many of us who found ourselves with human forms and vaguely human ways of thinking had chosen to observe. It was a diversion, if nothing else, and could provide a new social frame, if it proved useful.

"All done?" asked Arthur, a smile on his emerald lips.

It had been a small thing to take a seedling of an open line, with no ancestral memory, and place it next to Arthur's bound, struggling form. He had thanked me, of course, when his memories settled properly into their new home. He had always been a botanist. Now he could study himself, for centuries if he liked. It was my wedding gift to him.

"Yes," I said, and wrapped my creeper vines around his waist and my arms around his shoulders, and kissed him with the mouth I had stolen from a human Queen. The British Empire had claimed the sun would never set, and they had been wrong, because they had been thinking too small.

For the sun to be shining always, one needs more than a single world. It is vital to acquire a galaxy.

About the Authors

Bradley P. Beaulieu is the author of the critically acclaimed epic fantasy series, *The Lays of Anuskaya.* Along with fellow author Gregory A. Wilson, Brad runs the highly successful science fiction and fantasy podcast, Speculate, which can be found at www.speculatesf.com. Brad continues to work on his next projects, including a Norse-inspired middle grade series and *The Song of the Shattered Sands*, an Arabian Nights-inspired epic fantasy that will be published by DAW Books in the US and Gollancz in the UK. For more about Brad and his writing, please visit www.quillings.com.

Although not a zombie, **S.C. Butler** freely admits to needing more brains. His fantasy trilogy, "The Stoneways," was published by Tor Books, and his short fiction has appeared in **Beneath Ceaseless Skies**; **After Hours: Tales From the Ur-Bar**; and **The Modern Fae's Guide to Surviving Humanity**. "Heart of Clockwork" is his first attempt at steampunk.

Leah Cutter currently lives in Seattle—the land of coffee and fog. However, she's also lived all over the world and held the requisite odd writer jobs, such as doing archeology in England, teaching English in Taiwan, and bartending in Thailand. She writes fantasy set in exotic times and locations such as Tang dynasty China, WWII Budapest, rural Louisiana, and the Oregon coast. Her short fiction includes literary, fantasy, mystery, science fiction, and horror, and has been published in magazines as well as anthologies and on the web. Read more stories by Leah Cutter at www.KnottedRoadPress.com.

David J. Fortier grew up in Winnipeg, Canada, reading adventure classics and epic fantasies over the long winters. A true geek, he loves board games, superhero movies, video games, D&D, and comics. Naturally, his whiskey preference is rye, though he will not scoff at fine bourbon. He currently resides in Calgary, in the foothills of the Canadian Rocky Mountains, where he writes sword & sorcery, heroic fantasy, and a touch of other speculative fiction. Oh, and pirates over ninjas.

Brad Hafford is an archaeologist, teacher, writer and traveler. He holds a Ph.D. from the University of Pennsylvania and he also a graduate of the Odyssey Writing Workshop. He remains staunchly scientific in his studies and non-fiction, but loves to imagine about the myriad "what-ifs" in the world. These imaginings drive his fiction wherein he attempts to express the compelling stories of alternate realities that dance about in his head. "Fingers of Steam, Veins of Gold" was inspired by a trek through parts of Alaska, in particular the rusting hulk of an old steam engine left to die outside Skagway.

Jason Richard Hargenrader is an American speculative fiction writer living in Melbourne, Australia. Jason studied astronomy, English, and radio/TV/film at the University of Texas and graduated from the Odyssey Writing Workshop in 2013. When not corralling his toddler, Grace, you can find him following his Pyrenean Mountain Dog with a vacuum cleaner. He also lives with his beloved wife and cat. Learn more at jrhargenrader.com.

Gini Koch lives in Hell's Orientation Area (aka Phoenix, AZ), works her butt off (sadly, not literally) by day, and writes by night with the rest of the beautiful people. She writes the fast, fresh and funny *Alien/Katherine "Kitty" Katt* series for DAW Books, the *Necropolis Enforcement Files* series, and the *Martian Alliance Chronicles* series for Musa Publishing. As G.J. Koch she writes the *Alexander Outland* series. She also writes under a variety of other pen names including Anita Ensal, Jemma Chase, A.E. Stanton, and J.C. Koch. She can be reached through her website: www.ginikoch.com.

Gail Z. Martin is the author of **Ice Forged** and **Reign of Ash** in *The Ascendant Kingdoms Saga* (Orbit Books), plus *The Chronicles of The Necromancer* series (**The Summoner**, **The Blood King**, **Dark Haven** & **Dark Lady's Chosen**) from Solaris Books and *The Fallen Kings Cycle* (**The Sworn** and **The Dread**) from Orbit Books. In 2014, Gail's new urban fantasy novel, **Deadly Curiosities**, debuts from Solaris Books. **Iron and Blood**, a Steampunk novel, will be published by Solaris in 2015. She is also the author of two series of ebook short stories: *The Jonmarc Vahanian Adventures* and the *Deadly Curiosities Adventures*.

Seanan McGuire writes things. It is very difficult to make her stop. When not writing things, she can be found in haunted corn mazes, comic book stores, and Disney Parks. Seanan shares a crumbling farmhouse with three massive blue cats, a large collection of dolls, and a sufficient number of books to be considered a library. Seanan regularly claims to be the vanguard of an invading race of alien plant people. We see no reason to doubt her.

Jason Palmatier is a science fiction writer based in central Pennsylvania who has written numerous short stories and screenplays and is currently co-writing an independent comic. When not trying to create new worlds with just a keyboard and a dream he enjoys raising his three kids and sleeping. "Heart of the Empire" is his first professional sale.

C.B. Pratt has lived all over the United States, including California, New York and many stops in between. Having been a professional writer for over twenty years, she is ill-suited to any normal work and hopes to continue writing for the rest of her life. Independent publishing has allowed her to write the things she has always wanted to, including fantasy and steampunk. She is the author of numerous traditionally published books, as well as the *Eno the Thracian* fantasy-adventure series. **Steam Demon**, book one in a new steampunk series, will be available in 2015.

Tansy Rayner Roberts is the author of **Power and Majesty** and

Ink Black Magic among many other fantasy novels. She also writes crime under the name Livia Day. Tansy podcasts with Galactic Suburbia and Verity!, and won the Hugo for Best Fan Writer in 2013. You can find Tansy at her blog http://tansyrr.com/ or on Twitter as @tansyrr.

Ian Tregillis is the son of a bearded mountebank and a discredited tarot card reader. He is the author of the *Milkweed Triptych* (**Bitter Seeds**, **The Coldest War**, and **Necessary Evil**), as well as the critically acclaimed novel **Something More Than Night** and the forthcoming *Clakkers Trilogy*. His short fiction has appeared in Tor.com, Apex Magazine, Subterranean Press Magazine, and various anthologies. He lives in New Mexico, where he consorts with writers, scientists, and other disreputable types. His website is iantregillis.com.

Jean Marie Ward writes fiction, nonfiction, and everything in between, including novels (2008 Indie Book double-finalist **With Nine You Get Vanyr**) and art books. Her stories appear in numerous anthologies, such as **The Modern Fae's Guide to Surviving Humanity** and the award-winning **Hellebore & Rue**. The former editor of *Cresent Blues*, she is a frequent contributor of video interviews and short subjects to BUZZYMAG.com. Her website is JeanMarieWard.com.

About the Editors

Patricia Bray is the author of a dozen novels, including **Devlin's Luck**, which won the Compton Crook Award for the best first novel in the field of science fiction or fantasy. A multi-genre author whose career spans both epic fantasy and Regency romance, her books have been translated into Russian, German, Portuguese and Hebrew. She's also spent time on the editorial side of the fence, co-editing **After Hours: Tales from the Ur-Bar** and **The Modern Fae's Guide to Surviving Humanity** with her frequent partner-in-crime Joshua Palmatier.

Patricia lives in a New England college town, where she combines her writing with a full-time career as a Systems Analyst, ensuring that she is never more than a few feet away from a keyboard. You can find her on Twitter as @pbrayauthor, or visit her webpage at www.patriciabray.com.

Joshua Palmatier is a fantasy author with a PhD in mathematics. He currently teaches at SUNY Oneonta in upstate New York, while writing in his "spare" time, editing anthologies with fellow zombie and co-editor Patricia Bray, and founding the anthology-producing small press Zombies Need Brains LLC. His upcoming fantasy novel **Shattering the Ley** (July 2014) starts a new fantasy series, although you can also find his *Throne of Amenkor* series already on the shelves. He is currently hard at work writing the sequel to **Shattering the Ley** and designing the kickstarter for the next anthology. You can find out more at www.joshuapalmatier.com or www.benjamintate.com (yes, he committed pseudonym) or at the small press' site www.zombiesneedbrains.com. Or follow him on Twitter as @bentateauthor or @ZNBLLC.

Acknowledgements

This anthology would not have been possible without the tremendous support of those who pledged during the Kickstarter run from July 15-August 15, 2013. Everyone who contributed not only helped create this anthology, they also helped set up the small press Zombies Need Brains LLC, which I hope will be bringing SF&F themed anthologies to the reading public for years to come…as well as perhaps some select novels by leading authors, eventually. I want to thank each and every one of them for helping to bring this small dream into reality. Thank you, my zombie horde.

Signature Zombie: Jonathan S. Chance

Tuckerization Zombies: Julie Blackwood, Elizabeth Vrabel, Missy Gunnels Katano, Lori Joyce Parker, Jake Palmatier, Terry D. England, Brian Shay

Artistic Zombies: Vince & Diane Tate, David J. Fortier, Carla Larson, Ryan Leduc

Author Zombies: John L. Borbone, Andrea & Duncan Rittschof, Jenn Falls, Jennifer D'Ambrosio, Yankton Robins, Doug James, Kenya Mizzell, Rachel Sasseen, Niem To, Steven Mentzel, Galit A.

Sampler Zombies: Michael Trick, Brad Roberts, R.K. Bentley

All the Anthologies Zombies: Jennifer Della'Zanna, Michael Halverson, William Gunderson, Andrea Gygli Jennings, Jeff Ryan, Edward Willett, Kevin Niemczyk, Shannon Page & Mark J. Ferrari, Tory Shade, Paul Saunders, Jen Woods, Kristina

VanHeeswijk, Flights of Fantasy Books, Mi L. Holliday, Philda, Adam L. Crouse, Ronda Sanders, Kel "Selwyn" George, Devin La Salle, M.J. Fiori, Alex Newman, Morva Bowman & Alan Pollard, John C. Ness, Megan E. Daggett, Rachel Blackman, Cora Anderson, Wolf SilverOak, Rob Coke, Bill O'Connor, Danielle Hall, Konstantin Goreley, Teresa Home, Chris M.

Anthology Zombies: Robert E. Waters, Shauna Shoptaw, Beth Curtin, Andrew Croftcheck, MarnieCollette Walski, Rev. Dr. Brian Gray, Nick Watkins, Brian Y. Ashmore, Gregg Kern, Clare Deming, Alex von der Linden, Mike Douton, Mike Prosser, Rachel K., Terrell Scoggins, Kit Gordon, Ruth Stuart

Paper Zombies: Doug S., Daniel W., Jeffery Lawler, Jeremiah Whitmore, Colin MacDonald, Rebecca M., Jon K.G. Allanson, Lucinda Caughey, Steven Halter, Barbara Campbell, Chase Graham, Andy Vasbinder, Andrea M. Gregory, Hannah Schofield, Katie Rose, Melissa C., Donaithnen, Samantha, Cathy Brown, Ashley Dzama, Jackie Kessler, Sylvia Izzo Hunter, Twila Oxley Price, Steven Pratt, Angus Abranson, Mike Hampton, Lexie C., Jennifer Spadafino, batwrangler, Mean Mr. Fallywalker, C. Lennox, Matthew Markland, Vendela Cognition, Doug Bissell, Landon O., Roel Veldhuyzen, Marsheila (Marcy) Rockwell, John Leavitt, Bill McGeachin, Thea Maia, Ty Wilda, Sarah M. Heile, Taylor Sanfilippo, Becky LeJeune, Michael "The Mad Hatter" Pye, Peggy Wiles, Tim V., Peter R. Ellis, Sandra Komoroff, Peter Young, Marcus Gipps, Smashingsuns, Richard Arnold, Richard P. Bissmire, Anthony McDonald, Tibicina, Peter Ruggles, Mads Anders, Hans Ranke, Elizabeth Bear, Eric (squirmydad) Brown, Erin Kowalski, Lisa Kueltzo, Paul Genesse, Damon Eric English, Shawn Marier, Carmine Pellosie, Jr., Stephanie Ascone, Fen Eatough, Michael Moe, Jason Palmatier, Alice Bentley, Ron & Tara Oakes, Thomas & Leo Santilli, Colleen Reed, Michael Feldhusen, Sarah, Jeff Gulosh, Mike O'Toole, Pete Hollmer, Epiphyllum, Nayad Monroe, Sheryl Ehrlich, Geoggrey ford, Gwydion Vennema, D. Andrew McChesney, Kelli Neier, Jess Lethbridge, Carla Borsoi, Jonny Lynn, Alli Martin, Gary Ehrlich, Lisa Magruder, Sofie Bird, Nick

Laperouse, Naloth Halcyon, Jeff, Gary Phillips, Chaos, Jon McFarling, Cara Ellis, Tammy L. Garland, Scot Taylor, Fred & Mimi Bailey, Sean Collins, Lauren M. Roy, Sara Glassman, Pam Palmer, butterflywings, Joseph Cinek, Christine Swendseid, Robbin Wayward, James Turnbull, Silence in the Library Publishing, arzvi, Cheryl Losinger, Mark Kiraly, Paul McMullen, Kerry aka Trouble, Camron Saleh, Andrew V., Jasmine Stairs, PatK, Mariann Asanuma, Dan & Kat, Brooks Moses, Michael Wyatt, Nickolaus Eskew, Wooz, Julie Frost, April Steenburgh, Kimberly M. Lowe, Maggie Allen, Kendra Leigh Speedling, Kristie Strum, matthew, Christopher Mangum, Christopher Mansell, Peter Bernstorff, Cameron Paine, Ash Marten, DrTest

Electronic Zombies: Steven Saus, Jen Edwards, Karen, M.J. Fletcher, Rhel na DecVande, Emily R., Jon "Westy" Westenberg, Michele Dainiak, Mark C. Chu-Carroll, Andrew Barton, jennielf, C. Yau, @syntheticbrain, Yaron Davidson, Jackie D., K. Strawser-Booth, Candice Velasco, Josh Bluestein, Jonathan Foulkes, C. Budworth, Brook & Julia West, Fred Herman, Muriel Jackson, Ian Mond, David Wohlreich, Celeste Wetzel, Ellie Paxton, Justin Pinner, Gary Newcomb, Keith Hall, David Peek, Hendel Thistletop, Janni Lee Simner, Jason Rubenstein, Alan Thiesen, A. Chatain, Ian Simpson, Ichimonji10, Kate Gendall, Tom Conneely, Patricia Bullington-McGuire, Jack Vivace, Priscilla Spencer, Robert M. Everson, Samanda B. Jeude, Lynna Landstreet, Cliff Winnig, Aimee Kuzenski, Eagle Archambeault, Olai Amund, Jennifer Kahng, Stephanie Leary, David B., Gordon Waddell, Kyle Kinnear, Andy Miller, Lizzy Boden, Taylor Davis, Michael Coward, Olivia Gillham, Jeffry Rinkel, Steve Downey, Kristjan Wager, Lesley Smith, Jason Best, David Perkins, Jay Watson, James Weber, David Nicklin, josh green, Archaeron, Jan Gehrer, Erik DeBill, James "@realjimbob" Spinks, Bill & Laura Pearson, H., Orla Carey, Thomas P. Leahy, Ian Harvey, David Francis, William Hughes, Kari, Nathan Turner, Raymond Cypher, Kyle Bennett, Andrew Tudor, Jill Munro, Axel Wiklund, Mary Alice Wuerz, Robert Maughan, @competentgirl, sam murphy, Andy Armino @5thWall, Anastasia Talen, Elizabeth McCoy, James Husum, Rohith

Thumati, Maurice Strubel, Chris Harrison, Kai Nikulainen, Samuel Lubell, Nancy Campbell, John Murphy, Sheryl R. Hayes, Joanne B., Lisa Kruse, Thomas Cherneskie, Kayla F., Todd V. Ehrenfels, Peter Donald, Jesse McClusky, Doug Sarver, Tehani Wessely, Josh & Lisa, Carl Haynes, William M. Reed, Jerry Gaiser, Alexander Kevin Apgar, L.E. Doggett, Keith Chapman, Alexandre, Genevieve Cogman, Tahmi DeSchepper, Kevin J. "Womzilla" Maroney, Mark Martinez, Gregory A. Wilson, Jarrod Coad, Sol Foster, Emrys W. Hopkins, Gavran, Tony Fiorentino, Sonika Balyan, Khinasidog, Max Kaehn, Andy Cook, Katharine, Alan MacDonald, Dennis Ferruzzi, Angela Korra'ti, Michele Maakestad, Jake Haney, Ryland J. Kayin Lee, D. Miles Martin, Elizabeth Creegan, Kevin Flynn, Lianne Burwell, Jen Warren, S.M. Kennedy, Tera Fulbright, Alexander Smith, Derek Akerhielm, Ren Warom, Annika Samuelsson, Francis Budden-Hinds, TwShiloh, Matt Wagner, David Small, J.P. Goodwin, Michael Nichols, Christian Decomain, Catherine Sharp, Thomas Zilling, Laura Reid, Steven V., Mayer Brenner, David K. Mason, Brian Brunswick, Shiyiya LeCompte, Karne, Kaia Gavere, Helen Savore, Ben "Zhaph" Duguid, Brian, Sarah & Josh Williams, Heathyr Fields, Nojh, Anna McDuff, Zuhur Abdu, Tansy Rayner Roberts, Akimotos, Larisa LaBrant, Matt Hurlburt, Terese Ramin, Simon Julian, Thomas MacGregor, Alexey Romanov, Jan Meiners, Matt Pearsall, Ben Stanley, Celeste M., Heidi Cykana, Ginger, Dana, Sharon Wood, Elizabeth McKinstry, Kevin Heard, Jaime Wurth, Michael Hanscom, John "johnkzin" Rudd, Kelly Myers, Alicia & Howard Kleinman, Lorena Dinger, Stephanie Franklin, Leigh B., huskiebear, Muse, Ben Wolfe, Eleanor Russell, J.W. Alden, Joseph Asante, Jennifer Thorburn, Lightning, Carol J. Guess, Noel Coughlan, Deanne Fountaine, Rebecca Harbison

Friend of the Zombies: Andy Clayman, Bob Whitely, Deborah Dalton

Minion Zombies: Matthew Bongers, Svend Andersen

CPSIA information can be obtained at www.ICGtesting.com
Printed in the USA
LVOW11s0828081214

417754LV00005B/369/P

9 781940 709000